HEART'S DESIRES

HEART'S DESIRES

by

KATHARINE MARLOWE

DONALD I. FINE, INC.
New York

Library of Congress Cataloging-in-Publication Data

Marlowe, Katharine
    Heart's desires : a novel / by Katharine Marlowe.
      p. cm.
    ISBN 1-55611-226-2
    I. Title.
PR9199.3.M365H4   1991
813'.54—dc20   90-55335
                                                  CIP

Manufactured in the United States of America

10 9 8 7 6 5 4 3 2 1

Designed by Irving Perkins Associates

Dedicated to Brooke Forbes,
with love.

bull's-eye: 1. the circular spot, usually black or outlined in black, of the center of a target used in target practice . . . 7. a thick disk or lenslike piece of glass inserted into a roof, ship's deck, etc. to admit light . . . 9. the eye of a storm . . . 10. a large, round piece of peppermint-flavored hard candy.
(The Random House Dictionary
of the English Language)

AN INTERLUDE

At random moments, often when she was happiest, she'd have a sudden viewing of that scene. Like a full color slide from someone else's collection slipped mistakenly into the midst of her own, it would click into focus and she'd gaze at the carnage, breath held, eyes gone wide. She'd study the image then force it away, shaking her head to clear it of that reminder of those lives, that long-gone horror.

It happened this evening just as she tilted her head to one side to fasten on her diamond earrings. There she sat at the dressing table in the bay window of the bedroom, dressed but not zipped, her hair done, her reluctant concession to makeup (a bit of blush, lip gloss and mascara) completed, fairly well ready for a festive evening. It was rumored that certain members of the royal family would be in attendance to celebrate the tenth year, the four thousandth performance of the show. One of the longest-running productions in British history—discounting that old creaker The Mousetrap. *Ten years, four thousand performances. Everything Jeremy had ever dreamed of, complete with royals and celebrities queuing up to congratulate him, two best-selling singles and a cast album with record-setting sales. Quite the coup, really. Female leads had come and gone, more than a dozen of them, but Jeremy had never relinquished his grip on the role, had never for a moment broken any of the routines he'd established at the outset. Eight times a week he arrived at the theatre two and a half hours early, to look through the day's delivery of fan letters (some of which were explicitly sexual in nature), requests, accolades, and solicitations while sipping tea with honey and performing his vocal warm-ups. Then an hour for makeup and a further half-hour for deep breathing and even deeper concentrating before his first cue. And after the show he held court in his dressing room, thanking each and every one of the people who came to offer praise, murmuring a heartfelt "God bless," as they left. He reveled in it.*

Aly smiled, saw herself in the mirror, and had to look closely at the face in the glass, chagrined as always at the discrepancy between the brain that never aged but merely collected experiences and seemed gradually to grow larger and the face which changed no matter how young one felt. How could you still have the emotions and enthusiasms you'd had at ten and seventeen but look like a woman who'd lived a full forty-seven years? A great joke of fate, that: allowing the mind to remain fully fertile while the housing slowly lost its elasticity, its flexibility, its strength. Not that she was in such dreadful condition. It was more a matter of that shocking gap between what used to be and what was now. And she wouldn't even have been thinking such gloomy thoughts if that nightmarish slide hadn't projected itself onto her mental screen. But she knew all too well how certain events could inform a life, could alter and reshape it. After all, she had for many years now been counseling women who, thirty, forty and fifty years after the fact, were still attempting to come to terms with having been abused once or a hundred times—often by strangers but more often by people they'd been taught to trust.

All right, she told herself. She'd looked at the image. She'd shuddered as always as if violence lurked just beyond the bedroom door. It was time to put it aside. Time to get on with her preparations for the evening. Jeremy's gala evening.

Forgetting the earrings, she looked past the mirror at the street outside, watching a couple go past arm in arm, their faces animated. Young. So odd, to feel young one moment, then old and world-weary the next, then young again. It all depended on those interior views, those slides of a lifetime. Pictures of the people who'd come and gone through your life, some who'd stayed.

Voices. The housekeeper, her child, her husband. People waiting. Again she looked in the mirror, lifting her left hand to smooth the side of her hair. Then she looked at the diamonds on the surface of the dressing table and watched the way the light shattered on the facets. The image was receding quickly now, taking with it the bursting anxiety that forever accompanied that slide but leaving behind a tender residue, like a mental bruising. A little dent on the brain, a bit achey. Just something to remind you of Rheta, to probe that secret place where she resides in perpetuity.

"Any time this week would be good. Unless you'd prefer to spend the evening watching the foot traffic."

She laughed and turned from the mirror. "Caught me daydreaming," she said, looking over at the now open door.

"Is the Queen going to be there?" Teddy asked.

"Maybe," Aly answered. "'More likely it'll be Charles, or Princess Margaret."

"I wish I was going with you and not to Emma Clayton's birthday party," Teddy said unhappily. "Emma Clayton's fat and horrid."

"Emma Clayton," Aly said, "is merely chubby and really quite sweet. And I've told you it's very cruel to judge people by the way they look."

"Then why," Teddy said with an air that signified he'd just made an earth-shatteringly clever deduction, "does everyone dress up so?"

"Because it's fun," Aly said, and pulled him over to nuzzle the side of his neck, which made him giggle. "Now let me finish or I'll be late and your father will be cross with both of us. Won't you, Teddy's father?"

"Positively."

Teddy went to sit next to his father on the side of the bed and Aly looked at them in the mirror, and smiled. The slide had dwindled down now to the size of a pinhead—something so small it couldn't possibly upset or harm her.

PART ONE

New York, 1952

CHAPTER
ONE

THERE WERE three things Rheta Maxwell did each time another man went out of her life. First, she moved herself and the children into a new apartment. The idea was to start fresh in a place that had no associations with any previous man. Second, she hung the framed bull's-eye that she said had come from the bow window of the Cotswold cottage of her great-grandmother in a westerly-facing window of their new home. And third, she set about creating yet again her favorite *tableau:* the contented family happily ensconced in Rheta's bed, either eating a Sunday breakfast together, or listening to some radio program, or occupied with the reading matter of his or her choice. Rheta was pathologically dedicated to her construction of *tableaux,* utterly single-minded in the framing of these living portraits, but unaware on a conscious level of the repetitive nature of her behavior.

It seemed as if she couldn't believe in the actuality of any man's presence inside her life unless she had a physical image she could latch on to and describe to her mother and to her friends. And the image for her that best symbolized the perfect family was that warmly intimate bedroom portrait of herself, Cliff and Aly all snuggled up in bed with Rheta's latest beau. It was the ultimate cozy depiction of family life, and Rheta invariably glowed when describing it.

By the time Cliff was twelve and Aly was ten, their grandmother—Rheta's mother, the redoubtable Elizabeth Conover, known to the children as Auntie Lilbet—felt compelled to point

3

out to her daughter that Rheta's repeated efforts to create the quintessential family unit were becoming somewhat alarming.

"For an intelligent woman, you're an absolute fool when it comes to men!" Elizabeth told her daughter. "And it may be your god-given right to be a fool about men, but it is *not* your right to keep on and on inflicting this nonsense on the children. You've moved them so many times I'm amazed they know where to go when they leave school every day. Has it ever occurred to you," she asked, lowering her voice and narrowing her eyes slightly, "that you're setting a truly lamentable example for your children?"

"I don't know what you're talking about!" Rheta exclaimed. "I'm their mother and I'd be the first one to know if there was a problem."

Elizabeth paused in lighting a Camel to emit a gentle snort of disdainful laughter. "You're their mother, it's true. But you wouldn't recognize a problem if it fell on your head from a great height. You are so completely absorbed in your quest for the ideal man, I honestly don't think you know *what's* going on!"

"That's just crap!" Rheta replied hotly. "I'm aware of every last thing that's going on, and you know it. I'll remind you I hold down a very demanding job, and I'm still home to make dinner for those children every night of the week. *And* I take them out on weekends."

Elizabeth got her cigarette lit, sat back, recrossed her legs, and took a minute or two to study her daughter. It was always a bit of a jolt to absorb the physical details of her extraordinarily peculiar child. Rheta didn't look eccentric; there was nothing on the surface to indicate this woman's propensity for living on two entirely disparate planes. She did indeed hold down a very good job—she was the sales director for a large manufacturer of household paper products and had been steadily working her way up in the company since she'd been hired eight years earlier just after her divorce from Hal Jackson, the children's father. But she seemed incapable of keeping any kind of a hold on her private life. Since her divorce from Jackson, to whom she was married for somewhat less than four years, she'd gone through a second, very short-lived, marriage and had been involved with a further six or seven men. Lilbet had long since

4

lost track of the exact number of Rheta's paramours, which really was of no consequence, all things considered. What did matter, though, was the short-term and very intense nature of Rheta's relationships with these men; her refusal in the past several years to hire help, insisting that the children should do their fair share in the running of the household; and the possibly damaging effects of all this on Cliff and Aly.

Rheta seemed to have a natural predisposition toward unhappily married men who were torn between their obligations to their wives and children and their lust for her. Invariably, lust lost out and the men returned to their homes. Rheta could never understand why these men chose to go back to their drab, unintelligent, sexless wives instead of making a commitment to her. After all, she was attractive, overtly intelligent, and sexually aware. Why these men elected every time to return to their wives was incomprehensible to her.

"You scare the living hell out of them!" her mother told her often. "Men don't *want* a woman like you, Rheta. They want a female who'll allow them to be in charge, who'll let them make the decisions. They want women who make them feel *big*. You'd like to think you're the type any rational red-blooded man would want, and at the outset they always do. You're their every fantasy come true. But you're always engineering things, Rheta. And nobody likes that, nobody at all. I think you believe you can force things to happen simply because you want them to."

"That's not true!" Rheta said impatiently. "Why is it that everyone always thinks they know how to live my life better than I do?"

"Maybe," her mother said slowly, "because in this case they do. You don't want to see it, but one look at those two children and anyone could see they're not happy with the life they're leading."

"How can you *say* that?" Rheta cried, offended. "My children are perfectly happy! You're purposely trying to upset me!"

"Now why would I do that?" Lilbet said quietly. "Use your head! Think about this! I'm your mother. For all your foolishness, I love you, and I love Cliff and Aly. Why on earth would I say things with the idea in mind of intentionally upsetting you?"

5

Rheta had no answer. She sat back, her expression sullen, and lit one of her mother's cigarettes. She loved her mother, but she hated these conversations. It wasn't easy being Lilbet Conover's daughter, having for a mother a woman who believed no female should ever touch her face with her own two hands because it was a known cause of premature wrinkles; a woman who believed women should play-act with men in order to keep them happy; a woman whose early life in the South had obviously given her a warped view of northern reality. Lilbet Conover was a fifty-five-year-old Alabama belle who'd serve mint juleps to dinner guests and laughingly tell of the difficulty of finding fresh mint in Manhattan. Granted, she didn't try to dress the part, and her accent had toned down considerably after thirty-odd years in the North. But she was still as rigidly fixed in her ideas and attitudes as she'd ever been.

Her mother smiled, and Rheta relented, smiling back. It really wasn't possible to stay angry with Lilbet. She was too good-hearted and too good-looking. Rheta often thought that if she were as beautiful as her mother, she too might have had a thirty-year marriage to someone as wonderful as John Conover. But she'd inherited traits from both her parents, and not necessarily the ones she'd have preferred. She did have her mother's large eyes, but they were gray instead of Lilbet's deep blue; and she had her mother's fine complexion, for which she was grateful. But instead of Lilbet's delicately narrow, uptilted little nose, Rheta had her father's long, strong, prominent one that would have been a serious flaw had it not been balanced by the reproduction of his squarish jawline and rounded, jutting chin.

Being objective, she could see her attractiveness, and she knew men were drawn to her because of it. She just wasn't beautiful enough to hold them. Ironically, Aly had inherited Lilbet's looks. In fact, she looked more like Lilbet's child than Rheta did, while Cliff took after his father. He was already taller than most of his friends, and appeared older than twelve. He had Hal's slow, studied manner both in speech and action, as well as his father's judicious, even plodding, attitude. Imagine Lilbet saying she was setting a bad example for her children! Her kids were happy and very well-adjusted. She couldn't begin

6

to imagine why her mother would say a thing like that. Of course she'd only said it to get a rise out of Rheta. It was so obviously not the truth there could be no other reason.

THEY HAD this funny piece of glass that their mom always hung up first thing whenever they moved into a new place. It had a round thick lumpy middle that Cliffie once said looked like a squashed nipple. Even though Aly had been shocked and wildly amused by the description she had to admit it was very accurate. From the center outward the glass got thinner and less crumpled until, at the edges, it was normal. It would be hung where the sun was sure to shine through it, and after the furniture was carried in and they'd made their beds, Aly would go to check the windows to see where Mom had put the bull's-eye, and then, if it was still daylight, she'd get up close and look through it. Right away everything got bent and curvy; looking through the bull's-eye, everything got changed. Sometimes Aly would stay for ages, first with one eye closed, then the other, trying to make everything look right, the way it did when she looked out the ordinary windows. But no matter what she did, squinting, or opening her eyes as wide as they'd go, or looking with only one eye open, nothing was ever the way it was supposed to be. She couldn't stay away from the bull's-eye. Sometimes it would be like a reward she'd give herself for getting her homework done or for eating food she hated, like cod cakes. All the furniture might be the same, and everything would get arranged in the same way each time they moved, but somehow the only thing that really was the same, no matter what, was that funny piece of glass their mom said was very old and had come all the way from their great-great-grandmother's cottage in England.

Aly thought maybe the glass was magic. It was possible. All kinds of things were possible. It said so in books she got from the library, and Auntie Lilbet sort of said things like that too. Maybe not about magic, but about the way things could turn out. Like when Aly asked about her father, about why they only got to visit him twice a month and if maybe someday she and Cliffie could stay for longer, Auntie Lilbet always said, "Of

7

course it's possible, honey. Perhaps when you're a little older."
The way she talked, the sweetness of her voice and the music of
her accent were as convincing as the things she actually said.
Just listening to her grandmother made Aly feel better about
things. Oh, she knew there were rules and that she and Cliffie
had to pay attention to them or Auntie Lilbet might get upset,
but she never minded remembering to wipe her feet carefully
on the doormat before walking on the carpets, to wash her
hands before having anything to eat or drink, to make sure her
hair was brushed and her clothes were tidy before letting
Auntie Lilbet see her, because her Auntie Lilbet really was
magic. Just because they never talked about it didn't mean it
wasn't true. She knew Cliffie didn't think so because sometimes
he got mad having to wipe his feet and wash his hands all the
time, and said swears under his breath. Aly shushed him every
time because she knew he didn't really mean it, but Auntie
Lilbet might not know that and maybe she'd say they couldn't
come back anymore, which would be the worst thing that could
happen.

Cliffie said, "Don't worry about it, kiddo. She might throw me
out on my ear, but she'd never throw you out. You're her pet."

The way he said it made it sound like a bad thing, but she
didn't care. She liked being Lilbet's pet, even if there were lots
of things she'd have liked to tell her grandmother but couldn't,
for fear of making Lilbet angry. It was hard to know what
would make people mad, because it was different with everyone. As far as she could tell, there were things you could say
that could make anybody mad because there was always something people didn't like. So if you thought about it, there were
rules for absolutely everybody, not just grandmothers, and you
had to be careful all the time if you didn't want to go around
making everyone mad at you.

The most of what she could say to anybody Aly said to Cliffie
because he didn't care the way grownups did. And she knew
that even though he told her to get lost sometimes he was really
on her side and would stick up for her, like the way he'd beat
up those boys in the schoolyard that time in first grade when
they made a circle around her and wouldn't let her get past.

Cliffie had come shouting, throwing down his books and holding his fists up. The boys had turned to look at him and shrugged saying, "Aw, come on, guys," and gone away because Cliffie had scared them. He was her brother and she knew he'd always look out for her, so there was lots she talked about with Cliffie. But there was other stuff she couldn't talk about with anybody, not even her best friend Sharon Ackerman.

Sometimes she imagined herself sitting with Auntie Lilbet and telling her the icky way it made her feel when her mom would call her and Cliffie to come get into the bed with her and John, or Martin, or Adam, or Jerry or one of her "sweeties"— that's what she called them, "her sweeties"—acting like it was a big treat to sit in bed with them and pretend to be having fun just because Mom had a new "sweetie" and she wanted Aly and Cliff to play family. Cliff would bring a book and sit there and read, not saying a word, and Aly would watch her mom and the man, doubting other people did stuff like this. Aly would look at John or Martin or Adam or Jerry or the others whose names she couldn't remember anymore and decide they didn't look too happy. They'd smile at her mom as if they had to because they knew it would make her happy but not because it made them happy. Their smiling was kind of the same thing as her making sure to wipe her feet on the mat before she walked on Auntie Lilbet's carpets.

"What're you talking about, happy?" Cliffie said when Aly tried to explain this observation to him. "If it made them happy, don't you think one of them would stick around for a while?"

"Is it our fault they never want to stay?" Aly asked seriously.

"Why the holy heck would it be *our* fault?" Cliff said. "What's with you, Al?"

"I don't know," Aly replied, hoping Cliff would elaborate, but he didn't. Still, she couldn't help feeling a little guilty that none of the sweeties ever stayed for very long. Maybe if she acted more like she was really having fun when Mom got her and Cliffie to come into the bed, then maybe one of the sweeties would stick around and marry their mom. Then they'd have a family just like her friends' families, with a regular mother who didn't work and a regular father who did. There had to be something she could be doing to help make everything come out right. But no matter how hard she tried, she couldn't think what it could be.

There were times when she'd look across the dinner table at her mother, still in one of the suits she wore to her office, and think how pretty she was, almost like a fairy princess in a story, the magic child of magical Lilbet. Feeling somewhat dizzy, she'd gaze at her mother, amazed that this angelic-seeming creature was the same person who'd be in a rage for weeks when one of her sweeties went away; the same person who'd come hurrying in one evening to announce she'd met the man she'd always dreamed of; the person who, sooner or later, would let the new sweetie sleep over and in the morning would call for Aly and Cliff to come pile into the bed, urging them to give Martin or Adam or Jerry a great big hug, and be very mad with him later on if Cliffie didn't want to do it. She'd listen to her mother and Cliffie talk, not so much hearing their words but kind of riding on the rise and fall of their voices. She'd look at her brother who always looked exactly like himself, and at her mother who seemed to be a whole bunch of different people, and she'd get the same feeling she got when she looked through the bull's-eye: that regardless of what she said or did, she'd never be able to see things clearly or make sense of what she saw.

CHAPTER
TWO

THE WINTER of 1952, when Aly was ten and Cliffie was twelve, several big things happened. First, Rheta changed jobs and went to work as sales director for a manufacturer of office machinery. It was a step up, both in salary and in terms of prestige. "Very damned few women in positions like this, you know!" she told the children. "You've got a mother you can be proud of." The kids assured her they were already proud of her. She accepted their assurances then went on to tell them they'd be moving—which came as no surprise. They'd been expecting this announcement since Steve had left in the middle of the night seven weeks earlier to go home to his family in Larchmont.

"I've found us a great new apartment on East 55th," Rheta said with enthusiasm. "You'll love it."

"When do we go?" Cliff asked, looking over at the door to his room as if estimating how long it would take him to pack.

"End of the month."

"Gee," Cliff said. "Three whole days."

"Don't give me any trouble," Rheta warned. "I was lucky to get someone to sublet this place, not to mention finding the new one. It's all on my shoulders, you know, Clifford. It's not as if there's a man around to help me."

"Okay," Cliff backed down, reluctant to let her start in on her favorite subject. "Fifty-fifth and where, anyway?"

"Lexington. You'll love it."

Since they never knew how long they were going to be staying, the kids had stopped fixing up their rooms. They left a lot of their books and toys in boxes so it would be easier to move. The fact was that Dad's and Auntie Lilbet's apartments were more familiar than the many places they'd lived. It was like going home when they went to visit. And Dad was always so glad to see them. He'd have things lined up for the whole weekend. Aly went off to her room, terribly disappointed that they'd have to cancel their planned weekend with him.

She loved both her parents, but differently. Her mom was so unpredictable. You could never be sure when she came through the door how she was going to act, if she'd be all excited for some reason or in a bad mood and tell them to get their own dinner, she was going to bed. Dad was always the same, quiet and happy to see them, interested in hearing whatever they had to say. Neither of the kids could imagine their parents married. They just didn't fit together. Dad was solid and settled, easygoing. Mom was changeable, forever unsettled, and ready to believe every new sweetie was the man of her dreams who'd make their lives perfect. As far as the kids could see, she'd divorced the one man who could've done that—their dad. Lilbet said so too. Dad had fewer rules than anybody else, and there were more things you could tell him without having to be afraid he'd get mad.

"We'll make it next weekend," he told Aly when she telephoned him after dinner that evening. "I talked to your mother this afternoon and it's all arranged."

Aly gave a relieved little laugh and said, "Cliff counted up and said this is our eleventh move."

"I thought it was more," her dad laughed.

"Yeah. So did I. Anyway, Mom says she's got a two-year lease this time, so maybe we'll be staying."

"Maybe," he agreed softly.

CLIFF DIRECTED the movers, telling them where things had to go while Aly unpacked the kitchen stuff. This was the second move the kids had handled completely on their own because Rheta couldn't get away from work, and they were getting into a routine. By the time the furniture was in place, Aly had the dishes stacked on the counters ready to be washed. She'd flattened the cartons and stacked them to be stored for the next move. She'd smoothed out the newspapers that had been wrapped around the kitchenware and tied them into a bundle ready to go to the incinerator room. After filling in the dollar amount on the check Rheta had left him to give to the movers, Cliff went to the kitchen to dry while Aly washed.

It took just under two hours to organize the kitchen, then they went to get their bedrooms set up. By the time Rheta arrived at 5:40, it looked as if they'd been living there for months. They sat down to eat the pizza Rheta had brought home and afterwards Rheta selected a window, got the hammer and a nail, and hung the bull's-eye.

"Nice place, huh?" she said, looking around.

Cliff and Aly nodded, then glanced at each other. There wasn't a whole lot of difference between this apartment and most of the others they'd lived in. Doors, walls, windows, floors, and ceilings. Kitchen, bathroom, bedrooms. This place had a dining el, and a half-bathroom in the hall. Otherwise, it was like the others. Little square bedrooms for the kids, a bigger square bedroom for Rheta.

Aly just couldn't understand why they were always moving. She knew what Rheta said; she'd heard it enough times. But that didn't mean it made sense. People were supposed to have a home and live in it, not go moving every time their mother got a new boyfriend. And the worst part of all the moving was having to go to the school office. The secretary would give Aly this look, as if she was saying, "Why can't you people settle down and be like everyone else?" She'd let out a big sigh while she looked for the Jackson kids' records, then make a show of crossing out the old address and putting down the new one. It was Aly's turn this time, so first thing Monday morning she'd have to go to the office and stand by the counter until the secretary decided to notice her. The thought of it made her hate her mother for putting them through this so many times.

"DOESN'T IT make you mad?" Aly said. She was lying on her stomach across the bottom of Cliff's bed watching him sort

13

through his books before putting them on the shelf at the head of his bed. Cliff was very careful with books, and had actually screamed at Aly one time for dog-earing his copy of *Kim*.

"What?" he said distractedly.

"All the moving and everything."

He shrugged, ran two fingers down the spine of *Great Expectations,* said, "I think I'll read this again," and put the book on his pillow. "There's no point getting mad, Al. It won't do any good. She'll still be the way she is, whether we get mad or not."

She thought about that while he selected another volume from the carton in front of him, studied its first page, then returned it to the carton. "Well I'm fed up with it," she declared. "This is positively the last time I'm doing it."

Cliff laughed. "What're you gonna do, use your allowance from Lilbet to pay the rent on this place?"

"No. Maybe I'll just go live with Dad."

He looked over at her, his expression serious. "I were you, Al, I'd be very careful who I said that to. Unless you don't mind starting World War Three."

"It's not fair," she protested, knowing he was right. The one time she mentioned the idea, her mother had stared at her for ages before starting to cry. And after she'd finished crying she'd begun hitting herself in the chest while she'd talked to the walls, telling them what a terrible mother she was and how she deserved to lose her children; she was a failure across the board, which was why no one wanted to stay with her. Aly wound up feeling like the rottenest child who'd ever lived. And when they'd next gone to visit her, Auntie Lilbet had taken her aside to say, "Why would you want to go saying such hurtful things to your mama, Alyssa? You know how hard she works for you and your brother. It isn't easy for a woman alone. I hope you never have to find that out for yourself. So now don't let me go hearing anymore about this. Okay? You've got to try to be more thoughtful, and I know you'll do that, won't you?" Naturally, Aly had agreed. But it didn't stop her now from thinking longingly of how good it would be to stay in one place and live with her father. No matter what anyone said it wasn't fair that she couldn't even talk about living with her dad.

"Nothing's fair when you're a kid," Cliff said wisely. "You just have to live through it. Then once you're grown up you can have things the way you want them."

"Are you saying this is the way Mom *wants* it?"

"No," he said impatiently. "I'm saying you can choose."

"So if she can choose, then this *is* the way she wants it."

Cliff took a moment before answering. "Yeah, maybe it is."

"Okay, wait. You're saying Mom says she doesn't want things to be this way but really she does?"

"Right."

"Why?"

"Because she doesn't *know* she's doing it."

"How can she not know?"

"There's a part of your brain that operates without your knowing about it. And it can have you doing stuff your conscious brain has you saying you don't want to do."

"I never heard of such a thing!" Aly said doubtfully.

"Listen, kiddo, just because you haven't heard of it doesn't mean it doesn't exist. It so happens there was an article in *Time* magazine a couple of weeks ago telling all about the conscious and subconscious."

Since Cliffie never made things up, Aly had to believe him, even if most of what he'd said made no sense to her. She climbed off his bed and went to her room puzzling over the notion of people doing things even though they said they didn't want to. It was an idea that really intrigued her, and she promised herself to pay closer attention in future to see if she could actually spot people saying one thing but doing another.

THEY'D ONLY been in the apartment on East 55th a few weeks when Rheta arrived home one evening wearing an expression both kids recognized. They waited for her to break the news, knowing it was impossible for their mother to keep secrets.

Halfway through dinner, Rheta burst out with it.

"I've met someone you're really going to like," she declared. "He's absolutely wonderful, not a bit like any of the others." She looked first at Cliff and then at Aly. "For one thing," she said momentously, "he's *divorced!*" She paused and waited for their response.

15

"That's great, Mom," Cliff said.

"Great, Mom," Aly chorused.

"And," Rheta hurried on, flushed and beaming, "he's only three years older than I am. He loves kids. He's very good-looking. And guess what he does!"

"What?" the kids asked together.

"You'll never believe it!" Rheta laughed. "He's a detective on the police force. Isn't that amazing? I'm actually going out with a cop!"

"What kind of detective?" Cliff asked.

"Homicide," Rheta answered in awed tones. "Can you imagine?"

"Murder," Cliff said as if to himself. "That's amazing, all right."

Aly didn't know how to respond. She'd been taught to go directly to a policeman if there was trouble of any kind. Policemen were people who would help you. She couldn't imagine having someone like that sleeping over and their mom calling them Sunday morning to come get into bed with an officer who wore a gun and went to murders.

"Does he wear a uniform?" Aly asked, thinking at least a policeman would be helpful and kind. All the ones she'd ever said hello to on the street had always been.

"He's a detective," Rheta explained. "Plain clothes. No uniform."

"That's good," Aly said, let down. She'd hoped for a few moments she might be able to show off her mother's policeman to Sharon Ackerman. Sharon would be very impressed.

"You'll meet him Friday night when he comes to pick me up. We're going out."

"What's his name?" Cliff asked.

"Don. I just can't wait for you to meet him! I know you'll be crazy about him. He's so dear."

Because it was expected of them, the kids made a show of being friendly and enthusiastic when the new man arrived that Friday evening. But from the outset there was something about Don Hart that bothered Aly. He looked all right; he was actually quite handsome, with dark brown hair and kind of slanting brown eyes. He was tall and lean and Aly thought he looked more like a cowboy than a detective. He gave them kind of a shy smile and shook hands with Cliff, then sat down in the living room to wait for Rheta to finish dressing. Rheta always kept her sweeties waiting at the beginning, and the kids were to offer drinks and cigarettes, then keep the sweetie company until Rheta made her entrance.

Don said he'd have a scotch and water and Cliff went to get that while Aly opened the cigarette box and held it out. Don took a cigarette, lit it with a Zippo, then sat down in one of the armchairs. Aly leaned against the arm of the sofa, watching the intense way he smoked the cigarette, startled when he swivelled to look at her, asking "How old're you?"

"I'll be eleven in January. And Cliffie's going to be thirteen in March. How old're you?"

Don laughed. "Thirty-six."

"Oh. I thought you were thirty-eight."

He frowned, then shook his head, as if she'd said something stupid. But Rheta had said he was three years older than her, so somebody was fibbing.

Cliff came back, handed Don his drink, then sat on the sofa next to the arm where Aly was leaning.

"D'you like being a detective?" Cliff asked with genuine interest.

"It has its moments," Don answered flatly before tasting the scotch. "It's a job."

"I guess it's pretty gruesome dealing with murders all the time," Cliff said.

"Like I said, it's a job."

Cliff and Aly exchanged looks.

Rheta came in just then, putting a halt to the conversation. They all turned to look at her. Her long light brown hair was done up in a topknot, and she was wearing a new black dress that was, at ninety-five dollars, the single most expensive garment—outside of her wedding dress—she'd ever bought. Her gray eyes looked very large, her teeth seemed very white.

"You look wonderful, Mom," Cliff said.

"Yeah, Mom," Aly agreed.

"I'll go along with that," Don put in, getting to his feet.

"Cliff, be a sweetheart and fix me a drink," Rheta said, sliding

17

into the second armchair and reaching for the cigarette box.

Don at once had his Zippo out to light Rheta's cigarette, and Aly watched the two of them, intrigued. Don couldn't seem to take his eyes off Rheta, but then they were all like that at the beginning. After a while, something happened and then the sweeties would sit and talk with Cliff and Aly and hardly even look up when their mom came into the room. That was when Rheta would start talking about what cowardly bastards men were and how she wished to God she could live without them. But there was something different about the way Don looked at Rheta. He had a way of looking—at all of them—that made Aly feel funny. Partly it was the way his eyes slanted down, and partly it was the way he hardly ever smiled.

"So what d'you think?" Aly asked Cliff after their mother and Don had left.

"He's okay, I guess. Nothing special. I give him three months, tops."

"I don't know," Aly said. "This one's not married, Cliffie. It's different this time." She thought a moment, then said, "I kinda didn't like him."

"How come?" Cliff asked, twiddling the tuner dial on the radio.

"I don't know. He's funny, sort of."

"I wouldn't let it worry you, Al. Three months from now he'll be a memory."

"I hope so," Aly said fervently, wishing she could find words to fit the feeling she had about Don.

CHAPTER
THREE

VERY EARLY Saturday morning Aly crept into her brother's room and whispered, "Cliffie, wake up. Come on, wake up." When he blinked open his eyes, she said, "He already slept over!" then waited for him to absorb this.

Cliff sat up, asking, "Are you sure?"

"Positive. His coat's hanging in the hall closet."

"She's going fast this time."

"That's for sure. Cliffie, let's not be home when they get up."

"Where should we go at 7:30 on a Saturday morning?"

"We could go over to Lilbet's for breakfast. She loves it when we do that."

"She loves it when she *invites* us, Al."

"We'll surprise her. She won't be mad. If we stay, Mom's going to get up in about an hour and start making a great big breakfast, and she's going to expect us to get into bed with them and eat it. I don't want to."

After several moments' consideration he said, "Okay. We'll go see Lilbet. Just don't let me forget to leave Mom a note or she'll have a fit."

Their grandmother was actually pleased to see them. She told Pearl, the housekeeper, to prepare food for the children and Pearl said, "Yes, ma'am," as if Cliff and Aly hadn't already told her when they got there that they'd come to have breakfast with Lilbet.

"To what do I owe this honor?" Lilbet asked when the three of them were seated at the table with the morning sun pouring

19

warmly over them through the three large dining room windows.

"It was Aly's idea," Cliff said, with a look at Aly that said, "You explain it."

Aly's instinct was always to tell the truth, but in this case she sensed it wouldn't be smart. When it came to Rheta, Lilbet couldn't always be counted on to see the kids' point of view. "Mom's got a new sweetie," Aly said with a smile. "We thought we'd let them be alone." Cliff rolled his eyes. Aly looked quickly back at her grandmother. "This one's a murder detective with the police."

Lilbet drank some of her coffee while she took in this information. Then, carefully setting down her cup, she said, "Funny, Rheta didn't mention him to me."

Aly said nothing further but paid attention to her bacon and eggs. One of the things she liked best about Lilbet was the way she did things. The apartment always looked just so, with fresh flowers and magazines arranged on the coffee table, the pillows plumped on the sofa and armchairs, the drapes looped back with fancy cords attached to shiny brass hooks on the walls. The carpet always had vacuum cleaner tracks and the furniture smelled of lemon wax. When Aly once ventured to comment on this to her mother, Rheta got very angry. "My mother happens to have a great deal of time and money, and reliable staff to keep her place clean. *I* don't happen to have the same kind of resources, little girl." All she'd done was make an innocent observation, but Aly wound up not only having to apologize to her mother but to console her, too; assuring her she hadn't been criticizing Rheta's housekeeping, although she and Cliffie had been doing most of the work since Rheta stopped employing housekeepers and the cleaning lady who used to come twice a week. Aly learned to be cautious in her praise of others.

Lilbet was fully fashionably dressed at all times, even if she was just sitting at home on the sofa reading a novel. If Lilbet had been out shopping she'd stage a little fashion show complete with running commentary on each garment so Aly could see and admire the new things she'd bought. She loved spending time with her grandmother and considered the two weeks she and Cliff had stayed with Lilbet while Rheta was on her honeymoon with Jerry one of the best times of her life. She could hardly remember Jerry but she could recall every last thing she and Cliffie and Lilbet had done during those two weeks.

They'd just finished eating when Rheta called. Lilbet went off to talk to her and Aly looked guiltily over at her brother.

"Yes, I left a note even if you did forget to remind me," he said. "You worry too much."

"I can't help it. Anyway, you don't worry at all."

"I worry just as much as the next guy. This is not exactly the Nelson family, you know."

This reference to *Ozzie and Harriet* sent Aly in a new direction. "If we spend the day with Lilbet, we could watch television tonight. We could see the Jackie Gleason show, and *Your Show of Shows*. I love Sid Caesar and Imogene Coca!"

"Not a chance," Cliff said, but with reluctance. "Rheta's going to expect us home."

Lilbet returned saying, "Your mother wants you to go right home as soon as you've finished your breakfast."

"I told you," Cliff said quietly.

"What, honey?" Lilbet asked him.

"Aly wanted to stay and spend the day with you. I was telling her Mom would expect us home."

Lilbet gave her granddaughter a smile. "You really do love me, don't you, honey?"

"Sure I do," Aly replied sincerely.

"Did you want to stay, too, Clifford?" Lilbet asked.

"I'd like to, but I really think Aly and I should go home," he answered, casting a meaningful look at his sister.

"Cliffie's right, Auntie Lilbet."

"If you're sure," she said. "You know I always love having the two of you to visit."

"DON WAS very disappointed," Rheta scolded them. "We both were looking forward to spending the morning with you."

Aly apologized while Cliff started toward his room.

"Just a minute, sonny!" Rheta called. "Where d'you think you're going? You've got things to do around here."

He turned, asking, "What things?"

"I want you to take in the laundry, for one."

"Okay."

"And then I want you to pick up a few things from the market."

"Okay."

"And Aly, it's your week to vacuum. You kids have work to do, so let's get to it."

Cliff went off with a grocery list, twenty dollars, and a pillowcase full of sheets to drop off at the Chinese hand laundry. Aly sighed loudly, then opened the kitchen closet door to get out the vacuum cleaner. Rheta was letting them know she was annoyed. That's just too bad, Aly said to herself, getting the machine plugged in and turned on. Too too bad. This sweetie was different from the others, and not just because he was a policeman. It was his dark slanty eyes, and the way he looked at her. Nobody, not even her mom, was going to make her do something she didn't want to do. And she didn't want to get into bed with Mom and that man.

ALL TOO quickly it seemed as if Don was forever at their place. He worked strange hours, sometimes for a whole day and night. He started turning up early to have coffee with Rheta while she was getting ready for work, then he'd drive her to the office before going back to his own apartment to sleep for a few hours.

About six weeks after their mom began dating Don, Aly let herself into the apartment one afternoon, looked down the hallway, and saw Don come walking naked out of Rheta's bedroom. Without even stopping to think about it, Aly shot backwards out of the apartment, pulled her key from the lock, and raced back to the elevator. Feeling shaky, she sat downstairs in the lobby talking to Frankie, the doorman, until Cliff arrived.

"How come you're down here?" he asked her once they were in the elevator.

"I got home, opened the door, and there was Don in the hallway. *Naked!*"

"Are you kidding?" Cliff laughed.

"I am not kidding!" she said, offended that he'd doubt her.

"You're sure he was actually *naked*?" he asked her.

Aly nodded angrily.

Cliff said, "Oh, boy!" and held her back when the elevator doors opened. "We'd better talk about this," he said, and poked the G button to take them back to the lobby.

Frankie shrugged at seeing them emerge from the elevator, then hurried to open the door for a woman laden with groceries.

"Should I tell Mom?" Aly asked.

"I don't know," he said. "I think maybe if you do tell her, Don's gonna say you're making it up."

"But I'm not!"

"Okay, Al. I believe you. I'm just trying to figure out what to do."

"There's something wrong with this guy, Cliffie. I'm scared of him."

"Did he see you?"

"Sure he saw me! I opened the door and he came out of Mom's room without any clothes on."

"So we can't tell Mom we both saw him," Cliff reasoned. "He'll probably say he thought it was Mom coming home, and she'll believe him."

"Why should she believe him and not us?"

"We're kids," he said with a shrug. "Nobody believes kids."

"That's so unfair!"

He shrugged again. Then, seeing she was on the verge of tears, said, "From now on, when you get home from school sit down here and wait for me and we'll go up together. Okay?"

Aly looked around the lobby. "Okay," she agreed.

"If I've got to stay late at school, I'll try to let you know. Otherwise just sit here and wait for me."

"What if Mom gets home first?"

"Tell her you left your keys in your desk or something."

"Okay," she said morosely. "Maybe I'll tell Dad. . . ."

"Don't do that!" he exclaimed. "You'll just make trouble. Do as I've said and everything'll be fine. But for Pete's sake don't go telling Dad. He'd go nuts if you told him Mom's boyfriend showed himself to you naked. That'd be all we need. Just do what I said. Okay?"

"You'd feel differently if it'd happened to you," she sulked.

"Let's go up now. And if you have to tell Mom, don't say anything to her in front of Don. Wait till he's gone!"

Don didn't go. He and Rheta sat in the living room for hours talking and drinking scotch. At 9:30, Aly went to stand in the doorway to say, "I'm going to bed now, Mom."

Rheta looked over, smiling, and said, "Come give me a kiss goodnight, sweetheart."

Aly did, and straightened to go as Rheta said, "'Now give Don a kiss, too."

Aly stood gazing at her mother, waiting for Rheta to say she didn't have to kiss Don if she didn't want to. But Rheta said, "Go on. We don't want Don to think you don't like him, do we?"

No way out. Aly ducked forward, let her cheek touch against Don's, then hurried off, rubbing at her face where it had come into contact with his skin. She went straight to her brother's room, knocked, then opened the door. She walked in and flopped on the end of Cliff's bed, whispering, "She made me kiss him goodnight."

Cliff finished writing something in his three-ring binder, then turned to look over. "He's spending the night?"

"They're in the living room drinking scotch. They both smell of it. I hate the smell of scotch."

"It's not Dr. Pepper," he said in that grown-up tone he put on sometimes that made Aly's teeth ache.

"And you'd know that, wouldn't you?"

"I've had it a few times. After a while it's not so bad."

"You're such a liar. Anyway, yes, he's spending the night as far as I can tell."

"On a weeknight, too," Cliff mused. "She did this with Jerry, you know."

"God, Cliffie! Are you saying she's going to *marry* that man? Because if she is, then I'm definitely going to live with Dad and I don't care what anybody says. I mean it!"

"Calm down, Al. I don't know what she's going to do. I'm just saying."

"Well, don't just say. Okay? I'd die if she married him. He's so *awful*. Can I sleep in here with you tonight?"

"What for?"

"Can I or not?"

"I don't care. But I'm going to be up for a while, reading."

"That's fine. I'll just go get my blankets and stuff."

IN THE morning, Rheta crept around the kitchen, shushing them while she looked for the Alka Seltzer.

"Where's Don?" Cliff asked.

"Gone to work," Rheta answered, her voice husky from the scotch and too many cigarettes.

"You sick, Mom?" Aly asked.

"A little hung over," Rheta admitted. "Cliff, be a sweetheart and bring me a cup of that coffee when it's finished perking. I've got to get dressed or I'll be late." She pushed her hair behind her ears and stood looking at the two kids for a moment before going off to her bedroom.

Aly thought Rheta looked like a little kid with her hair hanging down and no makeup on, a pretty girl with great big eyes and tiny feet. It was only recently that Aly had realized how small their mother was. Aly wasn't eleven yet and she was almost as tall as Rheta. It gave her a funny feeling to be nearly the same height as her mother, as if the closer in size they got the more equal they were somehow.

Cliff got up to pour the coffee, and Aly said, "I'll take it."

"Okay by me." He went back to his cereal and *Great Expectations*.

"Are you going to marry the detective, Mom?" Aly asked, watching her mother sip the hot coffee before setting the cup down on the rim of the sink.

"His name is Don. And we've only been seeing each other a little while. Who knows where it'll end up."

"Does that mean you'd marry him if he asked you?"

"Maybe. I don't know. Go finish your breakfast now."

"Mom?"

"What, Aly? I really don't have time to talk to you now."

"Okay," Aly retreated. "Never mind."

25

"We'll talk when I get home. Okay, pumpkin?" Rheta looked at her in the mirror.

"Sure. That's okay."

It bothered her that she didn't get a chance to tell her mother what had happened the day before, and promised herself she'd tell her that afternoon. Then her mom would talk to Don and tell him he couldn't go around other people's apartments naked, upsetting the children. It just wasn't fair.

RHETA LAUGHED and said, "Don told me all about it."

"He did?" Aly was taken aback.

"Sure. He said you came charging in looking for me and caught him in the altogether."

For a few seconds all Aly could do was gape at her mother. Then her mouth got so full of words she could hardly get them out in any kind of rational order. "I did *not* go charging in!" she protested indignantly. "I was coming in the front door when *he* came charging out at *me*—and he was stark *naked*! I wasn't looking for you, Mom. Why would I be looking for you at a quarter to four when I know you don't get home until after six?" Aly was almost choking on her upset. "He *lied* to you!"

Rheta frowned.

"You don't *believe* me?" Aly was shattered. It was plain as day her mother didn't believe her. She was taking the word of a stranger against her own child's. That just wasn't right.

"Of course I believe you," Rheta said in a way that convinced Aly she really didn't. "I just don't understand why you're making such a fuss about this, Alyssa."

Aly turned to her brother for help.

"Mom," he said calmly, "what was he doing here anyway?"

"I told him he could stay," Rheta said in a tone that stated they had no right to question her actions and decisions.

"Did you tell him he could parade around in front of us naked?" Cliff asked in that same calm tone.

Aly looked back and forth between them, fiercely gratified by Cliff's defense of her. At least somebody knew when she was telling the truth.

"That's enough!" Rheta declared. "Don did tell me about it. Okay? Obviously it's not going to happen again."

"Does he have a key?" Aly asked. "Can he get in when we're not home?"

"Yes, he has a key. I gave it to him."

"Why?" Aly asked plaintively.

"Look!" Rheta said. "The two of you might as well know it right now: Don's moving in with us."

Aly felt as if she'd been hit in the chest. All the air went out of her lungs, and she wanted to sit down. This was the worst thing that had ever happened. Rheta didn't even care whether she and Cliffie wanted him there.

"Mom," Cliff said, as if he'd read Aly's mind, "don't you care what the two of us think?"

"Sure I do," Rheta replied.

"I don't like him," Aly whispered.

"You've hardly had a chance to get to know him," Rheta said coaxingly. "Don't you think you should give him a little time? He certainly likes the two of you."

"What does he like about us?" Cliff challenged her.

"You know," Rheta said, faltering. "He likes you both. Why wouldn't he?"

"I don't like him," Aly repeated more strongly.

"Give him a chance," Rheta pleaded, putting her arms around both the children. "He's shy and kind of quiet, but once you get to know him you'll see what a nice man he is."

Cliff put his foot down gently over top of Aly's, and she turned to read the message in his eyes. Then he said, "Okay, Mom, we'll wait and see." He increased the pressure of his foot and Aly said, "Okay, Mom."

At once Rheta brightened and suggested they go out to Luigi's for dinner. While they were getting their coats, Aly asked, "Why'd you do that?" and Cliff said, "Sshhh. We'll talk about it later."

"There's always the chance it was an accident," Cliff said. They were sitting on the floor of his room with their backs against the side of his bed, talking very quietly. "You don't know for sure that it wasn't, Al."

"No," she conceded, "but I know what it felt like, and it felt like he'd been waiting for me to come home."

"But how could he know it was you and not me?"

"That's true," she said, deflated, her argument shot full of holes. "He couldn't have known that."

"Listen, kiddo. You know and I know there's not a chance that this guy's going to work out any better for Mom than the others. But you also know how she is. She always starts off saying this one is it; this time it's going to be perfect. She likes him and she's happy. A couple of months, and he'll be gone and she'll be complaining what a jerk he was."

"So why bother to go through all that? It's just stupid."

"I don't know," he admitted. "But it's the way she does things. And she's happy, so it's no skin off our noses, really."

"I don't like that man, Cliffie, and I don't want him living here with us. He makes me nervous."

"Don't worry. I'll look out for you the way I always do. You can wait for me downstairs if you don't want to be up here alone with him. And like I said, by your birthday he'll probably be gone."

"But he'll be here for Christmas," she complained. "It's gonna wreck everything."

"No, it won't. And anyway we're going to Dad's on the twenty-sixth until the second. We're hardly even going to be here."

"I still don't like it," she said, finally giving up the fight, but secretly convinced Don was going to ruin everything. He never smiled, hardly ever talked—even to Rheta. He just sat in the living room with his big long legs stuck way out, smoking one cigarette after another and drinking something, coffee a lot of the time, or beer, and scotch when Rheta was home. He hardly ever ate, either, which was probably why he was so skinny and kind of mean looking.

DON MOVED in on the fifteenth of December, bringing two suit-cases, and several cartons of books and records. He slipped into their lives without fanfare, establishing himself in the apartment as if he'd made similar moves many times before and had learned how best to blend in.

He was a quiet man who seemed to have as little interest in the children as they had in him, except for the way his eyes seemed to follow Aly around all the time. It felt as if he was watching her, waiting for something, and it made her jumpy so that every time she left the apartment and breathed in the air on the street it was like she'd escaped to freedom. She dreaded going home each day, in case he'd be there, and sometimes spent hours in the lobby waiting for Cliffie or her mother to arrive. It was always Rheta who suggested they do things as a group, never Don. He never said no to going out with Cliff and Aly; he simply didn't extend himself. It was as if he didn't consider them real people because they were children, so it wouldn't have occurred to him to offer to take them to the zoo or the planetarium, to a movie or just for a walk—things most of Rheta's other men had done. Cliff and Aly were nothing more than noisy, irritating obstacles that got in the way between him and Rheta.

When he wasn't working, and Rheta wasn't home, he sat in the living room chain-smoking Lucky Strikes and drinking beer while he read newspapers or paperback novels, or listened to some football game on the radio. Every few days he'd get out a can of special oil and some rags, take his gun to pieces and clean it. When Cliffie expressed an interest in watching him do it, Don muttered something he didn't hear, but Cliffie got the message and went off to his room.

Both kids were polite, making a point of saying hi when they got home from school, but stayed out of his way. In the evenings when Rheta returned home, Don would shift over to the kitchen to keep her company while she cooked dinner. And once he sat down at the table with a glass of scotch and his Luckys he seemed to undergo a complete transformation. He'd laugh and talk and joke with Rheta; he'd even fondle her while she was cooking. If Cliff or Aly happened to come into the kitchen, Rheta would get red in the face and try to brush him away, but Don would look right into Cliff's or Aly's eyes and keep on patting Rheta's bottom, or hugging her around the middle while pressing up against her from behind, or kissing her on the back of the neck. Rheta would tell him to stop, and laugh with embarrassment, but Don looked as serious about what he was doing to Rheta as he did when he cleaned his gun. The kids would grab whatever they'd come for and get out fast. They didn't like seeing Rheta embarrassed or the proprietary way Don handled their mother. His expression seemed to say to them, Make sure you see this and understand it. Because I'm the one who's in charge here now. I can make your mother do whatever I want.

The lock on the bathroom door had been broken when they'd moved in. Until Don came along it hadn't been a problem, but now that he was living with them Aly was on edge every time she went to take a bath. Each time she started the water running in the tub, she kept her eyes on the door, certain Don was going to walk in on her. If she had to use the toilet she used the half-bathroom in the front hall that had a working lock. She kept putting off her baths but had to bathe sometime and finally asked Cliff to stand guard for her.

"What for?" he asked, making a face that said she'd gone completely nuts.

"Just because. Okay?" She didn't want to have to explain.

"No. Why the heck should I do that, Al?"

"I'm afraid someone's going to come in while I'm in the tub."

"Oh, come on," he said impatiently. "We all knock. Nothing's going to happen."

"It won't if you're sitting outside the door, keeping watch."

"I've got better things to do, kiddo."

"It'll only be just this once, and I'll be really fast."

Cliff relented. "Oh, for Pete's sake. Okay. But only this once. Let me just grab my book."

In the weeks between Don's moving in and Christmas, Aly bathed twice at her father's place and three times at her grandmother's. Since cleanliness was of great importance to Lilbet, she didn't question Aly's new habit of showering upon arrival. But the situation was getting Aly down and she even tried to repair the bathroom lock herself without success. At last, she asked her mother to do something about it.

"I'm not a baby anymore, Mom. I have the right to a little privacy."

"You should've said something," Rheta said with a smile that really irritated Aly, a smile that Rheta had worn when she'd given Aly and Cliff a little talk about sex the year before. "I understand about these things. I'll get Don to fix it."

Aly wanted to tell her mother to get somebody else to do it. She had the idea that Don would do something to the lock that would let him come into the bathroom if he wanted to. But after trying it a dozen times, she couldn't see how the door could possibly be opened from the outside, and felt somewhat more secure taking her baths, but her anxiety then transferred itself to the lack of a lock on her bedroom door. She began finding it hard to get to sleep at night. The moment she turned out the light she imagined she heard footsteps approaching her door, imagined she could see the knob slowly turning. She solved the problem temporarily by leaving the bedside light on all night. But then Rheta discovered she was doing this and wanted to know why. "I need a night light," Aly told her.

"Why, all of a sudden? You never needed one before. What's the matter, pumpkin?"

"Nothing," Aly told her, angry with her mother for not being able to see there was a problem. She was the mother; she was supposed to know when her children were upset. But she didn't see anything. "I just need a night light."

"You're sure there's nothing the matter?" Rheta persisted, stroking Aly's forehead with the back of her hand as if checking for a fever.

"I'm fine, honestly." If she couldn't see it for herself, Aly refused to tell her, remembering too vividly the way Rheta hadn't believed her about Don being naked that time.

"I'll get you a light," Rheta said, her expression bemused, "something small that won't use up so much electricity."

The bathroom door was now lockable; she had a night light in her room; but Aly was still apprehensive. If anything, her anxiety seemed to be growing daily so that she was watchful even when spending the weekend with her brother at her father's apartment, or visiting her grandmother overnight. Both her father and grandmother commented on her wary behavior, and she assured them both she was fine. "I've got a lot of school-work, that's all," she lied.

ALY WANTED to open the presents Christmas Eve instead of Christmas morning. If they didn't, she knew Rheta would order Aly and Cliff to climb into bed for a big family cuddle before the opening of the presents. But if the exchange of gifts was out of the way, the only excuse Rheta would have for getting them into the bedroom would be breakfast. So Aly first talked her mother into shifting to Christmas Eve for the opening of the presents. Then she talked Cliff into getting up early to make breakfast. "We'll take in two trays and say Merry Christmas and like that and then leave them to eat. By the time they're fin-ished, we'll be up and dressed and ready to go to Auntie Lil-bet's. You can sit and read until it's time to go."

"What's the point of all this?" Cliff asked earnestly.

"I don't like that man and I'm not getting into her bed for a cuddle. Just do it for me. Okay?"

"Yeah, okay. But I think you're cracked, kiddo."

"I'm really not, you know. One of these days you'll see I was right."

EVERYONE BUT Don knew how immediately and with what in-tensity Lilbet disliked him. She was charming and polite, but Rheta and the kids could practically see and touch her disap-proval. The fact that Don couldn't see he'd failed to win Lilbet over further reduced him in Aly's eyes. She believed people should be able to tell when other people didn't like them, and either do something about it or go away altogether. It didn't make sense that someone would stay around where he wasn't wanted. And Don definitely wasn't wanted in the apartment on Park Avenue at Seventy-sixth Street.

Aly studied the man the entire time they were at Lilbet's, able in this place to see him from a different perspective. He'd dressed carefully in a suit and tie with his shoes polished but somehow he didn't fit in. It showed in the way he looked at everything as if trying to guess how much it cost, and in the way he kowtowed to Auntie Lilbet. Aly actually felt kind of sorry for him. She could see him looking at Rheta differently now that he'd met her mother and seen where Lilbet lived.

Christmas dinner was served early, as always, at two o'clock. At four o'clock Rheta announced she and Don were leaving, ". . . but you kids can stay, if you like."

"We'll stay!" Aly said happily.

"I can speak for myself," Cliff said.

"You want to head on home, honey?" Lilbet asked him.

"No, I'll stay. I just like to make my own decisions," he said pointedly.

"You behave yourselves," Rheta told the kids. "And don't wear out your welcome."

"They could never do that," Lilbet said with a doting smile.

After seeing Rheta and Don to the door, Lilbet came back to the living room, took a Camel from the Limoges box on the coffee table, lit it, then sank down onto the sofa with a sigh. "Well," she drawled after a moment, "I swear I don't know where she finds them. Now you children didn't hear me say that," she said. "Did you?"

Gratified, Aly said, "Not me."

Cliff shook his head and went back to turning the pages of the leatherbound illustrated limited edition of *Oliver Twist* that was a Christmas gift from his grandmother. "He's not so bad," he said judiciously. "He's just not used to people like us. We're hardly a typical family."

"We're not so different, either," Aly disagreed.

Cliff shrugged and turned to the next illustration in his book.

"I have never judged people by the size of their pocketbooks," Lilbet said.

"That's not what it's all about," Cliff said, at last looking up.

"Oh, honey," Lilbet said sadly, "that's exactly what all this is about. Now," she clapped her hands together with finality, "we're not going to say one more word about it. We're going to enjoy our evening together."

As soon as the elevator doors opened they could hear the shouting. One of the neighbors had her door cracked open and was peering out, but quickly closed the door at the sight of the kids. Cliff already had his key out and the two of them automatically ran down the carpeted hallway toward the sound of their mother's distress.

With Cliff working the key and Aly turning the handle, they got the door open and raced to the living room to see Rheta and Don standing inches apart, faces twisted, hands clenched. The two went silent at once and turned to look at Cliff and Aly.

"I'm going out!" Don barked, turning to glare at the kids before snatching up his coat and stalking out.

The front door slammed. Cliff and Aly stood waiting for Rheta to say something. She pushed the hair back behind her ears, then lit a cigarette. "Notice anything?" she asked with a faked little laugh.

Neither of the kids understood.

"Look around," Rheta said, one hand on her hip, the other holding the cigarette near her mouth as she herself looked around.

Feeling somewhat stupid, Cliff and Aly exchanged glances— What the hell was going on here? they mutely asked each other—then obediently looked around the room.

"We've got TV," Aly saw.

"My big present for you two. That's why we left Lilbet's early, to come back and hook it up."

"What were you fighting about?" Aly asked as Cliff went over to inspect the set.

"I don't even remember, it was that stupid. Forget it." Rheta draped an arm around Aly's shoulders. "It isn't important." She looked at her watch and said, *"Racket Squad* will be coming on in a few minutes, if you want to watch."

Cliff turned on the set then took several steps back, waiting for the picture to come on.

"Are you going to stay and watch with us?" Aly asked, reluctant to move away from her mother's encircling arm.

"Sure. Get your coats off and we'll all watch together." Rheta sat down in the middle of the sofa, carefully tipping the ash from her cigarette into the ashtray on the coffee table.

"How come you don't tell him to go away?" Aly asked, throwing off her coat, then going to nestle close to her mother.

Rheta looked at her in surprise. "Why should I do that?"

"Well, you were fighting . . ."

"That doesn't mean we don't like each other. People disagree sometimes, you know, Aly."

"I know but you were shouting really loud. It sounded like you were killing each other."

Rheta laughed.

"We could hear the two of you all the way to the elevator," Cliff said. "It didn't sound like a 'disagreement.' "

"You're so adorable, the two of you; a couple of little worry-warts. It was a minor squabble. Don'll walk around the block a couple of times to cool off. Then he'll be back and everything'll be fine. You've got to understand he does a very difficult job. He needs to blow off a little steam now and again. That's all. You can understand that, can't you, pumpkin?"

Aly didn't at all, but she could see how badly her mother wanted her to go along on this, so she said, "I guess so," and gave Rheta a hug.

"One day," Rheta said softly, her cheek against Aly's, "you'll fall in love and it'll all make sense to you then. You'll see."

She might fall in love some day, Aly thought, but it wouldn't be with anyone like Don. It wouldn't, in fact, be with anyone remotely like the kind of men her mother took up with. Not counting their dad, of course. If she could, she'd find someone exactly like her father.

CHAPTER
FIVE

DURING THE week she and Cliff spent with their father, Aly made a point of phoning home every evening to talk to her mother and be sure everything was okay. She was convinced that as long as she spoke to her mother nightly nothing bad could happen to her. She knew it was a pretty dumb idea but hearing Rheta's voice made her feel better, and her dad and Cliff didn't mind if she called.

They had a terrific week. Their dad had taken the time off—"Not much goes on in banking the last week of the year," he told them—and he'd mapped out activities to please both the kids and himself. But first they had to exchange gifts. Aly got saddle shoes and insisted on wearing them daily. Cliff received a copy of *The Old Man and the Sea,* and carried it with him everywhere they went. Cliff had selected their present for their dad and Hal made a point of telling them several times how pleased he was with *The Caine Mutiny.*

They went to see *The Greatest Show on Earth* and *High Noon* and *Ivanhoe.* They visited the Metropolitan, the Museum of Modern Art, and took a round-trip ride on the Staten Island Ferry. They ate Chinese food down on Mott Street, tried Japanese in a place on Third Avenue near Sixty-sixth, and went to Luigi's for Italian.

As they'd done every year since the divorce, they celebrated New Year's Eve with Auntie Lilbet and a group of her friends. Dressed in their party clothes, they had wine with dinner and were allowed to stay up until midnight when they got to drink real French champagne to toast the new year. Everybody got hugged and kissed, and then the three of them left to spend their last night together.

Aly was reluctant to leave and clung to her father all morning, finally climbing into his lap right at the breakfast table and winding her arms around his neck. Cliff groaned and said, "You're going to strangle the man, Al."

"It's okay, Cliff," Hal said, smoothing Aly's hair. "Is something the matter, Aly?"

"I just wish we didn't have to go, that's all."

"You'll be coming for another weekend in a week. Plus there's your birthday. I was thinking maybe the two of us would go somewhere special for dinner. You wouldn't mind, would you, Cliff, if your sister and I made it an occasion?"

"I wouldn't mind. You really should read this, Dad," he said, at the end of the Hemingway novel. "Want me to leave it for you?"

"Sure," Hal Jackson said. "And I'll lend you the Wouk book when I'm finished. So, miss," he said to Aly. "Where d'you think we should have your birthday dinner? Any ideas?"

"I'll ask Lilbet. She'll probably know lots of good places."

Hal laughed. "She'll know places that'll put me in hock for the next five years. But you go ahead and ask her, honey. I'm sure she'll come up with someplace perfect." He was quiet for a moment or two, trying to interpret his daughter's mood. Aly had always been a good-natured, easy to read child. But in the last couple of months she'd been quieter, less spontaneous than usual. He knew she was approaching a time of life that was difficult for most kids, but he couldn't help feeling that what was bothering her wasn't anything so fundamental. Holding her secure on his lap, Hal looked over at Cliff, perennially tickled by how strongly Cliff resembled the boy Hal once had been: tall for his age, solidly built, and always lost in a book. Hal, too, had looked sixteen at the age of twelve. "How d'you feel about heading home, sport?" he asked his son.

Cliff shrugged. "Kind of the way Aly does, I guess. I wouldn't mind being able to stay. But then I wouldn't want to run out on Mom."

"What's going on?" Hal asked the children. "Seriously, what's up?"

"Aly doesn't like Mom's new boyfriend."

"You don't like him either," Aly accused.

"He doesn't bother me as much as he does you."

"What's wrong with the man?" Hal asked.

"He's just kind of quiet," Cliff said.

"Not when Mom's around he isn't," Aly disagreed. "He's weird and I don't like him. But Mom's in love with him even though they fight."

At this Hal was mildly alarmed. "Fight how?" he asked.

"She means they argue," Cliff explained. "'Loudly," he added.

"That would bother me," Hal told Aly sympathetically. "But it doesn't mean anything necessarily. Some people like to argue."

"That's what Mom says," Aly admitted, wishing she had the words to describe why Don bothered her. All she had was a feeling and it was impossible to explain; a strange feeling that sometimes faded away almost to nothing, and other times got so big it took up all the space inside her body so that her skin got too tight and felt like it might split open. Don would get this look and his face would turn sort of sharp; his eyes would go very dark and small, and the air around him would go noisy like a station on the radio that wasn't properly tuned in.

Hugging her father tightly, she said again, "I wish we could stay with you."

"You wouldn't want your mother to be lonely," he said charitably, so that Aly had to wonder, yet again, if he still loved Rheta. If he did, it must've made him very sad when she kept finding new men.

"No," she agreed, getting choked up. Her dad was such a nice man, always caring so much about things. "I wouldn't want that. But I don't want you to be lonely, either," she said, and started to cry even though she'd promised herself she wouldn't.

"Now, Aly," he said consolingly, patting her back. "Who said anything about my being lonely? You're such a mushy kid." He shifted to get a hanky from his pocket to dry her face. "No more tears. Okay? We can't send you home crying, or your mother'll think you had a lousy time."

"Come on, Al," Cliff said impatiently. "Dry up and let's get going. I think it's just adolescence, Dad," he said grandly, as if he'd long-since left that stage behind.

"You two are really something," Hal said, at last moving Aly off his lap. "I've got Winnie the Weeper over here, and Methusaleh over there. What a pair!" he said affectionately. "Make sure you've got all your stuff. Otherwise you'll have to wait a week to get it. I'm off to Chicago tomorrow, remember."

Before they left, Aly threw her arms around her father and hugged him as hard as she could. "I love you, Dad," she said fervently. "Will you phone us from Chicago?"

"Sure," he said, taken a little off guard by her ferocity, "if you want."

Somewhat embarrassed by his sister's emotional display, yet inspired by it too, Cliff kissed his father good-bye, said, "Take care of yourself, Dad, and thanks for a really swell week." Then he shook his father's hand, made sure Aly was safely in the back of the cab, and slid in after her.

RIGHT AWAY Aly knew something had happened. Rheta's face looked sort of lumpy; she was wearing way more makeup than usual; and she seemed different. Aly glanced at Cliff and he was looking back at her as if to say, We have to talk, kiddo.

"I made some tuna salad, if you guys're hungry," Rheta said after kissing each of them. "I thought I'd lie down for a couple of hours. We had kind of a late night last night and I'm a little pooped."

"Where's Don?" Cliff asked casually, hanging up his coat.

"He had to go to work. Something came up."

Both kids said, "Oh," and went off to their rooms to unpack their bags.

They met in the kitchen fifteen minutes later. Cliff buttered the bread while Aly got the lettuce and tuna salad from the refrigerator. Working side by side at the counter, they assembled some sandwiches, poured two glasses of milk, then ate leaning against the counter, their eyes on the kitchen door as they discussed in an undertone what might have gone on during their week-long absence.

"Did you see her face?" Aly asked.

"Looks like she's been crying," Cliff said a bit angrily.

"Why doesn't she get rid of him? She's not happy with him anymore. He makes her cry. So why doesn't she send him away?"

"Maybe," he said slowly, "he doesn't want to go."

"What're you talking about? If somebody asks you to go, you go."

"Some people, you can't tell them what to do. If you try, they just do the opposite. Don's probably one of those. It's hard to tell with him what he's thinking."

"You think Mom asked him to go?"

"Maybe," he allowed. "She doesn't usually let them hang around when it's no fun anymore."

"When was Don ever fun?" Aly asked sarcastically.

"Don't be a pain, Al. You know what I mean."

"Yeah." Aly paused to eat some more of her sandwich. "The two of *us* could ask him to go," she said at length.

"Oh, sure, Al! We'll just sit him down in the living room and say, 'Look, Don, Mom's had enough and she'd like you to go. So would we. Tell you what, Don. Why don't Aly and I help you pack? We're very good at packing.'"

At this, they both laughed, then sobering, finished their sandwiches in thoughtful silence.

"Do you understand any of this, Cliffie?"

"Not really," he admitted. "Guy-girl stuff doesn't interest me much."

"But this is our *mother* we're talking about! You've got to be interested in her."

"I am. I just said I don't understand it all that well."

"Neither do I," she said, downing the last of her milk. "I wish he'd go away. I wouldn't even mind if we had to move again. I truly wouldn't."

"Be patient, kiddo," her brother counseled. "It'll all be over soon enough."

"Not soon enough to suit me."

*   *   *

SHE FORGOT. It was that simple, that stupid. She forgot to wait downstairs in the lobby for Cliff to get home. She said hi to Frankie, sailed through the lobby to the elevator, got off on the eleventh floor, and let herself into the apartment. After hanging her coat away, she started down the hall to her room and was halted by the sight of Don sitting in the armchair in the living room, cigarette in one hand, a bottle of beer in the other. He was just sitting there, not reading or listening to the radio or anything. It was so quiet Aly could hear herself breathing. She said hi and moved to go on to her room.

"Wait a minute," he said softly, so that she had to stop in the doorway to hear what he was saying because it would've been rude to keep going when he'd asked her to stop. "I want to ask you something," he said, putting down the bottle of beer, then looking at his cigarette as if deciding he'd smoked enough and it was time to put it out. She watched him fold the cigarette over on itself in the ashtray, neatly, efficiently extinguishing it. She'd never seen anyone put out a cigarette that way before. Her mom sort of stabbed her cigarettes at the ashtray, making sparks and ash go all over the place. She had to keep picking them up and trying again before they'd finally be out. And Auntie Lilbet divided her cigarettes, pushing off the burning part, so one clump of tobacco would sit in the middle of the ashtray and keep on burning for several minutes, at last going out by itself.

"What'd I ever do to make you hate me so much?" Don asked, his eyes making her think of the entrances to dark alleyways she was afraid to go past at night.

The question made her feel terrible. "I don't hate you," she answered quietly. No adult had ever spoken to her this way. Something inside her chest started to lift and flutter, like a baby bird just learning to fly.

"No," he said seriously, "you do. You and your grandmother, both of you hated me on sight. Is it something about me?"

"I don't know what you're talking about," she hedged, anxious to end this awkward and perplexing conversation. "Nobody hates you, Don."

42

His mouth moved as if he was physically shaping words, working at them the way she worked bubble gum to get its consistency just right for blowing bubbles. His eyes were very dark, liquid. She wondered, with a pang, if he was going to cry. That would be awful, a grown man crying because he thought a little girl and her grandmother didn't like him. She really hoped he wasn't going to cry. The situation was painful. Don looked away at last and she took several steps into the room, drawn forward by her sympathy for him. She'd never given any thought to the fact that he was someone who might have feelings too. She put her hand on his arm, saying, "I'm very sorry you're not happy, Don. Maybe it's because we're not the right family for you. Maybe another family would make you happier." He put his arm around her waist. She pursued her thought in the hope that he might hear the sense of what she was saying and go away. "We're not like other families. And maybe a more regular family, a more ordinary family might be. . . ."

There was a moment of silence while she experienced disbelief, fury, betrayal—a dozen emotions simultaneously. The fury won out. She swung back then hit him in the face with her armload of schoolbooks, while emitting an involuntary shriek of protest. His forearm lifted but not in time to protect himself. She wasn't about to wait to see if she'd actually hurt him. She ran. Not wanting to wait for the elevator, fearful he'd come chasing after her, she headed for the fire exit and went pounding down the steel stairs, her footsteps echoing off the concrete walls, racing as fast as she could toward the safety of the lobby.

Before opening the door to the lobby, she took a deep breath to try to calm herself, then she went out and sat down in one of the chairs to wait for Cliff or her mother to get home. She could hardly stop shaking, and her anger surged every time she thought of how Don had tricked her, how he'd tried to get her to feel sorry for him, how he'd worked on her emotions and then done *that* to her. Maybe she hadn't hated him before, but she hated him now. She sat with her arms folded across her chest and her knees pressed very tightly together, determined not to cry in the lobby where everyone could see her.

*   *   *

"WHAT'S WRONG?" Cliff asked.

Mortified, she couldn't tell him.

"Cliffie, we've got to get him to leave."

He'd never seen her this way. Her face was white and all closed in; she looked sick. "Tell me," he urged. "What happened? Did he hurt you, Al?"

"I don't want to live here anymore," she said miserably, looking over at the elevator. "I want to live with Dad, or Auntie Lilbet."

"I sure wish you'd tell me what's up," he said, putting his arm protectively around her shoulders. He too looked over at the elevator, saying, "If you don't tell me, how can I do anything?"

Aly squirmed mentally as she thought yet again about what Don had done. She wished he'd die. She'd never in her whole life hated anybody as much as she hated that man. And she hated Rheta too for bringing him home.

"We can't stay down here forever," Cliff said at last. "He's got to go to work soon, and then we'll have the place to ourselves."

"I'm not going up there until after he's gone!"

Cliff sighed. "Okay." He withdrew his arm from around her shoulders. "Is it okay with you if I get some work done while we're waiting?"

"I don't mind," she said stiffly.

"Maybe you ought to talk to Mom," he suggested, fairly well defeated by her uncharacteristic reticence.

"Why should I tell her anything?" she said bitterly. "She never believes me. Nobody listens to kids. Except for Dad. Dad listens," she said, and started to cry. "I want to go live with my dad."

Putting down his math book, he tried to think of what he could say or do. Whatever Don had done it must've been pretty bad to get Aly so worked up.

"When I have kids, I'll always believe them when they tell me things. And I won't go bringing people home if my kids don't like them. Or make them give hugs and kisses to people if they don't feel like it. I won't make them do anything they don't want to do!" she vowed solemnly.

44

"Are you going to tell Mom?" he asked.

Her left shoulder rose then fell in a kind of half shrug. "She's supposed to look out for us, Cliffie. She's not supposed to let anything happen to us. It's not fair."

"I guess not," he said, completely at sea. "But if you don't tell her, then how can she do anything about it?"

"I'll think about it." She again folded her arms across her chest and stared over at the door.

Cliff watched her for a minute or two then moved to pick up his math book, asking, "Where's your books and stuff?"

"Upstairs," she answered, thinking if that man dared even touch her things she'd go get the big bread knife from the kitchen and kill him. She could see and almost feel herself stabbing and stabbing him. They'd probably come and take her away to jail, but when the judge heard what Don did he'd put Don in jail and tell her she'd done the absolutely right thing. Boy! she thought, seething. If Rheta didn't believe her this time, that was it! She'd go live with her dad. And if anyone tried to stop her she'd just run away, maybe go to Sharon Ackerman's house. Sharon's mom would look out for her.

ALY HAD to whisper the words into her mother's ear. Somehow whispering was less upsetting than having to say out loud what had happened. And if you whispered, it was a secret, and important. Rheta stopped her a few times saying, "What? I didn't hear that." And Aly went back and repeated what she'd just said, working up to the bad part, the part that made her feel so dirty and ashamed. ". . . then," she whispered, her heart knocking too fast and her throat dry, "he put his hand under my skirt, and he, he *touched* me." She moistened her lips and looked into her mother's eyes, waiting for the explosion. Rheta would go crazy and kill the man. Aly wanted to see it happen, wanted Don to be dead. He deserved it.

Rheta looked into Aly's eyes for what felt like a long time. Then, in a very cold voice, she said, "Why do you want to cause trouble, Alyssa?"

"What d'you mean 'cause trouble?' How am I causing trouble?"

"You have a tendency to exaggerate," Rheta said, "to blow things way out of proportion."

Aly's combined anger and disbelief made her head feel the size of a watermelon. "Don't you *care*?" she asked in a thick whisper, her upset making it almost impossible for her to get the words out. "Don't you care what he did?"

"He simply tried to show you a little affection, to be friendly," Rheta said wearily, unpacking groceries onto the counter.

Aly gazed at her mother, an odd empty sensation in her

46

chest. "I want to go live with my Dad," she said, dry-mouthed, struggling against tears. If she started to cry now, she'd probably never stop.

"I see," Rheta said coldly, letting it show the way she always did that she was hurt.

"I mean it," Aly insisted. This was one time when she knew she was right and she didn't care if her mother was going to try to make it seem as if she was the one who was hurt and not Aly. "I don't want to stay here. I hate that man and I refuse to live in the same house with him. He's a pig and a liar and you believe him over me. I'm going to live with someone who *believes* me when I say something."

"Fine," Rheta said. "If that's what you want, fine."

"I'm going to call my dad right now," Aly warned, positive Rheta would back down and see things Aly's way.

"You'd better tell him to bring a car so you can take all your things."

"Okay then, I will!" Aly marched off to the living room to the telephone.

Cliff followed, shaking his head slowly from side to side. "This is crazy," he said. "She's actually letting you go."

"She doesn't care about us," Aly said rancorously.

"Sure she does," he disagreed.

"I'm calling Dad now." Aly picked up the receiver. "Should I tell him you want to come too?"

"I'd better stay here, look out for Mom."

"It's up to you." She shrugged, and began dialing her father's number. It would serve Rheta right if everybody left her. She didn't deserve to have children when she wasn't even willing to take their word for things. Other mothers didn't act the way Rheta did.

AFTER LISTENING to everything Aly had to say, Hal said, "I'd better talk to your mother, honey."

"What for?" Aly wanted to know. "She doesn't care what happens to me. She told me to go ahead and call you."

"I know that, but it might be a good idea if I have a word with her."

47

"O-kaaay," Aly sighed. She put down the phone and went to get her mother. So profound was her sense of betrayal she could barely manage to speak to Rheta. "Dad wants to talk to you," she said, then leaned against the wall, listening to her mother's side of the conversation. It didn't take long. Rheta held out the receiver and waited for Aly to come get it.

"Well," Hal said, "I guess we're on, honey. I'll pick you up tomorrow afternoon."

Suddenly Aly realized this was actually happening. Her father was going to come the next day to move her to his apartment. She was leaving her mother and Cliffie. Yes, she wanted to get away from Don. She'd just imagined it could be done without her having to be separated from her mother and brother. But, she reminded herself, this was the way her mother wanted it; Rheta had chosen Don over her, so there was no going back now.

"Want me to help you pack your stuff?" Cliff offered, looking as stunned as Aly felt.

Aly could only nod; she didn't trust herself to speak. How could a mother just say Okay, go if you want to go? None of this was the way it was supposed to be.

The two of them set to work, clearing her books off the shelves, checking under the bed for shoes and stray socks. After about fifteen minutes, the tightness in Aly's throat eased and she was able to talk.

"D'you think it's awful of me, Cliffie?"

"Seems to me you're forgetting why you're doing this, Al," he said. "It's about Don, remember."

"I know. I don't want Mom to think I'm running out on her but I'm so tired of it all—moving all the time, new boyfriends all the time, some of them okay, some of them horrible. I only want to stay in one place for a while."

"I wouldn't mind that myself," he said, closing the flaps on a carton of books and toys. "You wait," he tried to be cheerful. "A few weeks and old Don'll be gone. We'll be in a new place and Mom'll be talking about what a clown the guy was. And," he reminded her, "it's not like I won't be seeing you at school every day."

48

Aly smiled, feeling a relaxing now of her chest muscles. "Hey! That's right. I was completely forgetting about school."

Rheta was too distraught to sustain her I-don't-give-a-damn attitude. Her baby was leaving her and she was already worrying about who'd make Aly's lunch, or if Hal would remember to give her busfare and make sure she had clean clothes. She looked across the table at her daughter who was poking at the food on her plate, and underwent a pang of guilty realization. Aly would be eleven in another few days; she was just a little girl. Precocious and outspoken, but she was still a little girl.

"Eat before your food gets cold, Aly," Rheta said, and felt Aly's eyes fall upon her almost like a physical blow. "Come on," Rheta said in a softer tone. "Eat up."

"I'm not hungry." Aly looked down at her plate. Without any warning tears overran her eyes and fell into the food.

"That's cute," Cliff said. "A new way to salt your potatoes."

Aly laughed, then sobbed. Rheta got up and went to give Aly a hug, her guilty conscience eased somewhat by Aly's clinging response.

"How come you want to keep him but not me?" Aly asked with her face pressed into her mother's belly, breathing in the scent that only belonged to Rheta, milky fresh and perfumed all at the same time.

"That's not quite the way it is," Rheta answered, although she could see how, from Aly's point of view, that's exactly the way it was. "Nothing's that black or white. And anyway, pumpkin, you've been wanting to go to your Dad's for ages. We'll just think of it as a visit."

"Why couldn't *I* stay and *Don* go?" Aly sat away, wiped her face with the backs of both hands, and looked up at her mother who, after a moment, returned to her chair.

"I don't know," Rheta sighed, looking without appetite at the partially consumed roast pork and mashed potatoes on her own plate. "I wish things were that simple."

"Why aren't they?" Cliff asked, genuinely puzzled by his mother's complicated thinking. "Sounds to me like Aly's right, that it's a choice between who stays and who goes."

"Well it's *not* that simple," Rheta argued. "And since Aly's all

49

set to go to her dad's tomorrow, we'll just leave it that way for now."

"What does that mean?" Aly asked.

"It means we'll see how things work out."

"Are you going to ask Don to go away?" Aly wanted to know.

"Don't nag me," Rheta said. "I have to think things over."

"How come what we want doesn't count for anything?" Cliff asked. "Why does that guy matter more than the two of us?"

"He doesn't," Rheta answered. "It's just . . . different. I mean, the two of you are always going to be my kids. But Don's. . . ."

"What?" Aly asked. "What's Don, anyway?"

"Let me think things over. Okay?"

"I'd really like to know," Aly persisted, a strident edge to her voice. "What makes him so special and us so not special?"

"If you're not going to eat, go do your homework or whatever." Rheta got up from the table to dump her plate in the sink, then lit a cigarette and waited until the kids went off to their rooms.

STRANGE NOISES began at the outside of her dream and started to move inside, changing the colors, making everything shaky and unpleasant so that the dream wasn't nice anymore. Aly wasn't happy with it and wanted to wake up. Thumping and people shouting. Her heart knew before her brain did, because she could feel how hard it was beating as she opened her eyes in the semi-dark and listened, her eyes automatically going first to the night light, then to the closed bedroom door. The walls seemed to be shaking. Low grunts and Cliffie yelling.

She jumped out of bed, opened the door, and ran down the hall to look in at what was happening in the master bedroom, then whirled, heart pounding even harder now, and tore into the living room to the telephone. When the operator came on, Aly said, "I need the police," and the operator said one moment please. Then a man came on and Aly tried to explain, her words tumbling over each other. "One of your detectives is hurting my mother. Hurry up and come right away!" She recited her name and their address, then threw down the phone and ran back to the master bedroom where Cliffie was sprawled on the floor with blood all over his face and Don was pulling Rheta's hair and hitting her.

"LEAVE MY MOTHER ALONE!" Aly screamed, looking for some weapon she might use against this monster. "LEAVE HER ALONE!" She threw herself forward, wrapped her arms around his leg and sank her teeth into his bare thigh.

Don yelped, released Rheta, and tried to swat Aly away, but she bit down harder. He moaned, then started shouting at Aly to stop. "Goddamn it!" he raged, whacking her across the top of the head.

"Don't you touch her!" Rheta cried, rushing to Aly's defense.

"Leave my sister alone!" Cliff yelled. He got to his feet, one hand cupped protectively over the lower half of his face. He moved across the room, did something out of Aly's sight, then in an entirely new voice that didn't sound like his but that commanded their immediate attention, said, "Okay, Al, get away from him. You too, Mom."

They all turned to see Cliff holding Don's gun. His hands were shaking so much the gun was going up and down. He had to hold on with both hands to keep from dropping it.

Aly wiped her mouth on the sleeve of her nightgown, trying to get rid of the taste of Don's flesh, as she instinctively positioned herself between Don and her mother. The intercom went off at the same time that somebody started pounding at the front door. Aly looked over her shoulder at her mother, explaining, "I called the police."

"Go let them in," Rheta said breathlessly, not taking her eyes off Don.

Aly ran to the front door and opened it to see two uniformed policemen. "Everybody's in here," she told them, leading the way at a run to the master bedroom.

The first officer into the room took the gun away from Cliff, asking, "Where'd you get this, son?"

"It's *his*," Cliff said disgustedly, nodding at Don who stood swaying back and forth in his underwear.

"What's going on here?" The officers looked first at the two adults and then at Aly.

51

"He was hitting my mother and brother!" Aly exclaimed.

"You want to press charges, ma'am?" the one officer asked, while the other took hold of Don's arm.

Aly realized all at once that Don was drunk. Things had happened so quickly she hadn't been aware of this before. But his glazed eyes and the unsteady way he stood listening to the two patrolmen made it very obvious.

Rheta rubbed her smarting scalp, trying to think. "I'd be grateful if you'd just get him out of here."

The first officer had found Don's shield on the dresser. Both patrolmen underwent a visible change in behavior at the sight of it.

"P.C. MacDonald will help you get dressed, sir," the second patrolman said to Don; then to Rheta, "We'll have him out of your way in a couple of minutes. If you and the children would step out here with me please."

In the living room, the second patrolman said, "If you don't intend to press charges, ma'am, we'll take him down to the station house and let him sleep it off in one of the holding cells."

"Good," Rheta said, gathering Cliff and Aly close to her. "I . . . uhm . . . really don't want him coming back here tonight. I'm not sure . . ."

"If I can make a suggestion, ma'am. If you don't want him coming around anymore, why don't you pack up his stuff and leave it downstairs with the doorman. Detective Hart can come by for his things tomorrow when he sobers up. And you might want to think about having your lock changed."

Rheta listened attentively to what the young man had to say, then remained with the children in the living room until Don had been taken away.

After they'd gone, Rheta went to make sure the front door was locked and the chain on. Then she put some ice cubes in a tea towel and made Cliff sit with the ice pack on his nose.

Aly watched her mother's every move, more frightened now than she'd been while the whole thing was actually taking place. Rheta took a piece of steak out of the refrigerator and pressed it against her eye. "Get me my cigarettes, will you, pumpkin?" she asked tiredly.

Aly went to the big bedroom to get them, pausing to look

around, noticing splotches of blood on the bedclothes and the rug. She grabbed the Luckys and the Zippo Don had given Rheta for Christmas and hurried back to the kitchen.

Rheta got a cigarette lit and inhaled deeply, then blew a big stream of smoke at the ceiling. "He didn't seem that drunk. You know?" she appealed to them. "He really didn't. I'm sorry for what happened. Are you okay, Cliff?"

"I'm okay," he assured her, sounding peculiar because of the injury to his nose. "You don't have to apologize, Mom. We understand."

"Sure we do," Aly agreed, although she didn't understand at all. She simply felt it was very important to stand by her mother now, to go along with Cliff's lead.

"You both should get to bed."

"What about you?" Cliff asked.

"I'll just finish my cigarette."

"So what's going to happen now?" Cliff asked. "Is he going to be coming back, or are you going to leave his stuff downstairs and have the lock changed?"

"I need to think. . . ."

"You're *not* going to let him come *back*?" Aly said disbelievingly. "Not after what he did, you're not. Are you?"

"He was drunk, Aly. He didn't know what he was doing."

"What if the next time he's drunk Aly and I aren't here to help you?" Cliff wanted to know. "Why do you want him around? What's so goddamned great about this guy that you'd take him back after what he did tonight?"

"I'm glad I'm going to my dad's," Aly muttered under her breath.

"I didn't say I'm going to let him come back. I don't know what I'm going to do."

"I was so scared," Aly complained.

"So was I," Cliff confessed. "But I really would've shot him if he didn't stop hitting you and Mom."

"I don't have to go to Dad's," Aly said. "I can stay here and help you if Don's not coming back."

"Go to bed now, the two of you."

Cliff lowered the ice pack and tentatively touched two fingers to the tip of his nose. "Stopped bleeding," he said.

"D'you think it's broken?" Rheta asked worriedly.

Cliff gave a honking laugh and said, "How would I know? I've never had a broken nose."

All three of them laughed for a moment, then fell silent.

"Go on to bed," Rheta said again, putting the piece of steak down on the kitchen table, then taking a final puff of her cigarette. "It's all over now. I'll see you in the morning. We'll decide then whether or not you guys are going to school and if I'm going to the office. Maybe," she said, trying to hold back a yawn, "the three of us'll take the day off and start looking for a new place."

Aly and Cliff each kissed her then went off to their rooms. Rheta lit another cigarette before going to her bedroom to examine herself in the full-length mirror on the back of the door, shaking her head at the sight of the scrapes and bruises all over her.

"You shouldn't let him come back," Aly said quietly from the doorway.

"I know," Rheta agreed.

"So if you know, does that mean you won't let him?"

"Aly, don't nag me. I'm in no condition to play twenty questions. I haven't made my mind up yet what I'm going to do."

"But why d'you even have to think about it? Why would you want him here? He's crazy."

"Please go to bed," Rheta said, controlling her voice and emotions with effort.

"Okay," Aly said, "but if it was me and somebody hit me and my children, I'd never let him come back."

"He's not coming back. All right? Now will you *please* go away and leave me alone?"

Aly closed the door and went back to her room. She sat on her bed in the glow of the night light for quite some time, thinking, going back again and again over the night's events. She knew it was awful of her but she couldn't help thinking her mother was crazy even to consider letting Don come back. It didn't make the tiniest bit of sense. Why would Rheta want someone so mean and nasty in their home?

At last, weary, she slid down in bed and closed her eyes. She was really very glad after all she was moving to her dad's place.

Sometimes, she couldn't make herself like her mother at all. Rheta made it just too hard, too complicated and confusing and hard. And when she'd had the chance she didn't say a thing about Aly staying, even though Aly offered when she didn't have to.

It was because, Aly decided, Rheta didn't really love her. If Rheta really loved her, she'd have believed her the first time when Aly told her about Don way back before he moved in. And she'd have believed her when Aly told her about the horrible thing Don did to her. It made her insides twist even to think about what Don did, and how awful it had been to whisper the words. But Rheta had accused her of wanting to make trouble, acting like Aly made the whole thing up just to get Don in trouble. How could she make a thing like that up? Rheta should've known just by the fact of Aly's telling her about it that it was true. She couldn't make up a story like that when she didn't even know people did rotten horrible things like that. God! She hated him so much. And she hated Rheta just as much because Rheta was stupid and a bad mother and couldn't tell when people were telling the truth.

Angrily turning onto her side, she decided she was very glad Rheta got hurt. Served her right. She'd be sorry.

CHAPTER
SEVEN

ALY DIDN'T tell her father about the previous night. Her mother had always insisted she and Cliffie weren't to carry tales back and forth so there was nothing unusual in her keeping secrets from her dad. In any case, she didn't want to have to talk about what had happened; she wished she could stop thinking about it—about the way she'd bitten Don's leg; the rage she'd felt; and the determination she'd had to bite right through his leg. She'd left deep bleeding impressions of her teeth on his thigh. He'd stood there, his eyelids drooping, swaying back and forth, blood trickling down his leg as the pair of patrolmen tried to establish what had been going on. Every time she thought about it a feeling of fury swept over her and she got a killing feeling that sent her fingernails digging into her palms, started her temples throbbing, and made a little pulse dance in her throat. She'd been mad lots of times before, but she'd never felt like this. There was the terrible anger, but an awful sadness; fear, too, and an enormous impatience with her mother for being unable to see and do the right thing in this situation.

If she, Aly, who wasn't quite eleven years old, could see what had to be done, then why couldn't her mother who was way more than twenty years older see it? Cliff sure saw it. And so would Auntie Lilbet and their dad, if they knew what was going on. While she sat in her cleared-out bedroom waiting for her dad to get there, it occurred to her that things she'd heard Lilbet say over the years about Rheta were true. Rheta really was a fool when it came to men. Don proved that. But why? How could someone be so smart in other areas and be so stupid about men? It made her want to take hold of her mother by the shoulders and shake her until all the foolishness came dropping out of her mouth and nose and ears like the coins she'd one time seen a magician make come pouring from a little boy's mouth, nose, and ears. She could picture the scene, seeing, instead of coins, little pellets flying out of Rheta's ears and mouth, falling all over the carpet. It made her smile. As if stupid ideas were like gum balls or something and you could shake them loose.

Cliff came to the door, his nose very swollen. "You all set?" he asked, looking around. "Aren't you taking your Raggedy Ann?"

"I'll get it another time," she said offhandedly. "What's Dad gonna think, seeing you and Mom? He's gonna know something happened."

"You better not say anything, Al. She's got this whole story worked out to tell him."

"It might be nice if she told me, in case he asks about it."

"She's coming in in a minute to tell you. You're in some beautiful mood," he said, looking hurt, as if he felt she was blaming him as well as Rheta for what was happening.

"What kind of mood am I supposed to be in?" she countered in a less biting tone. None of it was his fault, after all. "It's not as if stuff like that goes on every night of the world. You pointed a *gun* at that man."

"I pointed his own gun at him," Cliff corrected her. "The thing was heavy as hell, too." His face filling with renewed fear and disbelief, he said, "I was scared. Everything was so . . . out of control. I hated being so scared."

"But you said you'd have shot Don."

"I know," he said, that disbelieving expression holding. "I just wanted him to stop hitting you and Mom."

Rheta came down the hallway and Cliff stepped aside to let her enter the room. She'd done up her hair and put on makeup to cover the bruises. She looked very tired.

"Well," she gave Aly a bright smile that looked painted on, "your dad ought to be here any minute now. Excited?"

Aly nodded.

"Did you remember to take your toothbrush and your shower cap?"

"Uh-huh."

"It's going to be awfully quiet around here, isn't it, Cliff?" She looped her arm around Cliff's waist, smiled at him, then again at Aly. "I decided we'd tell your father we had a little accident in a taxi last night. That'll explain Cliff's nose and my bruises."

"Where was I when you two had this accident?" Aly asked, irritated at being told indirectly she'd have to lie to her father.

"You were with us," Rheta went on. "'You've got a bump on top of your head. Don't you?"

As a matter of fact, she did have a tender place on her scalp. It was where Don had pounded at her, trying to get her to stop biting him. She ran her fingers gingerly over the spot and slowly nodded, saying, "Okay. What about Don? Are you letting him come back?"

"Not for the moment," Rheta replied, her arm leaving Cliff's waist.

"You mean he *will* be coming back?" Cliff asked wide-eyed. "You're going to let that, that *drunk* come back here?" He was so upset at the prospect he was spluttering.

"I said not for the moment. All right? Leave me alone the two of you." Rheta turned and went off down the hall to the living room.

"She's stupid," Aly whispered contemptuously.

"I don't know what she is," Cliff said, for once sounding like a twelve-year-old. "He beat her up, for Pete's sake, but she'd let him come back. Kind of makes me wish I was coming with you to Dad's."

"You could still come with me."

He shook his head. "I don't really think she'll let Don come back, but I should stick around and keep an eye out for her. She's pretty upset, Al."

"Right! And we're not!"

"It's different for us." The intercom sounded and he said, "There's Dad. Time to get going, I guess."

When everything was loaded into the car, Aly went back into the lobby to say good-bye. Suddenly she got all weepy and could

58

hardly speak. She hugged her mother, saying, "I'll call you every night," and Rheta said, "It's okay, pumpkin. Have a good time with your dad, and make sure you do as you're told."

She exchanged awkward hugs with Cliff, to both their embarrassment murmuring, "I love you, Cliffie. Will you phone me?"

"Sure. Anyway, I'll see you at school tomorrow." Red-faced, he stood beside Rheta and the two of them watched through the lobby door as Aly ran out, got into the car with her dad, and drove off.

LIVING WITH her father was wonderful. Aly liked it so much she felt guilty and tried to play it down when she talked each evening to her mother. Their routine wasn't so different from the one she and Cliff had with Rheta. It was just more peaceful. Hal was a quiet man who rarely got angry. He didn't come home from the bank in the evenings and storm around for an hour, slamming pots and pans while he complained about the jerks he had to deal with. He came through the door with a smile, saying, "This is a real treat. I keep forgetting you're here. Well, what should we make for dinner?" He'd fix himself an extra dry martini while Aly rhymed off the contents of the refrigerator. Then they'd either cook a meal together or go out to one of the local restaurants for something to eat.

She felt so proud to be out with her dad. He was tall and nice looking. He wore suits he had tailor-made of very soft fabrics, and carefully starched shirts specially made for him by a place in London, England; he wore a cologne that smelled like lemons and a wristwatch that was waterproof. Everywhere they went, Aly held his hand and looked around hoping people noticed she was out with her father and that they were either stocking up on groceries, or buying new school shoes for her, or going to an early movie.

He almost never raised his voice, but quietly asked her to do things if she forgot, say, to clean the bathtub or to make her bed. He tried the first couple of days to make lunches for her but they were pretty bad, lumpy egg sandwiches or too much ham with no butter or mayo. So she took to making her own lunch. She felt very grown up, standing at the kitchen counter last thing before bed, preparing her lunchbag for the next day. It was funny but she didn't mind doing any of the things here that she'd minded like crazy at her mom's place.

Cliff said things were different there, too. "Don came banging at the door in the middle of the night last night," he told her in the lunch room at school at the end of Aly's third day with their father. "Nobody can figure out how he got by the doorman, but anyway, we were sound asleep and the next thing anybody knows there's this nut out in the hall banging on the door with his fists, begging Mom to open the door and let him in. And she would've, too." Cliff made a face. "Good thing I was there, Al. No kidding. Just because he was out there crying and saying how much he loved her and how sorry he was, and all this guff, she was actually going to let him in. He was drunk, naturally. Anyway, I wouldn't let her open the door and she was ready to get mad at me when Don decides since the begging and crying didn't work, he'll try shouting and threatening. So he starts hollering and we could hear doors opening and people telling him to shut up and go away or they're going to call the police. And Don's shouting back at them that he *is* the goddamned police, which was kind of funny. It shut everybody up for a couple of seconds. Then that guy from down the hall, you know the skinny one with glasses who looks like he works at the library? I couldn't believe it. This guy comes marching right down the hall and says to Don, 'You have five minutes to get out of here. I've called the police and I intend to file charges against you for disturbing the peace. If you really are an officer of the law you ought to be ashamed to be defiling your badge.' Can you beat it? Took all the wind out of Don's sails. He stood out there. We could almost hear him thinking. But he was too drunk to do anything as sensible as leave.

"So the next thing you know, I've got hold of Mom's wrist to stop her from opening the door because she's convinced Don's suffering out there and needs her help, and the police arrive. Mom opens the door in time to see the same two guys who came last week. They come over and say, 'You've got to stop harassing this woman and her kids, Detective Hart. You come with us now, sir.' Don got all meek and one of the cops stayed to talk to

Mom while the other guy took hold of Don. This cop was really okay and explained to Mom how some cops start drinking too much because of the pressures of the job, and how Don's a respected guy on the force and the other cops think a lot of him but sometimes when things start to get too much some cops just go right over the edge and maybe, if Mom wasn't planning to be seeing Detective Hart any more, it might be a good idea for her to move. It would be one sure way to put an end to Don's visits. Meanwhile, Mom's watching poor old Don staggering away down the hall toward the elevator with the other cop and you could practically see her thinking Don didn't mean to hurt anyone. Things were just too much for the poor guy at the moment. Anyway, I thanked the policeman and got Mom back inside. Of course the minute they saw it was pretty well over all the neighbors started going back inside, too. What a show! But the thing is I think I've finally managed to convince her to take the time this weekend to look for a new place."

"Did she actually say she would?" Aly asked suspiciously.

"She kind of said she might."

"I am so glad I don't have to put up with any more of that!" Aly declared, then saw Cliff's injured expression and said, "Don't tell me you like living that way with her!"

"Course not. But it's not her fault Don's the way he is."

"I didn't say it was. Nobody made her pick him for a boyfriend, though."

"Jeez, Al. Why're you being so hard on her?" He wet the tip of his finger and picked up the crumbs left on the waxed paper from his lunch. "Everybody makes mistakes. Everybody, even Dad. Nobody's perfect, but you act as if they're supposed to be. You hurt her, you know, the way you acted."

"The way I acted when?"

"All that business about the bathroom lock and making out like he was laying traps for you."

Terribly affronted, she cried, "But it was true! I was afraid he'd come in when I was taking a bath. And he was laying traps. I thought you *believed* me." She was so wounded by what she believed he was saying it was all she could do not to break into tears.

"I do believe you. I'm just saying you didn't help matters by

61

making such a fuss over every last thing the man did. If you'd just quietly told Mom how you felt, she'd've probably thrown him out right away. But you. . . ."

"That's not true!" she exclaimed. "She never would've! I told her all the things he did and she never once believed me. Not once!"

"Look," he backed down. "It's over now. I didn't mean to start a fight."

"I thought you at least believed me," Aly repeated, crushed.

"I did. I do. Forget I said anything. I've told you before I'm not all that good at understanding the stuff people do. I'm better with theories about things."

"How *can* I forget you said it when you *said* it?"

"I'm sorry. Okay? Can we change the subject now, please?"

Since apologizing was something her brother almost never did, Aly grudgingly showed her acceptance with a slow nod.

"So," Cliff said, striving to lighten the conversation, "what're you and Dad gonna be doing this weekend?"

"Nothing special," she answered. "Errands tomorrow, and then we're having lunch with Auntie Lilbet on Sunday. Tuesday night we're getting all dressed up and going out for my birthday. I can't wait. What're you and Mom gonna be doing?" she asked, then gave a little laugh. "This sounds pretty funny."

Relieved to see Aly was still capable of bouncing back fast from an upset, Cliff grinned and said, "I told you. We're gonna go apartment hunting."

"For sure, or are you just hoping?"

"Mom's right," he said, teasing. "You do nag."

"No," she said, lifting her chin, "I'm just extremely persistent."

Cliff laughed loudly. A bunch of the other kids turned to look at them. "Okay," he conceded. "You're extremely persistent. Jeez! You were like some wild dog or something," he said, shaking his head over the memory, "hanging on with your teeth in his leg. I swear I'll never forget that as long as I live. Boy, I'll bet that hurt."

"I hope so. I meant it to."

"I don't know one other kid anything like you," he said. "That's for sure."

"We're both very unusual children," she said seriously. "Everybody's always said so."

"We're not *that* unusual," he said consideringly. "Except in IQ, and maybe in height." He was silent for a moment, then asked, "Are you gonna stay with Dad for good?"

"I don't know. It's so nice for a change. I'd kind of like to stay, but it'll probably just be until school's over in June." She smiled impishly. "You guys'll get into trouble if I'm not around to keep an eye on you."

"Oh, right," he laughed. "We'll try not to mess up too much until you come back." He looked at his watch and said, "I've got a couple of things to do before the bell. I'll see you at lunch Monday."

"Will you call me if you find a new place?"

"You'll be talking to Mom. She'll tell you if we do." He got up, threw the wrappings from his lunch into the wastebasket, then gathered his books and left, turning to wave to her before going out the door.

She looked around. Three of her classmates signalled to her to come over. She didn't feel like finishing her sandwich, so she threw it away then went to join her friends. She really did feel so much better, now that she was living with her dad. She could imagine herself staying with him for good and never going back to Rheta. But then she'd miss Cliffie, and she had to admit she'd miss Rheta, too. Probably.

Smiling, she sat down at the table next to Sharon Ackerman who had the best lunches of anyone in their class. Sharon's mother did things to egg salad and to tuna salad that made them taste fabulous. Today Sharon had cream cheese and cucumber on pumpernickel with Thousand Island dressing, lettuce, and tomato. Aly's mouth started to water at the sight of the remaining half-sandwich centered on waxed paper in front of Sharon.

"Are you gonna finish that?" Aly asked.

"You can have it," Sharon said, and pushed it over to Aly.

"Wow! Thanks. I wish your mom made my lunches. They're so good."

"Is it true you're living with your dad now?" Theresa Ginetti asked.

"Uh-huh." Aly bit into the sandwich, her eyes half closing with pleasure at the crispness of the cucumber, the smooth cheese, the sweet tomato, the crunch of the lettuce, the tangy dressing, and the rich chewy bread. "This is *so* good!" she told Sharon.

"Is it true you had to move because your mother's boyfriend tried to kill all of you?"

The food lumped halfway down Aly's throat, and she stared at Beverly Skolnik who'd asked the question. Beverly didn't look mean or anything; she was just sitting there, like the other three girls, waiting to hear what Aly would say.

" 'Course it's not true," Sharon said loyally. "Is it, Al?"

"Of course it's not," Aly lied. "Nobody tried to kill anybody. We just don't happen to get along, so I'm living with my dad for now. Don's a police detective, you know," she told them, putting on a proud air and wondering as she did why she was saying and doing these things. "Police don't go around trying to kill people. You should know that."

At once Beverly turned to Theresa and said, "See! I told you it wasn't true." Beverly looked back at Aly. "Theresa said her mom said this uncle of hers who lives in your building heard the police had to come because your mother's boyfriend was shooting his gun off, trying to kill all of you."

"Well," Aly said, staring a bit sadly at the sandwich she knew she wasn't going to be able to eat now, "you can tell your mom to tell her uncle that he doesn't know what he's talking about."

"See!" Beverly said again. "I *told* you!"

Theresa looked cowed. "It's not my fault," she defended herself. "*I* wasn't the one who said it."

"Somebody said it," Sharon said, "and you heard and you just couldn't wait to tell the whole school. Could you?"

"It's okay, Shar," Aly said generously. "Let's forget it." Let's forget it, she repeated silently to herself. It was okay for her to say it to her friends but it wasn't okay for Cliff to say it to her. She'd talk to him over the weekend and tell him she understood now what he meant and that it was okay. She just hadn't understood before.

After school, Sharon walked her to the bus stop and kept her company until the bus came.

64

"I know what you said at lunch, but is it true?" she asked. "Did your mom's boyfriend go crazy with his gun and try to kill you all?"

Because Sharon was her best and oldest friend and because Aly knew Sharon always kept secrets, Aly looked around, saw the coast was clear, and said, "He was beating up Cliffie and Mom. He was drunk," she explained, wrinkling her nose. "He gets drunk a lot. Cliffie got his gun and said he was going to kill him. It was very scary."

"Holy cow!" Sharon whispered. "So that's why you moved to your dad's."

"I guess so."

"Boy!"

"Don't tell, Shar!"

"You know I never would. Wanna come over Sunday aft?"

"I'll call you later, okay?"

"Sure, okay."

The bus pulled up and Aly boarded, then ducked down to wave to Sharon as the bus pulled away. Once in her seat she wished she hadn't told, not even Sharon. It gave her a scratchy feeling in her chest, as if she'd given her promise not to tell, even though she'd never actually done that. Now Sharon knew, but her own dad didn't. And she could hardly tell him, not when they'd all told him that dumb story about the accident in the taxi. Boy! She hated to lie to her dad. Maybe Rheta really would go out this weekend and find a new place. Then things could be like they used to be. Except she'd always disliked the way things were. She sighed and turned to look out the window. Life was very complicated.

F RIDAY NIGHT Hal took Aly to see *Monsieur Hulot's Holiday*.
"Cliffie would like that movie," Aly told her father on the way
home. "'Maybe I'll go with him and see it again. He's crazy for
Charlie Chaplin, and this was a lot like one of his movies."

"That's true," her father said. "I had no idea you knew so
much about pictures."

"Cliff's the one, not me. I go to keep him company."

They stopped at the liquor store where Hal bought a bottle of
expensive French burgundy.

"Your grandmother likes good wine," he explained while
they were waiting to pay. "And I like your grandmother."

"Doesn't it make you feel funny sometimes, being friends
with Lilbet when you're not married any more to her daughter?"

"Lilbet's never allowed me to feel funny about it, honey," he
said. "We always got along, right from the first time we met,
when your mother and I started dating. After the divorce, Lilbet said she expected the two of us to keep on being friends,
and I was very happy about that. She's a remarkable woman,
your grandmother, a fascinating combination of lilting femi-
ninity and rock-hard common sense praticality."

"She has rules," Aly said seriously.

Hal smiled. "Everyone does. Some people follow theirs more
strictly than others."

"That's what I think, too," Aly declared, very pleased to have
her thinking confirmed.

When they got home, she asked her dad if he thought it was too late to call her mom and Cliffie, and he suggested she leave it until morning. "They might've decided to turn in early," he said. "All in all, it's been a pretty big week for everybody."

"I guess you're right." She grabbed a handful of saltines and a glass of milk, gave her father a kiss on the cheek and went off to bed.

Sunday morning they got off to a late start and wound up having to hurry to get to Lilbet's on time. It would've been rude, Aly thought, to ask to call her mother when she and her dad had only just arrived, so she promised herself she'd phone the minute they finished lunch.

Pearl, the housekeeper, had fixed Aly's favorite scalloped potatoes and Aly went out to the kitchen after lunch to have a visit with Pearl and to thank her for the treat.

"How're you gettin' on, darlin'?" Pearl wanted to know. "You havin' a good time livin' with your daddy?"

"It's great. I've even got my own personal bathroom," Aly told her, helping scrape and stack the dishes. "And I'm not saying anything against my mom, but it's so peaceful with Dad. No arguing, no fights." Suddenly she felt monstrously disloyal. "I love my mother, you know, Pearl."

"Darlin', everybody knows you do," Pearl assured her, filling the sink with hot water. "You don't need to explain that." Turning off the faucets, Pearl reached for her rubber gloves and pulled them on while she studied Miz Conover's granddaughter with her little face gone all thoughtful. To look at her, a body would never think she was such a deep-thinkin' child. She looked so like her grandmother it was hard to remember sometimes she wasn't actually Miz Conover's child. She sure as shootin' didn't take after her mommy or daddy, and the good lord only knew where she came by her deep-thinkin' ways. Clifford now looked like the kind of boy he was, a great big slow-movin' bookish child, but not Alyssa. She looked like a girl whose biggest concern would be what kind of dresses she had hangin' in the wardrobe; the kind who'd be fussin' over her popularity with the boys and frettin' how she maybe couldn't get the boy she'd set her mind to havin'. She had that same pale, wintery kind of colorin' like her grandmother, that same silky gold hair. But there was somethin' in the set of the girl's chin and the intensity of her eyes that was miles away from anyone else in the family. And she had an energy, a kind of electricity that made it seem—if you looked close—like she was vibratin'. She was snippy, and sharp, always ready for a laugh and always on the lookout for somethin' to be happenin'. "You're just feelin' a little guilty at changin' the way things are, eh?"

"Why is that?" Aly asked, reaching for a dish towel as Pearl began putting the dishes into the steaming water.

"The way I see it, most folks don't like changes too well. Even folks like you who've been changin' all their life long. There's changes and then there's changes, if you catch my meanin'."

"I do. And I think you're right. The thing is, I love my dad, too, and I'm so happy to get a chance to be with him, to get to know what he's like all the time. You know? I mean, all we've ever had is two weekends a month. How can you get to know what someone's really like if that's the most time you ever get to spend with them?"

"That's right," Pearl said. "You need the time for knowin' people."

"So, really, there's no reason for me to feel guilty, is there? I mean I've had almost eleven years with Mom, and now it's time for me to be with Dad. That's fair, don't you think?"

"Certainly seems so to me. And it's real nice for your daddy to be gettin' to know you too, eh?"

"Gosh! I never thought of that." Aly's features cleared. "I never even thought of that. You're a clever woman, Pearl. You understand human nature."

Pearl laughed hugely, her rubber-gloved hands immersed in the soapy water, her head thrown way back. "Lord!" she declared, her laughter abating. "I do love you, little girl."

Aly put her arm around Pearl's rounded middle and said, "I love you, too, Pearl."

"Lord God!" Pearl whispered, very pleased.

"Sometimes," Aly confided, "my mom is so stupid. I don't know what's the matter with her."

"She's not stupid, darlin'," Pearl said. "She just is what she's been taught to be. You and your daddy, the two of you're different in that regard. I don't think anybody could convince either one of you black was white or vice versey."

"Thank you," Aly said proudly.

"Oh, you're welcome."

"What do you mean she was taught?" Aly asked, puzzling over this.

"Well now, I guess I don't mean taught exactly in your mama's case. We get to be like we are for lots of reasons. Some of it's cause of the way we seen folks behavin', and some of it's just cause of what we got born in us."

"Oh!" Aly was quiet for a time, thinking.

"You best get along back to your grandmother before she comes lookin' for you."

"I have to call Sharon," she remembered, and hurried to do that.

"Can you come over?" Sharon asked.

"I don't think so," Aly told her. "I thought maybe I could, but I can't."

"Too bad," Sharon said, disappointed. "My mom made honey cake for you."

"She did?" Aly could almost smell and taste Mrs. Ackerman's wonderful cake. "Boy! Just for me?"

Sharon laughed. "Not just for you. I'll bring you a piece to school tomorrow. Okay?"

"Yeah. Boy! I wish I could come over. See you tomorrow, Shar." She hung up and went back to the living room, looking forward to lunch the next day with Sharon, and wishing she had a mother who did nice things like that for her friends. She hadn't brought anybody home from school for a long time. But maybe now that she was living with her dad she'd ask if Sharon could sleep over one weekend. Dad wouldn't mind.

IT WAS almost five when they got home from Lilbet's, and Aly went directly to the telephone. Nobody answered. "They must be out looking at apartments," she told her father. "I'll try again later."

She was allowed to stay up to watch Ed Sullivan's *Toast of the*

Town, and when it was over at nine she tried phoning again.

"Still no answer," she said, puzzled.

"They might've gone out for a late supper. You'll see Cliff at school tomorrow. Time for you to hit the sack now, honey."

She went off to bed wondering where her mother and Cliffie could be. It was pretty late to be out looking at new apartments. But then maybe they'd found a place and were taking care of the details, signing a lease, paying the first month's rent.

SHE GOT to school a few minutes early the next morning and scanned the kids outside, looking for her brother. It was the kind of cold day that made your face ache and your hands hurt if you'd forgotten your mittens. On top of that it was snowing. She hung around waiting for a few minutes then went inside, not to her own classroom but to Cliffie's. She watched the kids file in while she kept an eye on the hall. No sign of him. When the bell had gone and Cliffie's desk was still empty, Aly backed away as the classroom door was closed by one of the kids inside and stood staring at the door. One of her classmates went whizzing by, skidded briefly to a halt and said, "You're gonna catch it, you don't get a move on, Al. Didn't you hear the bell ring?" Aly signalled that she'd heard and her friend ran on, casting a bemused look back over her shoulder as she went.

Hands in her pocket she fingered her money, more than she needed, as she calmly turned, walked back down the hall and straight out of the school into the blowing snow. Head down to keep the stuff out of her eyes, she made her way to the bus stop.

Frankie was on the door and greeted her warmly. "Hey, Aly! How's it going? It ain't the same without you around."

"Have you seen my mother or brother this morning?" she asked.

"Matter of fact," he answered, "I haven't."

"Have you seen them at all this weekend?"

"Can't help you there, dear. I just come on this morning at eight, had the weekend off."

"Okay, thanks." She walked through the lobby to the elevator, feeling very overheated and heavy in her overcoat and

70

galoshes. She stood sweating while she waited for the elevator, a weird bitter taste in her mouth. She unwound her scarf, pulled off her hat and mittens and jammed them into her pockets before undoing her coat buttons, at once feeling lighter, cooler.

All the way up to the eleventh floor in the elevator she kept her eyes fixed on the floor indicator, swallowing the bitter stuff that kept coming up into her throat. Cliffie probably had the flu or something and Rheta had taken the day off work to stay home and look after him. Perfectly simple explanation, and she'd be in big trouble for playing hooky. Mom would have conniption fits but Dad would understand she'd been worried. Everybody knew she was a worrywart.

The elevator doors slid open. She stepped out and looked down the hall, feeling in her pocket for the key ring. She'd thought it was pretty mature to have keys to two different apartments. Only grownups seemed to have more than one key on their key rings. Kids only ever had one, if they had a key at all. She and Cliffie were two out of about maybe ten kids in the entire school who had to look after themselves until their parents got home from work. Everybody else had mothers at home waiting for them. Sharon Ackerman's mom was always there with food, amazing stuff like you'd get at a cocktail party or something. Little cut-out pieces of bread topped with special cream cheese Mrs. Ackerman mixed with chopped nuts and celery.

She couldn't have said why, but she rang the doorbell. That was stupid. Without waiting, she put her key into the lock, turned the handle and opened the door, stepped inside and quietly closed the door, to stand for a moment, her breathing shallow, taking off her coat then putting it and her books down on the bench beside the door. She called out, "Mom? Cliffie?" and her voice was like a pebble dropped into a well, hardly making any sound at all.

There was nobody home. She should put her hat and coat back on and get back to school before she got herself into serious trouble. She'd do that; she had the bus fare in her pocket and she'd head right back as soon as she'd had a look around. It was really something how she hadn't even been gone for a full week but already the place looked different. And it was so quiet she automatically tiptoed toward the hallway, very slowly stopping to look down the hall.

It was like magic. Outside there was a storm, with snow blowing right in your face so you couldn't see where you were going. But inside, all of a sudden it was so bright her eyes ached from the heat and glare of the beach and the sound in her ears was exactly the same as when she listened to Auntie Lilbet's big conch shell, this rhythmic repeating wave washing in over and over again.

What she told herself was laundry her mom must've thrown out into the hall for Cliffie to take to the Chinese man wasn't sheets and towels. She'd known all along that it wasn't but you could never tell. Sometimes your eyes could play tricks on you, like this one time when she'd been walking up Madison and she thought she'd seen somebody hiding in a doorway; she'd just caught a movement at the very edge of her eye. But when she turned her head to see, it was this big piece of dark plastic that'd blown into the doorway, and the wind was making it move. It didn't even look like a person. She'd only thought it might be because there was motion.

She could hear herself breathing in tiny little gasps. It was because she was so hot, coming indoors after being out in the cold. And the terrific brightness of the beach had her squinting, uncertain of what she was seeing. It had been the same way that time Dad had taken her and Cliffie to Bermuda for a week. The whole time they were there, except at night, of course, she'd had to scrunch up her eyes because it was so hard to see. She forced herself to open her eyes really wide now even though a voice in her head told her her eyes would get burned from the sun, and she came right up to the doorway of her mom's bedroom, took another gaspy breath and looked inside.

It was the sun that made everything look that way, she thought, remembering all the times she and Cliffie would hold their hands up right in front of a light bulb and laugh seeing their hands turned all red from the light shining through them. This was just the same thing, everything red from the light. She kept breathing in and out, in and out, a little more slowly. Then after a while she took several careful steps backwards, turned very precisely and went to the telephone in the living room.

When the man answered at the police station, she whispered her name and the address, her eyes all the time on the doorway, then she said, "I think you should send people. All three of them are dead."

She wanted to hang up but the man on the police station phone said, "Is this some joke, little girl?" and she went to laugh but it came out wrong, this stupid choking sound came out instead and she said, "They're all dead. I'll wait right here." She put the receiver down and sat looking at her hands front and back.

It didn't take very long. Frankie called on the intercom and asked in a doubtful voice if she'd called the police, and she said, "Yes, I did," and a couple of minutes later the same two patrolmen who'd come before were at the door.

She squinted up at the two men, recognized them and took the first one by the hand. "Come with me," she said. "I'll show you."

She led them down the hall where everything changed into the beach like in Bermuda that time, and she held on to the policeman's hand while the two men looked and then softly said swears. The one officer said to the other, "Go call this in, Matt," before directing Aly back to the foyer where he squatted in front of her, holding her hand with both of his now, asking, "Where's your dad, sweetheart? Is he around? Is there somebody we can call to come look after you?"

Working hard to control her peculiar difficult breathing, she managed to say, "I think you'd better call my father. It wouldn't be good to call Auntie Lilbet." She turned to look over toward the hallway. "No, Dad would be better." She recited the office number and the patrolman said, "Stay right here a minute, Okay?" and went to the living room where his partner was making calls, holding the receiver with his hanky, then came right back to Aly and took her into the kitchen where they sat down at the table.

"D'you think you could answer a few questions?" he asked her very nicely.

She nodded, and he got out a small notebook and a pencil to write down what she said.

After a while, she wasn't sure how long, her dad came. She never once cried, not until her dad appeared in the kitchen doorway and she saw his face. She gazed at him with her scorched eyes, able to tell that his feelings were exactly the same as her own. She reached out her arms to him and he scooped her up and held her very tightly. She wound her arms and legs around him, put her face down on his shoulder and took in a big deep breath full of his lemony smell. Then she cried.

AN INTERLUDE

Her dad said he didn't want her to be alone and since there were so many things that had to be done, he'd feel more secure in his mind if he knew she was safe and sound with her grandmother. When Aly balked at that, reluctant to have him out of her sight, he agreed, at Lilbet's invitation, to come and stay along with Aly at the Park Avenue apartment.

That very first night, everybody wanted Aly to go to bed early but she wasn't ready to sleep.

"Would you be mad if I asked to go visit with Pearl for a while?" she asked her grandmother.

"Now, honey, I can't think why you imagine that'd make me mad. You go right along and see Pearl. Just remember to knock first. It's always polite to knock first."

"I'll remember," Aly said, and went padding barefoot to the far side of the kitchen where Pearl had her room next to the ones she and Cliffie had always stayed in.

Pearl opened the door and said, "Come on in here and set down with me," and took Aly on her lap in the rocker. They sat for a time, rocking, Pearl humming low in her throat, and Aly stroked Pearl's satiny arm, putting together the words that made up her questions. When finally she felt the sentences all fit, she put her hand on Pearl's cheek to discover that the softness of her face was another kind to the softness of her arm.

"Can I ask you a question?"

"You can ask me anythin'," Pearl said, keeping the rocker going at a gentle pleasant pace.

"It's complicated," Aly said. "First I have to tell you about the dream I had last night. It has to do with my question. Okay?"

"Uh-huh, okay."

"Okay. Here goes. Last night, I dreamed that I had this little tin box and I was holding it in both hands. It wasn't very big, and it wasn't very special-looking. But in the dream there were people all around me, including Mom and Cliffie and even Don. All of them were trying to take the little box away from me and I couldn't understand why, but I knew I couldn't let them have it. I hung on and hung on, keeping both my hands wrapped tight around the box. Finally, everybody went away and left me alone and I still had the box. I held it for a long time wishing I knew why everybody wanted so badly to take it away from me. Anyway, Pearl?"

"Yes, darlin'?"

"When I opened the box, d'you know what was in there?"

"No, I don't."

"I opened the box and God was inside. That's why everybody wanted to take the box away from me. But I didn't even know God was in there!"

Pearl exclaimed, "Oh, my, my!" and firmed up her hold on Aly.

"It's my fault, isn't it? If I hadn't gone to live with my dad, if I'd stayed there, they'd be okay now, wouldn't they? Nothing would've happened, if only I'd stayed."

"You listen here to me!" Pearl said, her big hands closing around Aly's shoulders and holding her in place so Pearl could look straight into her eyes. "None of what happened is any of your fault! You hear me? There ain't a thing you could've done that would've changed a single bit of it. Not one thing. And if you'd stayed, little girl, the only thing you'd be now is dead. Understand me? You couldn't've done nothin'. Don't you never let me hear you say that ever again! Never! It wasn't your fault anymore'n it was mine. You hear me?" She searched deep into Aly's eyes, looking to make sure she was being heard.

"Honestly?" Aly asked. "Truly?"

"Honestly and truly," Pearl insisted. "What profit d'you think there might be for me to go misrepresentin' the facts of this matter to you, Alyssa?"

"None," Aly replied, watching Pearl's mouth shape her words.

"All right, then," Pearl said, satisfied. "Now just you put those foolish my-fault ideas out of your head for good'n always. Hear?"

"Okay."

"Good." Pearl directed Aly's head back to her shoulder and they rocked in silence for a time. Then Pearl said softly, "Tell me again about that dream, darlin'."

PART TWO

London, 1960

CHAPTER
NINE

JUST ABOUT everything Jeremy did was preconsidered. He weighed each action, every last gesture no matter how minimal. He knew at all times what sort of image he projected, how he appeared to others. He'd worked long and hard to perfect control over his exterior self so that he could at any time step outside of himself, check to be sure the impression he was making was precisely the one he wished, then slip back inside without anyone's ever being the wiser. Having been a lifelong observer of others, he'd managed to store up variations on behavioral themes to cover almost any conceivable situation. It was, therefore, quite out of the ordinary for him to do what he did on that Sunday afternoon in May of 1960. For the rest of his life the events of that day were the barometer by which he measured all other personal experiences.

He was standing just outside the doorway of a pub in the Fulham Road, having a pint with Andrew Slayne-Riggs, who was as usual moaning about the lack of suitable roles for his "type." No one had ever managed to define what sort of "type" Andrew might be. He seemed to fall between categories, his mannerisms too arch to permit him to play a credible juvenile and his facial features too shiningly youthful for a believable leading man. He liked to tell people he was a character actor who, unfortunately, had no exterior signs of character.

Jeremy nodded in all the right places, feigning sympathy, as he gazed up the road, taking note of strollers basking in the rare sunny weather, when along the pavement, a hundred or so yards away, came a most intriguing figure.

Jeremy was also a performer, and prided himself on, among other things, his ability to absorb detail quickly and accurately. It was an important skill, one that was useful at auditions when, by taking stock of the physical details of those in power, he could tailor his delivery to what he believed would be expected. What he saw on that day attracted and confused him. The confusion would outlast the attraction, although neither was destined to diminish appreciably with time.

This girl. She was obviously American. Her clothes, her walk, even somehow the set of her head all declared her foreignness. Americans fascinated him. They were so unimpressed by class distinctions, so energetically brash, so un-British. Americans always seemed to him to be terribly young and terribly old; old by dint of their great experience and young in how little affected by it they were.

This girl. She had wealth in her very coloring. Her skin had a matte pale gold finish; her hair was a thick intertwining of strands of gold and platinum; her clothes were champagne and cream and brandy. He'd never seen anyone so attractive who made such an overt effort to deny it. Not so much as the faintest smudge of cheek or mouth or eye color; horn-rimmed glasses to conceal round questioning gray-blue eyes. It seemed as if everything she wore had been chosen for its unobtrusiveness.

He couldn't let her get away. He extended his hand, and giving her his best smile, said, "Hello, come have a drink and let me introduce you to Andrew."

She stopped, her brows furrowing slightly, and looked past him at Andrew who gave her one of his sunniest smiles, under the impression she was someone Jeremy knew.

"Why do you want to introduce me to Andrew," she asked, "when nobody's bothered to introduce you to me?"

"Oh, I say!" Andrew exclaimed, very much the former Etonian. "How naughty of you, Gable!"

"Gable?" She looked at Jeremy, amusement creasing the corners of her eyes.

"Jeremy, actually."

"Is Gable your real name?"

"Uhm, no, actually."

"What're you, an actor?" she asked, her amusement growing.

"As a matter of fact, I am. Would you like a drink?" he asked, taken aback by her. Despite her looks he thought she'd be shy, and grateful for attention. She seemed anything but as she asked Andrew, "Are you an actor, too?"

"I'm trying desperately hard to be," he admitted with what she found to be charming candor. "I've had a few parts, but the competition's killing, really."

"I'll bet it is," she said sympathetically.

"What'll it be?" Jeremy asked. "You will have something, won't you?"

"Lemonade, please." She used the forefinger of her left hand to push her heavy-looking glasses back up her nose as she looked speculatively at Jeremy.

"Another pint for you, Andrew?"

"Not just yet, thanks." He took Jeremy's pint saying, "You'll need both hands free getting through that lot."

Jeremy set off toward the bar through the crush of people and Andrew turned back saying, "You're being an awfully good sport about this, really," and offered her another of his beamy grins.

"Oh, not really," she disagreed, enjoying the novelty of the situation. "I'm Alyssa, by the way."

"Smashing name," he approved. "Over visiting, are you?"

"No. I've lived here almost three years."

"You don't say! That means we needn't worry about you rushing off to catch your coach for the day trip to Hampton Court or any of that. Wonderful!"

Aly laughed appreciatively, very taken with him. "That's right. I've done all my sightseeing."

"Might one inquire how you come to be living so far from home—assuming, at the risk of life and limb, that you are indeed American?"

"What's the risk?" she asked.

"I recently made the fairly disastrous mistake of assuming another young lady was American. Charming creature living in Earls Court, which should of course have been the tip-off. The Canadians seem to favor Earls Court," he explained. "In any event, she got quite stroppy, didn't care in the least for being called American, although I honestly can't see what the fuss is about. You're all North American, aren't you? Just as we're all British."

"Not quite the same thing," she said. "But I don't see any need to get 'stroppy' about it."

"Ah, but that's because you're such a good sport."

"Are the two of you old school friends?"

"Me and Jeremy?" He craned around to look over at the bar. "Rather more like new school friends. We met a year or so ago at an acting class we both take now and again. Jeremy's the real thing, you know. Been at it since he was a lad. He sings," he said meaningfully.

"Sings?" He seemed to be speaking in a kind of theatrical code, with certain otherwise ordinary words having extraordinary meaning.

"Trained, that sort of thing," Andrew clarified. "I do envy him his voice. It's such a help in this business. Any twit can swan into an audition, but not everyone," he said sadly, "can sing."

"It's true," she agreed, glad to find no codes were involved here. "Some things are so . . . *provable*, aren't they? You just can't fake that kind of talent."

"Are you terribly young?" he asked earnestly, very drawn to her immediacy and understanding as well as to her exceptional good looks. He'd always been attracted to people who combined beauty and intelligence while managing not to be overbearing in either department. "I do hope that's not an offensive observation."

"I'm eighteen."

He smiled again, this time with relief, and she thought he had quite a delightful repertoire of facial expressions. "Eighteen," he stated, "is an eminently respectable age. I was afraid you were even younger."

"Well, I'm not," she confirmed. "So I guess we can be friends after all." She hadn't known she was going to say this, but the instant she did she knew it was the truth. The only other person she'd ever liked as well at first sight was Sharon Ackerman, and not even distance had affected their friendship.

"Wonderful! I expect we'll become very good friends."

"I think you're right," she confirmed.

"He's never right," Jeremy said, returning with her lemonade. "What is he supposedly right about?"

"It's between Alyssa and me," Andrew told him. "It hasn't anything to do with you, Gable."

"Of course it has to do with me," Jeremy disagreed, retrieving his pint from Andrew's hand. "Everything about Alyssa has to do with me." He said the words intending to be humorous, but as they emerged from his mouth they came on what felt like invisible cords of truth. If he chose to, he could swallow the words again; they'd disappear, but they'd remain forever attached to him.

"Did I miss something?" Aly looked from one to the other. "Did I turn myself over for safekeeping and forget about it?" Obviously, she'd landed smack in the middle of some kind of competition between these two.

Neither of the young men responded. Andrew studied her as he drank some of his lager, and Jeremy simply stared at her, feeling stupid and vulnerable and oddly undone as if he'd just heard of the death of a close friend. Somehow this American girl had come walking along the street and directly into his life. From one moment to the next he'd formed a dependency on and an attachment to someone he didn't know at all. It was frightening. He let out a gormless little laugh to mask his discomfort, and she directed her attention to him, her eyes absorbing him in a way that left him with the sense that she'd just ferreted out his every last secret.

He was tall and far too thin; he had red-brown hair, paper-white skin and tangerine freckles; his upper teeth stuck out slightly, and his hair was cut so short it made his ears look too big. He had enormous but quite graceful hands, and feet that seemed too small to hold him up. He was overeager; he tried too hard to be witty; he was visibly frightened of things he didn't understand, and desperately anxious to make a good impression. His taste in clothes was pedestrian; his speaking voice was a bit high; but his eyes were a remarkable blue-green, and his loneliness was almost palpable. Aly found him touching; he appealed to that same spot in her heart that responded to kittens mewling for attention from the depths of darkened doorways.

"You never did say how you've come to be here," Andrew remembered, "and whether or not you actually are American."

"My father got transferred, and I had a choice of staying on in New York with my grandmother or of coming with him. I decided to come with Dad. During school breaks, I go back to visit my grandmother."

"You're in school," Jeremy said, still caught up in feeling stupid.

"I'm studying psychology," she elaborated. "Just finishing my second year at university."

"Crikey!" Jeremy exclaimed involuntarily, impressed. "I thought you might be swotting for A levels or something."

"She's eighteen," Andrew told him.

"You never are!" Jeremy said.

"Of course I am," Aly assured him. "And you're, let's see." She narrowed her eyes and tilted her head to one side. "Twenty-five."

"Do I look that old?" Jeremy asked worriedly.

"That's not old," she said, wondering why the matter of age would bother him.

"It is in some circles," Andrew put in. "Our Jeremy's just gone twenty-three. *I'm* the one who's twenty-five."

"It's not old," she repeated, able to see it didn't bother Andrew.

"So Alyssa," Jeremy said anxiously, "where can I ring you?"

"Did I say you could?" she teased.

"Come on. If you won't let me ring you, how'll we meet up again?"

He said it lightly but she could tell he was serious. He was wounded in advance at the prospect of not being able to see her. For someone who made a big show of being light-hearted and amusing, he was incredibly serious underneath.

"We're in the directory," she told him. "Jackson, initial H., on Park Street. I'd better be going. Thanks for the drink."

"Where're you going?" Jeremy wanted to know, unable to curb his immediate and profound curiosity about her.

"I'm meeting a friend from school for tea." She gave Jeremy her glass then took a step away, said good-bye to Andrew, smiled and set off again along Fulham Road, feeling the heat of both young men's eyes on her back.

When she was out of sight Andrew asked, "Why did you do that? I quite liked her."

"She's not for you," Jeremy said firmly.

"Not exactly cricket, old sport," Andrew chided. "You intend to bring Lizzie along when you meet up with Alyssa?"

"We're splitting up, me and Liz."

"You are? Since when?"

"We just are," Jeremy insisted. "You ready for another?"

"I'll pass." Andrew looked at his watch. "The parentals will be keeping a watch on the drive, waiting for their darling boy to arrive. Drop you anywhere?"

Alyssa Jackson. She lived on Park Street with her father. She had a beautiful face she didn't want anyone to notice, and pots of money. She was tall, a bit on the thin side, bright as a new penny, and cheeky the way only Americans could be. He was going to have to clear everything out of the road to get to her.

"Drop you?" Andrew asked again.

"Oh, right. South Ken underground, if you're headed that way."

HE RANG the following evening. Her father answered and Jeremy put on his best voice to ask for Alyssa. Once they'd talked and she'd agreed to go out with him at the weekend, Jeremy went for a walk to plan what he'd say to Liz.

He should've known there'd be little in the way of a fuss. He let himself into the flat after his walk and said, "We've got to have a talk, you and me."

She put down her knitting and took a long slow look at him. "Mum said you'd never stick by me," she said reproachfully, lighting a Woodbine. "Mum always knows. I dunno 'ow she does it, but she always knows."

"It's just not working out, is it?" he said in a reasonable tone.

"I wish you'd made up your mind to that before, when there was still time for me to do somethin' about it." She laid one hand protectively over the top of her belly, casting a faintly disgusted look at him.

"I have every intention of honoring my obligations," he said loftily. "I thought we'd go see a solicitor, have everything put into writing. I'm not irresponsible, you know."

"You're a right bastard, you are," she said quietly, drawing hard on the Woodbine. "She told me I was daft takin' up with you, Mum did, but I said no, you was a decent bloke. Trust my mum." She gave a slow shake of her head. "Where'm I supposed to go?"

"Nowhere," he said quickly. "I wouldn't dream of asking you to move. I'm the one who should go. And I will. And I'll make arrangements to pay for the flat, as well as for the baby. It is my child, after all."

"Too bloody true," she said, her tone still quiet. "I suppose I'm lucky you're doin' it now instead of waitin' until after it's born. This way I've got a few months to sort things out, maybe get in a lodger to 'elp with the expenses."

"I told you I'll contribute."

"You don't 'ave nothin', do you, Jeremy? So what're you gonna contribute, if you don't mind me askin'?"

"You let me worry about that," he said. "I've said I'll pay and I will."

She smoked for a minute or two in silence, then said, "So when're you goin', then?"

"You'd probably like me to get out right away, wouldn't you?"

"Well, seein's 'ow I didn't know you was goin' in the first place, it don't make no nevermind to me when you go. Does it?" She put out the cigarette, looked at her knitting but kept her hands folded in her lap. For a few moments his resolve softened, watching her. She was very pretty; dark hair and brilliant blue eyes, warm-toned skin. He'd been quite content living with her; he'd even been looking forward—primarily with curiosity—to the arrival of the baby. They'd been together fifteen months and while she was far from the brightest creature he'd ever encountered, she was affectionate and undemanding. She worked as a barmaid at a pub in the Bayswater Road and had been planning to give up the job in another two months, when she was too big to go unnoticed behind the bar.

"Perhaps," he suggested, "you might be happier going back to your mother."

"I'll manage very nicely on me own, thank you. Bad enough she's gonna be tellin' me she knew all along you was never gonna stick with me, without me movin' back in to 'ear it full-time. I'll stay right 'ere, if you don't mind. So if you're goin', you might as well get your gear and go on. And mind you take the lot, 'cause you can't come back 'ere after tonight."

He hadn't expected this, but was nevertheless prepared to accede to her wishes. It didn't take him long to pack. All he had was one very large suitcase given him by his Gran, and two smallish cardboard cartons filled with theatre programs and books.

The whole time he was packing, Liz sat on the lumpy sofa of the furnished flat in Battersea and watched his every move. He wasn't going to miss trekking back and forth over the river, that was for certain, although every time he glanced guiltily over at Liz he had the feeling he might actually miss her. Still, he reminded himself, Alyssa was his future. And he had to be free for her.

CHAPTER
TEN

ALY HAD little interest in boys. The ones who showed an interest in her acted as if she was too good for them, or as if they knew in advance she'd never consider going out with them but they were asking her in spite of that. It bored her. It also touched a place at the rear of her mind that felt permanently irritated, rubbed raw by her continuing refusal to play out a role that was even remotely like the one her mother had played: of a female dependent on and conditioned entirely by her involvement with men. She wasn't like her mother, and the proof of that was her ability to deal with males while remaining uninvolved.

She found Jeremy Gable somewhat touching but overall amusing. She gave him points for boldness and persistence but had no intention of becoming serious about anyone at this point in her life.

Both Jeremy and Andrew called to ask her out. She made dates with both of them because she was curious about Jeremy and because when she'd talked with Andrew about being friends it had seemed a *fait accompli* even while she was speaking of it. There was something comfortable and familiar about Andrew; she knew they'd always find things to talk about. The two of them had similar backgrounds, even similar lives. Jeremy, though, was not so easily read nor so readily recognizable. She couldn't help wondering what drove him. That he was driven was, to her, as obvious as the seriousness positioned so close to his surface it was as visible as a fish in a stream of shallow water.

Jeremy got theatre tickets and took her to see *West Side Story*. During the interval he talked exclusively about the production and about the fact that although he'd auditioned for the show and could do a perfect American accent he hadn't been hired even for one of the secondary roles. With some bitterness he said, "They'll call me in six months to come in and replace someone. Typical, bloody typical."

"Why?" she asked, wondering if he wasn't a bit paranoid.

"I like to do things right," he told her. "They never have the time if you want to do things right."

She had no idea what he meant but in view of his upset she decided to change the subject. "When," she asked, "did you start performing?"

He smiled. "Oh, that was my gran. She's always loved me to sing for her. Got me started in the church choir when I was just seven; then she took me round here and there, and next thing you know I was on the radio regularly, doing shows, what have you."

"What did your parents think of that?"

"There's only me and Gran," he said. "Didn't I tell you that?"

"No."

"Oh, thought I did. My dad, he died three months before I was born. My mum, she died when I was two, and Gran took care of me right until I left school."

"How did they die?" she asked, curious about his grandmother. Was she one of those awful "stage mother" types who used children to satisfy their own ambitions?

"Dad, it was a construction accident; he fell off a building, something like that. Mum, some kind of seizure. I'm not sure."

"That's very sad."

"Nah, not really. I mean, it's not like I knew them. And Gran's terrific. It wasn't for her, I wouldn't have a career. Wasn't for her, I'd likely be the bloke delivering the post, singing with the church choir of a Sunday. No, she's always said my voice'll take me where I want to go, and she's been right so far."

The conversation then and later during their walk to Park Street was primarily about Jeremy. He did ask her questions, but she responded by asking him more about himself and since it appeared Jeremy Gable was his favorite topic of discussion he replied to her questions and didn't persist with his own. When they arrived at number 88, she shook his hand, said, "Thanks a lot for a nice evening," and left him standing on the pavement, feeling mystified and somehow duped. She'd got him to tell all about himself, and it didn't feel quite right now that he thought about it. He shouldn't have been so easily led. He was no fool, after all. He knew any bloke who spent hours talking only about himself came off looking right conceited. He set off home to his gran's place vowing the next time he took this girl out he'd see to it she talked about herself.

ANDREW TOOK her to dinner at a small French restaurant in Chelsea where the staff greeted him by name and seemed very pleased to see him. The owner fussed over Aly, exclaiming, "Andrew, you do very well for yourself, *mon vieux*. Such a beautiful girl!"

"Alyssa," Andrew introduced her, "this is Étienne, famous for his Gallic charm and flattering bullshit. Nice fellow, but you don't ever want to believe more than twenty-five percent of what he says."

Étienne shook her hand, gave a little bow, and said, "The same thing, my dear, is true of this young gentleman. But still, I am very fond of him." He draped an arm around Andrew's shoulders, extended a hand to show the way and led them to a table in a far corner. "Here, you can be *intime*," Étienne told them. "A nice *Bordeaux rouge* yes?"

"Do you like red wine?" Andrew asked her.

"Sure, that'll be fine."

"Étienne's a friend of my brother's," Andrew said, once they were settled. "Actually, Edmund has money in this place, I think. We're a frightfully secretive lot my family, so I can't be sure."

"How many of you are there?" she asked with a smile, happy to find her initial instincts about this young man holding firm. She really did like him very much.

"Six, if you can imagine it." He gave her one of his splendid smiles.

"Are you Catholic?"

"No," he laughed, delighted by her directness and naiveté. She was splendidly lacking in the world-weariness evidenced by the majority of girls he knew. "I think the parentals are just sex mad. Very non-U. Forever kissing in front of the kiddies, that sort of thing. Scandalizes the relatives, you know. Quite unseemly for a couple well into their fifties to be carrying on the way they do. Course as far as we kiddies go—I'm the youngest, by the bye; Edmund's thirty-four and the eldest—we think it's divine. We've all turned out to be frightfully huggie-kissie; makes people a mite nervous. They think we're a gang of sexual deviates, which of course we are." He laughed again. "Edmund's married to Olivia who's exceedingly low-key but great fun. They've got two kiddies of their own, Nicholas and Petra. Olivia's got this lifelong pash for Dostoevsky. The Corgi for God's sake's named Ilya. Aside from that, though, they're a damned good group. After Edmund come the two Pats; they're twins: Patrick and Patience, thirty-two, fraternals. Don't look a bit alike, although you can't tell them apart on the blower. Sound exactly the same, so you never know which one's ringing up. They're both married, but Patrick's is a tiny bit shaky. Mind you it's early days yet. They only just did the dirty deed eight months ago and we're convinced they'll get it sorted out. Mickey, his wife's a damned good sort, very sweet girl. Patience has a little bun in the oven, due"—he looked at his wristwatch, then back at Aly—"any minute. She's hoping for twins.

"Next we have Colin. He's thirty, been married for an entire decade literally to the girl next door, Emma. No kiddies and we doubt they ever will. Not the type. They're so utterly wrapped up in each other and their kennels they couldn't possibly fit babies in anywhere.

"After Colin, and before *moi-même*, comes darling Jill. Jillie's twenty-seven, single and a simply brilliant designer. She's got a shop in Chelsea and I predict she's going to revolutionize the fashion industry. Don't forget you heard it here!"

"I'd love to see her stuff," she said, caught up in his enthusiasm.

"Not your style," he said truthfully. "It's very showy, bold;

vivid colors, exaggerated cuts. Although you might like some of her tops. They're not quite so outrageous. I'll introduce you. I think the two of you'd get on."

"I'd like to meet her. And you never know, I might try something a little different for a change. I take it you're not especially whelmed by my clothes."

Andrew's eyebrows lifted questioningly as he gave her a challenging smile. "Not at all," he said. "I suspect they're a form of camouflage gear, but most attractive," he allowed. "So, now. I've done my *récitatif*. It's your turn."

She got out her Rothmans. He immediately reached for her lighter and lit her cigarette. In the half minute or so while she considered what she wanted to tell him she decided his instincts about her seemed to be as accurate as her own about him. Not since Cliffie had anyone shared this kind of an awareness with her. They knew about each other without having to throw out clues, lay out road maps, or explain endlessly. They were going to be friends, so there was no reason not to confide in him. She knew he would never betray whatever trust she chose to place in him. She had no reservations about Andrew. He came into her life as an entity; he was exactly who he was and he'd always remain that person. No matter what happened, he'd be just as he was at that moment. And there was something incalculably reassuring about that.

Everything about him delighted her. Not only was he intelligent and witty, he was nicely odd-looking. Of moderate height, solidly built, with dark brown hair that was already thinning at the crown, he had deep brown eyes, a strong quirky nose that took a pronounced turn to the left halfway down the bridge, a little boy's full rosy mouth, and a squared dimpled chin. He dressed with casual elegance in very good clothes that had seen much wear, and had a rumbling rich baritone voice that was a pleasure to hear.

"We really are going to be good friends, aren't we?" she said, her head tilted slightly to one side as she looked at him.

"Oh, absolutely," he concurred. "Never a doubt of it." It really did irk him to think that Jeremy had warned him to stay away from this girl. The cheeky sod had incredible nerve, really.

"My family's nowhere near as interesting as yours," she told him. "There's just me and dad and my grandmother. Actually, she'd probably fit right in with your people. She's always refused to admit she was old enough to be anyone's grandmother so right from the time we could talk we were taught to call her Auntie Lilbet."

"She'd definitely fit in," Andrew approved. "Who is 'we'?"

"My brother Cliffie and me. He and my mother are dead."

"Oh, I *am* sorry. That is too bad."

She took another puff on her cigarette, then said, "It was a long time ago. Anyway, my father's a banker, which makes him sound very boring, but he's a dear dear man and since we came to London, he's actually found himself a lady friend. My parents divorced when we were very little," she explained. "And he dated now and then but never seriously. I used to worry about him, work myself into crying jags imagining Dad all alone and needing us. So it's really great that he's got Serena now. They're very sweet together and I'm hoping they'll get married."

"And you're at the university, studying psychology," he contributed

"Right. Very ordinary."

"You'd like people to think so," he said cannily. "But no one who looks like you and has such marvelously conflicting qualities could ever be considered the least bit ordinary. Besides, as a matter of principle, I don't go about with ordinary people. Life is far too short."

She laughed.

"You're to tell me which weekend you're free to come down to Kent with me to meet the sibles and the parentals," he declared.

"Honestly? Are you sure you don't want to check out my table manners first to make sure I don't eat my mashed potatoes with my fingers, or maybe drink my soup directly from the bowl?"

He made an astonished face and exclaimed, "Good God! You don't mean to say one *doesn't* eat one's mashed potatoes with one's fingers? Oh good God! I'm simply lost for words. Wait till I tell the Pats! They'll probably go into cardiac arrest. Will you come to see me in my next show?" he asked without missing a beat.

"Well, sure I will. Do you know what it's going to be yet?"

"I've just auditioned for a new very experimental play they're doing at the Royal Court. Keep your digits crossed, old girl. They seemed to like me."

WITHIN A few weeks of meeting Alyssa both Jeremy and Andrew landed parts. Andrew didn't get the secondary role he'd gone after but to his amazement was given one of the four leads in the Royal Court production. Jeremy got ten days' work on a "Carry On" film, playing a good-natured bumbling bus driver. He hated every word and direction in the script and complained acrimoniously to Janie Grenville, his agent, who listened patiently then said, "I know you consider yourself dreadfully miscast, my dear, but you're *supposed* to be an actor, after all, and actors act. It's what I'm given to understand they do. Of course if you don't wish to sign on for the part, I've got better than a dozen other lads who'll leap at the chance. Up to you, Jeremy. Turn this down, though, my dear, and you'll have to look for representation elsewhere. You're far and away the most talented client I've got, but the bitching's wearing a mite thin."

Jeremy shut up and signed the contract. He disliked the part of himself that dealt with most situations with humor, and it galled him that people failed to see he wasn't actually funny. It further galled him when he showed his serious side to someone as important to his future as his bloody agent and all she heard was "bitching." What did it take to get people to recognize who he really was? Of course, if he could only stop larking about and show his true nature he was bound to get the kinds of serious roles he was meant to play. But he couldn't resist jumping in to fill conversational openings with self-deprecating jokes that he privately found dismal. He had to put himself down publicly in order to get people to like him, because if he revealed his true nature to all and sundry (discounting Janie for business reasons) he'd probably spend his life alone. And next to misrepresenting himself, the only thing he feared and disliked more was the idea of being alone.

Still, on the plus side, the money he'd get for the "Carry On" film would enable him to get set up in decent digs. Janie was a tough negotiator and she'd actually managed to get him a hundred quid a day plus expenses. He went to work learning his lines and developing his character. He might loathe playing a fool but he was a professional and he'd do the job better than anyone else possibly could. Before he even set foot in front of the camera, he'd know down to the last detail exactly how he'd play his part.

WHENEVER SHE took a break from her studies Alyssa found herself thinking about Jeremy and Andrew, making comparisons she knew were unfair, yet unable to stop herself. She'd never before had two men pursuing her at the same time and so determinedly. Andrew was by far the more self-possessed and knowledgeable of the two, and she felt infinitely more comfortable with him. But Jeremy touched her. He seemed so terribly needy, like a child at an orphanage trying desperately to get himself adopted by every prospective parent who came through the place. She was drawn to both of them, albeit for entirely different reasons, and found her mental scales perfectly balanced. She even boldly asked herself how she felt about touching or being touched by either of them, imagining, with a sudden overall flush, first Jeremy and then Andrew without their clothes. Neither image repelled her. To her consternation she could actually picture herself getting naked with either of them. She quickly pushed the pictures out of her mind, shocked by her imaginings. Sex was something you couldn't get away from; it was in every book, every movie, every play, every song, every last thing to which one might be exposed. But that didn't mean she had to involve herself personally in it.

She was well aware of the role sex played in human interactions; it was a direct part of her studies after all. People were driven to astonishing acts as a result of sexual needs. However, you didn't have to experience all things in order to understand them. A good psychoanalyst was empathetic, able to elicit from her patients the information that would permit one to be of real help. As far as she was personally concerned, the sexual drive was something on which she intended to keep a very tight control. But still. Wasn't it strange that she actually dreamed one night of making love with both Andrew and Jeremy at the same time? And in her dream, it was the most powerfully explosive, utterly satisfying experience imaginable. Incredibly, she knew precisely what to do and how, and performed in an exceedingly wanton yet physically gratifying fashion, as if she'd been doing it for years. It bothered her to awake in the morning with very vivid recall of the dream. Whatever it was her subconscious was trying to tell her, she was determined not to hear. She was in control of all the levels of her mind; she had the power to decide her actions, not her dreaming self.

She'd get up from her desk and go to one of her bedroom windows to gaze down at deserted Park Street—most of the houses contained offices, a few were private homes, and another few, like theirs, had been converted to flats—and concentrate on getting her mind back on track. Sometimes, if it were still daylight, she'd look through the bull's-eye which she'd hung just at eye level in the window and try, as she had when little, to force everything into focus. It was never going to happen, but the exercise was good practice. It fused her attention, brought back her sense of direction. She might go off to unlikely naked places in her dreams, but where she went in dreams had no bearing—nor would she allow it to have—on her daily life.

CHAPTER
ELEVEN

"YOU'RE STUDYING on your own time?" Andrew was impressed and a little bewildered. "Why, for God's sake? Hasn't anyone told you it's not *normal*? It's summer. You're supposed to be out having the time of your life, drinking too much and getting up to no good with the boys—one of them being me."

"I'm trying to stay ahead," Aly explained.

"Sorry, no good. Won't have it! I'll be there directly to fetch you. I've promised Jilly to bring you round to the shop."

"Andrew, I can't," she protested. "I'm right in the middle of something."

"Rubbish! I'm ringing off now, coming to fetch you."

He actually hung up. She stood holding the receiver for a few seconds, then smiled and put it down. She didn't honestly feel like working on such a lovely day, and she was interested in meeting Andrew's sister.

The char lady was making a lot of noise in the kitchen, as if to prove she was hard at work. Aly pushed open the door fully expecting to find Olive sitting at the table with a cup of tea in one hand and a noisemaker in the other. But Olive was down on her knees, her head in the oven as she scrubbed away at its interior while humming tunelessly under her breath.

"I'm going out," Aly told her, causing the woman to start and bump her kerchiefed head on the oven's interior. "Sorry. Didn't mean to scare you. I just wanted to let you know I'm going out, in case anyone calls."

Olive's upper half emerged from the oven. "Well blow me

down! Never thought I'd live to see the day when you, Aly, my girl, did something dead risky like going out for a bit of fun."

"I have lots of fun," Aly defended herself, returning the woman's smile. She liked Olive, considered her one of the better examples of British eccentricity. In her mid-thirties and quite good-looking, Olive claimed to come from a wealthy family who'd cut her off for reasons never disclosed. She'd taken up cleaning house, she'd told Aly, because it was all she knew how to do. Her style of dress certainly backed up her claims, although her hands looked as if she'd been scrubbing bathtubs and ovens for more than just a few years. She did have an attractive figure and good legs, and was forever telling Aly about the many men who were chasing her. "Can't leave me alone, the silly buggers," Olive would say, touching one sadly neglected hand to the nape of her neck as if searching for stray wisps of strawberry blonde hair needing to be tucked back under her kerchief. "I don't mind an evening out now and again, a bit of slap and tickle, but they can never be happy with just that. They're always wanting to tie you down, stick you in some semi-detached in Ealing and advise you to consider yourself lucky. Well I've been 'lucky' a time or two before, old girl, and I don't mind telling you I prefer things just as they are, thank you very much."

Aly was convinced Olive had a crush on her father. If he happened to be home when she arrived, Olive would thrust out her chest, straighten her spine, take pains to soften her voice and ask most solicitously how things were going and if there was anything special to which Mr. Jackson would like attention paid.

For his part, Hal confided to Aly he was genuinely fond of Olive. Joking, he said that if he hadn't met Serena so soon after their arrival in England, he might very well have asked Olive out on a date. "She's a good worker, very down to earth and quite attractive in her own way. I think we were damned lucky to get her."

Aly agreed, even though all they'd done was phone up a domestic agency. They'd sent Olive along and she'd been coming two days a week ever since.

Even Serena liked Olive, although Olive narrowed her eyes at the sight of the woman, and without fail muttered, "Wish she wasn't so bloody nice. I'd like this story a lot better if she was a miserable bitch out to enjoy your dad's money. Damned woman's got her own. You can tell by looking at her. And she's dead soppy over the man. I tell you. What can a body do?"

It was all true. Hal told Aly about Serena right after he met her. "She's rich as Croesus, an absolute knockout in the looks department, brain the size of a Bentley, and nice as the day is long. I think you're going to be seeing a lot of her, honey. I sure hope you don't mind."

Aly couldn't help liking Serena. In fact, she found it hard to imagine anyone not liking her. In her early forties, at five-foot-five or six, she had wonderfully exotic good looks: a fine heart-shaped face; blue-black hair in a most flattering short shaggy cut; slightly slanted, almost Oriental black eyes; a straight up-tilted nose; a wide very full mouth; and skin so white and flaw-less it was only the expressive lines around her mouth and at the corners of her eyes that saved her from appearing unnat-ural and doll-like. One of her eyeteeth was chipped, and gave her smile a hint of raffishness. She wore exquisite clothes. Even her most casual outfits were of the best quality and cut. She'd been a widow for more than ten years and said often that her greatest regret was never having had children. From the outset she treated Aly with a deferential interest that inspired Aly to trust Serena with the same immediacy and completeness as she did Andrew. Aly felt extremely lucky to have made two such good friends. It made her somehow less of an alien, more con-nected to a life that was so radically different to the one she'd known in New York.

She loved London, loved its shops and traditions and espe-cially its people. Aside from one or two awkward occasions when she'd encountered an anti-American newsagent and a classmate who wouldn't even deign to look at her, the majority of people she'd met had in common a marvelous sense of hu-mor and a curiosity about life on the other side of the Atlantic. She loved being able to go out for a walk at night and, if she cared to, purchase cigarettes, or chocolate bars, or half-pint containers of milk from the machines on the street. Now and then when she had trouble getting to sleep, or was roused from her sleep by one of her recurring nightmares, she'd get up and go out to walk, stopping en route to buy a Cadbury's hazel nut bar at one machine, and some milk to wash it down at another. She couldn't imagine machines like these lasting more than half an hour in Manhattan. They'd be ripped off walls, rivets and all, or carted right off the streets so the thieves could enjoy not only the cash but the contents to boot.

"So you off with that gormless wanker again?" Olive asked.

"I beg your pardon?" Although Olive invariably referred to Jeremy in deprecating terms, Aly refused to rise to the bait.

"Jeremy, Mr. Gable," Olive said. "He coming round to take you somewhere dead exciting like an empty rehearsal hall so you can watch him prance about performing?"

"You've seen him exactly twice in your entire life. Why do you hate him?"

"I wouldn't go so far as to say I hate him. I just can't stand the sort who're always on. I'll wager he never lets up, that one. I don't need to spend six months with someone to know I don't care for him. And Jeremy, Mr. Gable, fancies himself, my girl. I can't think what you see in him."

"He's very sweet."

Olive rolled her eyes.

"Well, he is," Aly insisted. "Some people are just easier to like, that's all. Jeremy takes some knowing."

"I don't have that much time, ta ever so."

The doorbell rang. Aly said, "It's Andrew. I'll see you later," grabbed her bag and hurried to the door.

"You're probably going to loathe Jilly's creations," Andrew warned her on the way to Chelsea in his Jensen. "Please don't feel you have to buy something. It's strictly unnecessary."

She admired the way he handled the sports car. He drove fast but well, with regard for her comfort. "I'll bet you drive like a maniac when nobody else is in the car with you," she guessed.

He grinned over at her. "Spot on! You're a clever little baggage. How did you suss that out?"

"I can tell. Rather than risk making me nervous, you drive carefully when I'm with you. I think it's very nice. I like that about you."

He stopped for a red light, popped the shift into neutral, and

100

again looked at her. "Do you frighten most people?" he asked. "I should think all this perceptiveness would be positively menacing to your average soul."

"I don't think anyone on this entire earth is frightened of me," she replied. "Including you."

"They would be if they watched and listened closely for a time. It's fairly unnerving to be with someone who's so . . . aware, I suppose."

"But that's my job. Or at least it will be. And anyway, I like understanding what makes people tick."

"Is that why you're seeing both me and Jeremy?" he asked, his eyes on the traffic ahead.

"Are you jealous, Andrew?"

"Well, of course, I am. I mean to say, it's not very flattering, is it? It's as if you're saying you find us fairly much of a muchness, interchangeable even."

"Oh, not at all," she said quickly. "The two of you couldn't be more different."

"Then why don't you choose one of us and put the other out of his misery?"

"Why?"

"Why?" he repeated. "Why. Bloody good question. Why. You must think of me as one of the over the hill gang," he said, as if to himself. "Not very fair of me, I suppose, pressuring you. Even if you are loaded with perspicacity, you're still scarcely more than a sprout, really. Old Gable's five years older than you, but here I am, *seven*. Must seem like centuries to you."

"It doesn't at all. And you haven't answered my question. Why do I have to choose?" One of the problems she had with Andrew was she could never be sure when he was joking. She suspected he was serious but it was always possible he wasn't.

"Because you're going to have to, sooner or later. That's the way these things happen." He pulled over to the curb, turned off the motor, shifted to face her and with one of his radiant smiles said, "Choose me!"

"Are we here?" she asked, looking around. She hated being put on the spot, especially this particular spot. She thought it was understood that she was simply friends with both of them. Now it appeared the matter was anything but understood.

"Yes, we're here."

"I'm not choosing anybody," she said. "Okay?"

"No, it's not okay. But never mind." He climbed out of the car and went around to open the passenger door, offering his hand to assist her. "You are a wonder to behold, fair Alyssa. *Choose me!*" he whispered urgently.

"I'm not choosing anybody!" she insisted, halfway convinced he was teasing her. "Stop saying that!"

Taking hold of her hand, he directed her along the pavement saying, "You know what I foresee?" He shielded his eyes with his free hand and gazed off into the distance as if he were scanning the limitless sands of the Kalahari. "I foresee a time when you'll shatter my poor weary heart by choosing that talented sod Gable because you feel sorry for the undernourished bastard. Promise me you won't do that!"

"Is this it?" she asked, stopping to look in the shop window. Mirrors and chrome cubes and only half a dozen carefully chosen garments. He really was serious and it made her horribly uncomfortable. She didn't want to hurt anyone, didn't want to be forced to select one friend in preference to another. Rather than confront him, she decided to play it lightly.

"Yes this is it," Andrew said, watching her take in Jilly's window display. "I think it's frightfully unfair, and I intend to fight it every way I can, right to the bitter end."

"Come on," Aly said, making her way to the door. "And stop all this whining."

"Whining? You can't tell the difference between grizzling and whining? You're not nearly as clever as I thought. I feel better already."

Jilly was busy, brittle, and nothing like as friendly and unaffected as her brother. As soon as it became obvious Aly wasn't going to buy anything, Jilly turned her attention to two other customers and managed without actually saying anything to make it clear that Andrew had wasted her time bringing Alyssa to the shop. Aly made polite noises about the quite ugly clothes and sent a silent message to Andrew to get her out of there. Obviously disappointed that the two girls hadn't hit it off, he said good-bye to his sister who half-turned, waggled two fingers at them, then turned again to her customers.

"Well," he said, once they were back in the Jensen, "that wasn't quite what I had in mind."

"She didn't like me."

"No," he said, "it doesn't seem as if she did. Do you mind terribly?"

"I mind a little, not terribly. I hate it when people decide they don't like you just because of the way you look, without even taking five minutes to get to know you even the slightest bit."

"Yes, that's about how I feel. I must say I've never seen Jilly behave quite so rudely." He sighed, started up the car, then said, "Would you like to come back to my place for a cup of tea, a drink, a bit of a look round, whatever?"

"Sure. Where d'you live?"

"South Ken, not far." He leered at her, lifted his brows and said, "Not afraid, are you?"

"God, Andrew! You're the least frightening person I've ever known."

"Well, fuck me! I'd say that puts me nicely in my place."

HER FATHER had to go to Hong Kong on bank business so Serena went with Aly to see Andrew in "Off the Hopper" at the Royal Court. It was a frenetic play, at some moments obscenely funny, at others incomprehensible. Andrew who was portraying a spectacularly erratic, not to mention eccentric member of the upper class, was gratifyingly good. He had an authority onstage that Aly hadn't expected. In fact, he was altogether far better than she'd thought he'd be.

"He always talks about Jeremy as being the one with the real talent," she told Serena. "He talks about it so much he managed to convince me it was true."

"He's a delight," Serena declared. "I do hope you intend to introduce us."

"You mean go backstage?"

"I should think he'd be most upset to learn you'd been to see the show without stopping backstage."

"Really? I thought maybe that would be kind of pushy."

"Actors love audiences, Alyssa. You want to remember that."

Serena was absolutely right. Andrew seemed to glow with

pleasure at the sight of them. He hugged Aly enthusiastically, then kissed Serena's hand, with a self-deprecating laugh declaring, "Forgive the *geste recherché*," then laughed again. "I'm so happy to meet you. Alyssa speaks very well of you."

They went out for a drink at a nearby pub, and Aly watched proudly as a number of people who'd seen the play stopped to compliment Andrew on his performance. He accepted the praise with grace and humility; always Andrew.

"Success suits you," Serena said sagely. "I rather suspect you'll have a good deal of it."

"Beautiful *and* kind," he said, and bent again over her hand. *"Encore le geste recherché,"* he said. "You may live to regret having been so nice to me."

"Not at all," Serena said with a slight shake of her head that subtly rearranged her shaggy tresses. "I adore having young men kiss my hand. It's divinely decadent." She offered one of her raffish smiles and patted his cheek. "Seriously," she said, "you'll do well. I can tell."

He sobered suddenly and looked into his Bell's. Just then he'd have given anything to be other than he was, to be someone who'd never been diligently schooled not to make overt and possibly unseemly displays of feelings. He was able to see at that moment how, despite his parents' affectionate shows, their children had always been given to understand that their mother and father were unique and that their behavior was confined strictly to the interior of the spacious Tunbridge Wells house. All his life these two people had acted out one code of decorum while instructing their children in another. The result was Andrew's present misery. He'd found someone who aroused every last instinct within him, but he could neither reveal them nor act upon them. He was hamstrung by his upbringing, and so he couldn't telephone Alyssa fifty times a day, or take her to his flat and make a telling display of his caring. Had he been any other man, he'd have stated his case and made it clear to her from the outset that whatever success he might achieve in his lifetime he'd never be able to savor it fully without Alyssa to share it with him. But because of a lifetime's rigorous training in self-control he was unable now to get past a reserve that had put down tenacious roots in the part of his brain that controlled speech. The most he could do was play the good-natured jester, offer cryptic little suggestions, pathetic hints, and hope these superficial clues would lead this girl he so adored to a discovery of the vast caverns of his emotions.

Alyssa put her hand on his arm and he turned to smile at her, gave her a light kiss on the lips, and with his face very close to hers whispered, "Choose me! I'm prepared to wait."

"Stop!" She gave him a push. "I've told you: I'm not choosing anyone."

What occurred next confounded Alyssa. Just a few moments, but she was to remember every detail vividly for years to come. The scene would replay itself for her at random, anguished moments and she'd experience again the awkwardness and confusion she felt then.

The three of them were jammed together on a banquette intended only for two. Andrew was as close to Serena as he was to Aly. Whichever way he turned his head he was only a matter of a few inches away from either one of them. As Aly watched, leaning slightly forward to see, he turned to Serena and said, "Tell her to choose me, would you, please. You see things, have influence with her. You know what I'm saying, don't you?"

Serena's black Oriental eyes were suddenly moist. She touched the tip of her finger to Andrew's lips, and murmured, "Poor darling. You know no one decides for anyone else. So sorry," she said, and curved her hand over his forehead as if he were feverish. A few seconds, then she smiled coaxingly and said, "Have your drink. There's a good boy."

It was a privileged communication Aly was only allowed to watch; she had no entry position. From the center row of the theatre of her insight she gazed up at the screen and viewed the action, saw the older woman's sympathetic comprehension and the young man's frustrated longing and knew she could make this come right if she could only somehow find a way into the script. But it wasn't written. She was limited to her role as audience; she had no idea how to circumvent the limitations imposed by her youth, by her lack of experience, and by her ignorance of the rules of this exchange. She sensed through her optic nerves, right through her central nervous system, the ways in which she might effect a satisfactory conclusion, but the knowledge of her senses refused to make itself known to her brain. She could only feel an ache of ineffectuality, and wished fervently she were old enough and sufficiently experienced to alter the course of events. All she could do was guiltily take hold of Andrew's hand while casting a regretful look at Serena, visually apologizing for her ineptitude. She wanted to possess Serena's understanding, her compassion. She hoped never again to feel as foolish and useless and abysmally young as she did just then.

"Never mind, sproggy," Andrew said sweetly, ashamed of himself for having attempted to elicit someone else's help in communicating his terrible affection to this girl. "I'll grizzle away at you some more tomorrow." He kissed her on the temple, then gulped down his Bell's. "Another round!" he declared, and climbed over Aly to push his way through to the bar.

Aly lit a cigarette then looked helplessly at Serena.

"Whatever you do," Serena counseled, "just be sure you play fairly."

"God," Aly sighed. "Now I'm completely lost."

Serena shook her head. "You're not at all," she said. "I quite understand, though. Once you acknowledge that you do, indeed, know what's happening you can't ever return to the safety of being a child."

"No," Aly agreed. "That's true. I have this feeling, Serena," she confided, finding it all at once a bit difficult to catch her breath. "It's as if I'm leaning against this transparent thing, sort of like being on the inside of a balloon; it's all elastic. What's scary is that I know if I lean hard enough against it, I'll break right through it."

Serena listened intently, her eyes locked to Aly's. "And?" she prompted.

Aly shook her head slowly and turned to watch Andrew returning with fresh drinks. She visualized him without his clothes, then placed herself beside him in the picture. It was an image with intriguing potential. She blinked it away, took a puff of her cigarette, then smiled at him. After he'd set the drinks down and climbed back over her to his place in the middle of the banquette, she breathed in deeply, inadvertently ingesting his scent while at the same time feeling the pressure of his thigh along the length of hers. She seemed to be pushing actively now against that balloon-like substance that separated her from the rest of the world. She could almost feel the gust of air and emotion that would come sweeping over her when she burst through that translucent membrane.

CHAPTER
TWELVE

To Jeremy the act of making love was, each time he engaged in it, an opportunity to fine-tune a performance of potentially award-winning caliber. He believed with all his heart and soul that one day he'd have a crack at a role that would allow him to put as much into it as he put into every sexual encounter. He knew with absolute certainty that when that role came along his fame would be guaranteed. He alone would have the passion for perfection, the dedication to detail, the undiluted commitment, that would make his name synonymous for all time with that role. He was destined for greatness, in line for accolades and royal benefit performances. In the meantime he simply had to suffer the indignities that came with miscasting, overcome his perennial inclination to play the fool, and struggle not to become discouraged.

For the present he got himself moved into a new flat off Kensington Church Street, and turned his attention to the conquest of Alyssa. He couldn't have said why he was so determined to win her over; he simply felt a need for her. He had to have her in almost the same way he had to have success.

He didn't actually plan any sort of sexual confrontation. He imagined it of course. He'd have to have been mad not to. She was a lovely creature, after all, and he was a young, healthy male. Just talking to her on the telephone got him aroused. So, yes, he had to admit he'd thought about it. But he couldn't have planned anything because Alyssa kept him so off guard. He diligently rang her two or three times a week, and she usually agreed to meet up with him—for a quick cuppa, or to take in a film, or just for a walk—at least once a week. What kept him on edge and in a state of ongoing uncertainty was the knowledge that she was also seeing Andrew on a regular basis. Instinct directed him, and he followed. The fact that Slayne-Riggs also wanted Alyssa proved to Jeremy the rightness of his choice. It didn't overly upset him to compete; he'd been doing it most of his life in one way or another. Usually he was up against other lads for roles, but a contest was a contest and he entered every last one of them determined to win. He intended to have Alyssa, and he'd do whatever was necessary to achieve that end. She was going off to New York in just a few days to visit her grandmother and would be away six weeks. There was all too little time to prove himself to Alyssa expecially since he was up against Slayne-Riggs who had all the right sort of things with which to compete: background, money, Eton, Cambridge, a flat in South Kensington, a bloody Jensen sports coupe, and one of those mellifluous upper crust voices it takes twelve generations of inbreeding to produce.

No, he honestly didn't plan anything. He simply wanted to see Alyssa before she went off to New York, and to make enough of an impression on her so that she'd remember him, even fall for him. In view of how obsessed with her he'd been since first sight of her walking along the Fulham Road it wasn't in the least unreasonable, he thought, to use whatever he could to convince her of his feelings.

She agreed to come out for a walk with him, maybe stop somewhere for a cup of coffee. He rushed directly over to Park Street to collect her. The door opened and she came out smiling, saying, "Hi," and looking as lusciously expensive as always in a white linen dress that must've cost a good hundred quid. He couldn't speak for a moment, so stricken was he simply by the sight of her. Somehow her beauty and wealth personified everything he longed for. She was to him far more than a good-looking young girl with a rich father. She was the living embodiment of a world to which he was determined to gain entry. She could take him a long way toward his ultimate goals simply by becoming a part of his life. After all if Jeremy Gable, *né* Brown, could win over someone like this girl, he must have more going for him than anyone suspected.

"Where should we go?" she asked, looking up toward Oxford Street.

"Come see my new flat!" he invited eagerly. "Maybe you'll have some suggestions on how to brighten it up. It's furnished." He made an apologetic gesture as he steered her over the road, heading toward Knightsbridge and the route that would lead them to the Kensington High Street. "But it's lovely and bright, very spacious."

"Sure, okay," she agreed, blinking into the sun. "The weather's been terrific this summer."

"It's because you're here," he blurted out.

"Jesus, Jeremy! I was here last year and the year before and we had the worst weather I've ever seen in my entire life." Sometimes he said things that were so stupid she had to wonder what she was doing with him. Stupid people were the bane of her existence. She knew it was an aspect of intolerance she badly needed to overcome if she was going to be of any use as a therapist, but she hadn't yet managed to curb her impatience when people started spouting flattering nonsense. She replaced her regular glasses with a pair of prescription sunglasses she got out of her shoulder bag and told herself not to be so harsh.

He truly hadn't planned anything. It was just seeing her standing there in the middle of his new flat, looking around and making polite comments about the place. All of a sudden he had this incredible insight. He realized she was merely human, another person, like him, and he had the right to try to show her how he felt. If he tried and it didn't come off, at least he'd have the satisfaction of knowing he'd done everything he possibly could.

She looked around, thinking it was quite a nice place. The room was about twenty by twenty, with a bay window into which had been set an old sofa. There was an electric fire on the left wall, and a grouping of table and chairs on the right. At the top of the room, to the left of the door, was a bed. A private kitchen and a bathroom, both perfectly adequate. "A few posters for the walls, maybe some plants and a couple of yellow or green pillows for the sofa and. . . ." She broke off in amazement as Jeremy seemed to launch himself at her from out of nowhere. One minute he was supposedly going off to make some tea and the next he'd crept up behind her to wind his arms around her midriff and start kissing her neck. "Jeremy!" she exclaimed. "What d'you think you're doing?" He never did answer. And after a few moments she was incapable of coherent thought, let alone speech.

He made a connection with a part of her she'd only very recently begun to suspect existed. It was liquid and highly volatile like some newly created but still experimental chemical explosive developed to be used in extreme situations where all other forms of diplomacy failed. He put his hands and mouth on her body, and she became her personal country's secret weapon, a missile that could be launched only within the confines of her own physical structure. She went rocketing off inside herself, colliding with the bones and tissues, the tendons, ligaments, and musculature that comprised her dark interior continent. She was a one-woman war zone, with full-scale battles taking place in the torrid regions, small skirmishes and minor contretemps being played out in the more temperate zones. She was a country without leadership, outer-directed by someone altogether foreign. Entirely subject to the whims of this foreigner, her country could only acquiesce as this interloper crossed over her border and assumed command. Her occupied territories were pillaged and sacked, then burned to the ground.

He'd made love to quite a few women, but he'd never known one to respond as Alyssa did that afternoon. All the while he had her there on his bed she was like some other person altogether. He'd never have thought that Alyssa, of all people, would go off the way she did. It was quite as if he'd inadvertently given her an electric shock, so frenzied were her reactions. He thought surely she must've had a go a time or two before, but when they got right down to it, he could tell he was the first and that rattled him some because he'd never been anyone's first. While he went at it, going dead easy, dead slow and careful because he never wanted to hurt her in any way, he couldn't help thinking he had one on old Andrew, didn't he? There could only ever be one first couldn't there? And Jeremy was the one this time. He felt positively triumphant.

He needn't have worried about hurting or upsetting her or any of that because she was so keen he didn't think she'd have noticed. She was crazy for it, wild like a gorgeous long pale animal. It gave him a fantastic sense of power to be able to take cool uncommitted Alyssa and turn her into this heated clinging creature who wound herself around him as if she thought maybe she could take the whole of him, from head to toe, right the way into herself; that he could bring her off one-two-three the very first time as if they'd been going at it together for ages, not like it was something she'd never done before and he'd been scared to death to try with her. He needn't have worried. She opened like overripe fruit and let him feast on her. And he couldn't resist the lure of her frantic embraces. The more she responded, the farther he was willing to go, until he grew fearful he might after all lose himself entirely inside of her. More and more she defied everything he thought he'd known about girls: She was bold when he expected she'd be diffident; her laughter was the kind that drew attention, rather than the polite behind-a-hand tee-hees he'd believed well-bred girls were taught; she was opinionated, outspoken, and loaded with confidence, but she was also kind and generous and forever game to try something new. Overall, she was completely unpredictable and it was that which kept him most on edge.

She was quiet for a good long time after and then all of a sudden she seemed to snap back inside herself. She said, "God!" sat up and put on her glasses. Most intrigued, Jeremy kept quiet and watched her.

In a state of shock and oblivious to everything but her own ravaged senses, she walked naked across the room to get a cigarette from her bag. She took a deep hard drag and stood staring out the window, forgetting she had no clothes on. After a minute or two, she shifted and looked down the length of the room to where Jeremy was stretched out on his bed, his arms folded under his head, his eyes on her. Her knees threatened to buckle, she felt so suddenly weak. Winding one arm around her middle she continued to smoke and gaze silently at Jeremy, trying to make sense of what had just taken place here. She glanced at her wristwatch and saw that the two of them had been writhing about on Jeremy's narrow bed for close to three hours. She'd allowed this man to do things to her she hadn't even known were possible let alone maddeningly pleasurable. "God!" she said again, taking another puff of her cigarette. Was this what Rheta . . . ?

"I really have to go home now, Jeremy," she said in a voice that didn't sound to her remotely like her own. She had the idea that everything she'd believed to be true about herself up until three hours ago had been part of an elaborate hoax she'd played, deluding herself, acting out some characterization she'd fabricated to conceal the truth. And the truth was. . . .

"Are you all right?" he asked, promptly sitting up.

"I'm fine. I just really have to go."

He began pulling on his clothes, saying, "I'll see you home in a taxi."

She took a final draw on her cigarette, looked around for an ashtray but couldn't find one. Her limbs heavy and not entirely in her control she walked the length of the room, crossed the tiny entryway and went into the bathroom to drop the cigarette into the toilet. She used a handful of tissues to wipe away the thick milky liquid oozing down her thighs, promising herself she'd have a good long bath once she got home. All she cared about was getting home, closing herself into her room to think. She badly needed time alone to try to come to terms with the new view of herself she'd been given.

They walked out to Kensington Church Street and when a taxi came along, she said, "You really don't have to see me home, Jeremy. I'll be fine."

"I don't mind at all."

"I want to have the time to myself," she explained, seeing the hurt again on his face. "I'll talk to you later," she promised, then reached out to kiss him, feeling the heat begin seeping into her belly the moment their mouths touched. "God!" she gasped, breaking away, then leaning back to kiss him again.

"I'm as much for love as the next bloke, darlin'," the driver said through the open window, "but tell the lad ta-ra and get in now."

"Will I see you again before you leave for New York?" Jeremy asked as he closed the taxi door.

"Call me tomorrow," she told him, then gave the driver her address. When she turned to look out the rear window, Jeremy was still standing on the pavement watching her go. Why the hell didn't he go home? she wondered irritably. Fumbling, she got a cigarette lit, then closed her eyes. She had no right to be angry with Jeremy. He hadn't forced her to do anything she hadn't wanted to do. But how had it all happened? She couldn't see any retrospective signposts that might have warned her. What she saw, though, with the late afternoon sun bleeding through her lowered eyelids, was that incarnadined *tableau mort* that now and then disrupted her sleep and jolted her into a state of heart-thudding wakefulness. At once her eyes shot open, panic a palsy in her veins as she sucked hard on the cigarette, swallowing lungfuls of acrid smoke to distract herself. Her mouth kept shaping the words, Oh god ohgodohgod, like some mantra designed to comfort her but which merely soothed her lips and tongue by providing them with something to do while the rest of her experienced small mental seizures over and over until, by the time she was out of the cab and paying the driver, she was so dizzy she could barely function.

WHEN SHE came down for breakfast the next morning her father greeted her as always with a wide smile and a kiss blown the length of the table saying, "Somebody dropped that off for you very early this morning. It was out front first thing with the newspaper."

Puzzled, she opened the envelope. Inside on a piece of paper torn from a steno pad Jeremy had written in a most constricted script, "I wanted you to have these. Love from J." There was a studio glossy of eleven-year-old Jeremy Brown and a 45 record in a faded yellow dust wrapper. She wondered as she studied the carefully posed portrait of the little boy if Jeremy was exceedingly clever or if he just had an unerring instinct for how to get to her. She was very touched by the photograph, and got up at once to play the record.

"What is it?" Hal asked as she headed for the hi-fi in the living room.

"I think it's a 45 Jeremy made when he was a little kid."

The eleven-year-old had had one of those hauntingly clear soprano voices that echo off the arched and vaulting ceilings of cathedrals, rebounding into the corresponding chambers of the hearts of listeners. Whatever she might have felt about him before, her feelings now slid over into a welling affection for the boy he'd been, the man he'd become. Repeatedly he probed an especially vulnerable spot inside her; he came back again and again to remind her she was susceptible. While she listened to the soaring soprano she saw herself frenziedly abetting him in previously unimaginable sexual acts and wanted instantly, desperately, to be with him and do it all again. This had to be love, she thought, aware of the pulse beating quickly, insistently in her throat. This had to be what inspired those books and songs and poems and plays and movies, those symphonies, those rhapsodies. God, if this was love, how was she ever going to get any work done? She'd be grounded, stuck in one place forever because all she could think about was having more of it, wanting more and more until she imagined herself shattering, fragmenting like some arcane incendiary device.

She didn't bother to call first. She simply ran over to Park Lane, flagged down a taxi, and went to Jeremy's place. He came to the door still in his pajamas, having been awake only long enough to brush his teeth and put on the kettle for tea.

She came charging into the flat saying, "Why did you send me those things?" and he immediately thought he'd been stupid, she was angry. But she didn't give him time to answer and went racing on, saying, "It was so sweet, the photograph. And the record. I listened and it was like that time Auntie Lilbet took Cliffie and me to St. Paul's, the one in New York, you know, not the one here, for a Christmas service and they had this boy's choir and when they sang, it was a carol service, I thought of angels and all of a sudden I knew exactly what heaven was. I knew *exactly*. It was so clear in my mind. But later on when I tried to describe it to them I couldn't get it right. I could see it all perfectly but I had no way to *tell* anybody."

He could barely follow, she was rattling along so fast. But she wasn't angry, didn't think he was a nutter, and that was what counted.

"Want a cup of tea, love?" he asked, hanging about in the entryway while she moved around his bed-sit, moving, moving, as if she had an engine inside her that'd been pushed into high gear.

"Sure, okay. I had breakfast with my dad. Well, I mean, he had breakfast and I drank some coffee to keep him company, and we talked but I was just waiting for him to finish and leave for the office so I could come over here and talk to you. . . ." She trailed off, stood still in the middle of the room and looked over at him.

She didn't look as cool and tidy as usual and it took him a moment to realize it was because her hair was down, not skinned back like always. It gave her a whole different appearance. Plus she had color in her cheeks today. "You look smashing," he said with a smile. "I'll just fetch the tea. Milk and sugar?"

"Sure, fine." She busied herself lighting a cigarette, remembered there wasn't an ashtray and went to the kitchen to stop in the doorway watching this tall tousle-haired young man pour boiling water into a teapot, his huge hands so surprisingly graceful, so surprisingly exciting. "Have you got an ashtray?" she asked, her throat gone thick.

"Will a saucer do?" he asked, opening a cupboard.

"Sure, that'll be fine." She took the saucer from him and returned to the main room, holding her cigarette in one hand, the saucer in the other, wondering if he could tell from the way she was behaving why she was there. And if he couldn't tell, what would she do? Was she going to have to come right out and ask him if they could do it again? God! This was terrible! Did Rheta . . . ? No, no. She turned to see that the curtains were drawn. Could anyone have seen the two of them yesterday? No. They were above street level. But still she did feel better with the curtains drawn, the room dim and quite cool. She was fairly overheated from her mad rush to get here.

116

"This is a treat," he said, carrying two cups over to the table. "Hungry? Fancy some eggs or toast?"

She shook her head and went to sit with him at the table, positioning the ashtray/saucer with great care to the left of her cup. "I'm left-handed, you know. Did you know that?"

"I'll be!" he said wide-eyed. "Me, too."

"When's your birthday?" she asked, words tumbling out of her mouth like little uncontrollable acrobats.

"The fifteenth of January."

"Are you being funny?" she said, and glared at him.

"Funny?"

"Did somebody *tell* you to say that?"

"You've lost me, love," he said apologetically, and took a sip of his tea.

"That's *my* birthday, the fifteenth," she near shouted.

"Nah!" he said softly. "Can't be. It's mine."

"This *isn't* funny!"

"No, honestly," he assured her, getting up to go for his wallet. "Look." He showed her his driving permit. "Date of birth, fifteenth of January, 1937."

She held his wallet in both hands and stared at the document with the feeling that she'd sampled the wrong Drink-Me bottle and gone plummeting down a dark hole to end up in Looney-Toons Land. She started to laugh, and it was so shrilly uncontrolled it frightened her. It unnerved him, too. He sought automatically to soothe her, getting up from his chair to come round to her side of the table and put his hand on her shoulder, asking, "Are you all right, love?" It was all she needed. She let the cigarette drop into the ashtray, let the wallet fall where it would, turned to press her cheek against his chest while her arms wrapped themselves tightly around him, and in seconds they were going at it even more tempestuously than they had the day before.

During a lull, he held her very close, possessively close, stroking the length of her arm, feeling the push of her breath against his shoulder, and listened to her whisper over and over, "I love you love you I love you." He drew her closer still, elated to have won her after all. "Love you too," he whispered back, the ex-

117

change of words firing him so thoroughly that he was immediately ready to have another go.

She repeated her declaration at every possible moment during their time together. The words seemed to help make everything real. If they loved one another, then nothing could be the least bit wrong.

S HE SAT on the floor with her arms crossed over Pearl's knees and her head resting on her arms while Pearl lazily stroked her hair, the two of them quiet for a time while Aly found words appropriate to the questions she wanted to ask. Throughout her entire time in transit—while she'd waited in the Ambassador's Lounge at Heathrow, all the way over on the TWA flight, and during the ride in from Idlewild in the limo Auntie Lilbet had sent to meet her—she'd risked confronting her memories, trying to match up what she recalled to what she was experiencing now. She was deeply afraid to have her thoughts confirmed, but couldn't escape her need to know. And only Pearl could provide the answers. She was the only one who'd tell the unvarnished truth.

Aly breathed in the scent that was uniquely Pearl's, a mingling of Ivory soap, lemon oil wax, vanilla, and Lentheric's Tweed perfume. "D'you think I'm like Rheta, Pearl?" she asked, then waited, very aware of her heartbeat, to hear what Pearl would say.

"Well, you sure enough don't look like her none," Pearl said, her hand rhythmically smoothing Aly's hair. "And you don't have your mummy's personality especially. So what way were you thinkin' you might be favorin' her?"

"The way she was. You know."

Pearl sighed. "You gone and fallen for some boy, little girl? That what this's all about?"

Aly raised her head to look up at her. "Maybe."

119

"Maybe?" Pearl's big hand reached down to cup Aly's chin. "You don't know?"

"How do people know? I mean, if it's something you've never done before, how could you know?"

"Hmmn. It's a fair question. Don't know that I have an answer. Lemme ask you this: What makes you think 'maybe'?"

Aly's face grew hot and she lowered her eyes. Pearl gave out a soft laugh and said, "You always have been a book I could pick up and read anytime, no matter where it was I happen to've left off."

Aly laughed with her, chagrined at being so transparent and yet grateful not to have to explain every last detail. It was why all her life she'd come to Pearl with anything of consequence that needed discussing.

"Done it and liked it, too, huh?" Pearl laughed more. "Well, I can remember it bein' a fine way to pass some time. I may be old but there's not a thing wrong with my rememory. What's got you worried, little girl? You gone and got yourself in the family way?" Pearl's face firmed apprehensively.

"I don't think so. I don't know. I never even thought about it," she admitted.

"Sharp girl like you and you don't do nothin' 'bout protectin' yourself? Shame on you, Aly! I thought you was smarter'n that. You don't never want to go trustin' any man to look out for you, 'cause they'll be too busy every time lookin' to please theirselves. And if you do finish up in the family way, it's your own blessed fault for bein' such a fool as to trust 'em."

"Jesus!" Aly said quietly, embarrassed.

"Didn't nobody ever *tell* you?" Pearl asked her. "I guess nobody did," she answered herself. "Wasn't nobody to tell you, I suppose. I can't see Miz Conover gettin' into a discussion 'bout somethin' so secret as sex even if she and the mister did tend to like it better'n most. Lord! I feel badly 'bout this, Aly. I shoulda talked with you, but truth to tell it never come into my head."

"I've known about sex since I was eight years old, Pearl. I just didn't think. . . ." She put her head back down and Pearl resumed stroking her hair. After a time Aly said, "None of the housekeepers Mom hired would stay with us more than a couple of months. It wasn't only because we were always moving, although that's what I used to think back then. Freda, the last one we had—I was about seven, I guess—she just all of a sudden one evening started shouting at Mom, saying Mom was the kind of woman no self-respecting person would want to work for, what with how she kept taking up with one man after another and how she was forever dragging her kids from pillar to post and expecting everyone to fall in line with her whims as if she thought she was special or something and the rules that applied to everybody else didn't apply to her just because her parents had money and she seemed to think it could buy her respectability. Cliffie and I started yelling at her to shut up and leave our mom alone. The two of us stood in front of Mom like guards, protecting her from the crazy housekeeper.

"Mom was shattered and furious at the same time. For days after she raged about the indignity of being accosted by someone in no way qualified to judge her on any level. After that we always looked after the apartments ourselves. For the longest time though I thought Freda was a lunatic or something. But then after . . . you know, later on, sometimes I'd recall things and when I thought about them I could see they weren't at all the way I remembered. And that included Freda who was really just an ordinary woman. There wasn't anything crazy about her at all. I'd interpreted events to suit myself."

"All children do that, darlin'. It's natural."

"Maybe. But Rheta wasn't natural, and the way we lived wasn't natural. I think Freda might have had a point. And I really need to know why Rheta was the way she was."

"Why d'you need to know?"

"Because I never want to be anything like her!"

"You think she was so bad, do you?"

"I don't know about bad, but she was *stupid*!" she said vehemently. "My God, she was the stupidest woman who ever lived!"

"That's not true," Pearl said quietly. "Maybe you'd like it to be, but it's not the truth. Your mummy was a lot of things, girl, but she wasn't stupid."

Sitting away from Pearl, Aly asked, "What was she then?"

"She was just crazy for men plain and simple. Once she found out what it was all about nobody and nothin' could keep Rheta and the men apart. Your mummy was foolish sometimes but she wasn't one bit stupid. And don't you never again let me hear you speak that way of her. You think she deserved to die so young? You think anythin' she ever did in her life was so bad she only got her just desserts bein' killed the way she was?"

"No," Aly whispered contritely.

"Smart's you are, there's lots of things you don't know about yet, little girl."

"I know," Aly agreed.

"Seems to me you've gone and got yourself into a situation you don't know how to handle, so you're blamin' your poor mummy for what's your own fault. And your mummy never in her life blamed anyone but her own self for her problems. You could do lots worse, you know, Aly, than to be like her. She wasn't evil like you seem to want to make her out to be. When she was a little girl, just like you, she used to come of an evenin' and sit 'n' talk with me."

"She did?" Aly asked tearfully.

"She surely did," Pearl confirmed, directing Aly's head back down to her knees. "Just like you," she repeated, her hand once again stroking Aly's hair.

"HONEY, YOU'RE just not yourself!" Lilbet was hurt, and Aly felt dreadful about it.

She apologized and went to give her grandmother a hug. To her complete dismay, the instant she was enclosed inside Lilbet's forgiving arms, she began to cry in huge sobbing gulps the way she had as a very small child.

"What's the matter?" Lilbet crooned, distressed by this extraordinary display. Alyssa was always such an even-tempered girl, never given to emotional outbursts.

Aly worked to pull herself together, for a few moments tempted to confide to her grandmother that she was scared to death she was pregnant. She was terrified to mention it. Lilbet would be scandalized, she was certain. And she hated to do anything that might jeopardize her relationship with her grandmother. It was something fixed in her life, something to which she could always look forward with pleasure because she knew in advance how her time with her Lilbet would be spent. They'd go shopping and Lilbet would insist on buying anything Aly might appear to admire. Aly would have to accept at least a few things or Lilbet would get upset; they'd go to the theatre half a dozen times, to the opera and ballet and a concert or two; they'd dine out in restaurants where the maître d's shot to attention the instant Lilbet came through the door and fuss, with just the right degree of obsequiousness, over both of them; they'd take walks and window shop; and on at least two evenings during her stay, they'd have quiet dinners at home and reminisce about safe subjects: the antics Rheta had got up to as a child, things Cliff and Aly had done when they were little. There was a blackout on the murders and anything remotely pertaining to them—and that was fine. Aly didn't want to remember, and Lilbet didn't want to know, so it was a simple enough matter to avoid the subject.

Directing Aly over to the sofa now, Lilbet sat down with her, keeping one arm around Aly's shoulders and with her free hand offering a lace-edged handkerchief. "I want you to tell me what's on your mind, Alyssa."

"I can't. You'll hate me."

"Honey, I could never hate you."

Agonized, Aly blotted her face with her grandmother's scented handkerchief and mentally weighed the risk. If she wasn't pregnant but went ahead and told, Lilbet would know what an idiot she'd been, behaving like some kind of brainless animal with Jeremy without even thinking about protecting herself. She hadn't thought about anything, let alone precautions. Jeremy with his clever instincts seemed to know things about her no one else had ever suspected. Or was it clever instinct? Maybe the truth was he'd simply been bold enough to approach her. Who knew why any of it had happened? She certainly didn't. In part she wished she could rewind the spool of the past and excise that segment. But in part she felt an ongoing fascination with her own sexuality. It was almost as if she'd accidentally discovered a seam at the point where her jaw gave way to her throat. A bit of gentle picking at that seam and it had unravelled. The face she'd always recognized fell away

123

like some *papier-mâché* construction and she was left gazing at a girl who looked faintly familiar but who had quite different appetites.

She couldn't possibly tell her grandmother about the numerous and greatly upsetting discoveries she'd made in only a matter of weeks. For one thing she had no explanations to offer, and for another Lilbet would tell her dad, so they'd both know. No, she couldn't do it. "It's nothing," she said, trying to get herself to smile.

"A nothing that'd make me hate you. That's a very big nothing."

"My period's due," Aly told her, inspired. "I always get a bit crazy. I'm sorry. I know I haven't been good company for you the last few days and I really am sorry."

"Well, why didn't you say so?" Lilbet said, appeased. "Have you taken anything? You should take some aspirin, or maybe Midol."

"What a good idea! I'll do that," Aly said, at last able to smile. "I'll wash my face right now and then we'll go out the way we planned." She got up, suppressing a desire to flee, and made her way to the bathroom where she sat on the side of the tub and stared at the imported Italian floral tiles Lilbet had had installed around the perimeter of the room when she'd renovated the apartment the previous year. Everything had been going so well—with school, with her life—until she'd accepted that invitation from Lydia Halliwell to come to tea. If only she'd refused, she wouldn't have been walking along Fulham Road that day. She'd never have been stopped by Jeremy, never have been gulled by him into meeting Andrew. She'd be continuing on with her life, contented, instead of spending most of her time praying she wasn't pregnant and eagerly awaiting some sign as proof of that. It was a goddamned nightmare! And the worst of it was knowing that if Jeremy magically appeared in front of her at that moment she'd shed her clothes and make love to him right there on the bathroom floor, with her grandmother within shouting distance.

Sighing, she got up and splashed cold water on her face. Why couldn't it have been Andrew? she asked herself. At least she knew and understood him. She seemed able to read Jeremy only superficially, and not well. He was capable of far more than she'd credited. And hateful as it was to admit it, what she liked best about him was what she'd least expected him to display a talent for.

Her face dry, she studied herself for a moment in the mirror over the sink. It was true, she didn't resemble Rheta. And she damned well wasn't going to behave like her.

When she returned from the bathroom, Lilbet said, "When I was a girl, I'd have to go to bed for days when my time of the month came around. There's no need ever for you to be embarrassed with me, honey. I understand these things. I'm not *that* old, you know, that I've forgotten what it's like."

"You're not old at all," Aly said with admiring fondness. At sixty-three, Lilbet looked and acted at least fifteen years younger, and turned a lot of heads whenever they went out for one of their walks. People routinely assumed she was Aly's mother and neither she nor Lilbet had ever discouraged anyone. They looked so alike it wasn't an unreasonable assumption. And there were times when Aly herself wondered if it mightn't actually be true. But of course it wasn't. She was Rheta's child, and like her in too many ways.

BY THE end of her six-week visit Aly was convinced she was pregnant, and feeling panicky. Although Lilbet didn't show it, Aly was sure her grandmother was as relieved to have her leave as Aly was to go. Despite her full-time effort to be worthy company, she knew she'd been less than a great success.

She'd written several times to Jeremy, but hadn't been able to put into words any of her true feelings. He'd replied in his cramped handwriting on more pages torn from a steno pad; outpourings of love and indiscreet sexual references that, despite their crudeness, inflamed her. She dreamed about him almost nightly, dragging him into her needy body like some improbable medicament she had to have to calm the palsied agitation in her limbs.

She exchanged letters with Andrew, too. He wrote lengthy

replies on crisp blue monogrammed airmail paper; splendidly witty anecdotes about his fellow cast members, descriptions of the weather that had turned, in her absence, typically British: cold and wet and relentlessly overcast; he outlined ideas he had for things they might do upon her return; he signed each time, "With all my love, Andrew," and she believed him, which was odd because Jeremy signed his letters fairly much the same way but she dismissed these salutations as affectations, merely words Jeremy thought she'd want to see at the end of any communication from him.

Things were a mess. She missed Andrew badly, but she missed Jeremy, too. She wished she'd never met either one of them. Now, less than four months after Jeremy stopped her outside the pub that Sunday everything was chaotic. It was so unfair. She'd discovered something she could do that was more pleasurable than anything else she could imagine, but there was a hefty price tag attached. If it turned out she wasn't pregnant, that she hadn't made a complete hash of her life, she swore she'd never get involved sexually with another man as long as she lived.

Throughout the trip home she excoriated herself for her weakness. Her dread of having her pregnancy confirmed was so overwhelming it seemed as if she could actually taste it—an unpleasant bitterness that rose from her throat and which she had repeatedly to swallow.

THE DAY after she returned from New York she went to see a doctor on the Bayswater Road whose name she'd picked from the telephone directory. After sitting in the waiting room of the surgery for quite some time, she was at last summoned inside to see the doctor. They completed the National Health form; she told him why she'd come, and he examined her. He said he thought she very likely was pregnant, but to be certain she should drop off a first-thing-in-the-morning urine specimen at the lab he used. She politely thanked him, went away, the next morning did as he'd told her, then hovered by the telephone waiting to hear the results.

In the course of the next three days, Jeremy phoned more than a dozen times. Olive took most of his calls, her father answered several; Aly herself spoke briefly to him twice and both times promised to ring back soon. Andrew called just once, on her first day home. She told him she was working and would call him in a day or two. He sounded disappointed but took her at her word and waited for her to get back to him. Jeremy's calls proliferated until Aly lost control and shrieked at him. "I *said* I'll call you! Stop *pestering* me! *I'll call you,* Jeremy!" She slammed down the phone, trembling with exasperation and anxiety, as well as regret for being so unkind, then paced up and down the front hall, wondering why Jeremy was hounding her, and why it was taking the doctor so long to get back to her.

On the morning of the fourth day Olive came out from the kitchen, without a word took hold of Aly by the arm, and hustled her back to the kitchen. Pushing her down into a chair, Olive lit two cigarettes, gave one to Aly, then said, "Right, then, miss! How long?"

Aly looked up at the woman prepared to play dumb, saw Olive was deadly serious and said, "Seven weeks, I think."

"Bloody hell! Which one of them is it?"

"Jeremy," Aly said wretchedly.

"Christ! You would pick the one that's all dick and no brains," Olive said disgustedly. "Why'n't you go after the other? He's the one with something to recommend him."

"It's not as if I sat down and played eeny-meeny, Olive. It just happened. And I'm still not sure anything even *has* happened."

"Seven weeks? You can be sure, dearie. What're you gonna do about it?"

"I don't know." Aly took a puff of the cigarette and gazed into space. "Just don't tell me what an idiot I am. Okay? I've told myself that several hundred times."

"Far be it from me to go calling the kettle black, my girl."

"You have a child?" Aly asked her, surprised.

"Didn't say that, did I?" she said.

"God! I couldn't do that."

"Don't go saying that. You never know what you could and couldn't do 'til the time comes when you've got to do it."

"No, I really couldn't," Aly insisted.

"Well, you change your mind, come to me. I might be able to help."

"Thank you," Aly said thickly as the telephone began ringing.

They looked at each other for a long moment, then Olive said, "You want me to answer?"

"No, that's all right. I'll get it." Leadenly, Aly got up and went to the telephone.

O LIVE WAS absolutely right. No one could say for certain what she'd do until a choice had to be made. Only then, with the weight of all the factors to be considered bearing down on you, could you decide what you had to do.

Olive made the arrangements and while Hal was away for three days in Geneva on business she went with Aly to a place in Worlds End. She waited downstairs in the stifling lounge while Aly went into one of the bedrooms of the narrow terraced house.

Aly stood near the door, her damp hands knotted in front of her, watching the elderly abortionist pull on a pair of rubber gloves. It appeared to be the only sanitary measure the woman planned to take, aside from tying on a flowery bibbed apron to protect her red wool dress. She turned and rather impatiently beckoned Aly over. "Come on, then," she said. "Off with everything from the waist down."

It was so embarrassing. There wasn't even anything to cover herself with. She had to stand there half naked in front of a total stranger waiting to be told what to do. And the old woman seemed so annoyed, as if Aly should've known without having to be told. She had to hoist herself up onto an old oak table and open her legs so the old lady could hurt her. Aly kept her eyes tightly closed and refused to make any sound whatsoever while the pain seemed to grow like something on fire inside her.

Afterwards Olive got Aly home in a taxi and spent the night

with her in case anything went wrong. "I'm not going off leaving you here on your own," she declared staunchly.

"It hurt," Aly admitted, the aftermath pain circling deep inside her like a tiny train chugging steadily around a narrow loop of track. Each time it approached the top of the loop the pain heightened, climaxed, then diminished; over and over, around and around. It was all she could do to drag her attention away from it. "I don't know why, but I didn't think it would. I was more bothered by the idea of undressing in front of that old woman than I was about what she was going to do. I mean, I didn't even think about it." She sniffed and wiped her face on her sleeve.

"I know," Olive said softly. "It's a right bugger. Still, it's done now. A day or two and you'll be right as rain."

Two weeks later she was threatening to return to Worlds End and have it out with that old woman.

"It's no use," Aly sighed, defeated. "I appreciate everything you've done. I truly do. But I couldn't go through that again. The very thought of it makes me feel sick."

"I've never heard of such a thing happening," Olive declared. "I've a mind to give that silly old git a good clout over the head. I should've known from the look of her she'd no idea what she was on about."

JEREMY ABSORBED the information soberly, blinked once or twice, said, "I see," then went quiet abruptly, as if his mind, like something airborne, had snagged on a tree branch. Aly lit a cigarette and sat studying his face, utterly unable to imagine what he might be thinking.

There were now two girls in London carrying babies of his, he thought, somewhat awed. He wanted to smile and actually had to work hard not to, well aware of how easily that might be misinterpreted. But inwardly he really did have to smile. Here he'd gone and put not one but two girls in the family way. He, Jeremy Brown, known professionally as Gable, had buns in two ovens; he, Jeremy, the one who during his school years could never get a girl even to go to the cinema with him, let alone out of her clothes and into a bed, had impregnated two very attrac-

130

tive and unfortunately fecund young women. He felt exceptionally potent, inordinately powerful. He'd made legal arrangements to take care of Liz. Now he'd have to make further legal arrangements, albeit of a decidedly different nature, to take care of Alyssa. He squashed his desire to crow. He'd not only beaten out Andrew and been first with Alyssa, he'd won game, set and match. He felt marvelous, absolutely euphoric.

"We'll get married! Absolutely. Yes," he said decisively.

Aly's head nodded up and down like a marionette's. He'd said what she'd wanted to hear; he'd do the honorable thing and make everything right. She puffed on her cigarette, trying not to succumb to a depression that lurked like a rapist in an alleyway, waiting for a likely victim to come walking by.

She couldn't bring herself to lie to her father. She told him she'd agreed to marry Jeremy, then watched the levels of disbelief layer down one after another on his face. At last, he said, "I'm sure you've given this a lot of thought, and if you think this is the best course, I've got to go along with you. Is that what you think, Aly?"

"I have no other choice. And Jeremy didn't hesitate for a moment, about saying we'd get married, I mean. I don't see what else we could do. And what I thought, since you've hardly had any kind of a chance to get to know him, I thought he should come to dinner. I asked him to come Friday. We'll have dinner and the two of you will get to meet each other properly. He's not at all a bad person."

"No, I didn't think he was, honey. I'm just concerned about your doing something you might regret later on. You haven't known this Jeremy all that long."

"I know," she agreed quietly. "I never wanted anything like this to happen, Dad. Are you ashamed of me?"

"Aly," he exclaimed. "Nothing you could ever do would make me ashamed of you. I'll admit I'm disappointed with this particular—situation, but it's not the first time in the history of the world a girl was a little pregnant when she walked down the aisle." He gave her a coaxing smile. "I take it you'll want to do this quietly, without any fuss."

"That's right."

"Well," he said, "since I'm not going to have to foot the bill for a big wedding, the least I can do is get you set up with someplace nice to live."

"Oh, Dad," she said, covering her eyes with her hands, "you're being too nice. You're not supposed to be so reasonable." She wept behind her hands, unable to meet his eyes.

"I don't have any choice either, Aly," he said soberly. "You and I and your grandmother are all that's left of something I used to think was going to last forever. I want you nearby. It's purely selfish, honey, and only partly for the sake of your comfort. Besides, from what I've seen of that young man he doesn't have two dimes to rub together. My daughter's not going to live in some crummy bed-sitting room if I have anything to say about it." He was silent for a few moments, then swore softly. "Shit! I don't much like any of it, Aly. But for your sake, I'll sit down to dinner with this fella, and all of us'll make the best of it. On the bright side," he said, reaching out to pat her shoulder, "I'm crazy about kids, and so's Serena. We don't want to go forgetting there's a baby involved in all of this."

It SEEMED that all she did during the week before the wedding was cry.

The most painful part of it was telling Andrew. She made a date to meet him at a pub on King's Road not too far from where he lived. They never did go in. He was waiting outside when she arrived, and without a word he took her hand and they started to walk. It was a gray bone-chillingly damp September day, very appropriate, Aly thought wryly, to the present circumstances of her life.

"I don't think I'm going to care one bit for this," he said after they'd walked without speaking to the Embankment. "All these weeks I've been waiting to see you, knowing in my bones it wasn't going to turn out the way I wanted. Why is that, do you suppose?" He leaned on the rail and looked down at the murky river.

She shrugged and busied herself lighting a cigarette, delaying as long as possible having to tell him.

"You looked tired," he said, turning to study her. "Did you not have a lovely time visiting your granny?"

132

"It was okay." She shrugged.

"This is truly dreadful, isn't it?" He made a comically grim face. "Might I have one of your cigarettes?"

"Oh, sure." She opened her bag and gave him the pack and her lighter. "I didn't know you smoked."

"Usually only post-coitally," he quipped. "Sorry. Bad joke."

They both watched the water for a time. Then, knowing she couldn't put it off any longer, she said, "I'm going to marry Jeremy."

He didn't respond and she turned to see his hand with the cigarette hovering in the air, a look of agony on his face. He felt as if she'd just driven a long knife right into his belly.

"Why?" he asked, sounding as if he were strangling.

"I'm pregnant," she confessed, mortified. Admitting this gave her the feeling she'd just stripped naked in front of him and given a brief and very crude demonstration of precisely how she'd managed to get herself into this state.

"Bad reason," he said, at last taking a puff on the cigarette. "Under the best of circumstances, that would be a bad reason for marrying Gable. In fact," he went on, "I'd be hard-pressed to come up with any single *good* reason for your embarking upon the ship of matrimony with someone so utterly undeserving of you."

"You're trying to be funny," she said flatly.

"I certainly am," he agreed. "It's in the best tradition of any good opera: laugh while your heart is breaking, that sort of thing."

"Oh, don't," she said, trying to keep some sort of control of the situation.

He flicked his cigarette into the water, then stood in silence gazing at the far shore, feeling the years of training, the whole nonsensical British tradition of stiff upper lip stoicism, and his confidence in himself all crumbling inside his chest, the fragments of everything he'd been taught from earliest childhood falling away from the central core of his being like rocks into a bottomless chasm. "Why are you doing it?" he asked, his voice squeezed by the pressure in his chest to barely a whisper.

"I went and had an abortion. It didn't work."

"Poor you," he said, unable now to look at her. "That is too bad."

"I don't like you when you're sarcastic, Andrew."

"No, no," he said. "It *is* too bad, most unfortunate."

"You won't even look at me," she accused, appalled at how badly this was going.

"I can't," he admitted.

"Why not? We're still friends. We always will be."

"Christ!" he exclaimed. She'd driven that long knife into him a second time. He doubted it was possible to survive such acute injuries.

"We will," she insisted, distraught and desperate for his reassurance.

"Marry *me!*" he spluttered, dangerously close to losing his dignity and fairly dazed with pain.

"I couldn't." She studied his profile, willing him to look at her.

"You really could, you know. I wouldn't mind. I quite like children. I'd even like his."

"You're not serious."

"Oh, but I am," he assured her.

"God! This is awful."

"It is, isn't it?" he concurred. "Truly awful. When I ran down the list of the many possible reasons why you've put off seeing me for weeks, I promise you none of this was even on the list. Silly of me, really. Do you know I wouldn't allow myself to imagine you with Gable. The thought of him anywhere near you made my teeth ache. And the thought of him *touching* you . . . I seriously underestimated him. Rather foolish, given what I know of him."

"What does that mean, what you know of him?"

He considered telling her about Liz but decided it was beneath him. "Never mind." At long last he ventured to look at her.

"What?" she asked, searching his eyes.

He shook his head, on the verge of disgracing himself.

"No, what? Andrew, you're so important to me. I've been counting on our being friends. I. . . ."

"*Why* are you doing it?"

"I have to, Andrew. I gave my word. . . ."

"You gave your word," he repeated disbelievingly. "You *gave* your *word* to a man for whom that particular nicety has no meaning whatsoever. Do you realize that? Do you love him?"

"Well, sure I do."

"Well, sure you do," he repeated, somewhat cruelly matching her intonation exactly. "That tripped easily enough off your tongue. Too easily perhaps?"

"What do you want me to say?"

"I love you!" he cried, the last remnants of his self-esteem falling noiselessly down, down. "*I'm* the one who loves you. And you love me. At least I believed that you did. Was I wrong? Did I only imagine there was something between us? Did I just imagine that?"

It was her turn to shake her head.

"Call if off! It's not too late. He'll only make you unhappy. Jeremy's not capable of genuinely caring for anyone. He doesn't know how. Not that he's a bad man. Please don't think I'm impugning his character. That's simply not possible where Jeremy's concerned. Because, you see, in order to impugn character one must have it to begin with. And that doesn't apply to Jeremy. He just *isn't* anyone. It's why the only logical place for him is in the theatre, because as an actor he can play out an endless series of roles, all of which will lend him the illusion of personally possessing character. Do you see? Can you understand that? Jeremy Gable is something a small boy created out of bits and pieces taken from here, there, and everywhere, and added to a God-given gift of a singing voice. He's a brilliantly talented performing automaton, but he's not real and it isn't in him to care deeply for anyone. But *I* can, Alyssa, *I* do. I never was all that interested in acting, really. It was something I did in school, a bit of a lark, nothing serious. Oh, dear God!" he lamented. "This is so un-English of me, isn't it?" He tried to laugh but couldn't bring it off. "I do apologize for making a scene. Really, what must you think of me! You've given your word and of course you're not going to call it off. You wouldn't, would you? Call it off, I mean," he asked forlornly.

"Andrew, I couldn't do that."

"No, of course not. Will you excuse me if I don't stay?" He was on the verge of tears and would not permit her to witness this final self-imposed indignity. "I really can't stay. You do understand." His face ashen and crumpled, he swivelled about and walked quickly away in the stiffly overcontrolled fashion of someone who's had too much to drink but who's determined to demonstrate his sobriety.

Dumbfounded she stood for a few seconds watching him hurry off. Then, with panic ballooning inside her chest at the prospect of losing him, she went running after him.

"Andrew! Wait! Don't run away from me!" she called, frightened because he wouldn't stop. "Please don't run away!" she cried, impatiently wiping her eyes with the back of her hand. "Everybody hates me for this, as if I planned it or something," she shouted at his back, all control lost. "You're not the only one. My dad's face looks just like yours, *just like yours,* Andrew! God! You're being so unfair!" she accused, almost out of breath and slowing down. "Oh, sure, you *say* you'd marry me and it wouldn't matter to you that I had Jeremy's baby." She couldn't run anymore, came to a stop and raised her voice at his retreating back. "It *would so* matter! It would! *I have to do what's right!* Don't run away from me!"

Her chest heaving, eyes and nose running, she stood panting. He went a few more steps, stopped, turned, looked at her for quite some time, then slowly walked back. He couldn't help it. He'd been taken from the start by the way truth seemed to burst out of her so unexpectedly, so very much in the fashion of young children who haven't yet learned to cloak themselves and their emotions in social disguises. She was so wonderfully, openly American and therefore unlike the people he'd known best in his life. Her eyes, her honesty, and the sweet self-deceit of her integrity drew at him in a way that he knew would spoil him for other women. At best, the females he met in the future would have one or two of Alyssa's qualities. But none of them would ever have her rare combination of vulnerability, truthfulness, and beauty lacking completely in vanity. She was, he thought, a magnificently wise child who would undoubtedly grow to become a magnificently wise woman. It was tragic, really, that Jeremy had succeeded in compromising her at a time when she hadn't quite made the transition from child to woman. Tragic.

"Don't you think I wish I could run away, too?" she sobbed.

"I'd love to, but it's no good for the children. It's no good for anyone. You *can't* do that to children. It makes them nervous and unhappy. . . . They need. . . ." She looked into his eyes, pleading. "Please don't run away and leave me."

He had no idea what specifically she was trying to say, but the emotional sense of it got through to him and he realized he'd only been prodding the edges of his own hurt without giving any consideration to hers. He understood all at once that it wasn't deceit but rather she was honoring some ethical code of which he was unaware. He had to respect her for it even though he was certain that her code, whatever it was, made no allowances for human error and had no flexibility to its rules. And since he did, in fact, love her and despaired of having to leave her, he unbent and lifted his arms to hold her, ironically attaining one of his fondest wishes only when she'd already committed herself to someone else. That unscrupulous prick Gable was to have the privilege of embracing the forlorn loveliness of this floundering child any time he fancied. Andrew had to make a concentrated effort to control his anger with Gable. Bad enough the despicable shit had to seduce the girl. The least he could've done was use a contraceptive. But, no. Using a contraceptive would indicate concern for someone other than himself, and that particular quality wasn't listed in Gable's credits.

"What am I to do with you?" he wondered aloud. "Could there possibly be a situation more hopeless?"

She shook her head.

"Your husband-to-be won't care one bit for my hanging about."

"I don't care," she said childishly. "You're *my* friend."

"Yes, I am," he agreed. "Unfortunately, I'm your friend who loves you."

"This isn't the way I ever thought it'd be, Andrew. I wish to God none of this was happening."

"On that, my dearest girl, I am in complete agreement." He let his cheek rest against the top of her head and inhaled the sweet fragrance of her hair.

"I would've chosen you, Andrew. I would've. I just thought it'd be later on. You know?"

"Not to worry," he said, finding himself able to play out the role of good sport. "You have my word I won't run away."

"You know what?" she asked, lifting her wet face from his shoulder to look at him.

He reached into his pocket for a tissue and carefully blotted her cheeks. "What?"

"I ruined everything, didn't I?"

"No, dear girl. I'm afraid Jeremy did that," he corrected her.

"Don't blame him. I was there, too."

"Come on," he said, anxious to keep her from confiding more than he was able to hear. "Let's go have a nice cup of tea, and we'll both feel heaps better. You'll see." He looped his arm through hers. "A cup of Typhoo and you'll be good as new."

She didn't laugh, but then he hadn't really expected her to.

I T WAS decided that Serena would give the dinner. Her staff would prepare and serve the food leaving everyone free to get better acquainted at a leisurely pace. But from the moment he came through the front door Jeremy was so obviously overwhelmed by the house and so determined to ingratiate himself that Aly was both sorry for him as well as irritated. "Just relax and be yourself," she counseled in a whisper while Serena and her father were fixing drinks at the far end of the lounge.

"I am," he replied, his expression blank.

"You don't have to impress anyone, you know, Jeremy."

His blank expression held. He really had no idea what she was talking about. Then, as if unable to help himself, his eyes wandered away like wayward children determined to explore the many splendors of this elegant house. Aly gave up and sat back to light a cigarette, thinking that with her help he'd soon stop fretting over the kind of impression he made and show the appealing unstudied aspects of himself. Reaching for his hand, she gave it a squeeze. He shifted and smiled distractedly then almost at once turned away again to continue his scrutiny of the room and its furnishings.

In a number of ways he really was like a child, she thought, fascinated. It was in part what she found so intriguingly contradictory, even endearing about him. She did wonder if others—her father and Serena, for example—found him as easy to read as she quite often did. At times, having had the opportunity to study him intently at very close range, she could

almost see his brain ticking over. But perhaps that very closeness distorted her view of him; perhaps it was like staring
through the bull's-eye, trying to force everything into focus
even though she knew it was impossible. Nor, being honest, was
her ability to read him a constant given. During the months
they'd known each other there had been just as many occasions
when his actions had struck her as all but incomprehensible.
The childlike qualities remained consistent, however, even
when he appeared to be making his best efforts at mature man-
liness. The only time he seemed entirely himself—neither childlike nor so easily read—was during lovemaking. But then she
too was another version of herself at those times. Being naked
was somehow a great deal more than simply removing one's
clothes. It was like shedding a layer of emotional protection so
that she felt closer to a potentially alarming level of personal
reality than at any other time. There was something quite dangerous about nakedness, despite the phenomenal pleasure
she'd thus far derived from it. It had to do with a faint nagging
fear that hovered on the very outer edge of her awareness. She
wanted both to acknowledge and identify the fear and to ignore
it in the hope it would go away of its own accord. Yet she
seemed unable to do either. She concentrated on going forward
one dogged step at a time, doing what had to be done. And
right now she had to familiarize her father with this young man
she was going to marry.

During the evening she found herself drifting away, first
from the conversation taking place over the drinks and then
over the very fine meal Serena's cook had prepared. She tried
to pay attention, but her brain felt fluffy and weightless and
kept floating off. Like foam being propelled by a vagrant lunar
tide, her thinking turned this way and that, touching briefly
against objects just below the surface before being pushed along
again. She looked at her father and then at Serena able to see
a kind of glow, a gentle golden radiance enclosing them. Lan-
guorously, her eyelids pleasantly heavy, she admired this
couple on the far side of the table; she studied their communication, wondering why it was that some people managed to
find partners who were very nearly perfect while others either
attracted or went after the worst possible mates. This business

of pairing was complicated, involving almost too many factors. Did you have to get to be over forty before you knew, finally, what qualities in another you could or couldn't live with? Or was there some cosmic system of preselection? Looking at Serena, seeing how happy her father was with her, Aly couldn't imagine what had appealed to him about Rheta. Rheta had been small and fair and flighty. Serena was tall and dark and somewhat fey but grounded, nonetheless, in very specific reality; she was eccentric in the most charming fashion, yet deeply thoughtful. She was the perfect partner for Hal Jackson. So what had he been doing with Rheta, who'd only seemed realistic but whose judgment in fact had been clouded by her perennial undiminished need for men?

Rheta had been a most intelligent woman who for reasons never to be known couldn't or wouldn't look past the surface of things. She'd given birth to two precociously bright children but had insisted always on assigning them mundane secondary roles, rarely admitting either to the children themselves or to outsiders—and that included the teachers who'd always wanted to talk about Cliff and Aly's exceptional abilities—that her children were, in fact, not at all ordinary. She'd kept Cliff and Aly so busy doing household chores and learning new routes to school that none of them had had the time to consider just how bizarre their life really was. Rheta's greatest talent, Aly thought, was her ability to delegate so many minor responsibilities to her children and to hold them accountable to such a stringent degree for their successful completion that Cliff and Aly had actually lived up to their mother's expectations, only at the very end venturing to question the reasonableness of her demands. Never mind that their marriage had only lasted a few years, what had drawn Hal to a woman who couldn't have been more different to the one he was with now? Or was that, quite simply, the answer? Was it Rheta's differentness that had been the lure? And was it Serena's soothing normalcy that so appealed to him now?

Aly gave her head a little shake and reached for her water glass, trying to match up the conversational fragments that reached her as she reined in her attention. Serena looked a bit puzzled, and was listening with her eyes slightly narrowed as Jeremy expounded on ... what? Aly turned and knew just from the set of his features that he was telling Serena and her father about his pet theory of perfection.

". . . they don't respect it," he was saying. "Everyone's too impatient; no one's got the time to waste on getting things right. And if you ask to have a bit more time to get things just so, well they've got no time for *you*, have they?" He was getting himself worked up and Aly thought she'd better stop this before he started ranting.

"Is your grandmother going to be able to come to the wedding?" Hal interrupted pleasantly.

"I meant to ask you about that myself," Aly said, grateful for her father's intervention.

"If transportation's a problem, we'll be glad to arrange something," Hal offered. "I know she's your only family."

"Well, actually," Jeremy said, a peculiar tight smile uptilting one corner of his mouth, "Gran's gone off to Penzance for a fortnight to visit her sister. She'd had it planned for ages, you see"—he looked first at Serena, then at Aly, and finally back at Hal—"and I didn't like to upset her plans." He trailed off rather lamely, that odd smile still distorting his mouth.

"Does she know we're getting married?" Aly asked, finding the story peculiar.

Jeremy gazed down at the table for a moment, his mouth working ever so slightly, as if he were pushing words like tiny seeds around with the tip of his tongue. Twin patches of color appeared on his cheeks and when he raised his head his eyes had acquired an artificial brightness. "Actually," he said, drawing the word out, "I've had to write to her. There's no telephone there, you see. I . . . ahm . . . I didn't want to upset her."

"Would your getting married upset your grandmother?" Serena asked interestedly.

"Oh no!" he answered quickly. "It's nothing like that at all. It's just that she had her heart set on this visit with her sister. I mean they'd been planning it for ages, and she's elderly, after all. You don't like to go changing things with old people, do you? I mean, it upsets them, doesn't it?" He again looked around the table, appealing to their understanding. Serena's brows had drawn together and she was gazing steadily at Jeremy, unable to conceal her bewilderment. Hal sat with his elbows on the table, chin in hand, blinking slowly.

"Don't you want her to come?" Aly asked head-on, and was taken aback to see pinpoints of anger spark to life in Jeremy's eyes.

"Well, of course I do!" he said, the patches of color spreading over his cheeks. "It's just that she can't be here, can she, if she's in Penzance with her sister?"

"We'll have coffee in the lounge, I think," Serena said smoothly, rising from the table.

Hal at once got to his feet, as did Aly, both of them anxious to avoid any unpleasantness, but Jeremy continued to sit there, as if determined to pursue his ardent self-defense.

"Come on," Aly said, touching his arm.

"Don't you ever do that again!" he railed at her in a barely controlled undertone.

"Do what?" she asked, anger beginning to sizzle in her chest. She'd never seen him like this and she didn't care at all for his irrational behavior.

"Don't you *ever* question what I say or do in front of other people!"

"You're behaving like an idiot," she declared, and left him there.

She smoked a cigarette and drank her coffee while she watched Jeremy work doubly hard to salvage the good impression he thought he'd made earlier, ignoring his visual pleas for help. She sat in silence beside Serena on the sofa. She chain-smoked, consumed several breath-stopping gulps of cognac with her second cup of coffee, and was about to refill her snifter when Serena's cool hand descended over the top of hers.

"Not good," Serena said kindly. "Not for you or the baby."

Aly leaned over to whisper, "I feel as if I hate him. What am I doing?"

With a laugh, aware of Jeremy observing them closely, Serena said, "I'm free tomorrow. Why don't I come with you? I know the area, and we can't have these estate agents taking advantage of you. More coffee, Jeremy?" Then, once Jeremy had resumed his conversation with Hal, she murmured, "I can't name a woman I know who didn't feel in the week before the deed was to be done as if she hated the man she was going to marry. Perfectly normal, darling, I promise you."

By 9:30, Aly was sending signals to her father, begging him to put an end to the evening. He nodded discreetly and ten minutes later looked at his watch, saying, "Hate to break things up, but I've got a 7:30 flight to Paris in the morning."

Jeremy thanked Serena effusively, complimenting her on the house, the dinner, her dress, even her hair. Serena took it all in stride, shook his hand, and said, "I expect we'll be seeing a great deal of you."

He then approached Aly, set to suggest they go somewhere for a drink or a coffee but she cut him off, not bothering to conceal her anger. "I'm going home with my father."

"Oh, right. Well, I'll push off then." He shook hands with Hal then gave Aly a kiss on the mouth, and instantly, responding to the softness of his lips, the fragrance that was uniquely his, she regretted sending him off this way. Why was she being so judgmental, so uncharitable? There was probably some totally legitimate reason why his grandmother couldn't come to the wedding and Jeremy being Jeremy he'd made everything more complicated than it needed to be. Just like his obsession with perfection in performance, he had a fairly rigid view of how things should be said and done. All these habits of his would change, he'd mellow once they were married and settled.

She gave him a smile and immediately his entire demeanor changed. He lost most of his stiffness, returned the smile, gave her another quick kiss and went on his way. It wasn't until she was sitting beside her father in the back of the cab that she realized her neck and shoulders ached from the tension she'd felt throughout the evening.

JUST AFTER the ceremony, when she and Jeremy and her father and Serena were on their way to where the chauffeur was waiting with Serena's Rolls Royce, Aly happened to glance over and see her father looking at Jeremy. His expression of dislike was so pronounced Aly wouldn't have been surprised to see Jeremy crumple in the road, doubled-up with pain. But Jeremy was walking blithely along at Hal's side, smiling to himself and fingering the pale pink rose pinned to his lapel.

Taking hold of Serena's hand, Aly held her back, letting the men get ahead of them.

"Do you dislike him as much as Dad does?"

Serena looked at Jeremy for a moment or two, then said, "Let me ask you something. Has everything always had to be a great challenge for you? Do you instinctively go after what promises to be most difficult?"

"Is that the way you see this?"

"I'm not certain how I see this," Serena admitted. "He says and does all the right things, but it doesn't quite ring true. Perhaps you'll bring him round," she said brightly. "It's been known to happen."

"You think he's phony?"

"Let's just say he's not one hundred percent real. He's an actor, after all."

"What a mess!" Aly muttered, convinced for the moment she'd just married someone no one could possibly like.

"Not to worry! At least the sex is good."

"How do you know that?" Aly asked ingenuously.

In answer, Serena gave one of her raffish smiles and patted Aly's abdomen with the flat of her hand.

"I don't even know if I like babies," Aly confessed.

"Oh, you will," Serena said. "Because if you show the least sign of not liking this one, I'll be off with the baby in the blink of an eye." She laughed gaily as if in anticipation of that eventuality. "I can't wait to play grandmother and have everyone go on about how I'm far too young for it. Divine!" She tugged on Aly's hand and they started again toward the car.

Jeremy's hair was very red in the sunlight, and his eyes today were more blue than green. He really was very sweet, Aly thought, and gave him an emphatic hug before they got into the car. He wasn't easy to get to know. But once people got to know him, the way she had, they'd see his sweetness; they'd come to care for him, the way she did. Everything would be all right now. She knew it would.

AN INTERLUDE

She'd never said a word to anyone but she'd worried about the baby since the failed abortion. What if that old woman had harmed the baby in some way? What if, after all she'd been through, the baby came out crippled or deformed? There'd been so much pain. Something had been damaged, otherwise she wouldn't have felt anything.

Everything to do with this baby had been painful—the attempt to get rid of it, the effort to push it out of her now. The midwife was the sort Serena laughingly referred to as "jolly hockey sticks," very gung-ho and let's get on with it, chaps, as if this was a football match and not a birth. Still, she was helpful and not at all unkind, just intent on seeing Aly put the maximum energy into breathing and pushing and concentrating on moving this child into the light.

Jeremy was away on location, but Olive would see to it he got the message. And her father was in New York, with Lilbet. Serena had gone up to Yorkshire to visit her sister. Only Olive happened to be around when the contractions started better than two weeks ahead of schedule. In a way, though, Aly preferred to be alone. If anything was wrong with the baby no one else would have to know. She'd take it and go away somewhere and make a happy life for it. That would be only right, only fair. She actually liked the idea of being alone with this baby that was shifting down in overlapping circles of pain she could almost see, like colored rings, white hot, glaring red, cautionary orange. Nobody had talked about the real hurt of it, the rending, rippling agony of your body trying to invert itself. It did feel that way, as if, if she pushed hard and long enough, she'd turn inside out and all her vital organs would be hanging, dangling on the outside, pulsing and purple, engorged.

"Come on come on come on," she whispered to the crown of that emerging head. "Come on come on." Panting and pushing, straining naked and unconcerned with anything but putting a perfect, undamaged infant into the hands of the enviably self-contained midwife. There was a long long moment when her head became a wind tunnel where a gale howled at maximum force as she gave everything in her to one massive final heave that sent the waxy little figure slithering out of her in a gush of blood-streaked fluid, its spiraling cord a miraculously ingenious creation.

The wind dying down, the pain quickly ebbing, the midwife ex-

claimed, *"A lovely little girl, a perfectly lovely little girl!"* and placed the squirming, wrinkled infant in Aly's astonished and grateful arms. Through a glaze of exhausted tears, Aly looked at the tiny puckered face and laughed inaudibly. Everything right where it was supposed to be, impossibly small curling fingers and toes, dark damp hair, eyes nose mouth; remarkable. "She looks like Jeremy," she told the busy midwife, reluctantly temporarily surrendering the baby. "She looks just like him."

"Come along now," said the midwife. "You're not quite finished here."

Everything else was easy, really. Another contraction or two and it was fairly much over; just a matter of getting cleaned up while a nurse tended to the baby, removing the waxy coating from her newborn's skin, swabbing her miniscule nostrils, running a thumbnail down the sole of each small foot, this and that and there she was, intact, perfect, Suzanne Lida Brown.

While she lay on her side on the brink of sleep gazing down at the baby in its cot, she realized that at that moment when the wind was shrieking through her skull and her thigh muscles were threatening to snap from the strain of being extended beyond the breaking point, at that moment when she'd been reduced to an utterly primal state, her mouth had opened and she'd cried out: M-O-T-H-E-R! She'd called for Rheta. MOTHER! Rheta. Mom. Rheta?

PART THREE

London,
1974

CHAPTER SIXTEEN

ALY DISCOVERED she'd married a man who viewed every new situation as an opportunity to engage in playing dress-up.

She first suspected it on the day after their wedding when Jeremy got himself all rigged out in nautical gear for the boat trip down the river Serena had arranged for them as an abbreviated honeymoon.

"You look very cute, Jeremy," she said of his peaked cap with mock naval insignia, his blazer and ascot and deck shoes, "very *H.M.S. Pinafore.*"

He reacted with a frown, turning to inspect himself in the mirror. "Cute?" he repeated doubtfully. "I don't think I care for that."

He was, she saw, absolutely serious about the image he'd created.

"Don't be silly. You look as if you just stepped off your yacht. You've given your crew the afternoon off and you're on your way to do a little sightseeing."

Seeing his frown become more pronounced, she abandoned her gentle teasing. Clearly he took this bit of role-playing very much to heart. It struck her as childish, but rather touching, and she had no desire either to hurt him or to spoil their outing. But as they set off to the landing stage on the Embankment and she noticed the jaunty swagger he effected to enhance his nautical image, she felt mildly embarrassed. With a pang she thought of Andrew, unable to imagine him behaving in this fashion. Immediately, she told herself it wasn't fair to compare the two. It would take time for her and Jeremy to adjust to being married, and it was wrong to start out by holding Andrew up as an example. She'd made a commitment to Jeremy and she'd make good on it.

She soon came to see that Jeremy culled from his wardrobe whatever outfit he deemed might be appropriate to any given day's appointments. Being up for the part of a cricketer in a film, he went off in whites after looking longingly at the cricket bat in the front hall cloakroom and finally deciding the bat would be too much. At other times she saw him rigged out in a three-piece business suit complete with bowler and rolled umbrella; in ripped jeans and torn sweater with his hair disheveled; he contrived the appearance of a French matelot, a rocker with greased hair and winklepicker shoes, a mod with Beatles'-length hair and a narrow-cut two-piece suit; he went to auditions dressed every time for the part. And quite often it worked for him.

She learned to disregard the irritation she felt at seeing him don one disguise after another and alter his behavior to fit. She told herself it wouldn't accomplish anything to criticize his methods. For one thing, he was utterly determined to succeed and she couldn't be sure that this role-playing wouldn't work to his advantage. For another, regardless of what she perceived to be his minor faults he was her husband and she was obligated to be loyal and to support his efforts. Even if he did behave in ways that irritated her, in all likelihood she probably said and did things that irked him as well. Couples didn't snipe at each other; they worked together over the long term. That's what a marriage was. It wasn't a series of haphazard alliances with a string of different men, but a dedication to one man, regardless of the small day-to-day annoyances. She wasn't Rheta. She could make her marriage work.

What upset her more than anything else was his endless harping on what he believed to be Andrew's unwarranted success. "It's monstrously unfair that someone with so much less talent than me should go from strength to strength simply because he was lucky enough to get cast in that dreary farce at the Royal Court," he said repeatedly.

"I wouldn't say he's less talented," she said carefully. "Andrew's just a different type, that's all."

"A different type," he scoffed. "He's no type at all. He just plays himself over and over."

"That's not true," she argued, stung by Jeremy's determination to denigrate Andrew's abilities.

Jeremy glared at her with such hostility that she decided to let the matter drop. Seeing that she wasn't going to pursue the matter, he assumed he'd won that round, and became suddenly amorous, trying to maneuver her down onto the sofa with the obvious intention of making love to her there and then.

"Jeremy," she protested, pushing him away, "I have to put the girls to bed. And I really don't want to do this now."

"You didn't used to mind," he said petulantly, his freckled cheeks acquiring color.

"I didn't used to have the responsibilities I do now. I wouldn't like Addy and Suze to find us making love in the living room. That sort of thing can traumatize a child, you know."

"Do me a favor," he said. "Don't give me another one of your lectures. To hear you tell it, there's nothing that won't traumatize them." Straightening his sweater, he said, "I think I'll go down to the pub for a pint," and went off with a sulky expression that was intended to make her feel guilty.

She refused to feel guilty. It was, after all, her right to say no. And Jeremy seemed to approach her with sexual intent at times when he knew she wouldn't be interested, as if he needed the rejection as proof of something—her inadequacy, her failings, something.

He couldn't leave the matter alone, though. A few days or weeks later, he'd start in again on Andrew. It positively galled him to have to have watched Andrew go directly from that production into a low budget film shot on location in North Africa, a blood and guts thriller that for some reason caught on and had people queuing up for hours in Leicester Square; a tuppence-hapenny flick that happened to have a damned good cameraman who made everything look shadowy and interesting, a script Jeremy grudgingly admitted was on the clever side, and an up-and-coming young director who took a chance on a

153

complete unknown as his leading man. And that was the making of bloody Andrew.

"Everybody wants him," Jeremy raged. "He goes from one
film to another to another, takes an entire *year* off to appear in
a revival of *The Seagull* in the West End, then back he goes to
work in one or two films a year. While I'm still slogging my guts
out, going to auditions like some nit fresh from RADA. And
why is it that every other time I come through my own front
door there's Andrew either busy nattering with you or playing
with the kids? Doesn't he have a place of his own?"

"Andrew and I are friends," she answered, working to control her anger at being forced repeatedly to justify herself.
"And he's very fond of Addy and Suze."

With a seemingly congenital disability to take in anything he
didn't want to hear, Jeremy sailed on. "And, naturally, he just
has to brag about his latest film, his latest play, never letting
anyone forget he's made good."

"Andrew does *not* brag," she said hotly. "Why must you always feel you're competing with him? You'd be all wrong for
the parts he plays. And he calls you every time he hears they're
casting for something you could do."

"Oh, right! Something *he* thinks I'd be right for."

"You've landed three very good jobs because of him, yet you
act as if he's out to sabotage you. This is very boring, Jeremy.
I'm tired of your constant attacks on Andrew. He's never been
anything but a good friend to you."

"To you, you mean," he said with slightly narrowed eyes.

"You're being ridiculous. I won't continue this," she said, and
went off to put the girls to bed.

JEREMY WAS offered work in the provinces, several completely
unsuitable small roles in films which he did despite his mounting dislike for the feckless bumblers the casting directors invariably had in mind for him, and kept track of every last
whisper of productions being mounted that might have an appropriate role for him. Whenever he did hear of something he
thought he could play, whether it was a film or stage work, he
went to any and all lengths to make himself visibly eligible. The

most notable instance was when he hired himself out as a cleaner at the theatre where the producers were holding auditions for a huge American musical being brought over from New York. Every morning he was there, performing his cleaning duties and singing his heart out—his voice soaring satisfyingly into the upper reaches of the theatre—when the producer, director, and choreographer arrived to begin the day's auditions. He put his back into the cleaning, of course, to lend credibility to his charade and he thought he could've taught the regular cleaners a thing or two. This three-week stint culminated one morning in the director standing on the stage apron with a hand shielding his eyes from the overheads as he peered out into the empty auditorium and asked, "Would you mind putting a sock in it, old fruit? That caterwauling's starting to get on my tits."

"Goddamned faggot," Jeremy muttered, and turned in his broom minutes later, going home to storm up and down the living room for more than an hour.

Initially, Aly was sympathetic to his disappointments. But as time passed and it seemed she was hearing endless variations on a single theme her sympathy dwindled. To compensate, she tried to be a tolerant audience to his regular diatribes, suppressing her exasperation at his refusal to accept his limitations.

"Perhaps," she offered, "you were so credible as a cleaner they simply didn't hear you, Jeremy."

"Ta ever so," he said caustically. "Lot of bloody good you are. Think I'd make a better cleaner than an actor, do you?"

"You have a fairly astonishing ability to turn things around," she said evenly. "That is not what I said."

"No, right. Forgive me, *Doctor* Brown."

For a moment she felt a hatred for him that was so overwhelming she could readily have struck him. She could almost see him sprawled, bleeding, on the floor. The image froze in her mind and all at once another image was superimposed over it. What looked like laundry flung into the hallway. But it wasn't laundry. And in the doorway beyond. . . . She shuddered, pushing the image away. "I have work to do," she said abruptly, and hurried upstairs to the bathroom where she splashed cold water on her face as she forced the image farther and farther away.

She must, she told herself, make more of an effort to be understanding, must not allow her anger and impatience to surface. It was dangerous to lose control. Lack of control could lead to broken marriages, to violence.

SOME MONTHS later Janie put him up for one more daft-bugger role in one more moronic comedy, and Jeremy went along to the audition dressed in his dapper best and in the upper crust accent called for in the script, read the male lead's lines. The casting director flipped back and forth through his script, confused, allowed Jeremy to finish his reading, then said, "Read the part of the waiter, would you, love? It's what I had you in mind for, actually."

With a sigh, Jeremy read the part, and was hired. He returned home from the studio at Twickenham so depressed Aly immediately sought to cheer him up, convinced he'd lost out yet again.

"I got the bloody part," he told her, watching with a frown as she lit a cigarette. "I wish you'd give those up. I can smell the smoke from halfway down the road."

"If you got the part," she said, ignoring his comments on her smoking, "what're you so pissed off about?" Her asking was merely a formality. She knew only too well why he was bothered but felt he deserved an opportunity to vent his disappointment. Very little ever went as Jeremy wished. It was as if he lived inside a small room whose walls were papered over, layers deep, with the script of his success. He'd travel the perimeters of this room repeatedly, reviewing the script, going over every last line in case there was some stage direction or bit of business he'd neglected to note that was responsible for his ongoing failure to gain the recognition he deserved. With obsessive perseverance he examined every last page of every last copy of the hundreds of duplicate scripts padding the walls of that private little chamber, but the script remained the same. He couldn't find a thing he'd missed in his countless prior readings. He was doing everything precisely as he should, so why wouldn't they recognize his superior gifts?

"It's the wrong part!" he exclaimed. "They should've given

156

me a chance at the lead. I could do it. I'd have done it a damned sight better than whoever they'll get who'll cost them a bloody bundle."

"Perhaps next time," she said, anxious to have done with a conversation they'd had far too many times.

She was fascinated by his dogged pursuit of an image that he was suited to only in his mind. As far as she was able to interpret it, he saw himself as a physically substantial, mysteriously romantic, classic leading man. In reality, he was a rather gangling, overly thin, patently youthful male, perfect for lightweight musical and/or comedy roles. She'd learned to keep this opinion strictly to herself. He was pathologically serious about this leading man image and viewed any opinion to the contrary as nothing less than betrayal. His needs were in so many ways identical to those of their daughters, his demands were couched in such infantile terms, that she sometimes treated him precisely as she treated Adele and Suzanne: with equal measures of indulgence, understanding, and strictness, all the while wishing he'd concede to the prevailing view of the casting directors, at least for the time being, and take pleasure in the work he was offered.

"Be patient," she counseled. "I'm sure eventually you'll get the roles you want."

"What would *you* know?" he demanded.

"Clearly very little on this subject," she answered, wishing briefly, fiercely, that she'd never set eyes on him. But then she'd never have met Andrew, and she couldn't imagine not having Andrew in her life. Next to Cliff and Sharon Ackerman, he was the dearest friend she'd ever had. She could talk to him. He listened. He didn't subject her to endless harangues, but rather attempted to divert and amuse her when Jeremy's behavior pushed her to the very edge of her tolerance.

"He's just Jeremy," Andrew said philosophically. "He's never going to change. There's little point to your wishing he would."

"But he makes things so much more difficult than they need to be."

"That's Jeremy," Andrew laughed. "I'll come round and take you out for a drink."

"Just come over and I'll give you a drink. It's too short notice for me to get a sitter."

157

"Twenty minutes," he said. "Help is on the way."

She laughed. "Mighty Mouse will save the day."

"Indeed, Madame," he sniffed. "I'd prefer some other soubriquet."

"I'll try to think of one before you get here."

"I should hope so. Mighty Mouse," he repeated disdainfully. "One would think you'd care more for my sensibilities than to refer to me in rodentlike terms."

"I'm sorry! Just come. Okay?"

"I suppose I'll forgive you," he said, then laughed. "Mighty Mouse. I'm crushed."

JEREMY WAS convinced he was at last on the direct path to stardom in '65 when he was cast as the second lead in a film to be directed by Oliver Metcalf. Metcalf was an American living in London who'd struck a nerve with his last three films. His movies were episodic and fairly hilarious, with much of the dialogue and action ad-libbed by the actors. He shot miles of film, then worked alongside the editor to assemble ninety minutes of the best footage. With the addition of quirky titles and end credits and a catchy score, Metcalf had become *the* director in Britain. For Jeremy, being cast in a Metcalf film was the precursor of inevitable fame. Granted he was yet again playing a bumbling fumbler, but once his foot was firmly in the door he'd soon enough be given serious roles that would allow him to demonstrate once and for all the true extent of his talent.

During the shooting of the Metcalf film, which was being done on location all over London, Aly went along several times to watch the set-ups, intrigued to see how Metcalf worked. She'd really enjoyed two of his earlier movies and tended to agree this time that Jeremy's career might just be on the verge of taking off.

Unfortunately, she saw at this time that his view of himself wasn't all that had been holding him back. To honor his concept of perfection he was in the habit of fussing with such extravagant compulsiveness over every last detail of every part he agreed to play that if one hadn't known better, one might have suspected he was acting out endless autobiographical sketches that required unqualified accuracy. He'd interrupt rehearsals to ask the director foolish-seeming questions about his motivation or his moves; he'd delay shooting because he couldn't quite deliver his lines the way he wanted. As a result, people disliked him and didn't bother trying to hide it. He was such a nitpicking self-involved performer that his genuine acting ability got overlooked, except by the film and theatre critics who invariably predicted great things for him.

There were four principals in the cast. The female lead was being played by a perky but really rather ugly young woman who'd shot to stardom in a British film of the late '50s that might have been written specifically for her. Mary Dunnigan had won all sorts of awards for her performance as a teenage mother on the dole in London's East End. She'd since appeared in more than a dozen films, none of which had lived up to her remarkable debut.

When Aly met her on the set of *Wotcha, Mate* she couldn't help feeling that Mary, too, was hoping to use this movie as a springboard to better things. Despite her friendliness and the general larking about that Mary joined the cast and crew in, she was as serious and self-interested as Jeremy. The primary difference between them, so far as Aly could see, was that Mary had the sense to make an effort to endear herself to her co-workers. Everyone seemed to like her—almost in direct ratio to their mounting dislike of Jeremy.

As the shooting progressed and Jeremy indulged himself more and more in nitpicking that delayed the production, Mary put her head together with the other two leads and they hatched a plot to make Jeremy's life as difficult as he was making theirs. Very simply, the three of them refused to speak to Jeremy off camera. They refused, in fact, to acknowledge him in any way.

"You brought this on yourself," Metcalf told him when Jeremy complained about the treatment he was receiving. "I was you, fella, I'd get my ass in gear and stop all this bullshit navel inspecting. Frankly, I think you've got real talent that could take you far, but if I'd known you'd be such a pain in the ass, Gable, I'd have hired somebody else for this part. So do us all a favor and get the fuck to work. Okay?"

When Aly attempted later on at home in the gentlest way possible to suggest to Jeremy that Metcalf and Mary and the others had a point, his face fell and he accused her of failing to understand. "I thought at least you'd see what I'm on about," he said in that manner intended to make her feel guilty.

"I do see," she told him. "Metcalf's being very fair about this because he thinks you're good, but if you keep irritating every-one you're never going to get what you want, no matter how good you are."

"Everyone's willing to settle for less than perfect," he said reproachfully. "Your good friend Andrew's a prime example."

"Why do you *always* have to drag Andrew into every one of our arguments?" she demanded tiredly. "I could understand your being resentful if he was the type who threw his weight around and played movie star with a vengeance. But he's not like that at all. The only thing he's changed about himself is his last name."

"Don't let's forget the hairpiece," he said snidely.

"You're on very shaky ground here, Jeremy!" she cautioned. "You're the guy who makes every day a fancy dress party."

"Even the name business is typical," Jeremy persisted, deaf always to reason. "Inverse snobbism, going as plain old Riggs to prove he's one of the lads."

"I'm not going to get into this with you again," Aly sighed, wearied and bored by the never-ending sameness of Jeremy's complaints. "I have work to do."

He made a face but for once didn't comment. She hurried to her office, anxious to be away from him. For just a moment as she sat down at her desk she wished with all her heart that Jeremy didn't exist. Then, filled with shame, she told herself she didn't mean that at all. Jeremy was her husband and the father of their children. She loved him. She did. And they had a very good marriage, really. Their marriage had already out-lasted Rheta's. Unlike her mother, she had the ability to sustain a relationship, to keep it functioning. And, as a result, her two daughters were growing up in a secure, consistent environ-ment. They'd never have to go through any of what she and Cliff had experienced.

CHAPTER
SEVENTEEN

IT WAS Jeremy's infrequent trips away for work that enabled Aly to regenerate her fondness and sympathy for him. His worst failing was as a father. Most of the time it appeared as if he viewed their daughters as competitors with him for Aly's affections. He either ignored them entirely, or he suddenly discovered them—playing the role of "dad" with a vengeance—and insisted on taking them out to the park for a walk, or to the zoo, or to the theatre. If the girls didn't live up to his performance expectations of them, he returned home with them greatly upset. Addy and Suze would come looking for their mother, confused and disappointed yet again at the end of another outing with their father. His wildly inconsistent and frequently moody behavior kept the girls almost permanently on edge.

Suzanne who was more like her father both in looks and temperament seemed to take everything most to heart. Adele, closer to Aly in every way, had more elasticity to her nature and was better able to bounce back. Aly spent a fair amount of time explaining to the girls the difficulties of an actor's life, giving them reasons why they should make an effort to be extra understanding of their father. Whatever her personal reactions to Jeremy might be, Aly tried always to paint a loving portrait of him for the children. She believed it would be unfair of her to prejudice the girls against their father. They would in time come to their own decisions about him. They didn't need to be burdened by their mother's emotional luggage.

"Daddy tries very hard to be good at his work," she told them. "Sometimes he gets let down and he has trouble hiding it. But that doesn't mean he doesn't love you very much."

"If he loves us," Addy said with fairly alarming perceptiveness for one so young, "why doesn't he tell us so?"

"Some people find it hard to talk about their feelings."

"Why?" Addy asked, her persistence reminding Aly of herself as a child.

"Not everyone's alike. We're all different and so we all have different ways of behaving. There are people like you, Addy, who like to ask lots of questions to find out why others do the things they do. And then there are people like Suze who find it hard to put their feelings into words. But you both have feelings all the same."

"I think Daddy's ever such a lot like Billy Winslow," Addy said.

"Why?" Aly asked her.

"Billy never shares his sweets or his crisps, even when his mummy says he must. He cries and says he won't and no one can make him."

Aly laughed even though she saw a fair degree of truth in this childish assessment.

"Billy's shy," Suze offered in a whisper, as if this explained everything to her satisfaction.

"Billy's mean and selfish!" Addy said, affronted. "And I don't like him at all!"

"You don't have to like him," Aly said. "But you should try to understand."

Suzanne's face was beginning to crumple, a sure sign of her upset, and Aly asked, "What's the matter, Suze?"

Breaking into tears, Suze cried, "I love my daddy! And Addy's horrid!"

"Of course you do," Aly said. "And Addy isn't horrid at all. She's just a very curious little girl. Aren't you Ad?"

"Yes," Addy said, pleased. "I'm ever so curious. But I love my daddy, too." She cast a defiant look at her older sister.

"You both do," Aly said, an arm around each girl. "No one's suggesting you don't. Now it's time for your bath. Run along and get your pajamas and I'll start the tub filling."

162

While the water ran in the tub in the hall bathroom, Aly looked over at the hook-and-eye lock on the door, all at once remembering how she'd begged Cliffie to stand guard in the hallway while she took her bath. Her girls would never have to be afraid their mother's latest boyfriend would invade their privacy, or make them fearful. They'd never be compelled to climb into bed with some new "sweetie" or give hugs and kisses to men they scarcely knew. No one who might harm them would ever be invited to share their home. Her girls were growing up safe, even if they did have a father who seemed to lack the ability to demonstrate his love for them. But at least he was where he was supposed to be: in his home, with his wife and children.

THERE WERE times when Jeremy's inability to recognize anyone's viewpoint but his own so infuriated Aly she felt capable of killing him. These occasions seemed to trigger her memories of that winter morning so long ago, and she worked doubly hard to keep a firm grip on her emotions. But he was so like his late grandmother in his capacity to see only one side to any given issue that Aly wished some catastrophic, but distant, event would just wipe him out. Were he to be rather quietly removed from their lives, she and the girls would be so much better off. She imagined accidents in which, before Jeremy had any chance to know what was happening, he simply ceased to exist. She saw herself and the girls clad in dark clothing, in attendance at the graveside, and felt a sense of relief that was fairly overwhelming. Then, on the heels of this, came monstrous guilt accompanied by self-recriminations. How could she think, even for a moment, that the girls might in any way benefit from the death of their father? She was being incredibly cruel and selfish. It was difficult to keep a marriage afloat. She knew that. So why, whenever there was a rough patch, did she indulge in these dreadful fantasies? Yet she couldn't help herself.

Gran, as she'd insisted she be called, had been a woman with only one viewpoint: her own. Like Jeremy, she viewed anyone who chose to disagree with her as not only wrong-headed but stupid. Aly had spent time with Gran on a half dozen occasions prior to her death in the fourth year of their marriage and had found it so intriguing to encounter the living source of every last one of Jeremy's bad habits, narrow opinions, and general disinterest in others, that she felt very sorry for the little boy who'd been forced through sad circumstances to grow up in the mold the old woman had cast for him.

Aly couldn't help thinking he might have been someone quite different if his grandmother had been even a little less ambitious and connivingly ruthless. Aly's own judgment of him was tempered by the understanding of how he'd come to be the way he was—but only for a time. As sympathetic as she was to his deprived background, it was hard to maintain her sympathy in the face of his ongoing refusal even to consider any alteration in his behavior, on any level. So, from time to time, she fell to painting detailed pictures of an existence without Jeremy. She and the girls would live calmer, less dramatic lives; they wouldn't have to feel they were obliged to live up to Jeremy's fantasy world expectations. Addy and Suze could simply be the children they were—argumentative, competitive with each other, and noisy; and Aly could get her work done without Jeremy's constant interruptions. Just as he'd been dismissive of her studies during her years at the university, he evidenced little respect for her career, and had no qualms about distracting her when she was trying to update her client notes. Since there simply wasn't enough time to see her private patients and write up the notes in the few minutes between appointments at the office, she'd brought the work home right from the beginning of her career as a psychotherapist. For at least an hour every evening, she closed herself into her office off the lounge, and every evening without fail, Jeremy opened the door without knocking to ask about something that could easily have waited.

Jeremy was as self-absorbed and childish, as frequently unreadable and as frequently transparent as he'd been at the outset. He was hopeless with money and trusted Aly and her father to manage the funds he turned over to her, but he also very arbitrarily felt he had a claim on her assets and reacted like a spoiled child whenever she rejected one of his more outlandish demands. His demands fell into several categories, outlandish being the most offensive. He'd ventured into that region only three or four times, and Aly remembered each occasion perfectly.

The earliest of his most memorably offensive demands, soon after their marriage, was for an absurdly expensive automobile.

"It's not as if we can't afford it," he argued. "And someone in my position has to maintain an image."

"First of all," she'd replied with a coolness she didn't really feel, "you don't need a car like that, especially not when we live a five-minute walk from the tube station. And secondly whatever your 'image' is, Jeremy, you don't need any car to help you maintain it. We've already got the Citroen which I personally happen to think is a piece of garbage, but which you just had to have because it was the 'in' car. I positively refuse to spend one more penny on *machinery*."

"I notice you don't apply the same rules to yourself," he came back at her. "You buy whatever you fancy."

"It happens to be *my* money. And the things I buy are usually things I need, not self-indulgences that cost thousands of pounds."

"Naturally you have to throw it up at me that I don't have money."

"Jeremy, drop this!" she warned.

He studied her face as if attempting to gauge just how far he could go. Evidently seeing he could go no further, he slouched into a chair and turned on the television set, wearing a hurt expression.

The next day he started in again on the car.

"I won't listen to this," she said, and walked out of the room.

The day after he tried once more.

This time she didn't bother to speak but simply left him talking to himself. And finally, at the point where she knew she'd physically lash out at him if he dared raise the subject one more time, he gave up. She wondered, from time to time, if he was trying to see how far he could push her before she snapped and completely lost control.

At the start of their marriage if he happened to admire something in a shop window she'd often insisted on buying it for him. Usually he fancied clothes, and since she preferred her taste to his, she hadn't minded spending the money to see him well dressed. Within a year, however, he took to admiring things in shop windows, fully expecting her to buy them. As soon as she saw a pattern being established she began ignoring his obvious hints. He was taken aback the first time she chose not to buy something he indicated he wanted, but tried pointedly several more times to draw her attention to garments he thought he'd like to have—a cashmere sports jacket, a pair of white flannel trousers, silk shirts. Finally, plainly disgruntled, he'd given it up. Accordingly, he looked considerably less well-groomed than he had when she'd been actively underwriting his wardrobe. Her money was a constant source of irritation to him, and he never missed an opportunity to accuse her of denying him while indulging herself. It took every bit of her willpower to ignore him on these occasions. He had certain failings—as did everyone—and she would not fall into the trap of concentrating on his weaknesses to the exclusion of his finer qualities. Unfortunately, as time passed, she found it increasingly more difficult either to make excuses to herself for his behavior, or to recall his finer qualities.

ALY AND Jeremy had been married eight years when Lilbet phoned from New York to tell her granddaughter that Pearl had passed away in her sleep the night before. Aly received the news like a blow to the solar plexus. Barely able to speak, she said, "I'll be over on the next available flight."

Seeing her distress, Jeremy became solicitous, asking, "What's the matter, love?"

"Pearl died," she told him, shattered, thinking of the many many times Pearl had held her on her lap and rocked her, comforted her. "I have to book a ticket," she said, and at once looked up the number for TWA. She was able to get a seat, and making a note of the flight number and departure time, next called Olive to ask her if she could please come stay with the girls for a few days. By this time, Olive worked four days a week for Aly, but was always willing to come look after Addy and Suze whom she adored and who adored her in return.

"What's happened?" Olive asked. "You sound right upset."

166

After Aly explained, Olive said, "I'll come straight away."

Aly thanked her and hung up.

The instant she put the receiver down, Jeremy let go. "You're flying off just like that, leaving us, to go to New York for the funeral of a *servant*? You're spending hundreds of pounds and upsetting our lives for the sake of an old colored charlady?" he asked scathingly.

Aly glared at him, filled with loathing. There were so many things she wanted to say to him that she couldn't speak at all. If she started to vent her grievances against him, she thought she might never finish. Her chest heaving, she stared at him for several long moments. Finally, very quietly she said, "Olive's on her way. I'll be back in three days. This is not a subject for discussion, so just drop it now!" Then squelching her anger flat, she went to explain the situation to the girls.

She lit a cigarette to calm herself and took time to look at the two children she and Jeremy had produced, marveling yet again at Suzanne's profound resemblance to her father and at how like herself Adele was. Suzanne was lanky and too thin, with pale freckled skin and thick auburn hair. Addy was solidly well-built with fair hair, gray-blue eyes and a stubborn chin. One at seven, the other just turned six, neither girl really understood about death, but they responded with upset to their mother's visible distress. Suze wanted to know, "Why can't we go with you, Mummy?"

"Where did Pearl go?" Addy asked.

Aly spent close to an hour answering their questions, hugging and reassuring them. Once in New York, she called them nightly while she was away. After every call, she and Lilbet reminisced about Pearl and all those years, those happy times, before Rheta and Cliffie died. And later in bed in the room she'd always had in her grandmother's home, she struggled to come to terms with her mounting dislike for her husband. She created a mental balance sheet and enumerated all the ways in which it was vital for her to make her best effort to maintain the marriage. What weighed most heavily was the welfare of the girls. For *their* sake she couldn't give in to her fairly overpowering desire to be free of Jeremy. For her own sake, she couldn't bear contemplating the possibility of being a failure in some-

167

thing as monumentally important as her marriage. She wasn't like Rheta. She had the personal glue to hold everything together. She'd overlook Jeremy's stunning insensitivity in this matter; she had no choice.

On her return to England, he was waiting for her at Heathrow, having apparently undergone a complete change of attitude. He didn't actually apologize—she'd never known him to do that—but he did ask how everything had gone and behaved generally with great concern for her then and for several days after. While she wasn't likely to forget his behavior, she did relegate the incident to a dusty mental file drawer, and was actually glad to pick up the threads of the family's day-to-day life. That, after all, was what was important. But every so often she'd remember his outburst, his referring to Pearl in that derogatory manner, and felt something sharp-edged and fiercely hot beating away inside her like a malevolent nonhuman fetus. She found, to her dismay, she was unable to forgive him. It worried her; she saw her inability to forgive in this instance as emblematic of personal failure. To compensate, she was especially sympathetic to his ongoing plotting and planning to advance his theatrical career.

After the film work dried up "inexplicably," he decided to concentrate on the theatre, to put his singing voice to work for him. Musicals were always being mounted in the West End. With the right vehicle he could bring audiences to their feet eight times a week, have them clamoring for more. Yes. Royal command performances, superstars dropping backstage after the show to congratulate him. Much more personal than film; direct contact with new people every night. He could expand onstage, perfect his performance nightly. It was ideal really, what with the weeks of rehearsal beforehand and then the nightly opportunities to polish every aspect of his role. Yes. It made good sense. It would work.

He signed on with the best singing teacher in the city, began attending dance classes on a regular basis to help him overcome his gawkiness, and started going to his old acting class again every week. He liked being with his peers.

"It makes me feel more in touch, more connected to the shows already in production and the new ones being mounted," he explained eagerly. "Should other offers come along—television, film, whatever—I'll consider them, but my goal now is the West End. Anything else will be strictly for the money."

"That makes sense," Aly said, and endorsed and underwrote this latest of his plans just as she'd supported his eight-year-long assault on the film industry. She continued to maintain the expense of the household and the children, and his income went on his ever-expanding wardrobe, on his many classes and instructors, on the socializing he insisted was necessary in order to keep himself visible to the people who counted. Aly didn't mind. Jeremy was, without question, exceptionally talented. There was also something admirable about his persistence. He had a vision, a dream, and he was determined to make it come true. And whatever irritation she might feel with him from time to time, she was never less than awed at seeing what he could do on a stage. She believed he deserved her support and the opportunity to continue his pursuit of the dream. It was her duty, after all, as his wife.

CHAPTER
EIGHTEEN

SHE PROBABLY wouldn't have taken any notice if Jeremy hadn't reacted as he did. They were all at the table, just finishing dinner, when the doorbell rang. Nothing extraordinary in that. Friends—either of theirs or of the girls—were always dropping by. Jeremy said, "I'll go," and was gone for so long that Aly told the girls to start clearing. "I'll see what's happened to him."

The front hall was empty, as were the lounge and den. Puzzled, Aly went from room to room, arriving upstairs at the door to the master bedroom in time to see Jeremy sliding closed the top drawer of his bureau.

"Who was at the door?" she asked.

He whirled around guiltily and eyed her for a moment, as if trying to assess how much she might have seen. "Oh! No one," he answered in so false a tone and with such a fake expression of innocence she had to wonder why his talent was limited solely to the stage. In reality he was an inept and uninspired liar. Fortunately for all concerned he rarely lied.

"No one rang the bell?" she said, able to see him resisting the temptation to open again that drawer he'd just closed.

"Someone looking for directions," he said with more conviction, and started past her out of the room. "There was no need for you to come following me."

"You were gone for ages." She descended the stairs at his side. "I thought maybe something was wrong."

"No. I was planning to wear that green jersey tomorrow and I couldn't remember if it was clean."

The girls were in the kitchen performing their assigned chores. Suze was rinsing the dishes and Addy was loading the machine. Even though Olive came every day and did whatever cleaning and laundry was needed, Aly felt it was important that the girls be in the habit of picking up after themselves. One day they'd be out on their own and, at the very least, they'd know how to do dishes and run a Hoover. It certainly hadn't done her or Cliffie any harm having to do chores. Aly automatically began removing the placemats from the table, returning them to the sideboard. Jeremy stood halfway between the dining room and the kitchen, as if unable to decide where to go.

"You're sure nothing's wrong?" Aly asked, surveying the surface of the table and thinking for at least the fiftieth time that it was badly in need of refinishing, before looking over at him. He exuded guilt. His eyes shifted as if in tempo with the shuffling of his thoughts. His lean body appeared to be trying to go in two directions at once, his shoulders angled away toward the door, his hips thrust slightly forward. His stance and the expression forming on his face reminded her suddenly, alarmingly, of scenes she'd witnessed in her childhood: men trying to avoid a confrontation with her mother while they attempted to explain why they were going to have to leave, go home. Their bodies had twisted in this same fashion, as if they were observing some arcane code of politeness while readying themselves to run.

"I do so dislike the way you go on and on once you get your teeth into something," he said, sailing into the offensive as he did whenever he had no wish to explain his actions.

Aly stared at him without replying. The remark was so absurdly untrue it didn't warrant a response. It was amazing the way he could attribute to others the very habits that made him so unpopular with so many people. He held his pose a bit longer then shifted both physically and in attitude, with a patently false sudden smile saying, "I must run or I'll miss the start of class." He gave her a hearty hug and kiss—proof positive he was guilty of something since she'd long since discouraged him from making physical displays in front of others—called ta-ra to the girls and went hurrying off to his acting class. He'd done something all right, Aly decided. She could almost smell it.

"Who was at the door?" Addy asked, closing the dishwasher.

"Apparently no one," Aly answered from the doorway, her attention caught by the sight of her two girls performing their brief domestic ballet. They seemed at last to have come past what Aly had feared might be a permanently combative stage and had now entered into an alliance based on equal measures of affection for one another, and secrecy. Boys had come into their lives and altered their perspective both of themselves and of their parents; they'd acquired a certain boldness, as if having recognized they were as much people in their own right as Aly and Jeremy.

Addy had taken to disparaging her father openly, decrying the things he said and did. "That's such rubbish!" was one of her stock replies to anything Jeremy might say. "He's such a nit!" was her favorite aside. Suze wasn't quite so rudely outspoken but she, too, found fault with Jeremy's occasional attempts to subject them to his parental authority. His concept of fatherhood, like the majority of his concepts, was predicated on things he'd seen and heard and read about. He seemed either to have no natural instincts about how to deal with his children or else chose to ignore them. Whatever the case, he had even less aptitude for dealing with Addy and Suze now than when they were toddlers. They knew it and were consistently offhand, even dismissive, with him. As a result, Aly occasionally had separation dreams wherein she and the girls went out looking for apartments and every place they saw looked ominously familiar. Aly kept saying, "No, this isn't right," and rushing them away to the next rental, and the next. But every apartment they saw was identical to the others: boxy rooms inside a larger box, a half-bathroom in the hall, and another bathroom with a broken lock.

"There was nobody there?" Suze asked, drying her hands on a tea towel. "That doesn't make sense."

"He probably sent them away," Addy told her sister knowingly. "The girls can't see you now," she mimicked her father.

172

"They're clearing up and then they've got their studies. Why don't you ring for an appointment? Speak to the maid." He referred to Olive this way, although he didn't dare do it within her hearing. The girls found this reference to their beloved Olive so insulting they'd turned it into a joke in order to deal with it. The one time Olive overheard him call her the maid, she'd marched right over to him, poked him hard in the middle of his chest and said, "Listen, you wanker! You want to watch what you say. Like to get above yourself, putting on airs and graces. I'm nobody's bloody *maid*, least of all yours, you useless git, and don't you ever forget it!" Jeremy had actually been afraid of her, his mouth dropping open, his eyes round as he backed away.

"The girls can see you Sunday at two," Addy intoned nasally, playing secretary.

Both girls laughed, and Aly said with a smile, "That's enough of that. *Do* you have homework?"

Suze nodded; Addy groaned, then grinned showing her hated braces. Aly went over to gather the two of them into her arms, permanently amazed by their solid reality, and hugged them briefly. "Thanks for clearing up. My turn tomorrow. Hit the road now, okay? I've got a couple of hours' work to do."

"Not to worry," Addy said. "We wouldn't dream of disturbing you."

"I'm most grateful." Aly pinched her younger daughter's cheek, and held on to Suze for a few seconds longer. "I'll be in to say good-night later. Okay?"

After the girls had run off upstairs, Aly lit a cigarette and walked through the downstairs rooms to her office. She never saw clients at home but did most of her paperwork here and had a complete set of duplicate files which she kept locked in a cabinet. She limited her private cases these days to twenty, averaging five clients daily Monday to Thursday. This left her with one full Friday free each week for her two groups of rape victims. She preferred to keep the groups small, a maximum of five. More and the groups seemed to degenerate into grievance sessions where little progress was made. With five the women seemed to pull together and were able to draw the support they needed from each other and from her. For her personal use, she kept notes of the group sessions, and it was today's notes she'd intended to write. But she couldn't get started.

She finished her cigarette and looked down at the desktop at the paper and her pen, then over at the doorway. Jeremy's bureau beckoned to her like some living thing needing her attention. She wanted to know what he was up to. She had the impression he'd hidden something in the drawer. He'd exuded such guilt it had been impossible to ignore. What *was* he up to?

Before she'd even made the conscious decision to go she was halfway up the stairs on her way to their bedroom. She wasn't in the habit of going through the girls' or Jeremy's things. Privacy was essential to everyone in a family. Once any member started violating the other member's right to it, in no matter how minimal a fashion, the family was in trouble. But Jeremy had lied, and he was obviously up to no good. This was one occasion when she felt justified in bending her rules, if not for her own sake, for the sake of the girls.

Legal papers, summoning Jeremy Brown to appear in court. For what? There was no explanation, only names and a date. It didn't make sense. Who was the plaintiff, Elizabeth Sparks? Aly returned the papers to the drawer and went back to her office where she lit another cigarette and sat for a time trying to remember if she'd ever heard that name before. She hadn't. What did it mean? Had Jeremy taken up with another woman who was trying through the courts to force him into some legal maneuver that would jeopardize their family?

It was ironic, she thought, that for some years she'd hoped Jeremy would take a mistress, redirect his attention to another woman. It would have been a relief in many ways. But she'd always been so convinced of his underlying need for what she and the girls represented in terms of security that she'd never for a moment believed he'd leave them. Now she was no longer sure of that. And the prospect of finding herself left alone with Addy and Suze frightened her. Not because she had any qualms about her own capabilities, but because as a single woman she'd be vulnerable to other men. And she knew all too well the results of vulnerability. She'd seen the evidence firsthand over and over.

She stared at the telephone for several minutes, then picked up the receiver and dialed Andrew's number.

His latest girlfriend answered and for a moment Aly couldn't recall her name. Then it came back to her and she said, "Diana, how are you? It's Alyssa. Is Andrew in?"

"Oh, right," Diana said frostily. "Hang on," and let the receiver drop with a crash, calling out, "Drew, for you!"

Aly waited, thinking that of all Andrew's women, this latest one was by far the most unpleasant. He'd been through a fair number of liaisons over the years, including one short-lived marriage to a woman who had, according to their mutual friends, looked remarkably like Aly but who otherwise couldn't have been more different. Aly had of course attended the wedding and to this day couldn't see the alleged resemblance to—God! She couldn't even remember the name of Andrew's wife. The marriage had lasted less than a year. He claimed he wasn't good matrimonial material and said he'd given up for good the idea of ever making a go of it.

"This is an unexpected pleasure," he said warmly now.

She laughed. "You always say that!" she accused. "You'd think we hadn't spoken in years."

"Nevertheless, it's a pleasure."

"Listen, Andrew. Does the name Elizabeth Sparks mean anything to you?"

"Not offhand. Let me think a moment. Elizabeth Sparks. No. Doesn't ring any bells. Why?"

"She's had Jeremy served with a summons. I wondered if you might know what it's about."

"Elizabeth Sparks," he repeated, thinking. Some woman was taking old Gable to court. Who'd do that? Why? Everyone knew Gable didn't have a thing of his own. All the money was Alyssa's. It was her house, her two cars; she paid the girls' school fees and Olive's wages. Elizabeth. The only Elizabeth that came to mind was an American actress he'd worked with on location in Arizona, and he sincerely doubted Jeremy had ever heard of her. Sparks. Elizabeth Sparks. It came to him all at once, and he sucked in his breath.

Instantly Aly picked up on it. "What?" she asked. "Do you know her?"

"I think she's someone I met ages ago," he said carefully.

"*You* met her? Who is she, Andrew?"

"I don't know that I want to get into this, Alyssa."

"What do you mean? Some woman you met ages ago has had Jeremy served with legal papers, but you don't want to get into it? Don't you think I deserve to know what's going on?"

"It isn't that I don't think you deserve to know. It's simply that I'm not at all sure I'm the one who should be telling you."

"Look," she said tightly. "Jeremy hid this damned thing in his sock drawer and tried to pretend it never happened. If you know what this is about I'd be very grateful if you'd help me out here. I need to know what's going on in my own home, Andrew."

"Alyssa, let me make a few inquiries and see if I can clarify this for you. I'm not about to leap in and start making suppositions. I think I may have some idea what it's about but I'd like to try to get some definite answers before I say anything."

"That's fair," she said, letting out her pent-up breath. "Will you ring me back as soon as you know something?"

"I'm only going to say one thing," he cautioned. "And that is: You won't like this."

"That's scary."

"Oh, it's nothing to be scared of," he told her. "You simply won't like it."

That night, she dreamed she was ten years old again and she was trapped in the apartment with Don. She ran from room to room trying to escape him, the rooms telescoping so that it took her heavy legs an age to get across them. Her chest heaving, terrified, she arrived at the front door and began undoing the many locks, fumbling with the chains and bolts that kept her trapped. So many locks. She had to stand on her toes to reach the ones at the very top of the door, then get down on her knees to open those at the bottom. She couldn't do it. Her hands wet with fear, her fingers slipped over the rounded knobs; she couldn't get a decent grip. It was too late. Don loomed over her, reeking of whiskey, and slowly put the end of the gun barrel to her forehead.

She forced herself to wake up and sat in the dark trembling, the back of her hair wet with perspiration. Beside her Jeremy slept peacefully.

"WHERE ARE we going?" Aly asked, tying a scarf on over her hair. Andrew's latest sports car was so low-slung she felt she was riding mere inches above the pavement, and the suspension was so tight she could feel every bump and rut in the road.

"Battersea," he replied, checking the rearview mirror as he pulled away from the house.

"Are you going to tell me anything?"

"I'm taking you to meet Liz—Elizabeth Sparks."

She studied his profile, able to see a certain resignation in the set of his features. "Who is she? Don't you think it's a bit too cold to be riding around with the top down?"

"Sorry." He glanced over. "Would you like me to stop and put it up?"

"No, that's okay. If we're going, let's go."

He took another quick look at her, feeling every bit as nervous as she appeared to be.

"What, I mean, how do you know this woman, Andrew?"

"Jeremy and I both knew her," he hedged, wishing bloody Gable would for once behave like a responsible adult. This promised to be an epic mess.

"I have a feeling everything's going to change now," she said, so quietly the words were carried away on the breeze.

"Sorry?"

Aly smiled at him. "Nothing." She shook her head, wondering how so much time had managed to get away so fast. Just a day or two ago she'd been out with Andrew in the Jensen, on their way to Chelsea to meet his sister. The shop was long gone. Jill had emigrated to Australia eight or ten years ago and apparently now had a flourishing boutique in Sydney. Andrew was an internationally recognized film star, and she was a practising therapist with two wonderful daughters and a husband who, it turned out, was given to lying and to keeping secrets. She dreaded learning this particular secret. Somehow it would change everything. She could feel the edges of her control

177

slipping, like a ripcord being slowly pulled through her fingers; her fear ballooning in gauzy billows. She'd created a marriage, a family, out of what she'd been given: two lovely children and a man who wasn't quite all there. Not that there was anything wrong with his brain. It was more that, as Andrew had warned her so long ago, pieces of him were missing. This was a subject she usually avoided. She was married; she'd made a commitment, and she'd honored it for fourteen years. Just because things weren't entirely perfect, one didn't simply give up and abandon the effort. A marriage, a family, entailed daily work.

She'd given her best but she'd known all along she was doing the work of two. She had no desire to change anything, yet sometimes she saw herself as a boring nonentity and yearned for a life that had motion, momentum. During those occasional moments when she allowed herself to consider her status, her discontent was so immense that to acknowledge its full extent would be admitting to failure in too many areas. Rather than make that sort of damaging admission, she concentrated on getting through each day, doing her best for everyone—the girls, Jeremy, her patients, and the psychically wounded who came seeking her help. She did her most successful and most rewarding work with the rape victims, perhaps because she cared so very much about them. She understood their losses, empathized with their fears. Sometimes what was taken away was so immense that nothing you ever gained could even begin to fill the desolate emptiness.

She couldn't shake the idea that she was on the verge of losing everything she valued, and the idea made her feel like a child again, and helpless. Other people were indirectly in charge of her future and she was powerless to control their actions. At best, she could only control her own, and yet her own best efforts couldn't prevent damage being done.

"I haven't been over the bridge here for years," Andrew told her, stopping to consult his *London A to Z*, reading half-glasses propped on the extreme tip of his nose as he searched for the street in the guide. "Here we are. Straight ahead, second left, then left again." He returned the *A to Z* to the glove box, tucked the glasses into his inside breast pocket, put the shift in gear, then looked over at her. "You said everything's going to change now. Was that it?"

She nodded.

"I'm afraid you may be right, sproggy." He gave her a rather sad smile.

"Don't say that," she whispered, her mouth dry.

"Things do change."

"Only some things. Your Diana can't stand me, you know."

"She's jealous." He shrugged, his smile less sad. "My women are always jealous of you."

"That's ridiculous! Why, for God's sake?" She couldn't help smiling.

"Because I like you better than I like any of them, and you know it."

"I don't know anything of the sort," she defended herself, falling easily into the long-term pattern of their habitual banter.

"Sure you do," he said, steering the car back into the flow of traffic. "You'll never admit it, but you and I both know it's the truth. Here we are," he said, pulling up behind a van. "Liz is the woman Jeremy lived with until you came along."

"I thought it was probably something like that," she said turning cold with dread.

"Let's get on with it." He climbed out and came around to the passenger side, offering his hand to help her out of the low-slung car. She stood beside him on the pavement looking around. It was a working class neighborhood, terraced houses lining both sides of the street, most of their facades in need of paint or repair. There was an odd emptiness to the street, not a soul in sight from one end of the block to the other. An off-license at the near corner and next to it a newsagent's. An orange cat came daintily over the road, its feet crossing just so one in front of the other like a fashion model along a runway. Aly watched, fascinated by its large slanting green eyes and natural grace. Cats never misstepped, knew always precisely where to place each clever paw. People could never be sure where it was safe to stand.

Andrew waited at her side, giving her the time she needed to orient herself. Her face, as ever, was completely free of

179

makeup, and her hair was pulled back and tied with a ribbon at the nape of her neck. The only external change was the absence of her old horn-rims. She'd taken to wearing contact lenses five or so years before and, if possible, she looked somehow younger than she had when they'd met. When they talked on the telephone, which they did almost daily when he wasn't away on a shoot, he sometimes forgot how young she was. He had the odd feeling he was aging far more rapidly than other people, but especially Alyssa. At thirty-two she could easily have passed for twenty-two or -three. For his part he avoided mirrors, with the feeling that there was a portrait in an attic somewhere that was daily growing younger—the reverse Dorian Gray syndrome. He shook off the mild self-pity, and gave her an encouraging smile.

"Christ!" she said under her breath, allowing Andrew to lead her up the front walk to the door of one of the terraced houses that reminded her of that place in Worlds End she'd gone to with Olive. Apprehension had turned her palms damp and made it difficult for her to take a deep breath. Her stomach was contracting unpleasantly.

The door was opened by a very pretty dark-haired woman who visibly shared Aly's apprehension. " 'Ello Andrew," she said nervously. "Been a long time, 'asnt it? You 'aven't changed a bit, look just the same as ever." She smiled, her eyes edging toward Aly. "Come in," she said, taking a step back from the door. "Come in, love."

CHAPTER
NINETEEN

"I DIDN'T WANT to go makin' no trouble," Liz explained, "but, see, it's been 'ard managin', everything bein' so expensive and me only able to work part-time now at the pub. I know I signed that paper 'n' all, but the solicitor said it wasn't reasonable for Jeremy to've got me to sign it the way he did without me havin' anyone lookin' out for me legal rights. At the time, you know, it seemed fair enough. But four pound don't 'ardly pay for nothin' these days, does it?"

"What exactly did that paper say?" Aly asked, finding it difficult to pay attention. The situation struck her as so bizarre she felt somehow lifted out of herself, moved beyond her body to become a witness watching the goings-on from over in the corner of the room. She recognized the signs of dissociation, understood quite clearly why it was happening, and was as fascinated by her own distress as she'd have been by one of her patients. It was peculiarly intriguing to find herself sitting, as it were, on both sides of the desk, playing both patient and therapist. She was powerless to apply to her own actions the same sensible advice she believed she gave to those who consulted her professionally. Like an exact mechanical replica, the Alyssa-doll communicated, making the appropriate responses. But throughout she was taking note, thinking what a good-natured, basically kind-hearted woman Liz was; how lacking she was in the bitterness most other women would have harbored toward Jeremy. As she listened, finding herself drawn to Liz's frankness and guilelessness, a terrible anger that had previously gone unacknowledged but which she suddenly realized she'd been holding in for many years seemed to take on a granular physical quality; like sand it began seeping through minute cracks in her self-control, displacing itself from behind the wall she'd so carefully constructed to keep it at bay, spilling forward against her awareness. She knew with absolute certainty that what she most feared was perilously close, and there was little she could do to prevent it occurring. It was merely a matter of time before the wall crumbled. All she could do in the interim was try through sheer force of will to keep it intact.

"I've got it 'ere somewhere," Liz said, and craned around as if trying to remember where she'd left the document. "It says, 'e'll pay the four pound every week and I'm not ever to talk about 'im and me."

Both Andrew and Aly were about to ask her to elaborate when the door to the lounge opened, and Liz beamed, saying, " 'Ere's my Donna now. Come say 'ello, darlin'."

With a jolt, Aly saw that the girl could have been Suzanne's twin. She had the same awkward height, thick auburn hair, and pale freckled complexion; the same deep-set brown eyes, and all but palpable shyness. At the sight of her, Aly knew what Jeremy had done. That seepage threatened to become an avalanche, and her heart knocked as if it had suddenly turned to wood. There was another child in the world just like Suzanne; they shared a father; they were sisters. The man Aly had married, the man with whom she shared her life, had known about this other child, this sister to their two girls, but had never once even so much as hinted at her existence. The reality of what Jeremy had done so surpassed her guesswork that she felt as if she'd been struck a physical blow.

"These're friends of your dad's," Liz explained to the girl. "She knows who 'er dad is," she told Andrew and Aly. "I've never made that no secret. I mean, I'm not supposed to tell nobody else, but that paper don't say nothin' 'bout me tellin' my own girl."

"How old are you?" Aly asked Donna, her mouth dusty, her heart a racketing wind-up toy. Her world was falling in pieces;

182

she could almost hear the columns tumbling, could see the debris accumulating.

"I was thirteen in October," she answered almost in a whisper.

Aly looked at Liz. "My daughter Suzanne turned thirteen three weeks ago."

The two women gazed at each other. Feeling the heat of their silent communication, Andrew said, "Donna, would you care to take a ride with me? I've got to pick up a script and I'd be glad of the company. You don't mind, do you, Liz?"

"I don't mind," Liz answered.

Color surged into Donna's face as she looked at Andrew. "You're him, aren't you?" she asked in her wispy voice. "Are you really a friend of my dad's?"

"I've known him a long time," Andrew admitted, concealing the distaste he felt for the man. Until the day before when he'd managed to track Liz down he'd had no idea there was a child involved. It sickened him to think that Gable had abandoned a pregnant woman in order to be free to pursue Alyssa. "Would you like to come with me?"

"Yes, please." Donna gazed adoringly at him. "I'm ever such a big fan of yours. We came on a school trip last year to see you in *The Merchant of Venice*."

"Aren't you kind," he said graciously. "We'll be back in about an hour." A hand under Donna's elbow, he directed the girl out of the room.

As soon as they were gone, Aly and Liz both reached for their cigarettes, glanced at each other, and laughed.

"I always liked Andrew. 'E was always a gentleman, if you know what I mean."

Aly nodded her agreement and took a hard drag on her cigarette. "You've raised Donna on your own?"

"Not that many blokes fancy takin' on someone else's kid." Liz shrugged. "I don't mind, really. She's a smashin' girl, does right well in school. Never 'ad a moment's worry with 'er, not like some who 'ave nothin' but trouble with their kids. My Donna's a good girl."

"I can see that," Aly said. "Suzanne's so like her it's uncanny."

"American, are you?" Liz asked interestedly.

183

"I've lived here for seventeen years. He"—she couldn't bring herself to speak Jeremy's name—"met me and broke off with you, didn't he? And he knew you were pregnant, too. Right?"

"Sure he did. I was in me third month by then. I'd been to 'ave the test 'n' all. Oh, 'e knew right enough. 'E went 'n' got you pregnant straight away too, didn't 'e?" She shook her head with disdain. "Fancy a drink, love? I've got some gin."

"I think we could both use one," Aly said gratefully.

"Won't be a minute." Liz got up and went out to the kitchen.

While she was gone, Aly smoked her cigarette, still stunned at having met Donna, Suzanne's older sister by five months. Prior to abandoning her, Jeremy had coerced a pregnant woman into signing some sort of binding, lifetime agreement in return for which he'd been paying her a paltry four pounds a week for fourteen years. In view of the fact that he'd never earned less than five or six thousand pounds a year every year in all that time his meanness was truly shocking. A monumental anger was building inside her, gathering to itself every minor irritation she'd ever felt toward Jeremy but brushed aside. Like one of those terrible terrorist explosive devices studded with bolts and bits of scrap metal, her anger was expanding to incorporate every last thing, no matter how minimal, Jeremy had said or done wrong in all the years she'd known him.

Everything seemed horribly distorted, out of focus, and she felt as if she were looking through the bull's-eye, struggling to pull things into a clearer definition. It made her head ache dully. Her eyes strained in conjunction with her brain; all her senses laboring to turn everything rational.

"Has he ever been to see you and Donna?" Aly asked when Liz returned with the drinks.

"What 'appened was 'e come 'ome one afternoon, sayin' we 'ad to talk. I knew straight off 'e was leavin' me. 'E took 'is gear that same night and that was the last I saw of 'im. 'E didn't even come to the solicitor's office when I went to sign the paper."

"Jesus!"

"Cheers, love!" Liz held up her glass then took a good swallow of her drink.

"Cheers." Aly drank some of the barely-diluted gin, welcoming the somewhat medicinal burn that relieved the aching in her skull, then said, "You need more money."

"I don't like to complain, but I don't fancy goin' on the dole, neither. I've always worked, but it's been a bit dodgy the last few months since I 'ad me turn. 'Avin' that op set me back good 'n' proper. It's taken me a while to get back on me feet. Otherwise, I wouldn't've made this trouble."

"I'm very sorry," Aly said, meaning it, and wondering what secret source of inner strength had prevented this woman from evolving into another Rheta. She'd stayed in the same place all these years; there were no men parading in and out to worry her child.

"It's none of your doin', is it?" Liz said openly.

"No," Aly agreed. "But you don't deserve to be treated the way you have, and that does very much concern me. I'll see to it that you and Donna start receiving a realistic amount you can live on."

Liz smiled again—she was a naturally cheerful woman, and Aly liked her more by the minute—and said, "No offense, but you seem right nice."

Aly returned the smile. "I know," she said. "What's a nice woman like me doing married to a son of a bitch like him? We had to get married, so I went ahead and made the best of it, but I wouldn't let myself think about it. I'm not going to be able to do that anymore, not after today. This changes everything. Right now the important thing is to see to you and Donna. In the future, if there's any problem, I want you to get in touch with me. Will you do that?"

" 'E don't deserve you," Liz declared.

"I'm so sorry for what you've been through," Aly said, nearly overwhelmed by a need to apologize for Jeremy's appalling behavior. She wondered if it would ever be possible to introduce Donna to her half sisters. Everything was so goddamned complicated. She could hardly walk through the front door and announce to the girls that they had a half sister their father had known about all along but hadn't thought worth mentioning. "We'll get it sorted out somehow."

Liz shook her head. "It's a right cockup, isn't it?"

"That's an understatement. God, I wish I'd known."

"Why?"

"It would have made a difference. So many things . . ." she trailed off, too readily able to envision the life she might have led.

"Never mind, darlin'," Liz said magnanimously. "It's just the way things are, isn't it?"

"WHAT ARE you going to do?" Andrew asked quietly, watching her light a cigarette then roll down the car window.

"I don't know, confront him, see what he says."

"You *know* what he's going to say, Alyssa. He's either going to lie, insisting none of it ever happened, or he's going to make Liz out to be the villain of the piece. He's certainly not going to admit his responsibility."

"He might," she said doubtfully.

Why, he wondered, could she never admit to her doubts about Gable? For years now he'd witnessed the way she side-stepped the sometimes remarkably insensitive things Jeremy said and did. It was as if in having committed herself to the marriage nothing short of either Jeremy's death or her own would permit her even to consider admitting their life together was less than ideal. On the one hand he admired her loyalty, but on the other he was bemused by her voluntary blindness. Fate had now provided Andrew with a viable opening, an opportunity to discuss Jeremy on a new level, and he was determined to get her to talk. Since his initial gambit wasn't succeeding, he decided to switch tracks and see if he couldn't reach her in another way. "She's a lovely kid, Donna," he said, "a dead ringer for Suze. I had to keep reminding myself who she was. Every time I looked at her I got a shock. I can't begin to imagine what it must be like for you."

"How am I going to tell the girls they've got a half sister?" She looked at him with an expression that seemed to beg for help. He wanted to put his arms around her, promise her it would all come right if she'd just admit the marriage was, and always had been, if not a mistake, definitely less than a great success.

186

"Do they need to know?"

"I'd want to know, if it were me," she answered thoughtfully.

"I suppose I would, too," he said. "Of course if you do tell them it's going to raise a lot of questions about their father."

"It raises a lot of questions about him for *me*, my dear. And please don't say you tried to warn me because it's all I've been thinking since we set out today. You tried to tell me what he was like but I wouldn't listen. No one ever listens," she admitted unhappily. "I think we just have to go ahead and make our mistakes, try somehow to learn from them. I remember sitting with you in that pub the night before the wedding, and you saying I didn't have to go through with it, no matter what I'd told Jeremy. The whole time you were talking I knew you were right, but I also knew I couldn't change anything. I'd given my word and I was going ahead with it. But Christ, Andrew! How could he *do* that? Swearing her to secrecy for four pounds a week, never even bothering to find out how his child was. What kind of man does things like that?"

"Jeremy does," he answered, encouraged by this break-through and not bothering to mask his distaste. "Maybe it's time you took a good hard look at him, Alyssa, and see just who he really is. I know you've got the girls to consider, but it's not as if you need Jeremy. The three of you could function perfectly well without him."

"You're underestimating Suze and Addy. He's their *father*, Andrew. Addy could probably cope if I were to make some kind of move. But I'm not at all sure about Suze. Anyway, we're jumping the gun. I can't just throw away fourteen years because I don't approve of something he did." Again, she saw herself and the girls looking at apartments, and told herself it was an absurd image. They had a home. They weren't obligated to uproot themselves.

"This is rather more than 'something he did,' Alyssa. And what exactly do you think you'd be throwing away?" he asked angrily.

"Don't push me, please."

"No, really. Answer me that and I'll let it drop for now. What would you be 'throwing away'?"

"Everything!" she exclaimed, her throat raw from cigarettes

187

and incipient tears. "Everything I've worked so hard. . . . Leave it be, please."

"You're still young, Alyssa. It's not too late for you to be happy."

"Happy?" She stared at him, wondering how he could be so familiar and yet so unknown. "I'm not a child. I have no ridiculous expectations."

"You think it's ridiculous to want to be happy?" He stared back at her. "You don't think it's your right to have some pleasure in your life?"

"I do have," she insisted, wondering as she spoke what, aside from the girls and her work, constituted her pleasure. It wasn't pleasurable to sleep every night beside Jeremy, hoping he wouldn't decide he wanted to make love. There was no pleasure to listening to his lengthy list of grievances or his equally lengthy list of plans. He was like a difficult tenant she tolerated for reasons that would make no sense to anyone else.

He reached with a forefinger to push a stray strand of hair behind her ear. "You've no idea, sproggy. None. I'd hazard a guess and say you've had moments here and there, but for someone whose job it is to understand people's motives you're hopeless when it comes to your own."

"But you understand me perfectly. Is that it?"

"I'm not saying that at all. I believe I have some inkling. You seem to dislike the idea of that, Alyssa. Why? It's not as if you haven't always known how I feel about you."

"This isn't the time to discuss it. I really must get back," she said.

"For once don't run away. Talk to me."

"What do you mean by that? You make it sound as if I've never discussed anything serious with you. That's not true and you know it. All these years, whenever something important's come up, you're the one I talk to. It's not as if *you* haven't always known how much I value your friendship." Why had he decided to make a stand now, of all times, when she was least prepared to deal with it? He wasn't wrong in what he was saying, but it felt like the worst possible timing.

He knew he was putting her on the spot, but he couldn't stop himself. He didn't want to lose her a second time and if he didn't state his case when he had the chance that might very well happen. "I'm not fond of playing the good sport," he said. "It's the game and all that, how it's played. But bloody hell, Alyssa, if one goes on and on with it, people begin to wonder."

"What game?" It was mid-afternoon but she was terribly tired, as if she hadn't slept for days. "What're you talking about?"

As an actor his timing was his biggest asset, but as a man it seemed to have deserted him. "I'm sorry," he backed down. "I should know better. I'm old enough, God knows."

She half-smiled. "For what?"

He could rarely resist an opportunity to try to amuse her, but this time he swallowed the quip that rose into his mouth and said instead, "I'll take you home."

As he reached to turn the key in the ignition, she put her hand on his arm—a gesture that it seemed to him she'd made hundreds of times before—and said, "We *will* talk, I promise. This just isn't the right time."

"Not to worry. I'll be around."

LATE THAT evening Aly walked through the house, pausing in each room to absorb the sight and feel of it. Jeremy's imprint was evident primarily in the family photographs in the lounge, and in the things he tended to leave lying about: a sweater draped over the arm of a chair, an Equity newsletter atop a theatrical magazine, an opened roll of Polo mints. He was fairly addicted to mints of one kind or another, and she recalled the time when he was performing in a farce in Hammersmith. He was in the habit of sucking on a mint until seconds before he heard his cue to go on. Then he'd put the sticky candy down wherever he happened to be.

One evening near the end of the run, he'd been whispering in the wings with two of the other cast members and was almost late for his cue. Depositing his mint on a tabletop, he raced onstage. One of the lead actresses came along and sat on the edge of the table for a minute or two before making her entrance. She played the entire scene with Jeremy's mint stuck to the back of her skirt. Since neither Jeremy nor the woman were especially well-liked, the other cast members furtively pointed it out to each other and laughed their heads off. The stage manager finally mentioned it to the actress after the curtain came down on the first act. Furious, she accused Jeremy of being a fool, and threatened to garotte him if she ever again saw his mints anywhere backstage. Jeremy came home to relate this tale with great indignation. Aly had been fairly repelled by the story, not only because Jeremy had some quite disgusting habits and was so inconsiderate of others but also because, in her opinion, only in the acting profession could people behave so badly in general and still win acceptance.

She was married to a peasant, she thought with a shiver of disgust, a man who had no compunction about leaving his half-eaten candies here and there so he could come back to finish them later; a man who'd abandon a pregnant woman in the hope of winning over someone who better fit his ludicrous image of himself; a man with little common sense and not the slightest shred of kindness. Why would any self-respecting woman want him? Did she *have* any self-respect? She'd long-since proved she could sustain an impossible marriage. Why then did it make her feel ill to contemplate ending it? She didn't love Jeremy; she scarcely liked him.

Completing her tour of the ground floor, she climbed the stairs and walked down the hallway to look in on each of the girls in turn. Jeremy was out for the evening and probably wouldn't return until very late. She had no interest in knowing where he was or what he was doing. Recently, she'd actively encouraged him to do the socializing he claimed was so vital to the furthering of his career.

Addy slept like a windmill, rarely still for long, her arms and legs making sweeping arcs as she flung herself from one side to the other. Addy was strong, intrepid. Everything about her was solid, positive. *I used to be like that*, Aly thought, remembering the positive force of her ten-year-old feelings, the strength of her convictions. She'd seen so clearly the demarcation between right and wrong, good and bad. Except where Rheta was concerned. With her, all the lines got blurred. Rheta was right and wrong, independent yet dependent, good and bad, dark and light, a combination of bewildering qualities. *I'm not like her. I'll never be like her*. With or without Jeremy, she'd never be a replica of her mother. So why couldn't she get rid of him? She pulled the blankets back over Addy, laid a hand briefly on her forehead, then crept out.

Suzanne slept in a fetal curl, hands tucked between her knees, her rich auburn hair appearing black in the darkness of the room. Suzanne was a nervous fledgling, a baby dove. She hung back, fearful of new people and situations, her emotions on display in her wide dark eyes, in her apprehensive gaze. From the beginning Addy had instinctively sought to protect her older sister, shielding her but never averse to squabbling with her, pinching and poking and prodding her, as if in the hope of toughening her up. Suzanne's diffidence served to keep Addy in check, to prevent her from going too far. The girls balanced one another and were powerfully bound together, just as Aly had been tied up in Cliffie. They would always have each other, even at a distance. Nothing, Aly vowed, would ever separate her girls.

At last, she went to her bedroom. Lighting a cigarette, she sat down in the slipper chair by the window and gazed over at the bed. This was the ongoing scene of the crime, the arena in which she grappled waking and sleeping with her demons. One was a deluded self-involved man capable of astonishing cruelty; the other her ten-year-old self who shouted angrily that the present Aly was being stupid and wrong-headed. "He's mean and selfish and you should throw him out!" The ten-year-old had more courage and good sense than she did now. How had she lost that ability to see things clearly? When? And why couldn't she bring herself to do what she knew had to be done?

191

CHAPTER
TWENTY

S HE HAD to get everything clear in her own mind, marshall her arguments and complaints before confronting Jeremy. But she was too preoccupied—repeatedly, exhaustively, reviewing not only her meeting with Liz and Donna but also a number of other pivotal moments—to sit him down for a serious dialogue. The anger that had started as a steady seepage had become a deluge sweeping over everything and leaving behind only the track of its own passage. What faced her now was a veritable mountain of upset that drastically reduced the available light and cast menacing shadows over all she saw.

Despite her fervent albeit unrealistic wish to believe otherwise, she knew unequivocally that a confrontation with Jeremy would put an end to their marriage. And while it was with a definite degree of relief that she was able to see this, she was reluctant to begin something that was bound to result in turmoil. Because she could only visualize negative results, her reluctance to confront him was compounded almost hourly.

She was haunted by recollections of her and Cliffie packing and unpacking their belongings, of directing the movers to put the sofa there and the chairs over there, of the two of them flattening the emptied boxes, storing them for the next move. She stiffened, remembering Rheta waltzing in to announce they were moving. She'd met a wonderful new "sweetie," or she'd sent Martin, or Adam, or Jerry, on his way. She relived almost nightly that final fatal weekend, the bus ride through the snow, the heat of the apartment, the glare of the light.

At the start of the week following her meeting with Liz she met as usual with her clients and was able to lose herself in their dilemmas. But by Thursday of that week, while listening to a first-time client stumble verbally over the minefield of her emotional life, she suddenly looked across her desk and realized she had no idea what the young woman seated opposite was saying. Tuning in, she paid the closest possible attention, trying to pick up clues both from the woman's demeanor and her halting words.

". . . she's my mother, after all. But, well, being my mother doesn't give her the right, does it, to . . . to take me over. I mean, it's as if she means to live my life for me because I'm making such a hash of it. And she'd do it perfectly, with no mistakes. I mean, I make her dreadfully impatient really because. . . . She says I will insist on doing things my way when everyone knows my way won't work. It's so terribly frustrating. After all, how does anyone know for certain one's own way will or won't work? I mean, it might work for me even though it didn't for her. Mightn't it?" She stopped and gazed expectantly at Aly.

"Could you give me an example?" Aly invited, hoping for more clues.

"Yes, well. All right. Just this past week. . . ."

An only child, twenty-two years old and quite pretty, working as a secretary to an oil company executive; still living at home with her widowed, obviously domineering mother who wanted to make all her daughter's decisions. Rheta had given them almost too much freedom, except when it came to the men. Then she'd expected them to climb into bed with her and the "sweetie" of the moment, ordered them to give so-and-so hugs and kisses. She and Cliffie had known almost every bus and subway route in Manhattan, and how to mix drinks when they were seven and eight years old. They'd known how to run down to the liquor store to cash Rheta's checks and pick up a bottle of Gilbey's or Bell's, which the store owners or managers allowed these kids to buy and carry home with substantial sums of cash. What sort of education was that for small children? How many other ten-year-old girls had seen similarly horrific results of their mothers' obsession with men? No, don't blame Rheta! It wasn't her fault, wasn't anyone's fault; not hers, or Cliffie's. But if things went wrong, if you didn't exercise the utmost caution, the end might very well come in a tide of blood. The most unlikely people could turn violent.

"Why don't you move out?" Aly cut abruptly into the young woman's narrative. "You're obviously capable of fending for yourself. You've got a good job, a regular income. Why not find a flat and make a break, take responsibility for yourself?"

"But she needs me."

Aly glanced at her notes, then said, "Georgina, what exactly do you think she needs you for? Is she financially dependent on you?"

"Well, no. My father left quite a lot of money actually."

"What, then?"

"She hasn't anyone else."

"She has no sisters or brothers, no relatives?"

"Oh! Yes, she does have quite a few relatives."

"She's not physically handicapped in any way, is she?"

"No, she's really very healthy."

"So," Aly persisted, "why does she need you?"

"I don't know. I mean to say, I'm her only child. . . ."

"Does it strike you as fair, any of it?"

Georgina looked down at her hands, cleared her throat, then raised her eyes, directing her gaze slightly to Aly's left. With a pang, Aly all at once realized she was probably subjecting this poor young woman to the same sort of pressure the mother did. She was demonstrating a most unprofessional impatience, even intolerance—all because of Jeremy. Now he was interfering with her work. Whether she liked it or not she was going to have to deal with him. It couldn't be put off any longer. Her daughters and her work were the most important things in her life. Nothing could be allowed to detract from her efforts and pleasure in either area.

"No, not really," Georgina answered. "I'd very much like a place of my own," she said with some enthusiasm. "I've a friend actually who's keen to share a flat, but I've been putting it off . . . afraid, you know, of what Mummy might say."

Relieved to find she hadn't done any harm with her fairly hard-line interrogation, Aly smiled. "Claiming one's independence, so far as I know, has never actually killed anyone," she said. "I honestly don't think you need therapy, Georgina. I think you need to ring up your friend and start looking for a flat."

"Truly? It wouldn't be wrong or cruel of me to go off on my own and leave Mummy?"

"Not at all," Aly said. "It's your right, as you said, to have a life. Your mother's lived a goodly portion of hers. Now it's your turn." Christ! It sounded so simple. Why did everyone have such trouble claiming what was theirs by right? And why did it frighten her to think of a life without Jeremy, even though she could hardly stand the sight of him these days? Because it signified failure. She'd devoted herself to the marriage, but she wasn't going to be able to make it last a lifetime. Rheta had taken up with married men, using Aly, and Cliff, and her own body to show these victims of the marital wars just what they'd been missing. She'd been driven to try to prove unprovable, unrealistic points. Her children had been part of the weaponry with which she'd approached each new conquest. Aly had taken note of Rheta's countless gambits, discrediting every last one of them in her determination never to duplicate, in any way, her mother's ultimately lethal mistakes. Aly had worked to demonstrate fidelity, loyalty, and maternal accountability in order that her children would grow up in a stable environment. Ironically, it now appeared that her efforts had been wasted. She'd failed, perhaps not in the same way as Rheta, but failed none the less.

Somehow she managed successfully to conclude the interview. Georgina, looking considerably lighter, younger, and more at ease than she had upon arriving, was standing now, saying, "Thank you ever so much, Dr. Brown. I'm most grateful," then rushed away in a big hurry to stake a claim upon her life. Aly envied her. If only it could be so simple a matter to reclaim her own life, recover the trenchant insights she'd had as a ten-year-old.

SHE TOOK great pains to find just the right moment, on an evening when Jeremy was home for a change, waiting until after the girls had gone to bed. She invited him to come into the

195

lounge, saying, "There's a matter I'd like to discuss with you."

Warily, his eyes narrowing slightly, he asked, "What matter?"

"Let's go in and sit down and we'll talk about it."

His reluctance was palpable. Like a small child convinced he was about to be reprimanded, he hung back, watching her every move as she got her cigarettes and an ashtray and settled into one of the armchairs in the lounge. He finally slid into the armchair opposite hers and played with a miniature brass gavel someone had once given them as a house gift. As Aly talked, he first rapped the gavel on the palm of his hand, then turned to beating it softly, rhythmically on the arm of the chair. He kept his eyes on the gavel, looking now like a surly six-year-old as he let her words—like innocuous soap bubbles—burst where they would. Sticks and stones could break his bones but her babble-bubbles could never harm him. He wouldn't even listen.

"How could you do that?" she asked him for the third time.

He shrugged and triple-rapped the gavel on the chair arm. It truly was like reprimanding an unruly child: frustrating and ultimately pointless, because he would not take heed.

"I'd appreciate some response, Jeremy," she said, thinking she sounded like an old maid schoolteacher, and loathing him for making everything, always, far more difficult than it had to be. "So far you haven't said a single word."

He shrugged again, still without looking at her, crossed his legs and began tapping his bony kneecap with the gavel. It was all she could do not to tear the thing from his hand and whack him on the head with it. She longed to beat him senseless, just pound his skull to mush. The need to commit mayhem seemed to coat her body like perspiration. Nothing and no one had ever aroused such violence in her.

"Don't you *care* that I'm deeply upset about this?" she asked him with genuine curiosity. She'd have dearly loved to know what was going on inside his head at that moment. She suspected he wasn't paying her the least bit of attention. Very likely he was mentally reciting lines for his acting class, or running up and down musical scales. Next to his singing voice, his greatest talent was his ability to ignore anything he didn't want to hear. Over the years she'd watched him retreat like a field mouse into the safety of his own skull; he'd poke his nose out, whiskers twitching, to test the air now and then, but he wouldn't emerge until all hint of danger was past. The first time he'd done it, some weeks after they were married, she'd been flabbergasted, unable to believe anyone could conveniently go deaf and dumb at will. But Jeremy could. The man was one hundred percent selective about what he saw and heard and took in.

It never failed to amaze her how differently the two of them perceived the same events. When he referred to films he'd done in the sixties, he invariably said, "I should've been concentrating on my singing, you see. That was my mistake. I wasn't right for those films. I'm a stage actor, really." His having in effect been blackballed by the other actors had never happened; he'd never been resoundingly rebuked by the director; he hadn't curtailed his own film career by being an anal-retentive, nit-picking, pain-in-the-ass perfectionist who had no real idea of how he appeared to others. No. None of that. He'd simply been aiming in the wrong direction. He was, however, headed in the right direction now, spending every day improving his vocal range, his physical control, his acting skills. To hear him talk about it, it had been his choice to leave films, not the filmmakers choice to leave him.

"You have to understand that finding out about Liz and Donna affects how I feel about you," she said, trying every way she knew to reach him. "Do you care about that?"

He shifted in his seat and at last looked at her, his eyes reflecting only boredom and petulance. She could see he was actually annoyed with her for taking up his time with what he considered pointless old news.

"Did you intend to show up in court?" she asked. "Were you planning to ignore the summons, hoping it'd just disappear, or were you actually going to go? *What* were you going to *do*, Jeremy?" Her voice was acquiring a sharp edge. She'd been trying for close to forty minutes to discuss this issue with him but he steadfastly refused to respond. The longer his silence held, the deeper her determination grew to force him to speak, and the more her dislike of him built. It was nearing midnight and she wanted to go to bed. She was up early every morning to have breakfast with the girls before she left for the office. Unless he had an audition, Jeremy usually slept until 9:30 or

10:00. It meant nothing to him to stay up until 2:00 or 3:00 a.m. She was very tired but had no intention of going upstairs until she'd broken through to him.

"*What were you going to do?*" she demanded, disliking every moment of this. She wished she had magical powers, the ability to cast spells. She'd close her eyes, murmur a few potent incantations, and when she opened her eyes again he'd be gone— from the house, from her life, forever. She hated him. It frightened her to feel the way she did about him. He seemed neither to know nor to care, which made her hatred and fear expand. Andrew was right. He'd always been right about Jeremy. Unfortunately it was no consolation because her refusal to accept the truth of Andrew's knowledge only made her a bigger fool, more of an ostrich. "Answer me, for God's sake!" she said shrilly, holding tightly to the arms of the chair to keep herself from physically attacking him. She could so easily understand now why people went berserk, killed their partners, threw their nagging mothers down flights of stairs. It was a sick feeling she battled to control, but it was a powerful one.

"What do you want me to say?" he asked. "You've decided everything. Whatever I say will be wrong." She waited for him to go on but he said nothing more; he simply resumed rapping the gavel on his knee.

"That's not the case at all," she said, studying with aversion his profile, his pale freckled skin, feeling violence like an injection of some narcotic substance racing through her bloodstream. If he didn't drop this pose, stop this infuriatingly childish behavior, she was going to do something dreadful. Her rage was overtaking her ability to think rationally, smothering it like a pillow held forcibly over an infant's face. "Listen to me, Jeremy." Her voice was quivering now, sinking into a husky lower register that, in itself, she thought, should have been a warning to him. "This isn't one of our minor differences of opinion, a case of the two of us seeing things from opposing viewpoints. This is about *facts*, about your having done something I find utterly, completely, reprehensible. I need to hear what you have to say about it. I need some kind of explanation of why you did what you did, because I can't go on living with you, pretending I don't know about Liz and Donna and what you did to them."

"I didn't do anything to them," he said, offended. "I've done nothing to them."

He didn't even hear the threat. Did he consider her so inconsequential that her threats meant nothing to him? Why did she even care what this loathsome man thought or didn't think of her? How, *how* could she have lived side by side with him all these years when almost every last thing about him repelled her? She hated the fact that he always left the bathroom in a mess whenever he used it; she hated the way he left his dirty clothes wherever they happened to fall; she hated his taste in clothes, in music, in reading material, even in food. She hated his delusions about himself, his tendency to be self-aggrandizing, his egocentricity that prevented him from viewing others as real and therefore worthy of his attention and respect. *She hated him.* This was the price to be paid, finally, for allowing your body to take control of you, for setting your intelligence to one side for half an hour or an hour while you wallowed in sensation. You found yourself yoked to someone who, under other circumstances, you doubted you'd allow to park your car.

"That's the whole point!" she exclaimed. "You coerced that poor woman into signing a document swearing her to secrecy, and left her to survive somehow with a child on the pittance you were willing to pay."

"I've paid faithfully every week," he defended himself. "I've never once missed a single week." He was getting very angry. How dare she imply he'd been irresponsible when, no matter where he happened to be, he'd always made sure that money was paid!

"You think coming up with that pathetic sum every week justifies your behavior? You have a thirteen-year-old daughter living in Battersea, but you've never once been to see her or even called to inquire about her health. You've contributed four pounds a week to her maintenance. What exactly do you think four pounds buys nowadays, Jeremy? Have you any *idea* what it costs to raise a child? Of course, you don't! How could you possibly when you've never had to give a single penny toward the maintenance of the two children who live in this house? I'll tell you something. You can't buy a week's food for four pounds. You can't buy a pair of shoes, or even a decent sweater. There's not a hell of a lot you *can* buy for *four pounds*!"

"I paid regularly every week," he insisted.

"Oh, Jesus!" Exasperated, maddened, she grabbed her cigarettes and lit one.

He waved impatiently at the smoke and made a face. "Must you?" he asked. "You know it's bad for my voice."

She bit back the rejoinder that sprang to her lips, waited a moment or two, then asked, "Weren't you even curious? Didn't you ever wonder what she was like, this other child of yours?"

He shrugged, studied the gavel, then began again rapping it on his knee.

"You'd like me to drop it, wouldn't you, Jeremy? You'd prefer it if I never mentioned it again. We'd continue on as before, and you'd be perfectly happy."

Another shrug. The gavel bounced off his knee.

"I *can't* drop this! I wish to God I could. But not this time. Can you possibly comprehend that what you've done is disgraceful? Can you even begin to imagine what it will do to Addy and Suze when they find out they have a sister they never knew existed?"

"They needn't know," he said unemotionally.

"*Yes*, they need to know," she disagreed strongly. "It's their *right* to be told. It's Donna's right to know them. They're *sisters*! Doesn't that mean anything to you?" She waited, but he didn't speak. Unbelievable, she thought, staring at his unyielding features. This man lived in a world entirely of his own devising, one that only intermittently touched against hers and the children's; it had different rules that were entirely elastic and subject to change without notice; it had carefully selected experiences and recollections, and a singularly non-judgmental view of his own behavior. His judgment of others was often harsh, expressed in scathing terms, but he was never less than completely tolerant of whatever he himself might do. His world was enviably convenient, its litter-free streets and roadways laid out in perfect right-angled grids with no surprising twists or turns.

200

This man was deaf to criticism, perceiving anything negative that might be said to him as purely personal antagonism felt by those less talented or less motivated or less perfect than he. Praise, on the other hand, was something he could never get enough of, regardless of the source. He accepted it as his due and could recite from memory every favorable review or comment anyone had ever made about him. What the hell was he? she wondered, seeing him for the first time as a likely sociopath. He had no conscience, no instincts toward right or wrong. People like Jeremy often committed atrocities, serial murders, rapes. They did whatever felt good to them and weren't in the least bothered by anything as cumbersome as a conscience. So why had she hoped she'd be able to have a rational discussion with him?

"I'm tired," she said at last, conceding defeat. Rheta's child to the bitter end, she thought grimly. Rheta's "sweeties" had always been the ones to call the shots, never Rheta. She'd merely reacted, in her own peculiar and often arbitrary fashion, to the dictates of the men. "I'm going to bed." She put out her cigarette then sat looking at him, exhausted now that the violence had ebbed from her system. "What are you thinking about, Jeremy?" she asked softly.

He looked at his watch, the gavel tilting toward her as he turned his left wrist. "I have an audition tomorrow," he said reproachfully, as if he knew in advance that her attempt to draw him into a dialogue would cause him to lose out on whatever part he was up for. Nothing good ever came of her efforts to communicate with him. He'd made this clear in any number of ways over the years. He'd many times blamed her for keeping him up too late the night before an audition, declaring that his resulting fatigue hadn't allowed him to present himself at his best. She was a handy excuse for his failures.

Her weariness temporarily overcoming her anger, she arose from the chair saying, "Well, if you don't get the part, feel free to blame me."

"How am I to be expected to sleep now, after you've made such a scene?"

For a moment all she could do was gape at him. Then she gave a brief, bitterly barking laugh, saying, "I think you'll sleep

201

like a baby, but I'd like you to use the guest room." Then she left. He and his righteous indignation were, she thought, perfect companions. Just as she and her dead mother were cut from the same bolt of flawed yard goods.

IT WAS one of those nights when she was never more than halfway asleep, and events and fragments of conversation repeated over and over maddeningly, causing her to turn from one side to the other in an attempt either to get away from these repeating loops or to trick her brain into subsiding to a less irritating level. But for hours Jeremy sat toying with the gavel while she threw words at him like blunted weapons that simply bounced off his impossibly thick skin.

Then she was wandering through the streets of Manhattan wearing her old horn-rimmed glasses that had been fitted not with prescription lenses but with miniature bull's-eyes that offered her a critically warped view of everything she saw. Struggling to see through these distorting glasses, she and Cliffie carried heavy boxes into a vast warehouse while Rheta stood in the doorway with Don urging them to hurry so they could come give her new sweetie a big hug and a kiss.

CHAPTER
TWENTY-ONE

"**A**LYSSA, WHAT are you waiting for?" Andrew simply could not comprehend Aly's procrastination. It had been almost nine months since he'd taken her to see Liz. He'd expected her to begin extricating herself from the marriage right away. But aside from that one useless conversation with Gable she'd told him about, she'd done nothing further. Andrew had gone off to Spain on a shoot for three months fully expecting upon his return to find her unencumbered. He'd telephoned immediately on his arrival home only to learn that, externally at least, nothing had changed.

He'd allowed himself to become very optimistic, floating on an adolescent high, buoyant at the prospect that he might, at long last, have a chance to stake a claim on this woman. Now he felt foolish and, perhaps unfairly, annoyed with her. Why the hell was she hanging on? And to what? What bizarre hold did Gable have over her that made it so difficult for her to leave him? Or did it even have anything to do with him?

"It's not quite so easy as you seem to think," she answered, wishing he wouldn't keep pressuring her. Andrew had from the beginning been someone she felt she could count on for all the things Jeremy failed to provide: sympathy, support, companionship, and absolute loyalty. It distressed her to have him insisting she take an action that might have irreparable effects. "Maybe you're thinking in terms of your own marriage, Andrew, and how easily you ended that. But the two of you had no history, no children. Regardless of the fact that you've never liked the idea of my being married to Jeremy, we've had almost fifteen years together. I can't just write that off because I found out something he did that I don't approve of."

"Isn't that putting it rather mildly? You seem to keep wanting to downplay it."

"All right. I deplore what he did. Does that help?" she snapped, her jaw jutting stubbornly—a telltale sign that she was in trouble and was masking it with anger.

"Let's not fight," he said, backing down. "That wasn't what I intended when I asked you to come out tonight." He struck a match to light her cigarette, noticing a faint tremor in her hand as she held the cigarette to her mouth. She look strained, shadows under her eyes, an atypical downcurving to her mouth. He'd been so intent on making his feelings known that he'd neglected to see her clearly. Now he did, and felt guilty. "I'm sorry," he told her. "The truth is I'm disappointed. I've been hoping against hope you'd make a break."

She gazed at him as she took a long draw on the cigarette, trying to find a direct path through the snarled underbrush of her feelings. He'd changed very little over the years. For his film work he wore a hairpiece, but made no effort in his daily life to conceal his baldness. She admired him for lacking the vanity that was so much a part of most actors, Jeremy in particular. But then Andrew was scarcely typical; he never had been. "We don't think of each other in the same way, Andrew," she said finally. "I think of you as my friend, my best friend really. You're the one I look to when I need to talk, to hear myself say what I think, how I feel. I turn automatically to you, because I know you'll be on my side." She shrugged at the childishness of the expression. "I'm never bored with you. And I'm prouder of you than I could ever say; proud I actually know you. You're so wonderfully good at what you do, yet it's never gone to your head. If anything, success has made you even more you. Of course you're older—we both are, God knows—and physically we've both changed. Otherwise you've stayed the same Andrew I've always known, and that's something I rely on. It really is. But you don't think of me in the same way as I do you. You've never accepted or believed in my commitment to Jeremy. You treat my marriage like an ongoing disaster that I'm going to walk away from one morning. Maybe that's what it is," she allowed. "That's probably exactly what it is. I'm not going to deny you've been right about Jeremy all along, but whether or not either one of us likes it, I'm *married* to him. We have two teenage daughters, Andrew. We have a life together, a shared history. I grant you it's not the history I'd have chosen, but I can't simply dump all that because something Jeremy did years ago infuriates and disgusts me. I *wish* you could see that from my point of view."

"Why do you assume I don't understand?" he asked patiently. "I have a part in that history, you know. I've been here, haven't I? And I happen, by the way, to think of you much in the same way you claim to think of me. Give me some credit, Alyssa. I'm not entirely stupid."

"You're not in the least stupid."

"Right, then. So why knock off all my nice pointed corners by trying to push me into that small round slot you've designated as my rightful place? And why ask me to honor your involvement with a man I wouldn't trust as far as I could lift him? If I did that, I'd have to give up on you. I'd have to walk away, because to honor your marriage to Gable would be declaring to all of us that you've got no bloody judgment and never have had. I happen not to believe that to be the case. I believe you know exactly what he is and why you're with him, and that in the not too distant future you're going to admit it's a complete farce and remove yourself from it with your dignity and intelligence intact."

She sat motionless for several seconds wondering if she underestimated everyone. Certainly she hadn't counted on Andrew's having thought things through as carefully as he had—possibly with more care and honesty than she'd taken herself. She had the feeling, looking at him now, that she was yet again trying to force a focus where none could possibly occur. Distortion was a concept she couldn't seem to accept. It made her queasy to think she was so far off track in almost every area of her thinking. Extinguishing her cigarette she said, "Let's get out of here, take a walk. Would you mind?"

At once he signalled for the check then turned back, regarding her with a somewhat guarded expression. "Please don't be angry with me, Alyssa. We've always been honest with each other. I can't, at this late date, start saying things I think you want to hear."

"I know. I just need some fresh air." She watched the waiter confer with the maître d' before presenting the check. Why did people become obsequious when dealing with celebrities or those with innate stature like Lilbet? It was something she wondered about every time she went out in public with Andrew, because whether he liked it or not he was recognized, and people paid close attention to his slightest request. Fortunately, he was unimpressed by his own fame and dealt politely and quietly with everyone. More than anything else, he disliked a fuss being made over him. "It's all fakery," he often said. "They think I'm actually the people I play. Frightening."

They left the restaurant and walked down Dover Street to Piccadilly. At the intersection, he took hold of her hand and they crossed the road, heading toward the Mall. It had rained earlier. The streets were still wet, but the chill autumn air was fragrant with the scent of matted leaves blanketing the damp grass. An occasional car travelled past but there were no other pedestrians nearby. She became aware of Andrew's hand, its warmth penetrating her hand. All those years ago, before she'd gone with Jeremy to his flat, she'd imagined herself naked in turn with both Andrew and Jeremy. She'd seen possibilities in all her imaginings, but Jeremy had dared to make a move and she'd responded in a fashion that radically altered her view of herself. It could have been either of them, but it had been Jeremy. And she'd been so undone, so disarmed to discover her own capabilities that she'd gone back to him again and again, never tiring of the often grating pleasure she'd derived from their encounters. She still slept with Jeremy now and then but disliked herself for being able to respond sexually to a man for whom she had such a wealth of contempt. Most of the time she discouraged his sexual advances because she despaired of the part of herself that could, with such brainlessness, enter so wholeheartedly into an activity that invariably resulted in some form of damage being done. When she did make love with Jeremy she couldn't help feeling every time that it was an act of punishment she allowed him to inflict upon her. Her orgasms were guilty spasms that left her diminished somehow. She and Andrew had never progressed beyond affectionate hugs, chaste kisses, and occasional handholding. Yet a sexual undercurrent ran beneath everything they said and did and she occasionally found it hard to ignore. It frightened her to have the breath catch in her lungs, to have her flesh suddenly begin tingling in response to Andrew's proximity. But because she loved him only slightly less than her girls she forced herself to ignore that potent undercurrent. She didn't dare even speculate on Andrew's reactions to this perennial tide, determined to keep their association purely fraternal.

"I don't love him," she admitted, feeling an immediate and terrible shame.

"I know that," he said without inflection. He'd always been able to read her, to recognize her moods. Of all the women he'd encountered through the years only she was completely known to him. He could tell from the line of her jaw, or the set of her mouth, or the particular light in her eyes, how she was reacting at a given time. He wanted so much to be on the privileged interior of her life that he'd worked extra hard at recognizing the outward signs that indicated her feelings, and it gave him a very real satisfaction to be so aware of her. "Do you ever wonder if Jeremy has had affairs?" he asked bluntly.

She turned to look at him. "I'll tell you something, Andrew. There have been times when I've wished to Christ he would. He flirts, all right. I've seen him do it at opening night parties, that sort of thing. But while he's doing it he keeps looking over at me to see if I'm noticing, if I'm reacting. When he sees that I don't care he just stops. I'd honestly be delighted if he got himself a mistress. He never will. There's no point to it for him. It's got to mean something. If it doesn't he can't be bothered. He's quite odd that way, I think. I mean, it's not as if he hasn't had ample opportunity, but I think he's written this little mental fable that has me cast as his warder. You know? He can't take up with another woman because I'd find out and castrate him. It's one hell of a handy rationale. For what, I couldn't say. But I think it's his modus operandi. In fact, I think women scare him. God knows, if I'd grown up with that grandmother of his, women would scare me, too. Christ! There he was married, with two small children, and she was telling him what to do and how and where and when to do it, as if he were still eight years old. And he obeyed her, too. 'Fetch me that newspaper, Jeremy,'" she mimicked the old woman's voice, " 'I've circled something I want you to read.' Or, 'You need to keep your throat warm. Haven't you got a decent scarf?' Casting this malevolent look at me as if I'd been sent by the devil to torment her gifted grandson. Anyway," she sighed, "she leached every last natural instinct out of him, including the ability to love. My mother died for love," she said, surprising herself. "I've never talked about it, not since it happened. I've tried never to think about it, although I've been having nightmares about it the past few months. The only person I ever actually told was my grandmother's housekeeper, Pearl."

"I remember you had a whacking great row with Jeremy over your flying back for her funeral."

"That's right." She glanced at him, then looked straight ahead, her eyes on the wet pavement. "She was a very wise woman, Pearl. She helped me deal with it. I'm still not sure I understand it all but at least, because of her, I don't blame myself for what happened."

"Would you like to sit down?" he asked, indicating a bench ahead.

She looked at the bench, then at Andrew, then again at the bench. "I feel odd, shaky. I want to tell you but just thinking about it makes me afraid."

"Then don't tell me," he said kindly.

"I have to," she said in so intense a fashion that he was able to see the child she'd been, as if that little girl's face had suddenly been superimposed over the woman's. He'd only seen her display such overt anxiety two or three times before—when she'd told him she was going to marry Gable; once when Suze was an infant and ran a fever of over a hundred and five and she'd been alone with the baby and had telephoned begging him to come; and that time her father and Serena had been in a smash-up on the Continent and she'd been unable to get specific details from the Austrian officials. Gable had said, "If they'd been killed, you'd have been told," and gone off to his singing class, leaving her alone to cope with her fear. The girls had been in New York with their great-grandmother, and Olive was off on a week's vacation. Frantic, Aly had telephoned to ask if he'd come be with her while she waited for news. He still couldn't get over Jeremy's cold indifference.

He gave her hand a squeeze and led her to the bench. "Why do you feel you have to?" he asked, sitting down with her.

"I don't know why, I just do," she said, searching his eyes in the dim orange-yellow glow of the streetlamp.

"I've never seen you quite this way," he said, alarmed by her fairly palpable dread. "Maybe this isn't a good idea. Some things should remain in the past."

"Some things shouldn't," she replied, opening her purse for a cigarette, trying to regain her composure. "I suppose I want to tell you to prove how much I trust you, to convince you how important you are to me. Or maybe it's for me. I don't know. I've arrived at a point where I can't seem to take a step in any direction. What you call my galloping indecision." She gave him a winsome smile and he automatically extended his arm across her shoulders as if to protect her. She briefly bent her head to his shoulder, wondering if she was taking advantage of him, using him to bolster her dwindling courage. Every day it was becoming more difficult to don her guise of normalcy, to carry on with her life as if her growing displeasure with her husband wasn't affecting her performance in every area. She straightened and took a puff of her cigarette. "Let me tell you about Rheta," she said, and gripped his hand as she began sketching word pictures on the dark canvas of the night.

He settled back to listen, anticipating the type of tale so many people had to recount, a family chronicle of relatively minor misunderstandings blown out of proportion due to the age of the children involved; recollections of incidents noteworthy only because of their being out of the ordinary as far as the family in question was concerned. Having known Alyssa all these years he'd never have guessed from any aspect of her behavior the extent of the tragedy. By the time she was telling— her voice a ragged whisper intercut with almost convulsive gasps for air—how she'd discovered the bodies, his view of her had been altered forever.

There was a long silence after she stopped talking. She at last released her grip on his hand to light a fresh cigarette and he concentrated on trying to quell the panicky hammering of his heart caused by her too-vivid description. His arm remained around her shoulders; he wouldn't have dreamed of breaking this connection. Looking at her now as if for the first time, it was his turn to feel deeply ashamed.

"I will never again," he said in a low voice, "make assumptions about another living soul. I'm ashamed to admit how many I've made about you. What a horrendous thing to have happen. Poor Alyssa. How dreadful for you! How very dreadful!"

"We all assume, Andrew," she said in a professional-sounding voice he imagined she must use with her patients. "It's our nature to do it—based on appearances, based on our experiences. Most of us do it every day. A lot of how we deal with others is instinct, but most of it is assumption. It's not wrong. We have to go by what we know, by what people show us. The rest is guesswork. That's why my appointment book's always full, why there's a waiting list." Losing much of that professional tone, she said, "When we run out of guesses and assumptions and our instinct's not working, we need help making sense of our lives. Unless we tell each other, how do we know what anyone's experienced? I still miss them, you know. Especially Cliffie. I'll see a boy walking along the street and my heart'll jump and I think it's him. But how could it be? Someone you love is dead but for the rest of your life you keep thinking you see him on the street, and you keep on missing him, even though you saw him *that way*, you know it's impossible. But knowing it's impossible doesn't stop you from wanting back what you had. It doesn't stop you from wanting to make sure nothing like it ever happens to anyone else you care about, doesn't stop you from worrying every day of your life that you're carrying her genes inside of you like microscopic time bombs."

"Will you despise me if I say what you've told me only confirms what I feel about your marriage?"

"How?" she asked.

"You've stuck with it for so long to prove you're not like Rheta. Am I wrong?"

"No, not entirely. Mostly it has to do with my girls, Andrew.

I want them to have the security Cliffie and I never had, the stability, the constancy. They don't deserve to have their lives disrupted because of my failure."

"What failure?" he asked skeptically. "Where, how, and in what way have you failed?"

"I couldn't make it work," she answered, knowing it sounded feeble.

"God himself couldn't make a marriage with Jeremy work!" he declared. "You don't think you're possibly setting somewhat Olympian standards for yourself, dear heart?" He reached for her cigarette, took a puff, then returned it.

"Feeling post-coital?" she quipped, feeling even closer to him now that she'd told him about Rheta and Cliffie. He'd got the point of what she'd been trying to say, grasped at once the reason why she'd told him.

He laughed softly and hugged her to him. "What are we going to do with you, Alyssa?" he asked, marveling at her resilience.

"I wish I knew." She turned her head so that she could feel the rough texture of his tweed jacket against her lips as she gazed at him. She wanted to say, I love you. The words, the sentiment were so close to the surface she could almost hear them asserting themselves. Unsafe, dangerous. Rheta usually had another man waiting in the wings. If she closed her eyes she could see those phantom figures, that queue of men stretching off to the horizon. No decent woman accumulated men like savings bonds to be tucked away in case of an emergency. She sat back and smoked her cigarette.

"I know I have to end it. I know I do. But every time I so much as think about it my insides start churning, my hands get wet, my throat goes dry, and I feel as if I'm going to pass out. It doesn't have a thing to do with Jeremy, believe it or not. The whole thing's about me, and about the girls. I can hardly stand to look at Jeremy now. Everything he says and does infuriates me. I hate myself for allowing him to live in the house, sleep in the same bed. I find every last thing about him reprehensible. When I manage to be objective, I can see we'd be infinitely better off without him. But there are unknowns, and they worry me. Do the girls feel about him the way I think they do? Or is their attitude typically teen-age? Will they blame me if I send

211

him away? Or will they accept that I had no other alternative?"

"Leave him, Alyssa. End it. The girls will cope. They're not babies. They won't be the first teenagers whose parents split up, and they'll survive in spite of your fears. It's not as if they'll be losing either one of you. You'll still be their mother; he'll still be their father. You'll simply be in different places, living separate lives."

"Just hearing you say that makes me feel sick," she said. "I have this vision of everything falling to pieces. No more home, no more family. I hate the idea of it."

"Of course you'll have a home. And what do you imagine will happen to the family? You think the girls will disown you?"

"It's possible, Andrew. The most frightening part of life is knowing that absolutely anything's possible, that we actually control very little. What if I do it?" she asked wildly. "What if I go home and say, 'Jeremy, it's over. I want you to leave,' and he says, 'No, *you* leave. The girls and I have talked it over and we've decided we want *you* to go.' I'd die, Andrew," she cried, shaking her head. "I can't *lose* them. I'd have nothing left."

"First of all," he said calmly, "that's simply not going to happen. And secondly, even if by some peculiar quirk of fate it did, you're always going to be their mother. No one can ever take that away from you. As well, you've got your grandmother in New York; and your father and Serena and dear old Olive here. Not to mention me and your other friends. Why do you think everyone's going to abandon you because you get a divorce? That didn't happen to Rheta, from what you've told me."

"I admit it's arbitrary and irrational. But it's how I feel, and I can't help how I feel."

"Look," he said. "I'm not committed to anything at the moment. There's a film in the offing, but I'll turn it down and stay in town. End it, Alyssa. I'll stand by you, see you through it. Just, please, for your own sake, put this bloody thing out of its misery and end it."

"Christ! I'm so scared." She crushed the cigarette under her heel then sat for a moment with both hands over her mouth.

"Do it before you're so paralyzed by your misgivings that you can't even contemplate it. Do you really want to be shackled to bloody Gable for the rest of your natural life?"

212

"No. The thought of that is almost as frightening as the thought of losing everything."

"Right. So when I take you home tonight, march right in there and tell him it's over."

"And you'll be there to pick up the pieces," she said accusingly, afraid he'd say he would, and equally afraid he wouldn't.

Stung, he said, "Tell me where and when I've made any reference to my own interests in this! Whatever I've advised, it's been with your well-being in mind, not mine. I'm not going to lie and say I don't have hopes where you're concerned. I do. I always have had. But don't try to make it sound as if I'm loitering with intent, hoping to capitalize on Gable's misfortune. Good Christ! After fifteen years you don't seriously believe I've pinned all my hopes on you, do you?" He glared at her for a moment, then said, "Don't answer that! It's a pack of lies. Not the part about your well-being, but the part about my intentions. I have been waiting. I'll probably spend my life waiting. That's just the way it is. I can't help my feelings for you any more than you can help having the fears you do. I'm sorry if that adds to your distress. I do try to be discreet, but it isn't always easy. Fuck it! Get yourself the hell out of it, Alyssa, and never mind about me! You and I aren't the issue here. Maybe one day we might be, but for now I'm just the one who'll hold your hand while you get through this. So would you finally do what's right for you? Will you go home and tell the man it's over. Would you *do* that, *please?*"

Her mind was filled with images of carnage—blood on the walls, the floors, the bedding; bodies robbed of their souls and left sprawling in impossibly contorted positions; dispossessed corpses that had once been people she'd loved more than she'd known. If you took the chance and pursued your heart's desire you risked far more than mere disappointment. But if you never took the chance you might be condemned to a living death. And what she had with Jeremy wasn't life the way she wanted to live it; it was a harrowing daily battle with her own mounting aversion for a man she had come to despise which, in turn, exacerbated her self-aversion.

Dumbstruck and profoundly afraid, she slowly nodded.

213

"**A**NDREW PLEASE don't refuse the film. I really don't want you to do that because of me."

"Have you changed your mind about asking him to go, Alyssa?"

"I haven't changed my mind. It just bothers me to think you're sitting around waiting for me to tell him. It's inhibiting. And besides, I know you were looking forward to this film."

"Are you sure?"

"Positive. It'll be easier for me if I know you're not counting the days."

"I don't know," he said doubtfully. "I hate to think of being a thousand miles away if you should need me."

"Please go. If I need to talk to you I can always phone."

"Promise me you won't put it off for another nine months."

"I won't do that," she said stiffly. "I'm just waiting for the right moment. You have my word that by the time you get back it'll be over."

"Well, if you're quite certain. . . ."

"It's a good part, Andrew. Take it."

He questioned her for several more minutes, then finally agreed to call his agent. "I want your promise that you'll get in touch if you need me."

"I will, you have my word."

After the call, she lit a cigarette and tried to pull herself together to deal with her next client. She felt as if a date had been set for her execution and she was attending to all the final details before the trap door swung open beneath her feet.

Jeremy was still asleep Sunday morning when she and the girls left to visit her father and Serena.

"Isn't Daddy coming?" Suzanne asked as they went out to the car.

"You know he doesn't enjoy these visits," Aly answered. "He feels uncomfortable."

"He feels *poor*," Addy laughed. "The staff make him frightfully nervous."

"That's unkind," Suzanne protested. "He's simply not accustomed to that sort of life. And neither are we, really."

"He'd jolly well like to be," Addy said incisively. "He'd love to have a maid and a cook and probably even a butler."

"Lots of people would," Suzanne defended him staunchly.

"Let's not bicker," Aly said quietly.

"We're not bickering," Addy said. "We're expressing our individual viewpoints."

Aly laughed. "Let's not. Okay?"

The girls settled back for the ride, and Aly concentrated on her driving, trying to guess how her father might respond to the news that she planned to split up with Jeremy. She was fairly confident Serena would support her position, but her father might ask her to reconsider. Then again he might ask her why she'd taken so long to come to this decision. It was pointless trying to anticipate their reactions. But she badly wanted their support, even though she planned to proceed in the unlikely event she didn't get it.

All through lunch, while Addy chattered away to Serena and Suzanne held a murmured conversation with her grandfather, Aly felt as if she were watching a film. She ate automatically, scarcely tasting the exquisite food, with a sense of being disconnected, of having lost her former ability to make contact with the people she most cared about. She watched admiringly as Serena gave one of her raffish smiles then replied to whatever Addy had said to her. Serena was the girls' grandmother,

215

the only wife they'd ever known their grandfather to have, and they adored her. How, Aly wondered, would they have responded to Rheta? What would they have thought of her, with her "sweeties" and her repeated moves?

"Mummy's daydreaming," Addy was saying, grinning across the table at her.

Aly looked up, saying, "Sorry. What did I miss?"

"Mummy has a great deal to think about," Serena said with a meaningful smile at Aly. "Doesn't she?"

"I guess I do," Aly admitted, drawn as always by Serena's deferential interest. "Not very nice of me to be doing it over lunch," she told Addy.

"I was asking," Addy said, "if anyone minds if Suze and I drag Granddad off to the garden room to play table tennis."

"I don't mind. He'll beat you," Aly said, smiling over at her father. "He always does."

"He does play a fierce game," Serena said indulgently. "He makes no allowances for age or infirmity. Last week he trounced his good friend Roger Deane. Poor Roger was fairly shattered."

"Roger talks a better game than he plays," Hal laughed. "He loses every time because he's got no backhand. So, you girls think you can beat the old man?"

Suze flushed and said, "No. But may I play?"

Hal said, "Of course. I'll take you both on." He got up saying, "Come on, you two. Maybe I'll teach you a few of my secrets."

Aly watched them head off to the garden room, her father with an arm around each of the girls, and for a moment she saw herself and Cliffie that last Christmas, on their way to the movies with their dad.

"Let's have our coffee in the lounge," Serena suggested. "We'll be able to talk quietly."

Getting up from the table, Aly went with Serena and at her invitation sat next to her on the sofa by the fireplace.

"You seem rather distracted," Serena said, pouring the coffee into two white Wedgwood cups. "And you look tired. Is something wrong?"

Aly accepted the cup Serena gave her and sat holding it with both hands, her eyes on the wood fire. "I'm going to ask Jeremy to leave," she said, then redirected her eyes to Serena.

"I see. And obviously you're dreading it."

Aly nodded.

"I can't honestly say I'm surprised. I've been expecting this for years."

"Have you?"

"Why have you stayed with him so long, darling? You've never loved him."

"Is it that obvious?" Aly asked fearfully.

"Only, I expect, to your father and me, and to dear Andrew. I shouldn't think the rest of the world would notice or care, one way or another."

"What a mess!" Aly sighed, and took a sip of the coffee.

"It needn't be," Serena said calmly. "Give me one of your cigarettes, would you? I'm too lazy to walk across the room for mine."

Aly gave her the pack and her lighter. "I don't know how the girls are going to take it."

"I doubt they'll be overly surprised. Children sense things. I'll wager they've known for quite some time that there's friction between you two. That doesn't mean they'll take it well. It's difficult to guess, really. Is that what has you so worried?"

"To some degree. I can't keep putting it off," Aly said. "But I wish I could just close my eyes and he'd be gone."

"You haven't answered my question, you know. Why have you put up with him for so long? I'm most curious about that."

Aly looked at her, finding her relatively unchanged. She was still wonderfully good-looking in an exotic fashion, although her hair was streaked now with gray. Her skin was as white and flawless as ever, her full mouth defined by clear red lipstick, a few more lines around her eyes which were subtly enhanced with dark gray eyeshadow and mascara, a touch of color highlighting her slanting cheekbones. "I made a commitment," she said quietly. "I tried to honor it."

"Admirable," Serena said. "But has it been worthwhile?"

"I don't know how to answer that. I thought I was doing the right thing . . . for the girls, primarily."

"Alyssa, I love you darling," she said, laying one cool hand on Aly's arm. "I'm sure you're well aware of that. I'm quite as fierce about my relationship to you as your darling father is about his

217

table tennis." She smiled and stroked Aly's arm. "I actually," she admitted, "refer to you as *my* girl. *My* girl, *my* divine grand-daughters. If you're going to do it, *do it*! You've wasted too many precious years on Jeremy, but you're still young enough to make a life with someone you do love. And don't worry about Adele and Suzanne. They'll make their own way."

"Why am I so afraid?" Aly asked, more of herself than of Serena. "I am, you know. I'm absolutely terrified."

"I suppose it's natural. Having never been through a divorce myself, I can't comment with any degree of authority. But the end of anything is painful. My first husband and I were only married six years. I'd expected we'd go on to have children, and grandchildren, that we'd live out our lives together. When he died I was devastated. It had taken me years to find a man who was interested in me for my own sake, and not for my money. Years. My parents had given up hope of my ever finding a husband. Not that that concerned me particularly. But I had to be *sure*. At last, I met Wilfred and I thought, now I'll be happy. Six years later he was dead of heart failure at the age of thirty-five and I was a thirty-two-year-old widow. For the next ten years I lived a perfectly useless existence, traveling a great deal and having rather too many cocktails before dinner. And then your father was transferred here from New York and darling Roger rang me up to say I simply had to meet his new associate.

"But I'm digressing," she said impatiently. "The point I wanted to make is: It's frightening to find one's self at the end of something. It's especially frightening the older one gets to be. You've done all you could and it's time now to move on. Whatever happens, it can only be for the best. Jeremy is one of the most singularly hateful human beings I've ever met. I grant you, I'm invariably impressed by his abilities as a performer. It never fails to amaze me that he can appear so lovable onstage when he's so utterly unlovable in reality. Let him go, Alyssa! You've proved you're capable of honoring your commitments. It's time now to have a bit of pleasure in your life."

"Why haven't you ever said any of this before?" Aly asked.

Serena shrugged lightly. "You never said before you wanted to be rid of him. One doesn't blithely volunteer one's unsolicited opinions. The thing about marriage is that one can never truly know what it is that holds two people together. If you'd asked my opinion, I'd have happily given it. And bear in mind, my darling, you do have two wonderful daughters. You're not going to be alone."

"What if I lose them?" Aly gave voice to her worst fear.

"How do you imagine that might happen?" Serena asked with a frown.

"They love their father."

"Oh, but my darling, you seem to be forgetting that they love you as well."

Aly smiled, relieved. "I was forgetting that," she admitted.

Just then Suze and Addy came racing in, with Hal following.

"He trounced us in no time flat," Addy announced, flopping down in one of the chairs with her legs over the arm.

"Sit properly, please," Aly said automatically.

"Sorry." Addy sat up as Suze came to sit close to Aly, looping her arm through her mother's.

"Would the two of you like to watch television?" Serena asked.

"Oh!" Addy said. "Serious conversation, is it?"

Suzanne's hand crept into Aly's as she whispered, "Would you like us to go, Mummy?"

"I want to talk to your grandfather and Serena. All right?"

"Yes, all right." Suze slipped off the sofa.

Addy sat a moment longer looking assessingly at her mother before asking, "Are we in trouble?"

"No, you're not in trouble," Aly assured her.

"Honestly?"

"Honestly."

"Okay," she said, jumping up and throwing an arm around her older sister's neck. "Come on, Suze."

"Go easy on your sister, honey," Hal said. "You'll strangle the poor girl. That kid's a pistol," he told Aly. "I get such a kick out of the two of them. Addy reminds me of you when you were her age."

"I know," Aly said. "Sometimes she'll say things and I know that's exactly the way I was."

"You were a pistol, too." He gave her an affectionate smile, then said, "You're looking a bit frazzled, Aly."

"I'm going to tell Jeremy he has to go, Dad."

"I kind of thought that's what it might be," he said soberly. "I've been expecting it."

"It seems that everyone's been expecting it," she said, chagrined to think she'd done such a poor job of concealing her dissatisfaction. "Have the girls said anything?"

He shook his head.

She wanted, all at once, to ask him if he ever thought about Cliffie, if he still missed him. But the timing was all wrong.

"When were you thinking of doing it?" he asked.

"Soon. This week," she answered, and felt her insides clench. "If I don't, it's going to get ugly, and that's the last thing I want. I'm hoping he'll hear me out and just quietly pack his belongings and go. I've gone over the accounts and figured out how much is his."

"Usually it's the other way around," Hal said.

"I know that, Dad. But he's always been hopeless with money, and he has to have something to get set up on his own."

"That ticks me off, Aly. So far as I can see, he's never contributed one red cent to you and the girls. Why the hell should you be giving him money?"

"She wants to be fair, Hal," Serena put in. "It's Aly's decision to make, not ours."

Glad of Serena's assistance, Aly said, "I don't want Addy and Suze to see their father leaving with empty pockets. He's going to have to find a flat, and they'll want to visit him. I've thought it all through very carefully. I have to do what I think is right."

"As far as I'm concerned, you might as well know I think he's been a poor excuse for a husband and an even poorer excuse for a father."

"Dad," Aly said unhappily, "I tried my best."

"Nobody's blaming you, Aly," he said quickly. "I know how hard you've tried. We all do."

"I feel like such a goddamned failure, as if I should've been able to make more of this than I have."

"Sometimes things just don't work out. It happens to the best of us. Remember?"

"I know, but that was different. It wasn't your fault."

"It's not a question of whose fault it is, honey. Your mother and I couldn't make a go of it. It didn't work. I know it sounds as if I'm blaming Jeremy and maybe I am, because I've never been able to warm up to him. But I imagine he's tried his best."

Aly looked at Serena to see how she was reacting to this talk about Rheta. She appeared merely interested and not in the least bothered. "Rheta was ridiculous," Aly said. "I've always had a horror of being like her in any way."

"Don't talk about her that way, honey," he said gently. "She was a lot of things, but she was never ridiculous."

"That's what it's been about, isn't it?" Serena guessed. "You've been trying to avoid your mother's mistakes, haven't you?"

"She made so damned many of them!" Aly said hotly. "The last thing on earth I'd want is to be anything like her." Why was she raging about Rheta this way? Why was she pushing aside the good memories, the happy times? "I'm sorry. I shouldn't have said that."

"Seems to me you've painted a pretty black picture of her," Hal said. "She wasn't a bad woman, Aly. I would never have cared for her if she had been. Her judgment left a little something to be desired, but she was never intentionally unkind, and she did her best for you and Cliff. She was *young*. Do you realize that? She was only a little older than you are now when she died."

"God!" She hadn't thought of that, and it jolted her. Rheta had only been thirty-five when Don killed her. Thirty-five. All those years ago she'd thought of her mother as old. But she hadn't been old at all. That was the child's perspective, and it was inaccurate. "I'm sorry, Dad," she said again. "I'm not thinking clearly."

"Things will sort themselves out," Serena said reassuringly, once more stroking Aly's arm. "And your father and I are always here if you need us."

"We sure are," Hal said. "So you just go ahead and do what you have to do, honey."

Aly drank some of the now cold coffee, thinking they were right. She was building this up too much. She and Jeremy would sit down together and talk. Then he'd leave, and she and the girls would get on with their lives.

CHAPTER
TWENTY-THREE

TIMING WAS crucial. She didn't want to talk to Jeremy in front of the girls. She'd tell them later of her decision. If possible everything would be managed discreetly, calmly. She had a horror of ugly scenes and throughout her marriage had gone to extraordinary lengths to avoid them. Rather than heave crockery at Jeremy when he became maddeningly self-important at the dinner table—he had to have an audience, no matter how small, and invariably opted to voice his grievances in front of the family—she'd either continue eating in silence or, if her appetite was ruined as so often happened, she'd light a cigarette and watch him try to deal not only with his theme of the moment but also with her hated tobacco addiction. The girls had long since stopped taking their father's periodic irascible outbursts seriously. Since his complaints usually concerned his career, Suze and Addy tended to listen with detached bemusement as if to an odd unscheduled radio program.

Nothing went as she'd planned. Jeremy didn't arrive home in time for dinner, nor did he telephone to say when he'd be back. Aly and the girls sat down in the kitchen to eat food from the Chinese takeaway. They were just finishing when Jeremy came bursting in.

"You won't believe it!" he crowed, hugging himself as if to keep from detonating from the sheer overwhelming force of his elation. Face flushed, his eyes burned as if with a fever.

"What?" the girls and Aly asked in unison, their attention caught by his almost drugged look of pleasure.

"Janie put me up for it. I told her I was tired of playing silly sods, but she put me up anyway. I went along just to please her, really. Well, I never dreamed . . . I mean, a series on the telly. It could do wonders for my career, even if it is another daft-bugger part."

"You've got a television series?" Suze asked, a flush now overtaking her features.

"You're going to have your own show?" Addy said, not sure if she should believe this. He often carried on about how this thing or that was going to be the making of him.

"They've signed me for twelve half-hour episodes," he told them excitedly, his eyes on Aly, waiting for her congratulations.

"That's wonderful," Aly said, unable to stop herself from wondering what he'd do this time to screw it up. It was uncharitable, she knew, but she couldn't help thinking it.

"You don't seem especially pleased." He narrowed his eyes slightly as if he was possessed of an internal barometer that measured the reactions of others and hers were falling well below the accepted mark.

"Of course I am," she told him, wondering if tonight would be the best or worst time to ask him to go. He'd be secure in the knowledge that he had work to do. On the other hand, he was at his neediest when he had a contract to fulfill.

"That's super, Dad," Suze said. "When is it going to be on?"

"We start shooting week after next," he answered, his eyes still on Aly. "Twenty-four weeks' work. Janie negotiated a very nice package."

"There's some food left, if you're hungry. I could heat it up for you," Aly offered, reaching for her cigarettes.

"I had a bite with the producer," he said, pacing the length of the kitchen, his long hands flexing at his sides.

Suze sat watching her father, twirling one long strand of hair around and around the fingers of her left hand. Addy, her chin cupped in both hands, looked first at her mother, then at her father, as if watching a rather dull sporting event. Aly smoked her cigarette in silence, fatigued in advance at the prospect of attempting to talk to Jeremy in his present mood, and frightened of putting it off. She'd promised herself she'd speak to him this evening and she didn't dare procrastinate any longer.

223

This felt like her last chance, and if she didn't do it tonight, she might never do it. She and Jeremy would go on together, performing their hobbled little dance, until she was too old and it was far too late to make a break.

"Do you have homework?" she asked the girls.

Addy made one of her faces. She had a seemingly limitless repertoire of wildly funny faces and never hesitated to use them on Aly, knowing she could always make her mother laugh. Aly did laugh, almost choking on a mouthful of smoke, then said, "Yes, but do you have homework?" which got all three of them laughing while Jeremy either ignored them or failed to hear.

"You could just tell us to bugger off," Addy said boldly, knowing Aly wouldn't make a big to-do over her swearing. "You needn't ask if we have homework."

"All right!" Aly laughed. "Bugger off, the two of you. And do you homework."

Delighted as ever by her younger sister's daring, Suze stood up, saying, "It's our turn to clear." She cast an uncertain glance over at her father who was on the return leg of one of his laps of the kitchen, then looked to Addy for some cue.

"Never mind. You owe me one," Aly said.

"We only owe you half," Addy corrected her. "Chinese takeaway doesn't count as a whole one." She grinned wickedly, then gave her sister a punch on the arm and went running off, calling over her shoulder, "Nice one, Dad! Congratulations!"

Jeremy halted his pacing to watch Addy go racing through the dining room with Suze following at a more sedate pace. They made little sense to him, those two girls, the younger one even less than the older. Much of the time he couldn't tell if Addy was being sarcastic or simply making a straightforward remark. Suze was her opposite, reluctant to say very much of anything. When she did speak it was in so small a voice she could barely be heard. He saw nothing of himself in the girls, and rarely knew what to say to them. They were too absorbed in fashion magazines, in rock stars, in lengthy giggling conversations with their equally incomprehensible girlfriends, and in boys who cluttered up the lounge on weekends. They were untidy, sometimes disrespectful, and a complete mystery to him; they gave him gifts at Christmas and on his birthday; they came along on opening nights whenever he appeared in a show and his associates and fellow performers made a great fuss over them, but even though he felt proud of the attention they received, he wasn't at all clear on what being a father was really supposed to mean.

Who was he? Aly wondered yet again. Was there another Jeremy inside that lanky frame struggling for ascendancy? Or had his hateful grandmother killed off that boy decades earlier? And what had attracted her to Jeremy? Had she ever actually been attracted to him? Or had she simply succumbed to her own need to perpetuate the pure physical pleasure he'd introduced into her life? She'd found him touching at the outset, but there'd been no particular attraction. It was to Andrew she'd always been drawn, on just about every level, but she'd learned to sublimate her very strong response to the physical aspects of the appeal he had for her. Sexual attraction was bound to lead only to trouble. Occasionally she felt tempted to caution her daughters regarding men. She resisted of course, well aware of how unreasonable that would be. She had no right to try to influence or to prejudice them. Besides they probably wouldn't pay any more attention to her advice that she had to that which Andrew and her father had given her.

But there were so many hazards to dealing with men. If you granted them intimate access to your nakedness, there was every likelihood the act would cost you dearly. Look what Jeremy had done to Liz! For that matter, look what he'd done to her! He'd bulldozed everyone and everything standing in his path in order to get to her. And for what? So he'd have someone to blame when things failed to go as he wished; a handy human hook upon which he could hang his inability to follow through on those unsubtle flirtations he occasionally tried on for size; a living accessory to add gloss, by reflection, to his public image. Rheta would never have tolerated ten percent of what Aly had put up with. Rheta might have allowed the men to decide on the timing of their arrivals and departures, but she'd never have put up with her "sweeties" deviating from what she saw as the acceptable course of their behavior. The men all had to be willing to participate in the *tableaux*; they had to be attentive and demonstrative; and above all, they had to be completely smitten by her. She'd never brought home a man who, at the outset, didn't get a glazed expression at the mere sight of her. Jeremy, once they were married, had never even pretended to be excited by her. Andrew was right, and so was Serena; she should have ended this long ago.

"You're sure you're not hungry?" she asked, preparing to clear the table.

He shook his head and watched her stack the plates then carry them to the sink. They'd pretty well killed off his excitement, the three of them. Here he'd landed a bloody series and they treated it matter-of-factly as if he'd done nothing more important than emptying the dustbins. His Gran would've been thrilled; she'd've gone sailing off, speculating on how the series would give his career a much needed push, how being on the telly once a week would make him a household name; how he'd have a new major credit to add to his resumé.

"Jeremy," Aly said, "we really have to talk."

His head jerked up and he looked at her round-eyed. "What about?" he asked, immediately alert to possible trouble.

"About us, about this family, about the fact that we don't have much of a marriage." He stood motionless, listening. She badly wanted a cigarette but didn't dare move to get one. Having started this, she was determined to see it through to the end. "We have nothing to say to each other," she went on. "The last time the two of us went out for dinner we sat three solid hours without talking. It was one of the worst evenings of my life. I felt as if I were sitting with a stranger, someone I'd never met before. I don't see any point to our continuing on this way, not when we have nothing to say to each other. Maybe the timing's right," she said, suffering all the symptoms she'd described to Andrew. Her hands were wet, her throat ached, and her stomach was clenched like a fist. "You'll be busy on this new series for months, and you know how you are when you're working. You get completely wrapped up in it. We never see you, and we don't dare interrupt if you're running your lines; not to mention tiptoeing around the house so we don't break your concentration. I think this might be a good time for you to move out, find a place of your own." She paused to allow him to respond. He didn't say a word, just continued to gaze fixedly at her. "I'm sorry," she said sincerely, the ache in her throat becoming worse. "More than anything else, I wanted this to work. But we're not going anywhere. You don't seem particularly happy, and I know I'm not. The girls get on your nerves with their music and their friends. It'll be better for all of us if we separate now."

"I see," he said thickly, his eyes fastened to her as if to a lifeline.

"We've given it fifteen years," she said, floundering. "There's no point to giving it fifteen years more, not when neither of us is happy. I, uhm. . . ." She had to stop, go for her cigarettes, get one lit—his eyes on her all the while—then start again. "I thought we could do it quietly, keep it amicable, for the girls' sake."

"You've discussed this with them?" he asked, his expression sliding into one that accused her of betrayal.

"Not yet. I wanted to talk it over with you first, naturally. I've been going over the accounts and I, uhm. . . . Well, you'll need something to help you get started in a place of your own." She reached into her pocket for the check she'd written that afternoon and handed it to him.

"I see," he said again, at last looking away from her to the paper in his hand. "Well, actually, I was thinking of leaving myself."

He had to say that to save face, she told herself, but it nevertheless infuriated her. Her carefully contained anger threatened to swamp her but she held it down. "This should work out perfectly, then," she said, drawing so hard on the cigarette it stung the inside of her lips. "I'll talk to the girls, explain everything."

He held the check with both hands as if he were reading a book, then looked back at her asking, "Is this all?"

The air seemed to leave her lungs in a rush. "*All?*" she wheezed. "Five thousand pounds and you ask is that all? I'm not obligated to give you anything, Jeremy. You do have your own bank account."

"I have a lifestyle to maintain."

"You also have an income to help you do it." She took another furious drag on the cigarette, a strange buzzing in her hands and feet as if live electricity had started coursing through her body.

"And what am I to use for furnishings?" he asked.

"That's what the check is for!"

"It's not going to pay for much, is it?"

"It'll pay for enough. You won't be living in a furnished bed-sitter, the way you were fifteen years ago. You've got plenty of money in the bank."

"I don't see why I shouldn't take a few things. . . ."

He was doing it, nit-picking, pulling threads from seams, poking away at what she was trying to tell him. It was why his fellow performers so disliked him, why directors would never use him more than once. It was the self-involved, inward-turned focus that made him something considerably less than human. And she despised him for it, hated the way his mouth shaped the words, loathed every last thing about him from the over-priced badly done caps some dentist had insisted would improve his looks to his bony wrists and ugly gray socks. She could scarcely believe she'd tolerated this utterly detestable creature for so many years. Her control simply evaporated; she felt it going but could do nothing to prevent it.

"Take whatever you goddamned want!" she shouted. "I don't *care* what you take! I just want you out of here! I want you to go now!" Her anger exploding to the surface, she threw her cigarette into the sink and went racing up to the bedroom. Heaving open the wardrobe doors she began dragging his clothes off the hangers, tossing them on the floor. When he appeared in the doorway, an amused smirk on his face, as if this were a scene from a play that he'd seen performed more effectively by some other actress, she grabbed up pairs of his shoes and started throwing them at him. He stood there, letting the shoes strike him, his smirk fueling her rage. *"I want you out of my life!"* she cried, winded from her exertions and maddened by his refusal to show any reaction. "I don't care where you go or what

you do! I'm sick of the sight of you, sick of everything about you." She sounded like Rheta! She could hear her mother's voice coming out of her mouth. She was behaving and sounding just like Rheta but she couldn't stop. She stormed to the door and pushed him out of her way, stopping dead in the hall at the sight of Suze and Addy standing just outside the door, their faces pallid and shock-filled.

She had to put her hand on the wall to keep herself from falling, the fear and anger blending dizzyingly inside her. This was where it happened, this was how the world came to an end. In the bedroom a man she'd tried to force herself to love was picking up his clothes from the floor, his movements lazily confident. The echo of her strident cries—Rheta's voice—hung like bands of livid color in the air, shameful banners of her lost control.

Addy asked, "What's the matter?" Her usually mischievous features were flattened by uncertainty. "What's happening?"

Aly opened her mouth but couldn't speak. She'd turned into Rheta; she was re-enacting a scene that had taken place with Jerry and Adam and Martin.

"Mummy?" Suze took several steps toward her, then halted. She looked into the bedroom where Jeremy had several suitcases open on the bed and was methodically packing his clothes. "Are you getting a divorce?" she asked, her eyes still on her father.

Aly could only nod. Her heartbeat was so tumultuous she wondered if the girls could hear it, if they could see her body pulsing; she wondered if as well as sounding like Rheta she now suddenly looked like her, too.

"Weren't you going to tell us?" Addy asked, moving to stand next to her sister to see what Jeremy was doing.

"Of course I was," Aly managed to get out.

"When?" Addy wanted to know.

She was angry. Aly wanted to beg her not to be angry, wanted her to wait and hear the facts, understand why this was happening. There were reasons, dozens of them, hundreds. If she could just catch her breath, overcome her suffocating fear she'd be able to explain herself, answer their questions.

"What did Daddy do?" Suze asked, stepping into the bedroom, stopping halfway between her parents. "What's wrong?" she asked Jeremy who paused in his packing to shrug and stare wordlessly at her.

"It's not any one thing," Aly said, thinking it was futile. How could she ever recite her lengthy list of complaints against him? Would they even sound reasonable? Probably not. Most people would think she was throwing away a perfectly good marriage, discarding something others would view as worth keeping. But they didn't know this man, didn't know how little he valued what so many people treasured—communication, his children, people in general.

"Where are you going, Dad?" Addy asked. "Have you got a place yet?"

"Not yet," he said uncertainly, looking to Aly for help. She had no desire to help him. She wanted the girls to see what he really was, how inept and unconcerned he was. But she hated to see anyone, even Jeremy, suffer. "Addy, please," she said. "Nothing's been settled." Experimentally she withdrew her hand from the wall and managed to remain upright, although everything seemed grotesquely telescoped and there was a loud rushing in her ears. The tension stretched between the four of them like an invisible filament. The slightest movement might cause it to snap. They'd be cast into darkness if any one of them made too sudden a move or gesture.

"Is it forever?" Suze asked. "We're never going to live together again?"

"I don't think so," Aly answered.

"It's what your mother wants," Jeremy said spitefully, intent on placing blame.

"Yes, it is," she agreed. "I'm sorry, but it is."

Without making a sound, Suze began to cry.

Addy cocked her head to one side, looking at each of them in turn, then she stepped into the room, took Suze by the wrist and said, "Your blubbering's not going to help." Leading her sister down the hall, she paused in front of Aly to say, "Will you be along to talk with us?"

"In a minute or two," Aly promised.

"Put a sock in it, Suze," Addy ordered, towing her sister into her room and closing the door behind them.

Jeremy finished packing the last of the suitcases, lifted them off the bed one by one, picked up the two biggest and carried them out of the room and down the stairs to the front hall. Taking the stairs three at a time, he returned, got the last case and positioned it next to the others. His movements exaggerated, perhaps for her benefit so that she'd see how deeply she'd wounded him, he put on his hat, opened the door, and began carrying the bags out to the car. His acting talent required distance in order to be effective. Up close, the mechanics showed. He needed the lights, and the makeup, and at least twenty feet separating him from the audience in order to be convincing.

Aly stood watching until he was leaving with the last bag.

He looked up to where she was standing at the top of the stairs, his expression that of the orphan child he'd been more than thirty years before, and said, "Well, I'll be going now," and paused, gazing up at her with such a lost bewildered expression that she couldn't help responding. In the last analysis, he was a child and always would be. He was stunted in such fundamental ways that there was no possibility he'd ever grow. And somewhere, very deep inside him, he had some inkling of the retardation. But it would be far too damaging for him ever to admit to it, because then he'd have nothing at all left to hold on to. She ran down the stairs to throw her arms around him, breaking into tears as she held him one last time; breathing in the so-familiar scent of him and remembering occasions at the very beginning when she'd cared for him, when she'd been profoundly touched by his silly pretensions and been made proud by his undeniable presence on a stage. She hugged him hard and abruptly released him, stepping back out of his embrace to see the same lost child expression creasing his face.

"Right," he said after a moment, his features clearing. "Well, good-bye, then," he said, and was gone. The door was closed. Blotting her face with a tissue, she listened to the sound of his car starting up, then driving off. Gone. She'd done it. She was alone with her girls. No blood had been shed, no mortal wounds inflicted. She'd gone a bit out of control, but only a bit. And she'd been able to regain herself despite the horror of hearing Rheta's voice issuing from her mouth. Andrew had said she could do it, and she had. She'd done it! It was going to be all right. Perhaps she'd telephone Andrew in Italy before she went to bed and tell him. He'd be so proud of her. Christ! She'd actually, finally, done it.

With a sigh, she went along to knock at Addy's door. The girls were sitting side by side on the bed, Suze still crying, still very red in the face. Aly sat down in the rocker.

"We've been talking," Addy said, looking exceptionally self-possessed for someone only thirteen years old.

"I'm sure you have," Aly said. "I'm truly sorry about the way this happened. It wasn't at all the way I planned it. I'm afraid I got very upset."

"It's all right, really," Suze sniffed. "I understand."

"So do I," Addy said. "I'm honestly not surprised. I've been telling Suze for ages the two of you were bound to split up."

"You have?" Aly was astounded. "What made you think that?"

"Oh, the way the two of you were ever so polite to one another, for one thing. Lots of things, really. Suze didn't want to believe me, did you, Suze?" Suze shook her head. "But I knew. I've thought a lot about it, actually."

"You have?" Aly repeated.

"I have," Addy confirmed. "You and Daddy aren't really suited to one another. He's not a very strong person, not in the way you are. He doesn't know how to fight the way you do. I don't mean actually fight. You know. I mean being strong, knowing what you want to do and doing it, that sort of thing."

"That's probably true," Aly said, impressed by her reasoning.

"Oh, I think it is true," Addy said earnestly. "Not having parents and being raised by his gran who, from the little I remember, was a frightful old cow, I don't think he ever learned. It's why he's so good when he's onstage, because that's when he can have everything the way he imagines it."

"I had no idea you'd given this so much thought," Aly said with a smile.

"I have," she confirmed. "I've thought a great great deal about it. And that's why, when he finds a place, I think I'd like to go live with Dad. You wouldn't need me the way he does."

Her child wanted to leave. She'd failed her. Aly's head nod-ded. "I see," she said, amazed she could still speak. "You're sure of this?" she asked, thinking it had to be a mistake. How could this be happening when she'd made such a monumental effort not to duplicate Rheta's mistakes?

"I'm sure," Addy said.

Aly nodded again. She wouldn't allow herself to give any hint of the pain, the monstrous scalding pain. She wouldn't com-pound the failure by revealing the hurt. Children invariably perceived displays of that sort as a form of blackmail. But it was possible, she now discovered, to scream without making a sound. And she knew, sickeningly, exactly how Rheta had felt that day she'd made her own announcement. Her eyes shifted to Suzanne. "Suze, do you want to go too?" she asked in a whisper, terrified by the prospect of having failed both her children.

"I want to stay here with you," Suze sobbed. "I hate this! Why does it have to happen?"

"I'm deeply sorry," Aly whispered, leaving the rocker, each movement—of shoulders, arms, torso, legs, feet—compound-ing the rending pain inside. "Go to sleep now," she said, bend-ing to kiss each of the girls in turn. "You're both exhausted. I'll see you in the morning."

She held everything in until she'd gone through the house checking the doors and windows, turning off lights; kept it all inside until the bedroom and bathroom doors were carefully locked. Then she undressed and sat on the tub floor with the shower creating a noise barrier that crashed down on her and allowed the racking cries to break her chest while she pulled at her hair, pummeled the pathetic flesh that housed her, and cursed herself for being fool enough to believe she could tamper with destiny by pandering to its whims. It didn't matter if you followed the rules, if you made not one of the mistakes Rheta made. It made no difference if you denied every last one of your instincts, whether healthy or not, and lived strictly ac-cording to the highest possible code of behavior you could de-vise. In the end you were Rheta's child, she lived on inside you, and that alone was what mattered.

AN INTERLUDE

She held her hand over her mouth and looked around the room wishing she hadn't come here tonight. Normally she enjoyed the slightly eccentric charm of Andrew's spacious flat. He'd acquired a number of precious antiques when the parentals sold off the family home, and had furnished the place around them, making the Chippendale desk, the étagère housing four Lalique bowls, and the pair of Queen Anne chairs the highlights of the lounge. He'd added a long clean-lined sofa, a low white marble coffee table that complimented the fireplace facade, and a deep blue Oriental carpet. The walls were Wedgwood blue with white trim; sheer white curtains covered the trio of windows overlooking the river. She loved this place; she loved this man; but she couldn't make love with him. It was something she'd thought she wanted, and had agreed to come to dinner this evening with the idea in mind that they might, finally, take that step. But here they were, not yet finished their aperitifs; the cigarette she'd lit after her first swallow of Bristol Cream was still burning in the ashtray. He'd leaned over to kiss her and she'd reacted internally as if she were having a heart seizure. Reaching for her cigarette now, she said, "I'm sorry but I really can't do this."

"You blame me, don't you?" he said sadly. "I pushed you to get rid of Jeremy. It didn't turn out quite as you'd hoped, and now you blame me."

"I don't blame anyone . . . except myself."

"But why, for God's sake?" he asked, mystified by her reasoning.

"It's been more than two years and Addy apparently has no intention of coming back. Doesn't that tell you anything?"

"Yes," he said slowly. "It tells me she has a soft spot for her father. I can't think why you'd interpret that as a strike against you. As you've pointed out to me any number of times, he is *their father. They* do *care for him. It does* not *mean she doesn't care about you." He waited for her to say something. When she didn't, hoping to lighten the mood, he laughed and said, "I wasn't planning to have you on the sofa prior to the first course."*

She looked directly into his eyes and said, "Yes you were."

"All right. I was. One can but hope." He picked up his glass and drank, then said, "Probably just nerves, sproggy. First time at bat since the split, and all that."

She shook her head, put out the cigarette and at once lit another.

234

"That doesn't begin to cover it." She wet her lips and looked at him. *"I do love you, Andrew. I always have."*

"And that depresses you, does it?" he teased.

"You probably should forget about me. I have nothing to give you."

"What's this all about, Alyssa? It's time to give old Andrew the push because the naughty boy wants to get amorous?"

She shrugged and at once regretted the gesture. It was Jeremy's favorite way to deal with questions he didn't want to answer. *"I thought I did too, but evidently I have a problem."*

"Is this a problem you've had before?"

She tapped the ash off her cigarette, then forced a laugh and shook her head. *"Well, Doctor, I'll tell you. Some time ago, I began to hate myself every time I allowed my former husband to touch me. At the end, we almost never . . . maybe on three occasions during that last year we engaged in activities of a sexual nature."* She made a face and averted her eyes.

"But you didn't love him. Surely that's a factor."

"You'd make a good therapist," she said, and shook her head again. *"Unfortunately, my feelings for Jeremy were never relevant to our sexual skirmishes."*

"Why don't you call it what it is?" he asked, increasingly perplexed. *"Lovemaking."*

"What he and I did together had nothing to do with love. We had encounters, activities, skirmishes. The only things we ever actually made *were Suzanne and Adele. Suzanne, as you well know, was an accident. Adele was a conscious decision on my part."*

"Fair enough."

"My mother, you know, thought she was in love every time she found some new man sexually appealing."

"What on earth has that to do with you?"

"Nothing. Everything. I might as well tell you now," she said, taking a deep breath. *"I'm going to New York, Andrew. Lilbet's eighty years old; she's not well, and I want to be with her. Suzanne's off to Cambridge in a few months and Addy's staying on with her father. I've listed the house with estate agents, and bought quite a nice flat off Sloane Square. Dad and Serena are going to keep an eye on it while I'm away."*

Dumfounded, he sat back and stared at her. *"For how long? And why haven't you told me any of this?"*

"I don't know," she said truthfully. *"I kept intending to, but somehow*

it was never the right time. Then, finally, I promised myself I'd tell you tonight. . . ."

"What about your practise, your patients?"

"I've given it all up. Christ!" She stubbed out her cigarette and stood up. "I think I should go. I hate the way I sound and I hate the way you're looking at me."

"I think I deserve a moment or two to absorb all this. Don't you? I mean, you've just given me one hell of a shock."

She sat back down and at once lit another cigarette.

"It isn't as if I'm not in New York several times a year," he said, thinking aloud. "But you seem to be saying you'd prefer it if I stayed away. Have I got that correct, Alyssa?"

"Perhaps," she said hesitantly.

"I see," he said, chastened. "You do blame me."

"I love you. I can't!" She broke off and looked wildly around the room. "I can't spoil it! We'd spoil it. We'd destroy everything we value in each other." She dropped the cigarette into the ashtray, jumped up, and hurried to the door.

"Do you hear how you sound?" he cried, racing after her. "Do you have any idea how ridiculous and unfair to both of us you're being?"

"We're spoiling it now!" she cried, struggling to get the door open.

"Don't run off this way, Alyssa. This isn't how one deals with anything."

"I couldn't bear to fail with you, too, Andrew. That really would be the end." Tears distorted her vision, turned her breathing uneven.

"You haven't failed. Why do you keep on insisting that you have?"

"I lost control completely that night I asked him to go. I screamed, and threw things at him. I was a disgrace, made myself look ridiculous in my children's eyes."

"You're not allowed to be human like the rest of us?" he asked incredulously. "You're not allowed to have moments of weakness? Come on, Alyssa. That's utterly unrealistic."

"You don't understand," she sobbed, at last getting the door open. "Don't run away, please."

"I can't stay here and make even more of a fool of myself."

"I see," he said unhappily. "And what am I to do?"

"I don't know!" she cried, escaping.

"Don't call us. We'll call you! Is that it? Have I got it right, Alyssa?"

he shouted as she ran down the stairs. "Is that it? Is it? Why couldn't you stay and try to work it out? Why?"

His words struck her spine like poisoned darts, but she kept going. One day he'd understand that she had to leave in order to preserve their feelings for each other, to keep what they had unsullied and safe.

PART FOUR

New York, 1978

CHAPTER
TWENTY-FOUR

S HE WAS thirty-five. It seemed old to her until when sitting with Lilbet, she was struck by the inescapable reality that actual aging had more to do with physical deterioration and less with emotional wear and tear. Lilbet was as acutely aware as she'd ever been; mind and eye remained in harmony; her talent for magnificent self-presentation was intact. But her flesh fell like a loose-fitting garment over her bones and despite her lifelong efforts to maintain its clarity her skin was now splashed with the telltale tea-stain blotches of age. While she was still beautiful, her beauty had become like the stately dominance of a cathedral—formidable and perennially impressive, but of the past. Aly knew, looking at her grandmother, how she herself would probably look at eighty, and it was oddly comforting to be able to see this softly-focused somewhat gauzy future portrait of herself.

"You can't be eighty!" Aly accused fondly. "You look nowhere near that old!"

"You, honey, look barely more than a child to me," Lilbet replied. "And it's nobody's business how old I am." Head held high, shoulders squared, spine straight as a yardstick, she said, "A lady never tells her age." She lit a Camel, puffed with satisfaction, then continued. "And she never complains, not if she wants folks to keep on coming around." She reached to tilt Aly's face toward the light, studying her intently for several moments before withdrawing her hand. "Just you remember to keep your hands away from your face and you'll never have a problem with your complexion."

Aly smiled. "I remember you used to say that to Rheta."

"Drove her wild. She always was stubborn, never wanted to listen to a thing anyone had to say. But I'm right, you know. Just think of all the dirt and germs on a woman's hands and it has to make sense." She took another puff of her cigarette, then daintily plucked a bit of tobacco from her lip with two manicured fingernails.

"How do you feel? You don't look as if you've had a sick day in your life."

"All those years in England, you've got an accent now. You know that?"

"I don't hear it," Aly said, "but Sharon said the same thing, so I guess I must have. Now, come on. Tell me. How are you really?"

"According to my doctor it's nothing short of a miracle I'm still around." She snorted and gave a slight shake of her head. "I don't have much faith in members of the medical profession. This youngster wants me to lie down and be dead because it says so in one of his textbooks. I refuse to die to accommodate some young man's notion of medical correctitude."

Aly laughed appreciatively.

"You laugh," Lilbet said, "but you simply wouldn't credit the number of my friends who've been good obedient senior citizens and died to accommodate some jackass doctor's diagnosis. Folks get old and it seems to turn them gullible. I may be old, honey, but I have no intention of taking to my bed and waiting to die there because some doctor says that's the way it's supposed to go. I plan to be taken by surprise," she declared. "I'll be having a cocktail and a cigarette and, bam, that'll be that. It's plain undignified to lie around, waiting for the end, like you've got nothing better to do."

"I agree," Aly said.

"Of course you do. Any sensible person would." She took one last puff of her cigarette and put it out. "Now, tell me. How are the girls? And your father? And that heavenly Serena?"

Aly dutifully launched into a rosy-tinted narrative about the family, filling Lilbet in on what the girls had been doing since

242

their visit with her some months earlier, and describing her own most recent stay with her father and Serena at the summer house in Cornwall. She wished Lilbet hadn't asked. As long as she didn't have to think about what she'd left behind in London she was fine. She was able to give herself over to her grandmother's world, to its rules and ceremonies and southern gentility; she could sleep in the same room she'd had in this apartment since childhood, and eat the food prepared by Lucille, the housekeeper who'd replaced Pearl ten years earlier; she could live out her role as beloved grandchild and pay lavish caring attention on the one person in her life who remained exactly where and who she'd always been. But the moment she was required to be the ex-wife of Jeremy Gable whose short-lived television series was currently being rerun, and the mother of Adele who preferred to live with the presently unemployed Gable, and of Suzanne who'd just started her first year at Cambridge pursuing her interest in modern English, she spun so rapidly down a tightly-coiled spiral of depression that she had to rely on her skimpy acting ability to conceal it.

She'd been successful in the three weeks since her arrival in maintaining a cheerful facade for Lilbet's benefit. She had, however, confided to her old friend Sharon Ackerman some of her true feelings. While there was a certain undeniable comfort in exchanging confidences with someone she'd not only known since kindergarten but who was also female, she missed her communication with Andrew. She missed their almost daily telephone conversations, his spontaneous invitations to dinner, and his attentiveness; she missed the sight of his face and the feel of his hand taking hold of hers to cross a street. She could still hear him shouting as she ran from him, and grieved over the loss of their friendship. No one could ever replace him. And she'd injured him so profoundly it was doubtful they'd be able to resurrect what they'd had. She missed him, couldn't stop thinking about him, and much of the time felt a constant dull pain in the base of her belly. Sharon insisted she needed to get out. "Play the gay divorcée," she advised. "Enjoy being single again!"

"There is no need for you to babysit me," Lilbet told her. "A young woman like you should be out socializing, not sitting indoors during the prime years of her life. And tell that darling Sharon I just adored those pralines. I wouldn't say no to another box."

"I'll tell her," Aly promised, and went off to phone.

SHARON HAD a wonderful face, with large glowing brown eyes and a wide ever-smiling mouth. Everyone liked her. Strangers on the street would stop to talk to her. She was big and round and generous in every way, from her inability to say no to panhandlers to her openness with friends. With Sharon it was never too late at night to be calling, never inconvenient, never a bother. Men all but lined up to get dates with her, but she refused to cancel out on a woman friend to accommodate any man.

"It's like when I was in high school and two of us would go together to a school dance. She'd get asked to dance. I'd hold up the wall. Then two hours later, she'd be coming over saying, 'I'm going home with Harold. Okay, Shar? You don't mind, do you?' And I always thought what a crummy thing that was to do, dump your girlfriend because some guy with sweaty hands, acne, and halitosis was willing to walk you home. Same thing in college. You'd make a date to go to the movies or something on a Saturday night. Last minute, she'd get a call from some lame-O with a hard-on and it'd be, 'I hate to do this to you, Shar, but Larry called and I couldn't say no.' After my sophomore year when the gonads brigade finally discovered I existed, I swore I'd never dump a girlfriend for some guy. No matter what. Drives men crazy if you say no. Have you noticed that?"

"I've never been in a position to notice," Aly said.

Sharon laughed loudly. "Yeah, that's right. The child bride. Jeez! We've got to get you a life, woman."

"I don't think we're going to find it here," Aly said, looking around the crowded restaurant. They'd spent twenty minutes at the packed bar waiting for a table to come free. "I've never seen anything like this," she said, watching men cruise the crowd, stopping to talk to women whose looks they liked.

"This is nothing. Late sixties, early seventies it was like those scabby islands in the Pacific that're totally covered with penguins or weird little birds, all looking to mate. These places," Sharon said, taking in the scene with interest, "women come looking for love and maybe a decent burger. The guys're all here to score. Shirts open to there, chest hair, and gold chains." She gave one of her booming laughs. "Thousands of polyesters died to outfit these geniuses." She glanced at her watch, then looked at Aly saying, "Twenty says you get hit on a minimum five times before we get to the coffee."

"You can't be serious," Aly smiled.

Sharon opened her oversized handbag, fished around inside, came out with a twenty dollar bill and said, "Here's my Mr. Jackson. Let's see yours."

"Never mind. I believe you."

"The burger is decent," Sharon said seriously. "So're the home fries. Otherwise, even with the free entertainment, I wouldn't put up with the bullshit wait. I hate waiting." She looked again at her watch. "Five minutes and then we go up the street for Mexican. Okay with you?"

"Sure. Jesus! I feel like a complete alien."

"Far as I'm concerned, sweetheart," Sharon grinned widely, "you are." She drank some of her red wine, her attention caught by a pair of men who appeared as out of place here as Aly did. They were both wearing suits and ties. The older of the two, mid- to late-thirties, was preternaturally good-looking, with deep-set dark eyes, a long sculpted nose balanced by a strong squared chin, slanting jawline, and well-shaped sensuous mouth. Olive-skinned, he wore his thick brown hair cut short and side parted. Touches of gray at the temple, manicured fingers holding the menu over the top of which he was gazing fixedly at Aly.

"That'll be numero uno for the night," Sharon decided, subtly directing Aly's eyes to the table by the window.

Aly looked over, her eyes made a connection, and her stomach lurched. She looked away at once, forcing a laugh. "Don't be silly," she said, and opened her bag for her cigarettes. She'd never had anyone look at her with quite such intensity.

"Mr. Jackson's going to have company tonight, woman. These weasels have never even *dreamed* of having a crack at something like you. Half of them've had drool running down

245

their chins since you came through the door. This's fun."
Sharon grinned again. "Feel kind of like a voyeur, but hey. Oh,
finally!" she said, as the hostess signalled to them. "A table after
only a three-day wait."

Every time Aly ventured to look in his direction it was to find
him staring intently at her. She worked to pay attention to
Sharon and to her dinner but those eyes drew at her and she
couldn't help glancing over, then at once averting her gaze,
feeling overheated and vaguely imperiled. She knew, without
actually knowing how or why, precisely what was going on in
the man's mind, and she wondered if there was something
about her that he seemed to recognize. They'd never seen one
another before, but he'd identified her, and she felt helplessly
transparent.

"Looks like a South American movie star, or an Italian count.
Probably just another weasel but with bucks," Sharon specu-
lated, enjoying herself as she worked her way through a me-
dium burger with Swiss, mushrooms and bacon, side of home
fries and a second glass of red wine. "Other guy's gotta be the
bodyguard. Check out the way the muscles strain the nice suit."
She shook her head. "Too much. How d'you like your burger?"

"Delicious," Aly answered.

"Burgers're about the only things next to Mexican I'll eat out
anymore. I cook French and Italian way better than most of the
restaurants charge you a month's rent. I make extra when I'm
doing a job, a wedding, bar mitzvah, party, what have you,
throw a few of this or that in the freezer. Always have plenty of
good stuff if people drop by. Ma says if she'd've thought of
going into the catering business like me, she'd've never stayed
married to the old man for forty-two years."

"I still remember your lunches," Aly said. "Every day I hoped
you'd want to share with me. Cliffie and I used to make our own."

"Ma always made extra for you. D'you know that?"

"No. How kind of her!"

"She was crazy for you," Sharon said proudly. "Thought you
were the most gorgeous kid she ever saw. She could never get
over what a sharp little number you were. Every time you came
over she'd *kvell*. Maybe some Sunday when I go visit, you'll
come with. She'd love to see you."

"Sure. I'd like that."

"That guy's in love, swear to God!" Sharon said in an undertone. "Amazed his lap's not filled with food. He hasn't taken his
eyes off you once. He doesn't make a move, I'll eat my hat. Oh,
okay. The bodyguard's going."

Aly laughed, feeling it ease the tension in her shoulders.
"You're wonderful," she said, deriving pleasure from the sight
of Sharon's glowing features framed by her mane of luxurious
auburn hair. "You really are."

"Everybody says so." Sharon held her napkin to her mouth,
then said, "Holy shit! This is too much!"

"What?"

"Just kind of slide your head around to one side and look out
the window. See it?"

"What?"

"The limo the size of Yankee Stadium."

"So?"

"Guess who just climbed into the driver's seat? Right! Nunzio,
the bodyguard. It's not even a rental."

"How can you tell?"

"The plates. What the hell're those two doing here?" she
wondered, reaching for her wine. "This is better than a double
feature. The polo player's having a cigarette now with his coffee, hasn't taken his eyes off you once. I gotta wizz. Be right
back."

Aly put down her knife and fork and reached for her cigarettes. Just as she got one lit, a pen and an open notebook were
placed on the table in front of her. "Write down your number,"
he said, in a husky unaccented voice.

As if mesmerized, she switched the cigarette to her right
hand and took hold of the pen, looking up at him.

"I'm Nicholas." At close range his eyes seemed to give off
heat. She nodded, lowered her head and quickly printed Dr. A.
Brown and Lilbet's telephone number. What was she doing?
she wondered, as her hand moved of its own volition, giving the
requested information. This was crazy. It was the kind of thing
she might have imagined Rheta doing. Rheta had met her men
in all sorts of unlikely places—bars, restaurants, jazz clubs,
supermarkets. "I'll call you," he promised, tucking the note-

book and pen into his breast pocket. She nodded again, reached for her cigarette and when she looked back he was leaving the restaurant. She watched the driver open the rear door. Nicholas slid into the car. A moment. Then the black machine with its dark-tinted windows slid out of sight. Was she trying in some bizarre way to replicate her mother's actions? That was ridiculous. She had no idea, really, of the things Rheta had done during her hours away from home.

"What'd he say?" Sharon asked breathlessly, hurrying back to the table.

"His name is Nicholas."

"And?"

"That's all he said."

"Are you *kidding*? My name is Nicholas, and that's it?"

"That's it," Aly confirmed, drawing hard on her cigarette. Her knees were pressed so tightly together her thighs ached. Once more she saw his slim-fingered, olive-skinned hand reach for the heavy gold pen, the leatherbound notebook. Long dark eyelashes, carved nostrils, perfect teeth, husky compelling voice. "Jesus!" she gave a shaky laugh, unable to believe what she'd done.

"What?"

"Nothing. I wouldn't mind another glass of wine."

Sharon at once swivelled around, signalling to the waiter. "So was he South American or what?"

"North American," Aly told her.

"Give us two more of this purple Kool Aid," Sharon told the waiter.

He guffawed appreciatively, cleared the table, and went off to get their wine.

"*And*? Jeez! It's like pulling teeth."

"I gave him my number," Aly admitted, heat and color flooding her face.

"He said 'My name is Nicholas,' and you went so crazy for the sound of his voice you gave him your number? I don't believe it!" Mouth open, Sharon stared at her.

"I know. I don't know why I did that. I think I've finally lost my mind altogether."

The waiter returned with the wine, asking, "Dessert, girls?"

248

"Women," Sharon said patiently. "Repeat after me: women."

"Dessert, women?" he parroted, beaming at Sharon.

"You got a menu or d'you recite?" she asked him.

"Carrot cake, pecan pie, ice cream," he recited.

"Nothing for me," Aly said, lighting a fresh cigarette, thinking she'd just done something monumentally stupid, and potentially dangerous. A woman didn't give her telephone number to a man she didn't know, not even one whose eyes signalled intimate recognition. You could wind up getting hurt, even killed, doing such impulsive things. Had it come to this? she wondered. Was she angling to have history repeat itself down to the last detail? In that fraction of a second after the trigger was pulled, did you feel the pain?

"What's the ice cream?" Sharon was asking. "It's not Häagen Daz, just bring a couple of coffees."

"Two coffees." He saluted, did a smart about-face, and went off.

"Nice buns. Cute guy altogether," Sharon said. "For someone about fifteen years old. You notice how after thirty everybody looks ten years old to you? What?" she asked. "You've got a face like a witness at a road accident."

"Why did I do that?" Aly said, stunned.

"He asked me, I'd've done it," Sharon said equably, "even if he is married. D'you notice that?"

Aly nodded, then held up her left hand. "Didn't seem to stop either one of us."

"That's the problem with the world today," Sharon said. "Nobody respects jewelry anymore."

Aly burst out laughing. Sharon patted her on the hand saying, "It's no big deal. I mean, hey! He calls, you can always say no. And you didn't give him your address, just the phone number, right? So don't worry about it. When he calls, you changed your mind. End of game."

"That's true."

"Sure," Sharon said. "And look at it this way, not everyone gets to give her telephone number to Sonny Corleone."

CHAPTER
TWENTY-FIVE

JUST BEFORE 1:00 A.M. that same night the telephone rang. Aly snatched up the receiver fearful of disturbing Lilbet and apprehensive always of late-night calls. They invariably signified bad news. She said an uneasy hello.

"This is Nicholas, Doctor Brown. I want to see you."

"But this is my grandmother's apartment," she tried to explain.

"There's only the one line?"

"Yes."

"Tomorrow you'll have a second one. Give me the address."

Wondering about her compliance, she told him, then lit a cigarette, aware of the pulse throbbing in her throat.

"Ten minutes," he said.

"You can't come here now!" Was he crazy? Was she? What was she doing?

"There's a service entrance, right?"

"Yes, but you can't. . . ."

"I'll be at the back door in ten minutes." A click, and she was listening to the hollow sound of a dead line.

She sat for a moment then jumped up and went to check that the telephone hadn't wakened Lucille or Lilbet. Evidently it hadn't. There was no sound to be heard beyond Lucille's closed door. And Lilbet, who always slept with her door slightly ajar, had fallen asleep in the midst of her nightly reading. Aly tiptoed in to set the book on the bedside table and turn off the light.

Aly's bedroom was separated from that of her grandmother and the housekeeper by the living and dining rooms. It wasn't likely they'd hear the rear service door being opened, or anything that might occur on this side of the apartment. Still, Aly stood barefoot in the dark kitchen with the service door cracked open, feeling fairly criminal and yet near palsied with excitement. She couldn't quite bring herself to believe any of this was actually happening, but she was reveling in every dangerous moment of it. She was thirty-five, the same age Rheta had been when she died. It seemed so significant. Were the women of this line of the family each destined to die violently at thirty-five?

There was a dreamlike deceptiveness to all that had transpired since Sharon pointed Nicholas out to her in the restaurant. Within the context of a dream, it didn't seem in the least unreasonable that he should telephone late at night, or that he should inform her matter-of-factly that she'd have a private telephone line the next day, or that he intended to see her there and then. In dreams all manner of peculiar occurrences took on the attributes of normalcy. One could fly; rooms had unearthly dimensions; people said and did things that had no daylight context. A door could ease open and a man could glide inside, reaching behind him to secure the lock; he could take hold of her, staking an immediate claim, and she could respond—as she hadn't done in years—directly through her nerve-endings, her hold on rational thought instantly diminished.

He acted with a lack of haste born of pure confidence, one hand secured in her hair directing her mouth to his, the other closing around her hip. Her bones turned to sawdust, she had to cling to him for support, quaking with anticipation and a continuing sense of danger. At last she had to push herself away, whispering, "Not here," and hurried him to her room where, with the door locked, he again took hold of her, and her brain, like a sparrow on a high tension wire, hovered weightlessly atop potential annihilation.

Only in a dream could such a voluptuous performance take place, with such rapacious participants avidly welding mouth to flesh, limb to limb, in heavy silence underlaid with the urgent

251

slippery shift of bodies contorting to heighten and accommodate pleasure.

He was determinedly gentle, knowingly inventive, directing her this way and that, introducing her to new sensations, regions of explosive responsiveness Jeremy had never thought to investigate. He nibbled and licked at her flesh as if she were some savoury delicacy he longed to consume, but very slowly. She in turn basked in the lean smooth length and breadth of this phantom's body, indulging all her senses as she touched and tasted and breathed him in. She explored his ears, his teeth, his ribs and knees and ankles, learning the varying textures that comprised his being; she examined the outer corners of his mouth, the spaces between his fingers, the span of his haunches, the architecture of his kneecaps. She went without shame wherever he directed, bending, spreading to absorb the pleasure, openly offering herself to give, to receive.

At last, they lay sated in her childhood single bed, and her brain slid back into its functioning mode. Taking hold of his left hand, she turned the ring on his finger, asking in a whisper, "Are you married, Nicholas?"

"Not anymore."

"Divorced?"

"She died."

"Oh! I'm sorry."

"You?" he asked, as if humoring her, as if speech did not come naturally to him, as if communication was only successfully accomplished through touch.

"Divorced. What do you do, Nicholas?"

There was a long pause. He sat up, reached for her cigarettes on the bedside table, lit one, then passed it to her. "You don't want to know," he said emphatically, so that a chill traversed her spine and she shivered.

She smoked the cigarette while he quickly dressed.

"Don't ask too many questions, Dr. Brown," he cautioned quite kindly in his distinctively husky voice. His fingertip traced the perimeter of her mouth, his eyes dark, unfathomable, boring into hers as his fingertip traveled across her cheek, over her chin, down the length of her throat, down to circle her nipple, then to push lightly into her navel, and down to the apex of her thighs. "The best thing is not to talk at all," he advised, his lips grazing against hers, his delicate probing returning her to a state of need. "This is what we're all about," he said, his lips brushing hers before he slipped away through the service door.

Despite her exhaustion, she stripped and remade the bed, then took a quick shower before going to sleep. It may have felt like a dream, but there was too much evidence proving it had been very real.

At 10:15 the next morning a serviceman from New York Telephone arrived to hook up the second line.

"I didn't want any late-night calls disturbing you," Aly told her grandmother, wondering just who Nicholas might be that he could, so effortlessly, accomplish the near impossible.

"I thought I heard the phone ringing last night," Lilbet said, head cocked to one side as she regarded Alyssa. "Everything all right at home?"

Aly smiled. "A call late at night somehow has to be bad news, doesn't it?" she said. "That's how I always feel too. No, everything's fine as far as I know. It was just a friend." A friend? Nicholas wasn't a friend. She didn't even know his last name, or where he lived. She knew down to the finest detail the shape and feel of his entire body, but he didn't qualify as a friend. And what was she, to do the things she had, with this man she didn't know? Recalling her ravening eagerness, her shameless hunger, made her squirm. How could she have done any of that?

"You look a mite peaky this morning, honey," Lilbet observed.

"Do I?" Aly wandered over to the fireplace to look in the mirror over the mantel. Incredible, she thought, eyeing her reflection. She didn't look like a woman who, only hours before, had been nakedly fellating a stranger while he rubbed her between his fingers as if gauging the quality of a piece of silk; a woman who'd sat spread-legged on that stranger's lap, encouraging him to feed himself into her as if she were the music and he were a spade-headed cobra. How could she have done such things in her grandmother's home? Her behavior was con-

253

temptible. "I suppose I do look a bit tired," she agreed with her grandmother. "I'll have to go to bed early tonight." And maybe later her new telephone would ring, announcing the return of the taciturn but prodigal Nicholas. What was she *doing*? she wondered, guilt-stricken as she looked over at her grandmother. Why hadn't she told the telephone installer there'd been a mistake, that she had no need of a second line? She was not only allowing someone else to dictate the rules to a game she was covertly playing on Lilbet's turf, she seemed unable even to question any aspect of it. Something that began this way, in secret and with so much about it that was wrong, could only end badly. Did she really want to die? Was she actually determined to end her life suddenly, violently, as Rheta had? It couldn't continue, she decided. She was defiling her grandmother's home, destroying the sanctuary she'd always found here. The next time Nicholas called she'd tell him she couldn't see him again. But she *wanted* to see him again, wanted to see and feel his perfect body bearing down on hers, filling her so completely with sensation that there was no room for thought.

Lucille brought in the mail, several letters for Aly and a number of envelopes and magazines for Lilbet.

"I'd dearly love to know how my name's managed to get on the mailing list for every registered charity in the known universe," Lilbet said with energy, tearing in half most of the envelopes without bothering to examine their contents.

"How do you know that's what those are?" Aly asked. "I could never tear something up without at least opening it."

"Honey, I can spot folks who're after money while they're dropping the letters in the box. These things"—she waved an envelope in the air—"have a feel to them. Begging letters," she said dismissingly, ripping the last of them. "I give where I want, when I want. I truly *hate* solicitations. And I hate those folks who get on the telephone of an evening and introduce themselves, then try to get you to buy brooms or light bulbs. I want light bulbs or a broom, I'll go get me some from Mr. Shuster over to the hardware store on Third Avenue. I'm certainly not going to go buying them from some woman calling up in the middle of my dinner. Who all's writing to you?" she asked.

Aly lifted the letters from her lap. "Suze," she smiled, "and one from Addy. This one's from Dad, and I think this must be from Donna."

"You keep in touch with that girl?" Lilbet asked.

"Her and her mother," Aly said. "I'm very fond of them both."

"I wasn't accusing you of anything," Lilbet said. "I think it's truly big-hearted of you to feel the way you do. A lot of women wouldn't."

"It'd be their loss, just as it's Jeremy's loss. Do you know he's never so much as *seen* Donna?"

"Not a nice man," Lilbet agreed, opening the first of the envelopes she'd chosen to keep.

Aly watched her grandmother for a few moments then looked down at the sheaf of letters in her hand. Her entire body was stiff. The movement of her head felt mechanical, like some piece of machinery badly in need of maintenance.

Donna wrote to say she was happy at the art college and while she hadn't made a final decision yet she was leaning toward packaging design, although the challenge of set design appealed to her too. "Mom's fine, back to work at the pub full time. She's in high spirits, been seeing a very nice man going on for two months now, and she says to say hello, sends you her love. . . ."

She read on to the end of the letter then glanced over at her grandmother who was leafing through the new issue of *Town and Country*. "Only reason I subscribe to this," Lilbet said, "is 'cause of the horoscopes." Opening the back cover, she directed her eyes to the December forecast for Aries. Aly lowered her head, feeling her neck creak, and went on to the next envelope.

Reading between the lies of Suzanne's letter, Aly sensed she was having some difficulty adjusting both to Cambridge and to living alone. "I can't think why anyone would bother to cook an entire meal simply for one's self. I've stocked my small larder with tins primarily. I expect I'll gain masses of weight, eating stodge, eggs and chips, beans on toast, but it's such a lot of bother cooking. I am enjoying my studies enormously, although there's a great deal more reading to be done than hours in the day to do it. Sorry to grizzle. I miss you and wish you were nearer. Ad and I talked the other night and discussed perhaps coming to you and Lilbet for Christmas. Would that be possible? We'd both like it. Ad says she plans to write, so I expect you'll get letters the same day from both of us. . . ."

His hands very slowly traced her outer dimensions as if he were molding clay, recreating her in a shimmering image; or as if he were painting with a white-hot liquid that, in cooling, shuddered down to its final form. She was obliged to remain motionless in order to assist him. The strain of keeping still made her muscles quiver, caused her entire body to tremble. Her nipples shriveled, her eyes kept wanting to close. It was a form of exquisite torment.

Her father wrote, "We were thinking of bringing the girls over at Christmas for ten days during their school break. Serena's anxious to see some exhibit or other at the Museum of Modern Art. I've completely forgotten what she told me—DaDa or MaMa school or something. You know me, honey. I'm hopeless when it comes to things like remembering artists. We thought we'd treat the girls, stay at the Sherry Netherland. Serena's mad for the place, apparently always stayed there as a girl when her parents visited New York. Anyway, let me know how you feel and whether or not Lilbet's up to it. If it's a bad idea, no feelings hurt. . . ."

When he'd completed his shaping, he cooled his creation with his tongue, going back over the outlines he'd set down, taking care to make contiguous lineaments so that the effect was of completeness. "Don't move, Doctor," his husky voice instructed. "Don't move. I'll just do this now. . . ." He had an artist's commitment to his endeavors, and a visionary's zeal about her personal terrain, apparently viewing her as a ready convert. She came so easily to his point of view.

". . . and I can't *wait* to be at the university," Addy wrote. "I'm so bored at school now. Suze probably told you we had a lovely natter the other evening and discussed coming to see you and Auntie Lilbet at Christmas. I do hope you'll say yes. Serena and Grandfather have said we could come. Please say yes.

"Jeremy's all atwitter determined to play the lead in a major new musical in the West End to be put on next year. It's all he ever talks about. He's actually changed to a new singing teacher because the wife of the show's composer studies with this one and he's got the idea he'll become fast and hard friends with the wife so that she'll put in a good word for him with her husband when it comes time to cast the show. He's also eating hugely in order to *look* right for the part, masses of potatoes and puddings. It's too funny, really. But he's dead serious, as always, and he's been working to lower his voice, doing all these droning scales and what-have-you. He's already gained half a stone and he's got himself rigged out in dead peculiar gear, 'mentally preparing' (as he calls it) for 'The Part of a Lifetime'!!!!! It's to be a musical version of *The Blue Angel* and Jeremy insists he's going to play the professor. If he doesn't get it there'll be hell to pay. He's already dressing and eating the part, not to mention talking in very scholarly tones. Except what he says doesn't make very much sense.

"Please say yes we can come. I do miss you, and I'm longing to see Lilbet. What are you doing? Are you working? Do you miss me? . . ." .

He rendered her liquid, molten, with a tensile surface that vibrated, then plunged beneath the surface in one fluent motion, and paused to study his effect on her. Satisfied, he withdrew—a sword momentously drawn from its perfect sheath.

Not sure of what she'd read, Aly had to go through all the letters a second time, then looked up to see her grandmother watching her. "What?" she asked, lighting a cigarette.

"Good news?"

"I think so. My father's proposing he and Serena bring the girls to visit at Christmas. How would you feel about that?"

"If I'm not dead, I'll feel just fine about it," Lilbet laughed.

"Please don't say things like that," Aly said quietly.

"You're not yourself," Lilbet declared, reaching for a Camel from the Limoges cup on the table beside her chair. "What's bothering you, Alyssa?"

"Nothing, honestly. That phone call," she ad-libbed, "it woke me and I had trouble getting back to sleep." She was reminded of the visit she'd made years before when she'd spent almost every moment of her stay here worrying she might be pregnant. She'd apologized endlessly for destroying Lilbet's pleasure in her company. She was here now to be with her grandmother until that inevitable death Lilbet so liked to dispute arrived to sweep her into its inky embrace. Lilbet had every right to expect Aly to join her in her jovial defiance.

257

Setting aside her letters, she got up and went over to kiss her grandmother on each cheek, saying, "You've got this impossible radar. It homes in on the subtlest changes in my moods. If I had that gift people would be queuing up for days to get an appointment to consult me."

"Speaking of which," Lilbet said with a pleased smile, "what's going to happen to your practise with you leaving indefinitely? And by the bye what's your movie star friend up to?"

The reference to Andrew was like an ice cube slipped down the back of her dress. She covered her reaction in the move back to her chair, in retrieving her cigarette from the ashtray, in placing the letters behind the ashtray on the table. Andrew. How was she ever going to live through this? "First of all," she said, "I'm not sure I want to continue my practise. I need some time away from it. I've been thinking I might rework my doctoral thesis into a book. Non-fiction self-help books do very well, and . . . I don't know." She sighed. "As for Andrew, I'm not sure what he's doing at the moment. I'm afraid we've had a falling out. I, uhm. . . ." She had to stop. She was going to cry, and that was the last thing either of them wanted or needed. She busied herself lighting a fresh cigarette from the one she was finishing.

"Use the table lighter, honey," Lilbet said disapprovingly. "That's such an unattractive habit."

"Sorry," Aly managed, dusting ashes off her sleeve.

"A falling out, you say?"

"Yes. I'm afraid so." *Last night she'd done with a stranger everything she'd been unable to allow herself to do with Andrew. She'd accorded Nicholas the ultimate intimate knowledge of her she'd withheld from Andrew for almost eighteen years. What kind of perversity was that? Or was that putting too genteel a name to her behavior? She'd behaved like a trollop, and with a man who had the power to arrange telephone installations at night, who was so assured of his power that no one—least of all her—ventured to refuse him. He'd evidenced satisfaction in his choice of her as a sexual partner, gazing into her eyes as if immensely gratified by the response he'd known he'd find there. He'd moved over her, inside of her, with the control and gratification of a man who'd at long last found the woman he'd been seeking—the per-*

258

fectly acquiescent, febrile female he could bend to his whims, perhaps even destroy.

"You surely do surprise me," Lilbet said. "I was convinced you'd be telling me any time now you were planning to marry that fella."

"Why would you think that?" Aly asked, forcing herself to pay attention.

"Oh, honey," Lilbet chided. "Any fool could tell from hearing you talk about him how you feel. Or am I a silly old woman with cancer in her brain as well as everywhere else?"

"No, you're not," Aly said hoarsely.

"Well what on earth *happened*?"

"I don't know."

"You don't know? What was this falling out over?"

"Auntie Lilbet," Aly pleaded, "I can't discuss it. I'm sorry, but I can't."

Lilbet puffed thoughtfully on her cigarette, then said, "Catch him back before it's too late, honey. He looks and sounds to me like a truly decent fella. And lord knows, after living all those years with that fool Jeremy, I think you deserve someone decent. So you listen to your old Aunt Lilbet, and you catch him back. You hear?"

"I hear," Aly got out, pushing her mouth up into a smile. *It was too late. The telephone would ring tonight or tomorrow night or the night after that and Nicholas would come to strip her of her clothes, he'd put her down on that narrow bed she'd slept in since childhood, and she'd open her arms and legs, take him in like bitter medicine that would make her feel better; Nicholas would take away the pain, perhaps forever.*

259

CHAPTER
TWENTY-SIX

THE NIGHTS were indistinguishable; they merged to become one lengthy night that went on and on. Nicholas telephoned, then appeared at the service door three or four or five times each week. Just the sound of his throaty voice on the other end of the line turned her receptive. "I'll be there in ten minutes," or "fifteen minutes," and her limbs turned rubbery, prepared to flex in whatever manner necessary to accommodate his remarkably gentle thrust.

Naked under her robe, she'd stand barefoot on the cold linoleum floor by the rear door, waiting for the light rapping of his knuckles that signalled his arrival. Quaking, she'd get the door open, gorging herself on the very sight of him—his good looks a hastily consumed hors d'ouevre that whet her enormous appetite.

"Doctor," he'd greet her, showing his very white teeth in a smile as she quickly locked the door, then took him by the hand to lead him to the safe little island of her childhood room.

He arrived with odd offerings. Bars of Godiva bittersweet chocolate he shared with her before disappearing into the night, a sack of imported Clementine oranges he fed her segment by segment, or a large cluster of fat seedless grapes. One evening he brought an entire roasted chicken and they devoured it, tearing it to pieces with their hands. Then he licked her fingers clean. He arrived on a Thursday night with a single long-stemmed red rose and laid it with extreme care between her breasts. On other nights he presented her with a pale pink rose, or a yellow one. He gave her a bag of penny licorice sticks, a Yo-Yo that glowed in the dark. He lit two sparklers and sat with her on the side of the bed as they waved them slowly in the dark. He came with White Castle hamburgers, with freshly-baked bialis, with Tootsie Rolls and a bag of Kraft marshmallows; with scented oil they massaged into each other's flesh. He fed her slippery roasted red peppers, crisp dill pickles, and Nathan's hot dogs. He gave her a leather-bound notepad and a solid gold pen to keep on the table beside the telephone, a trim compact shortwave radio, a Hermès scarf with huge pale pink water lilies and cool green leaves, a delicate gold chain he fastened around her neck, and a pair of tortoise shell hair combs.

Initially when she tried to thank him, he said, "From Nicholas to the Doctor. Don't thank me, and don't buy me anything. Okay?"

When they spoke at all, it was either the giving of whispered commands, "Turn this way, Doctor," or the confirmation of success, "Nicholas, I'm almost there," the pleased murmurs of mutual congratulation. "Can't get enough of you, Doc." "It was wonderful."

Her nights were an ongoing odyssey to the remotest shores of sensuality that brought her to each morning glutted yet disoriented. Her life had been split precisely down the middle and she had to exercise the greatest care to prevent her nocturnal self from accidentally spilling over into her daytime self. She felt like the worst possible fraud. But just as she'd been unable to sever herself from Jeremy, so she felt incapable of separating herself from the greatest purely physical pleasure she'd ever known. She felt guilty, and anxious, and was convinced this peculiar relationship with Nicholas could only end in disaster.

"YOU DON'T feel like going out, come over here. I'll cook," Sharon said. "It's been weeks I haven't seen you. How's your grandmother, everything okay?"

"She tires easily," Aly said. "Otherwise she's remarkably well. They say she isn't, but I'd swear she's in remission."

"Doctors. What do they know? God willing, she'll live another fifteen, twenty years. So, what time're you coming? I've got *stuffed cabbage,"* she said, making it sound like "Want some candy, little girl?"

Aly laughed. "What time?"

"Seven-thirty, after my dose of the nightly network man bites dog. Okay, gotta go. Bring some wine, your choice of color."

Lilbet was settled in with Lucille for an evening of gin rummy and Benny Goodman records. "Half-a-cent a point," Lilbet was saying as Aly came into the living room.

"Since when?" Lucille wanted to know. "We been playing quarter-a-cent ten years, all of a sudden it's half a cent?"

"It's your chance to build a nest egg before I pencil in my dance with the Grim Reaper. I'd think you'd jump at it."

Dealing with efficient speed, Lucille said, "Hnnh! Be okay if you didn't win most all the time. But you cheat, Lilbet Conover, and we both know it. More like you got it in mind to win back ten years' worth of salary you been paying me."

Lilbet picked up the board card, a three of spades, fit it into her hand then studiously rearranged her cards before putting down a three of clubs.

"Well, now we know you're not collecting threes," Lucille said, taking the top card from the deck.

"You off, honey?" Lilbet asked without taking her eyes from the cards.

"I'll be back early. I've left Sharon's number on the pad by the phone in case you need me."

"You have a nice time," Lilbet said, glancing up with a smile, "and be sure to thank that sweet girl for the pralines."

Aly went around the table to kiss her grandmother's cheek, feeling Lilbet's shoulder lift under her hand in affectionate acknowledgment.

"You're discarding the ace of hearts?" Lilbet asked in disbelief, eyebrows arching.

"You make it sound like I was throwing away the Mona Lisa, for pity's sake," Lucille replied. "I don't happen to need that ace."

"I can certainly use it." Lilbet whisked the card off the table. "You run along now and enjoy yourself, honey," she told Aly.

"We'll probably still be at this when you get home," Lucille said with a grin that showed her strong white teeth.

Aly patted the housekeeper's arm, watched the game for a few more moments, then left to walk the dozen blocks to Sharon's apartment.

"So DID the Prince of Darkness ever call you or what? Sharon asked, finally pushing her plate away and reaching for her goblet of wine.

Aly didn't know how to answer and stalled, drinking some of her burgundy before lighting a cigarette.

"Swear to God you're the worst," Sharon laughed. "Everybody else, they're on the phone to me the minute the guy steps into the shower. You, it's the Chinese water torture to get a word out of you."

"Do you remember my mother at all?" Aly asked, leaning with elbows spread on the table.

"A bit. Why?"

"Nothing. I just wondered."

"She was small, I remember. And gorgeous. Didn't look like anybody's mother I knew. Plus she worked, which I thought was very glamorous. I know you guys moved about every other week, and there were a lot of boyfriends. A shitload of boyfriends, which I also thought was very glamorous. A lady ahead of her time," Sharon said philosophically. "I liked her."

"Did you? Why?"

Sharon sat back holding her goblet, trying to decipher Aly's expression. "Why'd I like your mother?" she repeated, as if the question were nonsensical. "She was different, interesting. I liked her. Why'd you like *my* mother?"

"Because she was homey, warm, domestic, all the things Rheta wasn't. She made those fabulous lunches."

"Made me into a fat lady," Sharon corrected with a laugh. "Every calorie I ever owned I got honestly from my mother, a woman who could be the poster girl for anorexia. I liked your mother, Al. I liked Cliffie, too, although he was such a genius it made me nervous just to say hi to him, like my inferiority was showing. He couldn't help it. Neither one of you could, I know. But it's always been a testament to my great love for you, kiddo, that I hung out with you guys at all. Most of the kids at school

263

were plain blown away by the two of you. What'd you have against your poor mother?"

"Why do you say that?"

"I can tell by the way you talk about her, always calling her Rheta, never Mom. Your kids call you Alyssa?"

Aly shook her head.

"Right. Call you Mom, don't they?"

"Something like that." Aly stared into the depths of her wine. Addy referred to her father as Jeremy. Suddenly, it was highly significant.

Sharon waited, watching Aly make a visible effort to marshall her thoughts. She was as impeccably turned out as ever, in beige wool slacks with a matching cashmere pullover, her hair slicked back in a long braid, but she lacked her usual composure. It showed in the slightly anxious set of her mouth and the way she was chain-smoking.

"What's the matter, Al?" Sharon asked solicitously.

Aly looked up and gave her a dim smile. "I honestly wouldn't know where to begin."

"Dive in anywhere," Sharon invited. "I've got all night."

"I told Rheta I wanted to live with my father. Not even a week later she and Cliffie were dead."

"And?"

"I betrayed her," Aly said grimly.

"Excuse me. Just how, exactly, did you do that?"

"I left them. I hated the way we lived, and I hated her for making us live that way."

"You were a little kid, for chrissake. You wanted to be settled. That, by you, is betrayal?"

"Addy chose to go with Jeremy," Aly admitted, feeling again the shame of her failure. "He's probably the worst father in the history of the world, but she prefers to live with him."

"I can't believe what I'm hearing," Sharon said, pulling back in close to the table. "You're equating one thing with the other? You wanted to live with your dad, that's one thing. Your kid wanted to live with hers, that's another. Show me the connection!"

Aly hadn't expected to have to defend her thesis. Caught off guard she could only stare at Sharon, groping for explanations.

264

"What's up with you, Al?" Sharon asked, concerned. "You're talking nutsy shit here. This about your grandmother?" Aly shook her head. "What then? Give me something to work with, something that makes sense."

This was headed in a direction Aly didn't wish to go. And yet she was anxious to have Sharon's opinion, to hear another woman's views on any number of issues. Too much of the time she felt cut off from people, especially women. Even though her clients had been primarily female they'd come to her for counseling and she could hardly solicit their reactions to her own problems. "I'm shattering your lovely image of me, aren't I?" Aly said jokingly.

"I'm a realist, Al," Sharon answered seriously. "Fat people kind of have to be. The world tends not to encourage overweight romantics. I never *had* any 'lovely image' of you, kiddo. To me, you've always been my best friend from grade school whose mom and brother got murdered. That was very very rough. Still have the newspaper clippings, as a matter of fact." She looked over at the far side of the room as if pinpointing precisely where she'd stored those yellowed pages. "Made a hell of an impact on me," she went on. "Here you were this gorgeous kid, smartest one in the whole class, and you actually wanted to be friends when most of the other kids were into name-calling and lousy jokes. So a lovely image I've never had. You were my friend Al who went and got herself pregnant first time out. Shmuck," she smiled. "My friend the shrink who's batty as a bedbug, like every other shrink in the goddamned world. So what else is new? But lovely image, uhn-uh. Could you tell me maybe why you're the heavy because twenty-five years ago you wanted some order to your life so you decided to go live with your dad?"

Aly returned her smile, with a shake of her head saying, "Forget I said any of that, will you? It's the wine talking."

Sharon picked up the bottle, held it close to her face and said, "Shut up already," then plonked the bottle back on the table.

With a laugh, Aly asked, "You thought of me as your best friend?"

"Well, sure. We were."

"Yes, we were," Aly agreed, suddenly wishing she could have

it all back—her mother and Cliffie, the awful apartments, the moving, the chores, all of it. She'd do things so differently now. Gulping down a sob, she cried, "What a bore!" and snatched up the napkin to blot her face. "And the stuffed cabbage was so good, too."

"Oh, this is great!" Sharon laughed. "What're you having—a breakdown?"

"I hope not." Aly lit a fresh cigarette thinking how her body seemed to be riddled with dangerous devices: hooks, razors, hair-thin unbreakable wires;—so many interior hazards. She might be killed simply by drawing too deep a breath, uttering too-emotional words, thinking oblique thoughts. Her mind roiled with images of her calisthenics with Nicholas, their late-night, for the most part silent, meetings. All she knew of this man was his surface. And she couldn't help believing that the major part of her appeal for him was her lamentable willing-ness and her overt gratitude. Because regardless of her guilt and anxiety, regardless of her supposed intelligence, her body was burningly grateful to Nicholas for his skilled ministrations. But she still loved Andrew. Her grandmother was dying; she had a daughter who preferred to live with her father; her prac-tise was no more; and she had no idea where Andrew was. His silence was absolute.

"What?" Sharon asked.

"Nothing. Sorry." Under cover of night she could do things that made her daytime self cringe with embarrassment. Why did darkness somehow sanctify acts that couldn't withstand day-light scrutiny? "Some of my clients," she said, ad-libbing, "get up to fairly amazing antics."

"Yeah? Do tell." Sharon Groucho-ed her eyebrows and smirked lasciviously.

"I had one who had a long-term strenuously illicit affair right under her mother's nose. Literally."

"Oh, this is good." Sharon made 'give me' gestures with her hands. "Come on. I love hearing about your whacked-out cli-ents. Makes me feel so normal."

"Her paramour came to her house late at night, sometimes four or five times in a week. She'd wait for him at the side door, then they'd creep into her room and make love while the

266

mother was sleeping in the next room. They didn't dare make any sound at all, not even so much as a whisper. They also didn't dare use the bed, so they performed on the floor. The odd aspect to the relationship has to do with the fact that my client scarcely knew this man; they rarely exchanged more than a few words. In essence she lived one life at night and an entirely different one during the day."

"What's the deal?" Sharon asked, puzzled. "I mean, how old was this 'client' for one thing? And what was with the mother?"

"Ah, yes. She was in her mid-thirties, the responsible child who undertook to care for the aging parent. Fairly classic scenario, so far as all that goes."

Sharon stared fixedly at her for a long moment, then pointed a finger at Aly, declaring, "That's chutzpah, Al, serious goddamned chutzpah! You're fucking 'I'm Nicholas' with your grandmother and the housekeeper right there?"

Aly's mouth dropped open. Before she could speak, Sharon let out a whooping laugh. "Fuck me, Alice! Aren't you just chock full of surprises! You've been making out with him for how long?"

"Since that night in the restaurant," Aly admitted, her face afire.

"You really thought I'd buy that corny client routine? Jeez, Al! That's like when we were kids going to the drugstore to buy Kotex and we'd always say, 'It's for my mother,' because God forbid the guy behind the counter should find out we're standing in front of him bleeding. So, tell me. You've got to do it where you eat, if you'll forgive me?"

In spite of her discomfiture Aly had to laugh. Then, sobering, she said, "I unplugged the telephone two weeks ago so he'd think I was out or away, something. But while I was out with Lilbet for her doctor's visit, Lucille came in to clean and plugged it back in. He came to see me that night and it was as if it'd been three months, not just three days. I feel like an addict." She took a puff of her cigarette, using the time to search Sharon's eyes for signs of disgust. Seeing none, and glad of this rare opportunity to unburden herself, she continued. "We really don't talk. The telephone rings and he says he'll be over in ten minutes. I had my period last week. He wasn't a bit bothered.

267

Jeremy used to act as if I'd contracted syphilis, wouldn't come near me during my periods. Nicholas went into the bathroom for a towel. That's all, just a towel. Anyway," she sighed heavily. "Every morning I tell myself I'll disconnect the phone, put it away, that'll be the end of it. But every night I'm there waiting for him to call. I don't know a thing about him, not one blessed thing."

"Except he's fabulous in bed," Sharon put in.

"Astonishing."

"Lucky old you."

"You don't think I'm a slut?"

"A slut? I should think you're a slut?"

"I feel like one."

"Nice," Sharon chided. "Granted, it's a tad on the tacky side to be fucking 'I'm Nicholas' right under Auntie Lilbet's nose, but what's the big deal? Think you're the only one ever had a good time getting her rocks off? Why don't you go do it in his limo or something, it gives you the guilts making out at grandma's, Little Red?" she laughed. "Try his place, a hotel, whatever."

"For some reason that seems to be out of the question. I broached the subject a few times at the beginning, but he went very tense and said we were in the safest place possible."

"The *safest* place? Weird," Sharon said. "So answer me something. What's happened with your movie star buddy? You haven't mentioned his name once since you got here the end of October."

Aly took a breath so deep it seemed to catch painfully on tiny sharp hooks implanted at the base of her ribcage. "Here I am, as you say, fucking Nicholas"—she winced as if the word gave her physical discomfort—"but unfortunately I couldn't make love with Andrew. Couldn't do it. Could not."

"You're in love with Andrew," Sharon said, "Different ballgame."

"I love Andrew," Aly declared, razors in her throat. She would be killed either by her nefarious relationship with Nicholas, or by these treacherous interior implements.

"We all know that," Sharon said patiently. "And?"

With a shrug, Aly said, "And nothing. We've fallen out. It's over."

"So this thing with the Godfather, it's what, revenge?"

"Christ! Could that be it?" Aly wondered aloud. "No. It's something else entirely. I don't know what precisely, but not revenge, nothing like that. I'm not proud of my involvement with Nicholas, you know. But I seem to need him, although I couldn't tell you why."

"If you say so."

"You don't believe me?"

"Sure I believe you. Lighten up, Al. We've all done our fair share of egregious fucking."

A moment, then Aly howled with laughter. *"Egregious?"*

"Positively. Me, I had this gorgeous black boyfriend my senior year. Gregory Raines. Dear God above, was he gorgeous! We didn't have a thing to talk about. He was on your classic football scholarship, studying his divine buns off so he'd have something to fall back on when the football career turned to shit. Sweetest guy. We fucked our hearts out. Scandalized most of the senior class. Not to mention my mother and father, nice Jewish racists that they've always been, they'd have had coronaries they found out I was *shtupping* a *schvarze*. Naturally I said I didn't care, but I cared. They're *my* Jewish racist parents after all. Never mind. We did it every chance we got," she confessed, her face aglow with recall. "Best I've ever had. Lasted maybe four months total, then without even discussing it, we had one final, sensational farewell session, and that was that. God, Gregory Raines! I still think of him, hope he's got a nice chain of drugstores somewhere out in the Midwest. What a honey!

"Let there be no doubt in your mind, kiddo, that what went down was seriously egregious fucking. And a good time was had by all. I can assure you, Al, you are not the only one ever indulged in a little gratuitous friction. And, trust me on this, when it next happens across my path, I'll be ready, diaphragm in hand, to indulge in a little more. What I can't figure here is how come for a change the Wasp has the guilt? I'm the one supposed to be red in the face, beating my breast, not you."

"Maybe I'm doing it for both of us," Aly said.

"I knew you'd come in handy for something. Here, drink some more of your fency-shmensy wine."

They clinked glasses and Aly said, "Thank you for letting me tell you all that. It helped. I feel much better, not quite so horribly guilty."

"Hey, kiddo! You know me. I love a good story."

CHAPTER
TWENTY-SEVEN

WHEN ADELE took up residence with Jeremy, Aly lost faith in her motherhood, lost her previous ease with her daughter. Their conversations were, to her ear, stilted and even contrived, lacking spontaneity. Addy, however, seemed relatively unchanged. She approached her mother with the same wicked wit, the same borderline disrespect she'd always shown both her parents. But Aly couldn't respond as before. Addy's decision to split the family down the middle was a declaration of preference that couldn't be ignored, so Aly dealt with her from the disadvantage of knowing she'd failed in some crucial way as a parent. Every visit with her younger daughter was very like being dragged back to the scene of a fatal mishap; she suffered while trying to maintain a calm exterior. She could no longer gather her clever caustic child into her arms and hug her tightly, feeling the resilient flesh aligned to her body, while Addy emitted delighted squawks of protest. They still embraced but there was distance between them now. Aly was too fearful of further rejection to attempt to bridge it, and Addy was evidently unaware of it.

With Suzanne matters were as they'd always been, warmly unconstrained. Aly had seen her settled at Cambridge, then left to come to New York, content in the knowledge she wasn't a total failure. Their exchange of letters reflecting their continuing closeness was proof of that. She was also quite certain those she wrote to Addy gave no hint of the rift she felt between them.

Now they were coming for a fortnight's visit. It was on everyone's mind that this might well be the last time they'd see Lilbet, and so Aly hoped to make it a memorable Christmas. She shopped with care, making the purchases Lilbet had requested as well as a large number of her own, anxious to prolong the festivities on the day and to please the girls.

While she worked her way through the crowds on Fifty-seventh Street headed for Tiffany's she considered her affair with Nicholas, asking herself truthfully who she thought she was punishing. Rheta was beyond pain. Nothing Aly could say or do or think would ever again have an effect on her mother. Did she really believe she was behaving as Rheta might have? Not even remotely. For Rheta, strangely enough, the family was the thing. Her *tableaux* were all family portraits; only the father figure changed with alarming frequency. In all probability, Rheta would never have risked Lilbet's wrath by smuggling some man into the apartment late at night. No. Rheta brought her men home in broad daylight, for her children's approval. On one level she'd cared what Cliff and Aly thought of these men. On another level it was of little consequence to her what Cliff and Aly thought of them. What a dichotomy! How could anyone have been expected to reconcile Rheta's habits with anything resembling equanimity?

Rheta, were she alive today, would be every bit as scandalized by Aly's behavior as Lilbet would be if she knew. So, Aly could hardly claim she was emulating her mother. Rheta hadn't been looking to get herself murdered. She'd simply had the bad luck and poor judgment that put her in Don's path. *But you,* Aly told herself, *are angling to get yourself, if not killed, at the very least, in trouble.* Jesus!

She would have to break off with Nicholas, to tell him next time he called she'd be unable to see him again. The longer their late-night assignations continued the more contempt she felt for herself. Her behavior was despicable, reprehensible; its genesis was not rooted in her mother's history. It was her own garden of stones and she was tending it with a vengeance. No matter how badly she might want to cast the blame back onto Rheta, it simply wasn't possible, given the hard facts. The very thought of anyone in the family discovering what she'd been up to made her start to sweat in spite of the lancing cold of the day.

She wandered around the main floor of Tiffany's looking into the display cases but seeing only inward. Until she put an end to this business with Nicholas she wasn't going to be able to take an honest step or utter an honest word. She'd fallen into a daily battle with herself, her common sense and self-esteem fighting for ascendance over her need to be ministered to sexually, to be fondled and rubbed, to be stroked and pierced. No small thing, her physical need. All she had to do was let her mind brush against the subject and her body began readying itself for another educated assault. This had to stop. Had to.

That night when the telephone rang she drew a deep breath before saying hello, prepared to say no, he couldn't come.

"I need a favor, Dr. Brown," Nicholas said urgently, without preamble. "Be downstairs in ten minutes." Without waiting for her reply, he disconnected.

His tone made her forget her resolution. She hung up, then hurried to dress, wondering what sort of favor she could possibly do for him at twenty-to-one in the morning. Whatever it was, she fervently hoped it would balance the scales, thereby enabling her to say good-bye to him once and for all. She could not, and would not, see him again after this.

The limo pulled up just as she emerged from the building. The rear door opened and Nicholas climbed out. That he was critically overwrought was evident in his every move.

"I appreciate this," he said, his arm sweeping out to hasten her into the back seat. Despite the cold he seemed to be perspiring, the hair damp at his temples.

She didn't answer, her eyes going to the other passenger already in place. As she opened her mouth to protest, Nicholas swung into the car, the door closed, and they were moving down Park Avenue.

The young man slumped in the corner of the seat was taking shallow breaths, his eyelids half lowered, his face bleached of color. His right hand was out of sight beneath the overlap of his topcoat. Blood was dripping steadily into his lap.

"What's happened to him?" Aly asked fearfully, looking over at Nicholas who was sitting on the edge of the facing seat.

"Little accident," Nicholas answered curtly. "We've got a place you can patch him up."

"Patch him up?" she echoed, dragging her eyes away from Nicholas to look again at the injured young man whose eyes were slitted closed against the pain. His breath whistled slightly as he sucked in air, then exhaled with extreme caution as if the action of his lungs heightened the pain. She turned again toward Nicholas whose face was tight, his mouth thinned with anger or upset. "Oh my God!" she exclaimed, glancing again at the other man, the meaning of this favor at last registering. "I'm a doctor of psychology, Nicholas, not a medical doctor. I can't help him. I'm sorry. He's going into shock. I can tell you that much. He needs attention right away."

There was silence. Then Nicholas said hoarsely over his shoulder, "Pull over, Ben!" He shifted his weight to one side as he reached into his trousers pocket. "*I'm* sorry," he said, as the overlong vehicle swerved sickeningly to the curb. With great agility he climbed out of the car then leaned in to offer her a hand out. "My mistake, Doc. I just assumed. Here." He pressed some bills into her hand and looked penetratingly into her eyes for a moment. "Forget this. Okay?" She nodded dumbly, and he swung back into the limousine, saying, "Grab a cab home. I'll call you. *Go*, Ben!" he ordered, closing the door, then moving closer to the man now sagged against the far door.

She stood on the sidewalk and watched the limo shoot off down the avenue, then, tires squealing, it turned west out of sight.

"Jesus!" she whispered, suddenly aware of the cold and the all but deserted avenue. She was at Fifty-ninth Street, almost twenty blocks from home. There wasn't a cab in sight. Remembering, she opened her hand and looked at the money Nicholas had given her—two hundred-dollar bills. "Jesus!" she said again, feeling like a whore. She looked up Park, took several steps and stopped. Sharon's place was closer. But could she arrive unannounced at this time of the morning? She couldn't possibly, not without some kind of explanation. And she knew it would not only be unwise to tell anyone of this, it would truly

274

be dangerous. Suddenly, very clearly, she understood that she didn't want to die. She absolutely did not want to die.

She'd go home. But there were no cabs. And she wasn't properly dressed. No boots, no purse or hat or gloves. All she had was the money Nicholas had given her and her keys. She crossed Fifty-ninth looking at the two bills, sickened by the attachment they represented to a man who drove around at ungodly hours with someone bleeding to death in the back of his limousine. There was a mailbox on the corner. She crossed the street, folding the bills in half, then in half again, pushed the money through the mailbox slot then wiped her hands down the sides of her coat and walked on, arms folded tightly across her chest, head bent against the wind.

The doorman gave her a suspicious look as she squished through the lobby in her sodden shoes. She rode up to the eleventh floor staring at her feet, her face and hands stinging from the heat. Once inside the apartment she removed her shoes, poured herself some cognac, then went noiselessly through to her bedroom where she dropped the ruined shoes into the waste basket, and swallowed half the cognac in one go.

While she waited for the tub to fill she sat on the rim and drank the rest of the cognac. Why had she written Dr. A. Brown in his notebook? Dr. Brown. It was so pretentious, not the sort of thing she did normally. She never referred to herself that way. But she hadn't, for some reason, wanted him to know her name. Brown was Jeremy's name, not hers. And he didn't even use it. He called himself Gable, for God's sake. But since he'd never legally changed his name, he'd been obliged to marry as ordinary Jeremy Brown. He'd been mightily vexed by that. Perhaps it was time to reclaim her rightful name, to be rid of Jeremy once and for all. She was Alyssa Jackson, daughter of Hal, daughter of poor misguided Rheta.

From where she lay in the steaming water she could see the bedroom window. Being night the curtains were, of course, drawn. But behind them hung the bull's-eye, and she wondered why she'd brought the ridiculous thing with her. It hadn't been a conscious act. She'd been packing and had looked around to see if she'd forgotten anything. Before she even knew what she was doing, she'd unhooked it from the window and tucked it into her bag between some sweaters. Then, having brought it, she'd had no choice really but to hang it. Now every morning when she drew the curtains it was the first thing she saw, and invariably she stood for a few seconds gazing out at the deformed view offered through the bull's-eye. What sort of idiocy was that? she asked herself, running more hot water into the tub and wishing she'd thought to bring the cognac bottle with her into the bathroom. Who in their right mind made a daily exercise out of staring through a misshapen lump of glass, trying by sheer force of will to push things into perspective? People confined to institutions did things that were more rational than that.

Where was Andrew? Had he gone off on location for another film? Probably. And most likely he was consoling himself with his female co-star, or one of the legions of women who were forever writing him astonishingly suggestive letters. But he'd never do any of that. He'd always said he made it a point never to become involved with co-workers or with fans. He restricted himself to women he met legitimately one way or another. *Don't call us, we'll call you.* There wasn't an actor alive who didn't quote that line at some point or another. Even Jeremy had derisively spouted it after unsuccessful interviews.

If she closed her eyes she could readily picture herself making love to Andrew. Why was it that daydreams and fantasies could convince you with their potency when reality never traveled the same smoothly-paved roads? Daydreams dispensed with all the negatives—obstacles, emotions, circumstances—and made possible everything reality forced you to acknowledge was impossible. In her reveries she could rewrite her personal history; she wasn't Rheta's child but her own woman, suffering no guilt for her alliance with Nicholas, a man who was undoubtedly engaged in criminal activities; in her daydreams she was inner-directed, self-assured, and an ideal mother; she was perfectly balanced mentally and emotionally—and able to declare herself without the need for pathetic subterfuges like the hypothetical case history she'd fabricated for Sharon.

Jesus! Had that man been shot? Or stabbed? Obviously Nicholas hadn't taken him to a hospital because questions would have been asked. She laughed grimly, the sound bouncing back at her off the tiled walls. He'd thought she was a medical doctor, and that because of her involvement with him she'd be willing to circumvent the code of ethics of her supposed profession and treat a gunshot victim without reporting the incident. She, the woman who nearly fainted when four-year-old Suzanne's fall at the playground resulted in a deep gash on the vulnerable underside of her chin; who couldn't have dealt with a sprained limb let alone a gushing wound.

It had all happened so quickly. No more than four or five minutes between the time she climbed into the car and her being deposited back on the sidewalk. But every last detail was etched as if with acid into her recall: the young man's camelhair coat, the waxy caste to his features and his partially lowered eyelids, the blood pooling in his lap; Nicholas's gravity, his almost military tone of command; the driver Ben's silent obedience, his face as open and bewildered as a child's. Who were these people with their hand-tailored clothes and arcane pursuits? And why was she involved, even peripherally, with them?

In bed she sat with her knees drawn up, lit a cigarette, and thought about Rheta and Cliffie, consciously confronting that scene of carnage that so often of late reappeared in nightmares. She felt again the heat as she approached the doorway and saw the bodies, saw the blood splattered on the walls, the floor, the bedding. Her heartbeat accelerated to a giddying rate and she had to close her eyes, rest her head on her knees for a few moments while the scene receded and the coppery taste of blood faded from her tongue.

When finally she slept her dreams twisted and squirmed like helpless creatures caught in some massive, steel-jawed trap. Inscrutable Nicholas with his ominous appeal stood beside Don's body, asking her to help patch him up. "I've got a place," he said, "where you can do it." Then, before she could state her lack of willingness or ability, he said, "Never mind," and forced Sharon to minister to the corpse. With apologetic eyes, Sharon applied a froth of egg white to the tidy blood-encrusted hole between Don's brows. "Everybody does it," Sharon explained, smoothing the egg white with a stainless steel spatula. "It'll be okay, kiddo."

Sharon refused to be made aware of the danger, refused to heed Aly's frantic warnings. "He'll kill you!" she cried, unable to cross the threshold and physically prevent Sharon from reviving the odious drunk. "Can't you see what he did to them?" she pointed a trembling finger at the remains of her mother and brother.

"I'll do them next," Sharon said blithely, watching the egg white congeal, forming an unblemished new skin.

"What on earth is the girl doing?" Lilbet asked.

Aly turned to see her grandmother, skeletal in white chiffon, hair and manicure perfect. She'd risen directly from her coffin to make one last stand on Aly's behalf.

"It's all right," Aly lied, gingerly taking hold of Lilbet's wasted arm. "I'll take care of it. You go back and lie down again."

"Make sure you do, honey," her grandmother said, sniffing indignantly. "We can't have this kind of thing going on in my home."

IT WAS obvious at breakfast that Lilbet had taken a turn for the worse. She had no appetite and surreptitiously swallowed two of her pain pills with her coffee. Aly felt guilty, as if in some way her waking and sleeping actions were somehow responsible for her grandmother's deterioration. She told herself that was absurd but she felt guilty nevertheless and longed to be able to do something to ease Lilbet's visible suffering.

"Now don't you go fussing over me, honey. You know I hate to be fussed over. I'll be just fine. You go on about your business and don't give me another thought."

"I don't have any 'business,' " Aly said with a smile, determined not to be sent away like a small child. "I thought I'd have a quiet day, maybe let you show me how to cheat at cards."

Lilbet lifted her chin imperiously. "Lucille's a poor loser, that's all. Course I don't cheat," she said, a glint in her eye. "Darling John Conover always said a good card player has no need to cheat. Do you remember your Uncle John, Alyssa?"

"A little," Aly answered, although in fact she could recall very little of her grandfather who'd died when she was six. The image that came to mind was of a courtly man with graying hair and soft-spoken ways. She could remember her grandmother bustling about, prepared to attend to his slightest need. And she could remember the affection they'd displayed toward one another, their kisses hello and good-bye, their great deference.

"I miss that man," Lilbet said sadly. "He was the love of my life. I knew it the moment I set eyes on him. It was the gas that killed him, you know, that mustard gas those Germans used in the first war. He was an officer, not in the trenches. But the wind blew that gas everywhere; they all breathed it in. It wasn't till years and years later we found out about the damage to his lungs." She shook her head. "Terrible it was to see him struggling to breathe. It was a blessing, really, when he finally went. I'd remind myself of that whenever I got to missing him badly, tell myself he'd earned his peace. Truth to tell though, honey, I never thought I'd live on all these years without him. Not that I didn't have my chances to marry again. No, I certainly didn't lack for opportunities. But I knew no one else could ever be for me what your Uncle John was. It's a pity we didn't have more children. We tried. They just never came."

The way she said it gave Aly an image of a roomful of children waiting patiently for a summons that never occurred; she could see a cluster of small faces growing pale and wearied with waiting.

"Rheta was his pride and joy," Lilbet went on. "She could do no wrong in that man's eyes. I've always been grateful he never had to know of that tragedy. Poor Rheta. You must miss her."

Aly was momentarily nonplussed. She'd spent so many years working to be different from her mother, so long conscientiously trying to avoid the traps into which Rheta had fallen so blindly, and then in the past few weeks she'd made such an absurd and fairly pathetic attempt at trying to be Rheta, that she'd given little if any thought to the actual loss of her. She had actively missed Cliffie, but beyond anger, she hadn't investigated her feelings for Rheta. Now Lilbet's question prompted her to examine this neglected area and, to her surprise, she found a region of longing that had remained undiscovered all these years.

"Yes, I do," Aly answered, suddenly able to remember any number of happy occasions. "I try not to think about her," she said truthfully, and had to wonder why she'd so diligently refused to see there'd been anything good to remember of the woman. She'd never forgiven Rheta for her mistakes, especially her last one. Jesus! she thought. How cruel! She herself had made errors in judgment that were of epic proportions. Look at Jeremy! And Nicholas! Fair was fair, however. She'd no more forgiven her own mistakes than she had her mother's. She'd been more tolerant of Jeremy than she'd ever been of Rheta. Why was that? Because Jeremy couldn't be held responsible for her flawed logic. "But I do miss her," she said wonderingly, feeling all at once an ache in her arms that only embracing her mother could satisfy. Poor Rheta, poor deluded Rheta who'd tried to console all the unhappily married men she could find and who had died trying. At least she'd honored her code, misguided as it was.

All at once she longed to see her girls, to discover if they were as angry with her and as indignant as she'd been for so long with Rheta. She'd been remiss; she'd neglected to provide them with a forum for dissent, for discussion. It wasn't too late to sit down with them, with Adele in particular, and try to remedy what had gone wrong.

She looked at her grandmother and saw Lilbet's face contorted with the effort to bear her pain silently and discreetly. At once she reached to hold Lilbet's hand, asking, "What can I do?"

"The pills will go to work in a minute and I'll be fine," Lilbet told her, dredging up a wavering smile. "I told you I won't be fussed over."

"But we might be able to get another prescription, something stronger."

"Anything stronger, honey," Lilbet said, "and I'll be a drug addict. Now see," she said, color slowly returning to her features, "I'm feeling better already. Naturally if you're going to sit watching my every move things're going to look worse than they are. So stop looking so closely, Alyssa," she counseled wisely. "Go fetch that gift-wrap and let's do up some of the presents."

Aly had no choice but to do as she'd been asked. There were some things she could and would seek to remedy in the very near future, but Lilbet had chosen the manner in which she planned to go, and Aly had no right to argue with her or to attempt to influence her to go via some alternate route.

CHAPTER
TWENTY - EIGHT

THE FOLLOWING night Nicholas telephoned just after midnight. Again he gave her no chance to speak. "I'll be there in ten minutes," he said, then hung up.

Greatly annoyed, she disconnected the telephone, then hurriedly dressed. When he arrived at the rear service door she was waiting with the telephone, the radio, the scarf, the pen and notebook, and the gold necklace.

"I can't see you any more, Nicholas," she said, holding the items out to him.

For the first time he appeared at a loss. It was evident people rarely if ever said no to Nicholas, and it was something he was unaccustomed to dealing with. His handsome brows furrowed, his well-shaped mouth fell slightly agape. "Because of the other night," he guessed, accepting the things without looking at them.

"Not just that,".she said, thinking how odd it was that they were at last having something resembling a conversation when there was no likelihood they'd ever have the opportunity of another. "I have children, Nicholas, obligations. My grandmother's terminally ill. This is her home and I've dishonored it."

That seemed to make a strong impression on him. He nodded solemnly, saying, "You should've told me. I would've made other arrangements."

"I did try to tell you. It doesn't matter now." She looked into his thickly-lashed dark eyes finding him no less beautiful than before. She imagined his mother must have marveled over the magnificent child she'd produced; she must have gazed into his perfect features again and again, awed by his flawless golden skin and choirboy's eyes. Aly imagined his looks were both a blessing and a curse, and felt a pang of sympathy.

"I'm not too good at talking," he said regretfully, suddenly becoming aware of the items in his hands. "You can keep these, if you want."

She shook her head. "I can't."

"I'll take this," he said of the telephone. "But I want you to have these." He pushed the necklace, radio, scarf, notebook and pen back at her. "I bought these specially for you. Keep them," he said softly.

His feelings were so obviously on the line that she couldn't refuse. "All right, Nicholas," she said. "I will."

"You're a good person," he said seriously. "I could tell that right away. I never wanted to get you involved. . . . You know?"

"I understand. Thank you." She was touched by this declaration.

He took a step away from the door, his eyes on the telephone. "Maybe I should've taken you out, bought you dinner. But I wanted to keep you special." He was having difficulty finding the right words to describe how he'd felt. "I liked you, a lot," he said, looking up again at her. "I never knew anybody like you."

"I liked you, too, Nicholas. In many ways, you've been a big help to me. And," she smiled, "I've never known anyone like you, either."

From inside the apartment Aly heard the sound of footsteps approaching quickly, and Lucille calling out her name. "I'm here!" she called back and turned to look one last time at Nicholas. She whispered, "Good-bye. Be careful please."

He nodded, touched a finger to his lips then held it to hers. "Good-bye, Dr. Brown. Take care of yourself." He gave her a winsome smile as she quietly closed the door.

"You'd better come!" Lucille beckoned. "Your grandma's not right."

*   *   *

IT TOOK Lilbet six hours and forty-three minutes to die. She refused to be taken to the hospital or even to allow Aly to call her doctor.

"I want to be here in my own bed," she insisted. "I won't go with a bunch of starchy strangers poking needles in me, trying to force me to stay alive another few days or weeks. Just give me my pills and visit with me."

Aly gave her a double dosage of the pain killers, then drew a chair close to the bed and sat holding her grandmother's hand.

Lucille hovered anxiously in the doorway asking what she should do.

"We could all use some coffee," Aly told her. "If you wouldn't mind."

Glad of something to do, Lucille went off to the kitchen.

"I've made arrangements for Lucille," Lilbet said. "Light me a cigarette, would you, honey?"

Aly did and Lilbet took one puff then left the cigarette to burn out in the ashtray. "Made arrangements for all of you," she went on after a time. "Damned lawyers've been after me for years to make sure all the loose ends were tied up. Keep this place, Alyssa. It's always been your home. You might be glad of it sometime."

"I will," Aly promised. "I love this apartment."

"Good." Lilbet nodded, pleased. "I was looking forward to seeing your daddy and that darling Serena and the girls. I always did love Christmas. My favorite holiday."

"I know."

"City's changed since we first came here. You noticed that?"

"Some," Aly agreed. "And it's so different from London. Although London's not what it was when Dad and I moved over years ago. I used to love to go for walks late at night. I'd stop and buy a carton of milk from a machine, walk along looking at the houses. The restaurants were dreadful," she smiled. "I was desperate for Luigi's, all the good restaurants here. Now, you'd think twice before walking out alone at night in London. And the vending machines are long gone. There are some fairly decent restaurants, though. But I preferred it the way it used to be. Here, it's dirtier and a whole lot more dangerous. I don't think I'd want to raise children here, the way you and Rheta did. Children get mugged nowadays for their lunch money."

"So I hear," Lilbet put in.

"I feel very—split, most of the time. You know. I mean, this is my home. I was born here. I spent the first fifteen years of my life here. But London's my home, too. I think I'd like to spend part of every year in each city. Maybe then I won't feel as if I don't actually live anywhere."

"I know what you mean," Lilbet said. "When we first came up here, what bothered me most was the *smell*. The south didn't smell the way New York does. And the all-fired rush everyone's in all the time. I come from a slow-moving kind of life, where the people have time to stop and say hello, where everything doesn't have to get done this very minute. It's amazing what a body can get used to, isn't it?"

"Yes, it truly is."

Lucille brought in a tray with coffee, saying, "Here you go. Just the way you like it," as she set a cup on the bedside table. "How is it?" she asked Lilbet sweetly, her fondness for the old woman obvious in the way she smoothed Lilbet's hair.

"Tolerable," Lilbet answered, taking hold of the housekeeper's hand. "Alyssa, you'll excuse us for a minute, honey?"

Alyssa wandered into the living room and stopped to look at the silver-framed photographs grouped at one end of the mantel. Everyone was there: Lilbet and Uncle John on their wedding day, a studio portrait of Rheta and Hal with Aly and Cliff at two and four, Hal with Serena on the lawn of the Cornwall house, Adele and Suzanne and Aly together in one armchair, even a small picture of Pearl. She picked up Pearl's picture with a smile. Only Lilbet would have a photograph of her late housekeeper and long-time friend. All her life Lilbet had been a closet liberal, and only since the mid-sixties had she emerged to declare openly she'd always voted Democrat; her hero was Eleanor Roosevelt, the only president's wife who'd had any real gumption.

No matter how often Aly looked at these photographs it felt as if she were viewing them for the first time. They revived any number of memories, provoked disparate reactions. Rheta

285

looked young and vulnerable, yet defiant; intelligence sparked in her eyes, stubbornness resided in the thrust of her rounded chin. My mother, Aly thought. This is my mother. Aly was now some months older than Rheta had been when she died. Another month and she'd be thirty-six; already she'd survived a year longer than her mother. It shook her again to realize how very young Rheta had been. All the more reason to forgive her. She'd probably have outgrown some of her sillier ideas about men, given a bit of time. And without question there were infinitely worse mothers. Rheta couldn't have known Don harbored a murderous rage. She'd just been looking for love.

Experiencing a surging fondness for this woman she'd scarcely known, Aly held the photograph in her arms and wondered why it was that so many things only made sense when it was too late, and there was no chance left to make important declarations. Carefully returning the photograph to its appointed place on the mantel, she vowed to set as many things right as she was able and as soon as possible. She'd squandered far too much time trying to demonstrate her infallibility when all she'd proved was that she was merely human, as Andrew had attempted to point out to her.

JUST AFTER three that morning she gave Lilbet another double dosage of the pain killers, then resumed her seat and her grip on Lilbet's hand, keeping a close watch on her grandmother's face. Lilbet was leaving her. She could see it in the way Lilbet's view had turned almost entirely inward and how she gazed attentively, lovingly, at scenes that played solely for her. Whatever it was she saw, it seemed to please her. The medication slowed her down, softened her, subdued her movements. Her smile when it came was dreamy, distracted.

"What do you see?" Aly asked softly, stroking the fine old hand she held gently with both her own.

"Folks I thought I'd forgotten," Lilbet answered, her accent thicker and more lyrical, as if she'd traveled back sixty or seventy years. "My darlin' mama and her sister, my Aunt Rose. My dearest friend Katie-May who lived right next door. The two of

286

us in summer we'd crawl under the front verandah. It was cool under there. We'd look out through the latticework, eavesdrop on the ladies rockin' right overhead, cover our mouths with our hands so they didn't hear us gigglin'. Lord, the things we heard! The ladies rockin' away, talkin' 'bout their men, their friends, their aches and pains, their best recipes. Me and Katie-May we could make a day of it under the verandah, 'ceptin' for meals. They'd be callin' for us and we'd have to scamper out, dustin' ourselves off, then come strollin' around the side of the house like we hadn't been there the whole time spyin' on them." She laughed soundlessly, then stared into space as the pain took hold of her attention and stole the words from her tongue. Her hand closed hard around Aly's, and Aly held on, willing the pain away.

"Little devils, were you?" Aly prompted, anxious to keep Lilbet distracted.

Lilbet took a long deep breath, her grip on Aly's hand easing. "Good as gold, we were. Katie-May had a bit of a wild streak, sassed back now and again. Everyone said it came with the red hair and the freckles, that streak. Pretty as a picture, Katie-May. See her clear as day, as if it was yesterday. Died in the great influenza epidemic back in '18, Katie-May did. Cried my heart out. I always thought Katie-May and me, we'd get to be old ladies together and sit out rockin' on the verandah, with a pair of impish girls hidin' out underneath listenin' in on every last word. Lotta folks were taken. My Aunt Rose, Cousin Herbert, Uncle Si, some other friends. Terrible thing that was, the Spanish influenza. So many died." She sighed and turned her head slowly. "It's like lookin' at myself," she smiled, "seein' you sittin' there. Like a mirror. Gives me the oddest feelin', as if I'm one person in two places."

"I hope I get to look as good as you when I'm your age."

"Poo! You'll be better. I surely do love you," she said tiredly. "I just wish darling Cliffie had had a chance."

"So do I," Aly agreed wholeheartedly.

"Quite the pair, the two of you. Used to amuse me no end listenin' to you two chatterin' away to each other. Like a couple of little old people you were. Had some truly bitter arguments with your mama about the way she was raisin' you. She never liked to listen. So headstrong. But goodhearted, really. She never in her life meant to harm anyone."

"I know."

"She didn't, Alyssa. Don't waste your life blamin' poor Rheta for what she couldn't help. It does no good blamin' people, I've found. You've got to get on with things, just get on. Blame-placing's no more than a waste of time. She had these ridiculous ideas about men. Lord knows where she got 'em, but she had 'em, sure enough. That last one, I knew the minute I set eyes on him he was bad. I was afraid for you, afraid he'd molest you. He had a look to him that gave me the shudders. Your mama and me, we had the biggest fight of our lives over that man."

"I didn't know that."

"Well, we did," Lilbet said with some energy. "I told her if she didn't get rid of him I'd have to take you away from her 'cause I feared for your well-being."

"You did?"

"I most assuredly did. As fate would have it, you solved the problem all by yourself by movin' in with your daddy. I was already takin' steps to become legal guardian to you children. At least until Rheta came to her senses and got rid of that *animal*."

"Why didn't you ever tell me?" Aly asked, sent reeling by this piece of information.

"There wasn't any point, was there? You moved over to your daddy's and not one week later, well . . . I thought Cliffie would be all right, being a boy. To this day, I rue the fact I didn't march over there and bring your brother home with me. I was giving her two weeks," she said. "Two weeks to come to her senses."

"Oh, God!" Aly bent over and rested her forehead on the side of the bed. Lilbet squeezed her hand, saying, "We've all got something we find hard to live with, honey. That's mine. I didn't act when I should've, so I lost my only child and my grandson. It's hurt me every time I've thought of it. I was just thankful you weren't harmed. Although I did worry how seein' them would affect you. All those nights when you went to Pearl, climbin' into her lap and her rockin' you to sleep, I worried you'd come away scarred. But you turned out just fine, Alyssa. Turned out a woman after my own heart."

Aly blotted her eyes on her sleeve, then straightened up, managing a smile. "You set me a good example," she said, pressing a kiss on the back of Lilbet's hand.

"I see you still got that funny old piece of glass of Rheta's," Lilbet said.

"The bull's-eye? That's right, I do."

"Bull's-eye. That what that thing is?"

"But you know it is," Aly said. "It came from your grandmother's cottage in the Midlands."

"Say what?" Lilbet looked confused. "Who ever told you a thing like that?"

"Rheta did."

"Well, if that don't beat all," Lilbet chuckled. "She always had a fanciful nature, that girl. My grandmother never set foot in England, honey. She was born just outside Lexington, Kentucky on a farm where her daddy bred horses. Rheta found that old piece of glass over on Seventy-third Street one afternoon when we were out for a walk. She must've been five or six, couldn't've been more. They were tearing down a big old house and she spotted that glass thing in the debris and nothin' would do but that we take it home with us. Your Uncle John took it over to Mr. Shuster on Third Avenue and he rigged up the frame, so Rheta could hang it in her window. She loved that silly old thing, took it with her everywhere she went."

"I thought it was magic," Aly confessed to Lilbet's amusement. "The way Rheta made a ceremony of hanging it every time we moved, and that story about how it'd been in the family for generations." She laughed helplessly. "I practically prayed to that thing, for heaven's sake. I've been moving it around with me the same way my mother did."

"Just an old piece of trash," Lilbet said. "Where'd Lucille get to?"

"I think she's sitting in the kitchen. Want me to get her?"

"I'd like to say good-bye."

"Of course," Aly said, and went for Lucille.

*   *   *

AT 7:23 that morning Lilbet died. She exhaled a final time and was still. Aly and Lucille looked at each other, then back at Lilbet. Aly released Lilbet's hand and slowly got to her feet, and she and Lucille embraced without a word.

Aly sat down at the telephone to make a number of calls while Lucille went to make a fresh pot of coffee before getting dressed. There was a lot to be done. The phone calls were only the beginning. But when she'd completed the last of them, she lit a cigarette, finished her second cup of coffee, and told Lucille there was something she had to do. "I'll be with you in a few minutes."

"You hungry?" Lucille asked.

"No, but I think I'd better eat something."

"That's sensible. I'll fix us some breakfast."

Aly thanked her and walked through to her room where she drew the curtains. The sight of the bull's-eye elicited a response from her that was half laugh and half cry. "Jesus, Rheta!" she said, reaching to unhook the glass from the window frame. "All these years, you had me believing it was magic and all the time it was nothing but refuse from some stranger's house." She held the thing in her hands considering the countless times she'd looked through its thickened center and tried to force what she saw into focus, believing that if she could do that she'd somehow be in control. And the whole time it had been a childhood whim of her mother's. Thinking of it in those terms, those ten years she'd shared with her mother—the moving, the men, the endless *tableaux* of contented family life she'd attempted to effect—had been another whim of her mother's. Not so childish, perhaps, but whimsical to a large extent nevertheless. "You sold me on a hunk of glass, Mom, and I bought it completely." She really had to laugh. Then she sat on the side of the bed and cried for a time, exhausted but exhilarated too. Lilbet had known; Lilbet had planned to rescue her and Cliffie. She'd have been removed from Rheta one way or another, so betrayal was not an issue. The issue had become common sense and Lilbet's determination to see to it that her grandchildren were taken out of harm's way. It was far better that Aly had made her own decision. She knew in retrospect that she and Cliffie would have defended Rheta and their right to remain with her. And that

290

defense would have resulted in Aly's dying along with her mother and brother. She'd saved her own life by insisting on going to live with her father. That could, in no light, be construed as a bad thing.

She wrapped the bull's-eye in the previous day's *Times*, dropped the package into a plastic garbage bag, then took the bag to the incinerator chute and listened to it smash into untold pieces as it traveled twelve floors to the basement. Then she dusted off her hands and returned to the apartment to deal with the death of her grandmother.

CHAPTER
TWENTY-NINE

EVERYONE AGREED that Lilbet would have wanted them to celebrate the holiday. So Lucille and Sharon took over the kitchen on the twenty-fourth, the day after the funeral, and began cooking and baking while Hal discreetly took the girls off to see the tree in Rockefeller Plaza and to do some last-minute shopping. Serena and Aly closed themselves into the master suite to wrap the last of the gifts Aly had purchased.

"You must have been at this for ages," Serena commented, surveying the sizeable mound of presents.

"Lilbet had a long list," Aly said, reaching for her cigarettes. "She was taking care to say good-bye to everyone properly."

"I shall miss her." Serena crossed her elegant legs and looked around the room. "She had character, and superb taste. This is a lovely room."

Aly, too, looked around. "It feels strange that she isn't here, strange at breakfast, strange all day long. Yet she's everywhere, all around me. Even knowing she wasn't going to recover, somehow I didn't actually believe she'd die. Death is the strangest thing of all," she said, sadly. "It stays with you in ways no other experience does. I sat with her and held her hand and watched her life disappear like smoke. All I could do was watch, but I couldn't help thinking there had to be some way I could delay it, or even stop it altogether."

"I expect you'll feel that for a long time to come," Serena said with an empathetic smile. "You seem to be bearing up quite well."

"She died the way she wanted to. I'm relieved for her sake that it's over. You know, we talked every day for hours. It was as if she wanted to pass on to me a verbal family history. She told me about her parents, about her childhood, about Uncle John and my mother. There was a lot I didn't know, a lot that's made quite an impact, especially some of the things she told me about Rheta. It's helped me gain a perspective on my mother, given me what I hope is a more realistic attitude toward her."

"You've forgiven her," Serena guessed.

"It's about time, wouldn't you say?"

"It's not for me, or anyone else for that matter, to say. There's no schedule that I know of for emotional matters. Some never do forgive, or forget. Some manage to do it early enough so they're able to enjoy the balance of their lives. Really, it's a matter of degree, don't you think? It has to do with the scope of the parental 'crime' so to speak, how much of our present dissatisfaction we place at their feet. In your case, I've always thought you'd done remarkably well."

"I can't imagine why you'd think so," Aly said, surprised. "When you consider the scope of some of my errors in judgment. Jeremy, for example."

"Yes, well. But unlike the majority of your peers you stuck with it, probably far longer than you should have. You did all you possibly could to make a go of it."

"I stuck with it, Serena, because Rheta never managed to hold on to anyone for very long. I was only showing I wasn't like her."

"Of course that does put a different complexion on it."

"I've wasted too much time proving points," Aly said strongly. "At least proving those that had any behavioral bearing whatsoever on my mother. What I realized, talking to Lilbet these past weeks, was that it didn't really matter if I was like my mother in certain areas because Rheta wasn't who I'd thought she was. I worked so hard at being unlike her that I neglected to be entirely myself. I've rarely trusted my instincts because I had this absurd notion that they were genetically impaired; I'd inherited all kinds of flaws, not the least of which was my interest in men. So to demonstrate I wasn't remotely like her, I stuck with goddamned Jeremy for all those years. In retrospect, it was idiotic."

293

"What, may I ask, is wrong with being interested in men?" Serena asked with amusement.

"Not a thing, under normal circumstances. Unfortunately, I've never approached my dealings with them from anything even close to normal circumstances. I've been thinking hard about this the past few days, trying to get to the bottom of why I've felt for so long the way I have. I can lay that particular problem at Rheta's feet. She was, as Lilbet said, a complete fool when it came to men. Having seen her in action," she said sardonically, "I hardly wanted to emulate her. So, of course, I went to the opposite extreme. Although I've never actually put the concept into words, I had the feeling that love was good but sex somehow equated with death. After all, Rheta was forever falling in love, but from my viewpoint what she really fell into was sexual attraction and she kept trying to elevate it into something nobler. All those men that came and went, all the times she moved us, and expected Cliffie and I to perform like trained seals with her latest 'sweetie,' I hated her for it. She subjected us to her transient emotional life and insisted we behave as if it were normal when we were surrounded on all side by kids who really did have quote—normal—unquote families. I really don't think it ever occurred to her that we were in a position to make comparisons, that our judgmental skills were fairly well developed by the time we were ten and twelve. Jesus! I'm ranting."

"But you say you've forgiven her. Have you forgiven yourself?"

"Some. I need more time to come to terms with everything, especially the girls."

"Give me one of your cigarettes, will you?" Serena asked, extending her long pale hand. "I've left mine somewhere." She waved vaguely, with a smile indicating the rest of the apartment.

Aly gave her the package and her lighter and admired the way, without affectation, that Serena made the act of lighting a cigarette into something worth watching. "You are the most watchable woman I've ever known," Aly complimented her. "You always look wonderful and you move like a force of nature."

Serena laughed and gave her head a shake so that her glossy

silver-streaked hair shimmered in the light. "A force of nature, indeed! You must come to stay with us in Cornwall one weekend soon and see me first thing in the morning. That'll put paid to your lavish compliments. But I thank you." She gave a gracious nod of her head before returning the cigarettes and lighter. "That tendency toward being complimentary may very well be a genetic impairment. Your father suffers from it too. However, I wouldn't dream of inhibiting either one of you. It's so very good for the ego. What is it you think requires coming to terms with *vis-à-vis* the girls?"

"A fair amount. I've done them a great disservice. I haven't told them certain things I think they deserve to know."

"About your mother and brother?"

"That's part of it. I can't help feeling that once I've had a good long talk with them I'll be able to resolve certain other issues."

"Andrew?" Serena gave one of her raffish smiles.

"Are you a witch?" Aly smiled back at her.

"Very possibly," Serena answered. "One never knows. Do you recollect that evening you and I went to see him in that play at the Royal Court?"

"I'll never forget it."

"The poor dear tried so desperately to convince you of his feelings, but you seemed frightened more than anything else. I always wondered why you were so fearful when it was glaringly apparent that he adored you."

"I didn't want to think about it," Aly admitted. "I felt as if I was held together with pins and Scotch tape. The slightest wrong move and I'd come to pieces. Everyone was so anxious for me to be all right, not to be adversely affected by what happened. I didn't want to disappoint Lilbet, or my father, so I directed all my energy to showing them I was fine, that it hadn't destroyed me. It was a mistake. I should have asked for help. But you see I thought they'd think less of me, that I was weak."

"Sad," Serena said thoughtfully. "How very sad."

"I didn't want anyone to feel sorry for me. But of course they did. It would have been impossible not to. I feel sorry for that little girl now, when I think about it. I was so hard on her. I insisted that she behave as if everything were normal. And nothing was normal. It's unfortunate that it took me so long to see that. But," she said with a regretful smile, "at least, thank God, I see it now."

"I THOUGHT we should have a talk, and this seems as good a time as any," Aly began nervously, looking first at Suzanne and then at Adele. Her daughters had become women and she marveled, as she had so many times before, at their independent growth and progress. They would continue to grow, with or without her. The bonds between parent and child were so tenuous in some ways and so indissoluble in others. Veritable chasms could open between you, yet in spite of time and separation or disagreement, you'd forever be their parent; worrying nights about their health and safety, praying no male with an abiding rage toward all females decided to exercise his fury at their expense; hoping they succeeded in living lives less fraught with secret fears, with secrets.

"Sounds rather ominous," Addy said. "Feels rather ominous too, actually, being in Auntie Lilbet's room. How can you sleep in her bed? Doesn't it bother you?"

"Not in the least. It makes me feel close to her." Aly looked at each girl in turn wondering how three people with entirely different points of view could ever begin to agree. Yet for the most part they managed to do just that.

"It wouldn't bother me," Suze said, looking over at the bed with its coverlet and banked lace-edged pillows. "I should think it's quite comforting."

Addy shrugged, conceding. Aly smiled, aware how much Addy liked to say things purely for effect; she was someone who liked to set fire to people's eyes, to send their breathing crazy, and to watch them try to apply their logic to her random remarks. She'd argue with anyone about anything, and didn't care especially about winning. It was the heat of the exchange Addy enjoyed, the leap of energy, the heightened rush of blood through previously benumbed veins.

"There are some things I think you both should know," Aly

said, "things I should have told you a long time ago. Your knowing might have made a difference."

"To what?" Addy asked curiously.

"To why, for example, you chose to go live with your father," Aly answered, feeling herself tighten in anticipation of her daughter's negative reply.

"I never thought you'd actually let me go," Addy said somewhat angrily. "I thought you'd say it was out of the question. But you didn't say anything at all. And I thought, well, fine. She doesn't care, so I might as well go live with dear Dad."

"Of course I cared!" Aly defended herself. "How could you possibly think I didn't?"

"You didn't try to stop me."

"Jesus!" It was true. It hadn't even occurred to her to try to stop her. Aly lit a cigarette, thinking this through. "That's because it was history repeating itself, because it had happened once before."

"What do you mean?" Suze asked. "When?"

"When I was ten, my mother took up with a new man. She'd had a lot of men after she divorced your grandfather. And every time she broke up with one, we had to move, start fresh in a new apartment. We'd just moved again when my mother took up with Don." She filled them in on the events that had led up to her announcing she intended to go live with her father. "Rheta didn't try to stop me. She didn't argue, she just looked wounded. I thought it served her right for taking up with someone so awful. So I moved in with my father. And I was happy. Guilty, but happy. I was getting his complete attention, not even having to share him with Cliffie. I kept thinking it couldn't last, she'd demand I come back, and I wanted to enjoy every minute of it while I could. Life was settled, peaceful. There was no one sitting in the living room oiling his gun, no one popping out at me naked or making me squirm with the way he looked at me, no one making me feel afraid all the time, afraid even to take a bath without getting my brother to stand guard outside because the lock on the bathroom door was broken. I didn't have to watch that man mauling my mother, or striking her and Cliffie, or me, for that matter, or threatening us.

297

"Anyway," she said, a little shaky at having to go back in detail over this unsettling territory, "the Monday morning after my first weekend at dad's place, Cliffie didn't show up at school. I'd been calling the apartment all weekend but nobody answered. Dad and I thought they'd spent the weekend looking for a new place, because Rheta had pretty much promised she wouldn't let Don come back. When Cliffie wasn't at school I just knew something was wrong. So I left and went back to the apartment, very afraid of what I'd find. I was scared, and kept trying to convince myself there was a perfectly good reason why they hadn't been answering the phone. It was out of order, or Cliffie had a cold." She stopped for a moment, in the grip of an exact replication of her emotions on that morning. She was ten years old again and driven forward by a fear so dark and thick it was like swimming in congealing glue. "They were dead," she said, seeing Cliffie's body in the hallway just outside Rheta's bedroom, and Rheta and Don inside the room. She cleared her throat, and lit another cigarette. "There'd been a tremendous fight. Cliff had obviously tried to defend my mother and, apparently, Don killed Cliffie first. He'd beaten my mother before he shot her. Then he'd put the gun between his eyes and killed himself."

Suzanne chewed on her fist, in tears. Adele gaped at her mother, her eyes horror-filled.

"I had the idea, you see," Aly rushed on, anxious to be done with this, "that if I'd stayed, if I hadn't left them, it wouldn't have happened. Everyone told me that simply wasn't the case, but I still felt guilty. I'd left them, and they died. What I hadn't known until just a few days ago is that Lilbet had been planning to take Cliffie and me away until Rheta got rid of that man. When I insisted on going to stay with my father, Lilbet was relieved. She'd intended to remove Cliffie from Rheta's custody the following week. But, by then, it was too late. If I'd known that, perhaps I'd have felt differently. As it was, all I could think was that I'd deserted my mother and brother. I had the idea that if I'd stayed, none of it would have happened. Just before she died, Lilbet made it very clear that if I had stayed, I'd have died with them. For some reason, that had never occurred to me. Rheta was to blame in my eyes because she'd been unforgivably stupid. And I was to blame because I'd abandoned them. So," she sighed, "that's why I didn't ask you to stay, Addy. I saw history repeating itself and I viewed it as my failure. I'm afraid you viewed it as my lack of caring. But I did care, terribly. I just couldn't speak, couldn't say a word. I'd failed you and you were letting me know it in no uncertain terms."

"I'm sorry," Addy said soberly. "I had no idea."

"Of course you didn't. How could you? That was my true failure. If I'd told you both about this a long time ago you might have understood why I acted as I did. But that's hindsight," she said, "and doesn't help."

"I thought I was being frightfully mature," Addy said sheepishly, "but I really didn't want to go with Jeremy. He's so *wet!*" she lamented, which made everyone laugh. "Well, he is, and you know it! Now that he's going to be playing The Professor in the bloody *Blue Angel* he's become impossible. Honestly! He's had his teeth capped again and they're ridiculous, far too big and white, so now he looks like a grinning squirrel. How could you have married him, really?" she chided. "It's quite embarrassing to have to admit to anyone he's my father."

"He's not all that dreadful," Suzanne defended him. "Although the caps actually are frightful."

"There's one last thing I wanted to tell you," Aly said. She paused for a moment trying to think how best to put it, saw no perfect way, so forged ahead with the simple truth. "It isn't my intention to sway your feelings about your father. He is your father, after all, and always will be. What I think of him has to do with me personally, what you think of him is your private terrain. I've never tried to influence you where he's concerned and I never will. But you have to know this: You have a half sister. Donna is a few months older than you, Suze, and looks enough like you to be your twin. She's a lovely girl and I've been. . . . No, I'll tell you the plain facts. Your father was living with another woman when he met me. Liz was pregnant and he abandoned her to pursue me. I didn't know a thing about any of this, and I probably never would have known if Liz hadn't been forced to institute a law suit against him for increased financial assistance. He's never so much as seen Donna and, beyond the four pounds a week he's paid since her birth, he's never displayed any interest or had the slightest bit of curiosity about this third child of his. Finding out about Donna and Liz was the end of the marriage for me. I couldn't go on living with him after that, although I dragged my feet for ages about confronting him. What he did to Liz and Donna was unforgivable, which is why I've assumed financial responsibility for the girl. I think you know I'm not exaggerating when I say your father never would. He saw the whole thing as a nuisance, something getting in the way of his goddamned career. Sorry," she said. "I'm just so angry about this." She took a calming breath and said, "I hope you'll want to meet her. Your father didn't feel you should be told, didn't see the relevance."

"That bloody tears it!" Addy swore. "I thought he was gormless, but not bad really. He's a sod! I'd *adore* to meet her. Wouldn't you, Suze?"

"She looks like me?" Suze asked, looking dazed.

"Almost identical. She even speaks like you."

"Crikey!" Suze whispered. "What's she like?"

"Lovely. Would you like to read some of her letters?"

Both girls said they would.

"I wish you'd told us all this before," Suzanne said. "I'd have liked to know. It must have been so dreadful for you. Poor Mummy."

"I was lucky, you know. I had Lilbet and Dad and Pearl. People were very kind to me."

"And your super friend Sharon," Addy contributed.

"Yes, and Sharon," Aly said, pleased by the way everything had gone, and wondering why she'd been afraid for so long of confiding in her girls. "I'm very touched by the way you're reacting about Donna."

"Did you think we'd turn up our noses and play at being too good for The Professor's bye-blow?" Addy asked archly.

Aly laughed. "One of these days your wit's going to get you in trouble."

"It's *always* had me in trouble," Addy snapped back. "I am your child, after all."

"You didn't inherit that wicked tongue from me," Aly declared.

"I quite agree," Suze said with a smile. "She came along with it ready-made."

"Well, now that we've got all that out of the way," Addy said, making a face at her sister, "and seeing how we've launched 'Truth-and-Honesty Day,' there's something Suze and I have been wanting to ask you."

"Absolutely." Aly spread her arms in a gesture of openness. "Fire away."

"Why have you broken up with Andrew?" Addy asked. "We were both so sure you'd marry him. What happened?"

"We were just friends, Addy. We didn't 'break up.' We had a falling-out, I'm afraid."

"You can't really be this thick. Can she actually be this thick?" Addy appealed to Suze.

"You're not, are you, Mummy?" Suze appealed to her.

"No," Aly conceded. "This is something I've got to work out." She looked from one girl to the other, then said, "Are the two of you giving me permission to take up with Andrew?"

"It's hardly up to *us*," Addy said dramatically, one hand over her heart, "to be giving you permission to do anything. We simply wondered what happened. We kept expecting some sort of announcement. Then suddenly no more Andrew."

"He's such a love," Suze said warmly. "Is it a serious falling-out?"

"I'm not sure."

"It's Christmas," Addy said puckishly. "Why not ring him to say happy holidays?"

"I'll think about it," Aly hedged.

"Don't be a ninny," Addy said, giving Aly a fierce hug before grabbing Suze by the arm. "Call him this very minute."

"Stop dragging me about!" Suze said, shaking herself free to embrace her mother. "We love Andrew," she whispered to Aly, "and we want you to be happy. I know you've been unhappy for ever so long."

Addy again took hold of her sister's arm and towed Suze to the door saying, "Be sure to send him our love."

"I have no idea where he is!" Aly protested.

"He'll be at home, for heaven's sake. Everyone knows no one

301

shoots over Christmas." Addy wagged her finger saying, "Make sure you do it now, or you'll have no plum pudding."

"There's no plum pudding in any case," Suze said. "Sharon said it's boiled rubber with booze and she wouldn't dream of asking anyone to eat such a thing."

"Really?" Addy was saying as they went off. "What d'you suppose she's planning to offer instead?"

Aly lit a cigarette and looked at the white telephone on Lilbet's writing table. What harm could it do? It was as good a way as any to offer an apology, to try to set things right.

She got up, her hands suddenly cold, and walked over to sit down at the table. She wasted several moments opening the drawers to look at Lilbet's embossed stationery, the cards and envelopes neatly aligned. The door opened, Addy stuck her head in and said, "Call him, Mum. It'll be all right. He's always been soppy for you." She grinned and shut the door.

Feeling as if she might faint, she lifted the receiver and got the operator, recited Andrew's London number, then waited, convinced he wouldn't be there. The double rings started and she was suddenly overheated. Then he answered and for a moment she couldn't speak. He said hello again, his voice echoing as if through a vast tunnel that spanned the considerable distance between them.

"Andrew," she said, her throat too dry. "It's Aly. I thought I'd call to wish you a Merry Christmas."

There was silence, and then he laughed. "Hello, Sproggy," he shouted down the line. "Have you come to your senses finally?"

"Maybe," she laughed. "I'd love to see you, Andrew."

"That can be arranged," he said cheerfully. "In New York, are you?"

"That's right."

"All is forgiven? Lassie come home?"

"Are you crazy?" she asked, smiling.

"Of course!" he bellowed. "Do you realize I'd about given up hope? It's been almost three bloody months, woman! I was beginning to believe you'd gone for good."

"Obviously, I haven't."

"Good, good! I must ring off now. I've a plane to catch."

"Oh!"

302

"Yes," he shouted. "If I run like the bloody devil I can catch up with the producer. Has his own jet! I've only just come through the door. Haven't even opened my bags."

"Everyone's here," she said, resisting the impulse to shout back at him. "My father and Serena, the girls."

"Wonderful! Expect me when you see me! Happy Christmas, Sproggy."

She put down the receiver ready both to laugh and to cry. No recriminations, no unpleasantness, just Andrew, rushing to be with her. "Jesus!" she whispered, then got up and went to join the others.

AN INTERLUDE

"Why did he invite us?" Andrew wondered aloud. "Ah, dear heart, haven't you got a tissue? Mustn't wipe one's nose on the sleeve of one's best suit. It's so déclassé."

Aly handed him a Kleenex and he held it out to Teddy saying, "You'll find this infinitely preferable to velvet, piglet."

Teddy giggled and rubbed the tissue over his nose.

"He invited us," Aly said, "because it's the tenth anniversary of 'The Blue Angel *and it's a gala occasion. Besides, aren't you just a little bit curious to know what Jeremy's been doing all over hell and gone for ten years?"*

"Not really," Andrew replied. "Are you ready for your *gala, piglet?" he asked Teddy, dropping to his haunches to make a show of dusting his buttons and adjusting his collar.*

"Daddy, you're so silly," Teddy said with a show of sorely-tried patience. "It's Emma Clayton's ninth birthday party and I expect it'll be as horrid as last year. I hate Emma Clayton. I don't even want to go. I'd much rather go to the theatre with you and Mummy. Or spend the night with Addy in her new flat. She said I could."

"Sorry," he said, straightening. "We've committed you to the rigors of this evening. You'll just have to soldier on, I'm afraid."

Aly laughed, fastening on the diamond earrings Andrew had given

303

her when Teddy was born. "Soldier on," she repeated. "He's eight years old, for God's sake, and you're telling him to soldier on."

"All good souls soldier on," he said. "It's in the British tradition."

"Teddy has dual citizenship," she reminded him. "Zip me, please."

"You look wonderful," he said, planting a kiss at the nape of her neck.

"Not in front of the child, please," Teddy said, wrinkling his nose.

"What did you say?" Andrew roared, swooping down on him as Teddy backed away.

"I said," he giggled, "not in front of the child, please!*"*

Scooping him up, Andrew swung him in a circle, howling, "The child? The child*? What's all that about, I wonder?"*

"It's what Serena said to Grandfather when we stayed," Teddy said. "They were having a cuddle and I was watching."

"Naughty, naughty," Andrew said, setting him down. "Why were you watching?"

"Because they're old*," Teddy declared.*

"Oh, well, that's all right, then," he said. "Where's Emma's gift?" he asked. "You'd better fetch it. We have to leave now if I'm to be back in time to take Mummy to see old Gable in his ten-thousandth performance, or whatever."

Teddy picked up the package from the bed, saying, "I'm ready."

"Then give poor old Mum a kiss and we're off!"

Teddy trotted over and Aly bent to give him a hug. "Have a terrific time," she said. "And don't forget to say please and thank you. Suze will pick you up at 9:30. Okay?"

"Okay."

"And Olive will be here if there's a problem. Okay?"

"Okay."

"And if it really is an awful party, and you're having the worst time of your entire life, telephone Suze and ask her to come for you early. Okay?"

"Okay, but I know it'll be horrid, so I'll probably ring Suze straight away."

"Don't you dare," Aly warned.

"I told you I hate Emma. I hate all girls."

"Of course you don't," Aly said. "Go on, now. And I'll see you in the morning."

"Come on, piglet," Andrew beckoned, his hand out.

Teddy trudged toward him and Andrew muttered, "Grouse, grouse, grouse. What a grizzler!"

"You don't have to go to Emma Clayton's horrible party."

"And jolly glad I am about that, too," he said, marching him off to the car.

"Don't forget to wear your seat belts!" Aly called after them.

"Never do!" Andrew called back, then said more quietly, "Frightful nag, old Mum, isn't she?"

"I'll say!" Teddy agreed heartily.

Aly laughed and went to the telephone. "I wanted to warn you," she told Suze. "Teddy's rebelling. He'll probably be calling you five minutes after he gets to the party."

"Forewarned," Suze said. "If he does, perhaps I'll take him out to dinner. It'd be a shame to waste that lovely new suit."

"Everything all right?" Aly asked.

"I've got masses of exams to mark, but yes. Will you be going to the party afterwards?"

"I doubt Andrew could stand it. You know how he feels about your father."

Suze laughed. "The whole world knows how Andrew feels about Dad. Never mind. The show's not bad, really. You'll have a good time."

"We'll talk tomorrow," Aly said. "And thanks again for collecting Teddy."

"Happy to. Donna said she might stop by. So if little Ted rings up in a tiz, he'll have the two of us to console him."

"He'll be in heaven."

During the interval Andrew said, "Quite the performance, isn't it?"

"The part of a lifetime," Aly answered.

Andrew looked at her for a long moment, then touched his forefinger to the tip of her nose. "You make this old chap very happy."

"Old chap," she scoffed. "You're fifty-four, not eighty."

"Yes, but you've got all your hair."

She laughed. "But only slightly more than half my marbles."

"And I wouldn't have you any other way," he said staunchly.

"You'd have me any way you could get me, and you know it."

"True, but not in the lobby of the theatre with so many watching." He looked around furtively, then slipped an arm around her waist. "They all envy me, you know."

"Do they?"

"The ones with half a brain do, definitely."

"The half-wits, you mean?"

"I'll have to restrict your visits with Sharon when next we're in New York," he said. "She's influencing your speech patterns."

"He's played this part here for four years, then two years in New York, two more in Los Angeles, and now here for another two. I think he intends to play it for the rest of his life."

"He'll have to," Andrew said judiciously. "It's the only role he's ever likely to be offered. Did you hear what Oliver Metcalf said when he was offered tickets for tonight's performance?"

"No, what?"

"He said the idea of twice as much Jeremy by the pound was two times more than he could stand," Andrew laughed appreciatively. "Rather nice turn of phrase, I thought."

"Do you really want to see the second act?" she asked.

He looked closely into her eyes, then said, "Only if I must."

"Then let's go to Le Caprice and eat at the bar. You know they'll genuflect when they see you coming through the door."

"There's nothing wrong with a bit of genuflection now and then," he said, steering her through the crowd toward the doors. "I fancy one of their eggs Benedict appetizers, a bit of smoked salmon, a glass of Bordeaux, possibly some peas mange-tout.*"*

"You've memorized the menu!"

"Many's the lonely evening I whiled away at the bar of Le Caprice, waiting for you to come to your senses and ditch that insufferable cretin Gable."

"Wait! I'll get the violin."

He stopped her on the pavement and chucked her under the chin. "Give us a kiss, then."

She gave him a kiss, then took his hand saying, "It's a nice evening for a walk."

"Indeed it is."

She glanced at him sidelong and smiled. "I'm very happy."

"I should bloody hope so!" he bellowed in his parade-ground sergeant

major's voice. "I work damned hard at it! I'm not bloody Gable, you know, not governed by sod's law, you know."

Hugging his arm, she laughed. "One day they'll arrest you, Andrew, take you right off the street for role-playing in public."

"Hah! Not a chance. My good lady doctor wife will plead insanity on my behalf." He turned to look at her. "Won't you?"

"Always! Absolutely!"

"I really do fancy those eggs Benedict," he said. "And a bit of smoked salmon."

"I love you, you fool." She studied his face, seeing his affection for her shining in his deep brown eyes. "I like your face," she told him, running her finger down the length of his quirky nose, and across his always appealing mouth, to his dimpled chin. "I love you."

"Of course, you do. You'd be mad not to," he laughed and, tightening his arm around her waist, directed her across the road.

91001170

Marlowe, Katharine
Heart's desires